LONGINUS

LONGINUS

BOOK I OF THE MERLIN FACTOR

STEVEN MAINES

Purple Haze Press

LONGINUS

BOOK I OF THE MERLIN FACTOR

Copyright © 2006 by Steven Maines

Purple Haze Press books may be ordered through booksellers or by contacting:
Purple Haze Press
PMB 167
2430 Vanderbilt Beach Road, #108
Naples, Florida 34109
www.purplehazepress.com
239-513-3313

This is a work of fiction. All of the characters, names, incidents, organizations and dialogue in this novel are either the products or the author's imagination or are used fictitiously.

COVER DESIGN:

Ingrid Rofkar

ISBN 978-0-9773200-3-5

Library of Congress Control Number: 2007926635

Printed in the United States of America

ACKNOWLEDGEMENTS

I would like to thank the following people for their constant encouragement, support, input & love:

My wife, Michele Genovese-Maines.
Laney Clevenger. Rev. Cheryl Jensen. Ann Maines, Barry Maines, Sharon Maines & Chris Maines. Geoffrey Patterson. Tom Woosley. Ingrid Rofkar. My editor, Arlene Uslander.
& Wilbur.

I also wish to express my great appreciation to the following people:
Vaishali, Elliot Malach, Stephanie Buenger,
Maxine Chavez and Purple Haze Press.

I

My duties put me in charge of one hundred men. It was nearly a thousand years into the existence of my beloved Republic. It was no longer a Republic, however. Rome was now an Imperial State, with the façade of a Republic in the guise of the Senate. My title or rank was Centurion, and my name was Longinus. Centurion Longinus.

To recall it now, in my present state of existence, in the memory of my soul, my spirit, is to relive it again in the flesh.

You see, the memory of the soul is not memory as we think of it when we are in human form. It is not a conglomeration of images and sounds and feelings impressed on the pathways of the brain. Instead, when one truly recalls an event of the soul's existence, it is instantly relived, or lived all over again in what you would call *real time*.

When I truly recall, or relive a life, I am going immediately again to that place and time. Of course, time does not exist, per se. But, as humans, we tend to internalize this no-thing we call time, so for the sake of argument, I will use it here. All Time and thus all Creation, exists at once, on or at different dimensional aspects of the Universe. By tapping into my soul's memory, I can travel back to any point in time in my soul's history or past. In other words, when one taps into an event in the soul's memory, one becomes the participant-observer, destined to play out the drama again.

But enough of that. This is about my life as Longinus at the time of the crucifixion of the Christ.

Some have cursed me down through history. Some believe that I became a devout and learned Christian, and even sainted me. Some think that I left Rome and her Legions and traveled to Gaul with the mindful intent to join the Celts and Druid sects. Still others believe that I was condemned to walk the earth forever, never being allowed to die, ever to walk in my own living hell for my act, my so-called sin. They are all wrong. And, they are all correct. Except this last one. How absurd. I laugh at it now, but did not find it at all humorous at the time.

In this life, I am Centurion Longinus, formally known as Gaius Cassius, Centurion in the Emperor's Legions; Centurion of the Roman Guard in Jerusalem, circa 0033 of the Common Era. I am not to be confused with General Gaius Cassius Longinus, who conspired against the great Gaius Julius Caesar some seventy years earlier, or the other Gaius Longinus, who was a Greek philosopher two-hundred years later. I was Gaius Cassius Longinus, Legionnaire and Centurion. I remembered nothing of my True Merlin Nature in this life until the event that changed it forever, and even then, it took many years for me to be open to it and remember it, or realize it. The event I refer to is the one for which many others cursed and condemned me.

My *sin*? I am he who pierced the side of the Christ while he hanged from his cross.

It was a simple thing, really. My orders were to accompany King Herod's palace guards to the site of the crucifixion and to stand guard myself—not to have a mere Legionnaire, a common foot soldier, for this duty—to stand next to this crucified one and keep his followers at bay until he died.

Hours and hours had passed. People had come and gone all day, weeping and wailing and gnashing their teeth with despair at the sight of their "Savior" and his two companions spread out and dangling upon their wooden beams. The sky had become grotesquely dark and ominous at one point, instilling a palpable fear among the mourners and the curious who had gathered. I, too, felt a twinge of irrational foreboding at first, but quickly dismissed my dread as ridiculous. I was simply witnessing an unusual weather-storm for this time of year. That this man was being crucified at the same time was mere coincidence. And, I believed that. Until, that is, the Earth shook.

It only lasted for a moment, the shaking. But, it left no doubt in my mind that it was directly correlated to this dying man on the cross.

In that moment, I looked up at him. Though the sky behind his body was dark with clouds, there was a beautiful, unearthly glow emanating from around his slumped head. He muttered something then. Something like, *they know not what they do.* Though somewhere deep within me, I knew this man to truly be a Holy man, connected to a power—perhaps, to The Power above us all—my heart was still the hardened stone of a soldier of Rome, impassionate and immune to all but death and orders. My orders here included staying with the doomed One until he was dead.

Some versions of my duties, or what took place next, proclaim that I was a hero; that my next act actually saved the Christ's skull from being crushed. It was the custom at that time in this particular region that one who was hanged from the cross would remain there until dusk only. No prisoner was to be left on the cross overnight. If he had not died by dusk, his skull would be crushed by a soldier standing guard, thus insuring death. It was brutal, yes. But nothing I haven't seen in many a battle. Besides, by that time, there was no feeling left on the part of the condemned, as he long since would have passed into unconsciousness. But instead of having his skull crushed, this man that hanged before me had another fate. Here is what really happened.

His eyes closed, his chin on his chest, the Christ appeared to be in the state of eternal sleep, his spirit departed. The only way to be certain that he had passed on was to reach up with my spear and prod. This I did, to the gasps of horror of the remainder of those present, which included his mother and another woman to whom she clung. What did I care? I had my orders. I pierced his side, between his ribs. A sickening moan came from his mouth as blood and body fluids seeped down the length of the protruding blade and shaft from his ribs. Some of it even spattered on my face and into my eyes. Contrary to what some believe, however, my poor eyesight was not suddenly and miraculously restored to normal at the touch of the Christ's blood and body fluids. In subsequent years, however, my eyesight became nearly perfect the older I got, instead of degenerating with age, as is usually the case.

Before I could withdraw my instrument, I felt a vibration come from the body on the cross. It came down my spear and into my own body. It paralyzed me. The air around me instantly filled with a static tingle, like a localized lightening charge. I felt as though I were floating. A man's voice then whispered to me, saying, "What have you done, my child? What have you done?"

An Otherworldly fear overtook my mind and with all my strength, I cursed and yanked on the spear, finally pulling it free of the body. I spun around to see who had said the words to me. But no one was close enough to have whispered and be heard, save for the two women, and, as I said, it was a man's voice.

Confused, I looked back up at the man on the cross. His now vacant, dead eyes stared at me from a corpse no longer occupied by the spirit. Or, so was my assumption, until I had heard what had happened three days later. But for the moment, I gave the orders for him to be removed from his death-perch. His loving, weeping mother and a few others moved forward to take him away.

I stood there for a few moments, staring at his mother and then staring at him. The voice once more whispered in my head, and I found myself saying out loud, "What have I done? By the Gods, what have I done?" I felt a tear roll down my cheek, though inwardly, I felt no emotions. But, again, somewhere inside of my being, I knew who this Man truly was; an emissary from God or the Gods. Nevertheless, I convinced myself that I had followed and executed the orders given to me with my usual exemplary proficiency. Commendations would be forthcoming, I was sure. However, my conscience and spirit would show me something else.

That night I was able to keep sleep at bay for a long while. I knew that if I gave into slumber, I would have to face my conscience, my fears and truths of the day's events, and this, of course, I could not allow. So I spent the night in the arms of the local whores. When one would tire, I would find another to play with. This went on throughout the night. I spent nearly half-a-year's wages that evening. I was possessed, so to speak, by the gods of sex. I could not be satiated. I had the virility of ten bulls. I would no sooner spend my seed in one woman, when I would rise and swell again. On more than one level, I hoped the night would never end.

But it did finally end. As dawn approached I drifted off into a strange slumber in the arms of the two women sharing my bed. Unwillingly, as my eyelids began to close, I found myself glancing in the direction of the corner of the room. There, propped up against the wall, was my spear. Though I had thoroughly cleaned his blood from the blade—actually, I had cleaned the blade three times, the last one especially being quite unnecessary—the blade now gleamed crimson with blood once again. Impossible!! It must be the light within the room! But nay, it was clearly blood that dripped down the blade, seeping along the shaft as well. I tried to disentangle myself from the limbs that lewdly entwined my body, but found that I was paralyzed, as I had been momentarily on the field of crosses the previous day. My eyes, though I endeavored to keep them open, closed of their own accord.

Images thrust themselves at me in my mind's eye. Horrifying images of death and destruction, of torture and foulness beyond human comprehension; of wars and rumors of wars being fought on the planes of the heavens, as well as of earth; of Evil reigning in the minds and hearts of men the evils that he can and will inflict on his fellow man. The visions showed the fall of my beloved Empire and the rise of another; then the fall of that one and the rise and fall of another, then another, and so on. They showed the swift boats going to new lands and the killing and torture of humans unknown. They showed men flying in great machines that rained down fire and death. They showed flying objects that carried no man, but delivered swift and massive destruction and fates worse than death. They showed bodies alive but burning, screaming for their very souls. Could this all be true?

This and more I saw in the sleep of that dawn. Then the voice, the whispered voice from the field came to me. "Fear naught," it said. Even so, terror infused my being. I tried to speak, but found that I could not. I continued to see the horrific images play out in front of my mind, as the voice continued: "This and more shall you see, for I tell you now that you have been chosen. You will not leave here until this world is consumed. Until this world has run its course, shall you wander and learn and teach. You will long to leave, for death, on many an occasion, but true death will never come, because it cannot. Ah, you think this to be punishment, but it is not, not at all. There is nothing for which to be punished. It is your *desire*."

At the ceasing of the words, the words which came from I knew not where, nor from whom—though, much later, I would come to realize it came from the depths of my own being, the eternal, ever-present Oneness of all within, and not from anything at all external—I realized that my fear was of this world. That was all.

At the ceasing of the words, the images increased in speed and ferocity until all I could see was the earth from the vantage point of the stars. She was now a very old and very dead planet. I was not completely aware at the time of what I was looking at, but knew, nonetheless, that it meant the utter annihilation of all existence as I then understood it.

In the trance state—the dream state—I screamed. With my entire being, did I scream. A silent one at first, but it grew, and it grew.

I heard the scream far off in the distance and tried to move away from it. But instead, of moving away from it, it simply grew closer. As it did, I realized that it was my own voice; my own scream emanating from my own body. A bright light exploded in front of me, and I found myself in the bed, swimming in a pool of my own fetid sweat. The two women were trembling at the foot of the bed, staring at me as if I were the foulest of Demons. I sat up, breathing hard and looked at the spear, the blood now dried as if it had been there forever.

I looked back at the women and, in unison, they jumped back as if I were going to pounce and devour them in one-felled swoop.

"What do you stare at?" I bellowed.

"I...we...you became violent, thr...thrashing at us as if the devil was in you," squeaked one.

"Truly," moused the other.

I rubbed my head, trying to make sense of the vision or dream I had just had, as well as what these women were saying.

"Leave me," I finally mumbled.

Slowly, the women backed away toward the door. Just before they passed through it, though, one of them, Irena, a beautiful, green-eyed, dark-haired, Roman-Hebrew woman whom I had known since first being stationed at this hole of an outpost, stopped and boldly brought up a fact. This was her...house, so to speak, after all.

"Longinus, there is one other matter..." she hinted.

Ah, Irena. She was ever the business woman. Her eyes always conveyed a strength and confidence that were accentuated by the high cheekbone structure of her lovely face. If I was meeting her for the first time, I would assume she was noble born. But, I knew better. I nodded to the clump that was my clothes and armor near the spear. "There is coin in the bag on my tunic. Take what you will."

She did as she was bade. But then, curiously, as she stood from retrieving the money, she stared at the spear as if transfixed by enchantment. She had not been on the field of crosses on the previous day. She could not have known how I had used the instrument, nor had she been a follower of this so-called Anointed One. Yet, there she stood, under the spell of the spear. She reached out to touch it.

I exploded, leaping out of the bed. "No!" I screamed, violently grabbing her arm and throwing her across the room back onto the bed with the strength of three men.

She bounced off of the skins of the bed, smashing her head against the wall.

"Do not touch it," I snarled at her, caring not whether she had died from the impact. She had not. She lay clutching the back of her head and whimpering, blood oozing between her fingers.

Irena then looked up at me weepily, yet angrily. I suddenly felt like the ass that I was. I tried to mouth an apology, but nothing came out. Irena's green eyes flashed a mixture of disbelief, fear, and above all, defiance. Irena. I so loved her boldness. With as much dignity as she could muster, she collected herself, stood, and walked toward the door. Taking the other still trembling woman, girl, really, by the elbow, they both left me alone with my apparent dementia.

II

I sat in the deafening silence of the room for over an hour, staring at the spear against the wall. Aside from, or because of, the apparent permanent blood stain on it, it now looked like any other spear of a Legionnaire. But I knew otherwise.

I finally came to my senses and began to put on my clothing, my uniform, my duty regalia. I did so as though in a fog, as if my body was detached from my very essence; as if I were watching someone else donning his uniform. *It doesn't matter,* I kept telling myself. *What's done is done.* The soldier in me was clearly trying to reassert himself.

But it did matter. Nothing would ever be the same again. Ever. I reverently approached the spear, half fearing it might come to life. But ultimately, that's not what I began feeling from it. I paused, sensing its…what was it? Divine energy? It seemed to glow. I finally shook my head, nonsense, plucked it from its resting place, and departed the stuffy room.

The sun beat down harshly as I stepped outside. Curse this region! Perhaps if I asked the General for a transfer to the homeland. The gods knew I deserved it. Yes, a transfer would not be too much to ask.

A crowd had gathered at the far end of the street. They seemed to be watching something, or someone. I couldn't really hear anything. Two of my platoons were there as well, milling about, apparently not too concerned with whatever was causing the crowd to gather. Still.

A Legionnaire trotted by, oblivious to me, clearly quite intent on joining his comrades down at the end of the street.

"You there!" I yelled at him.

The young man stopped and looked at me. Recognition appeared on his face, and his eyes grew large. He trotted up to me, saluting fist to chest much too hard and crisply, clearly trying to impress his Centurion with the polished moves. *Green, this one is,* was all I thought. My thoughts, however, quickly returned to the reason why I had stopped him. I nodded toward the crowd. "What goes on down there?" I asked.

"The people...," his voice cracked.

Inwardly, I had to smile. This lad couldn't have been more than fifteen summers. He cleared his throat, and tried to deepen his voice with age and authority.

"The people," he began again, "are listening to someone speak, Centurion. I believe it is one of those who followed the Jew-King that was hanged yesterday." This last part, the lad spat with sardonic contempt.

"Hold your tongue, boy, or I'll have it on a platter!" I bellowed angrily, though I must confess that I wasn't sure why I was angry. "You know nothing of this man."

The boy-soldier before me began to tremble, fearing my wrath and clearly confused as to what possible transgression he could have committed.

"Dismissed!" I barked.

Again, his crisp, forced salute. He almost fell over his own feet in his flight away from me. I watched him run toward the crowd; and then I turned toward the tavern next to the place where I had spent the night of debauchery, now intent on finding food.

But something stopped me. I slowly turned and found myself looking back down the street at the crowd once again. The next thing I knew, my feet were moving, seemingly of their own accord, guiding me forward toward the crowd.

A string of thoughts and voices went through my mind. *Why am I going there? What do I care what one of His followers has to say? Well...what if this person speaks against Rome? No. He never did, did he? I heard tell that he even said, 'render unto Caesar, that which belongs to Caesar,' so why would a follower of his say otherwise? Besides, his own people condemned him to death.*

My inner dialogue, or argument, went on like this as I walked toward the crowd. "Silence!" I finally declared out loud, apparently none too quietly, for two women stared at me from a nearby doorway as if I were mad.

No matter.

The voices stopped. I decided to go check on the situation anyway. It was my duty, after all, to investigate any impromptu gathering. *I am a Roman officer here,* I reminded myself.

The lad whom I'd stopped a moment before saw me coming and alerted his comrades, all of them snapping to attention as I approached. I simply gave them a curt nod and maneuvered my way into the crowd to get a better look at the cause of it.

A man, a Jew by the look of his unkempt beard and Levite robe, stood on a table in the center of the crowd. He was talking to a couple of other men in a normal, though slightly raised, conversational tone, a combination of awe and reverence laced into his speech. The crowd here was pressed tight, straining to hear what this person had to say.

The dirty, sweating bodies around me began to become oppressive. But it didn't seem to matter, as I found myself drawn into this moment, to hear what this man was saying. Though I could only pick up snippets, he was clearly talking about the man hanged the previous day—his, Teacher, he was saying.

"But he told us! I'm speaking the truth!" he insisted.

"Impossible!" said another. "No one rises from the dead!"

"Did he not command Lazarus to come out of his tomb?" countered the first man.

"So it is claimed, but, I was not there to see it."

"I was. And I tell you, *that* happened. So shall this. On the third day," declared the man on the table.

My heart began to thump. "On the third day?" I found myself saying out loud.

The crowd turned to me in unison, fear suddenly spreading on the face of the two men who had been conversing. Clearly, they had mistaken my reason for saying the words.

"No, no," I said. "I sincerely wish to know. For myself. Not for any other reason. Not for State reasons, certainly. Please."

The two men looked from one to the other. They were Hebrew. The first, the one on the table, stepped gingerly down to the ground, all traces of fear evaporating from his craggy face. He was older than the second by far.

He then stepped forward and looked me squarely in the eyes, peering into my soul, I felt. Apparently satisfied that my inquiry was of a true and sincere nature, he spoke. "So said my Lord."

He continued to look at me, assessing me. I suddenly felt vulnerable. I could have arrested this man for the way he dared to look a Roman in the eye, for the way he was inspecting me at the moment. But I simply stood there. He then looked at my spear and his eyes grew wide.

"You!" he said. "You are the Centurion who pierced my Lord's side."

A murmur rose from the crowd. I stood my ground. *Where are my men*, I found myself thinking. But I needn't have been concerned. The man reached for the blade of my spear. I jerked it back out of his reach.

"Please," he said. I looked closer at him. Covering the lower part of his craggy, aged face, he had a scraggly grey beard. He wore an old and tattered robe—though of which tribe I could not tell—its hood covering most of the top of his head, though I could see wisps of thin grey hair hanging limply near his temples. His eyes were kind and full of depth. Still, he was just an old man. That's all he was. He was harmless.

I felt myself compelled to put the blade of the spear within his reach. He touched it tenderly with his hand, caressing it almost lovingly. A tear rolled down his cheek and he put his lips to the metal, kissing it respectfully. I felt a moist drop descend my cheek as well. I was moved beyond words, though I knew not why.

"Thank you," he said, looking into my eyes. Slowly, he turned and walked into the crowd, the people moving with him. Soon, I found myself standing in open space, the crowd having dispersed.

"Sir?" a voice said. I looked up to the source of the voice. It was my young legionnaire, along with his fellow soldiers. "Are you well? You've been standing here for a while now," he said hesitantly.

I blinked as if waking from a dream. "Quite well, soldier," I said smiling. I looked from his face to those of the others. Boys, all of them. They could not have been more than sixteen summers. "Come," I said. "Let's find food." We began to move off, and I took one look back at where I had stood with the crowd and the man who had kissed the blade of my spear.

I looked at the weapon myself, cradled in my hand, feeling the power it held. Something was moving me, beginning to shape my destiny. I could feel it, but denied it in that moment. Sometimes, the Universe will move us whether we acknowledge it or not. Destiny will not be denied.

That night, true sleep was a foreign thing, kept at bay by the deep thoughts, voices and images within my mind. I saw many things in my tumultuous dreams. Again, as before, they were things that were violent and seemed to be off in the future. But there were also things that were pertinent to the present, to me. One voice in particular, came through.

It *was* familiar. It was *his*, the One from the Cross.

"Longinus," he said to my dreaming mind. "Longinus, I will see you again. You will see that I live. In heart, mind and body, I live. All will see that they, too, will live forever—that they have always lived, always will."

I knew not then what he was saying. I now know, however. It is a wondrous thing. Why do we not give in to these Truths? We spend millennia and then some, hearing these things, but not listening—not listening to the Spirit within which houses all Truth, houses our very Truest Self.

I awoke in a sweat and more fatigued than when I retired the previous evening. I looked at my surroundings. I was in the same room as on the night of His death; the same room of debauchery; now two nights ago. For an instant I was confused.

In my fogged mind, I thought it was the night of His death. I thought that perhaps it had all been a dream: the death, the night of debauchery, all of it. But then I saw my spear leaning against the wall in the corner, dried blood still caked on parts of the blade, in spite of the many times I'd already scrubbed it, and I knew it was no dream. I didn't remember coming to the same room on the previous night, but obviously, I had. Too bad it wasn't all a dream.

Something was rattling around in my brain. Was it something about today? Yes. That was it. But what? There was indeed something about this day that was to set it apart. But in that moment, for my life, I could not remember.

I lay there for some time, soaking in the newness of the day. Or rather, absorbing the newness of my Self, for that is actually how I felt. Inexplicably. After a time, I slowly got up and splashed water on my face from the basin that had been left for me. Then I donned my uniform and breastplate. Taking the spear in hand, I headed out in search of food.

"Ah, Longinus," came the sweet, familiar voice. Something in it this time, however, gave me pause. I turned to see Irena's eyes piercing me with feathered contempt. What could she be angry about? Was it my outburst from the other night? Perhaps. But it wasn't like her to hold a grudge. Still, she was vexed by something. "I demand payment," she blurted out.

"For what? I already paid for my room, gave *you* something for the night. I told you to take what you wanted from my coins, which you did," I said.

"The girl!"

I was confused. "Irena, I was with no one last night, so I don't owe you…"

"…She left. You had us both two nights ago—all night long. And in the morning, you scared demons out of the girl, myself as well, for that matter. But I know you. I took it as just another of your moods." She paused briefly, calming herself before continuing. "We've known each other a long time. I won't pretend that there's…something…between us as man and woman, because there's not. It's business. Which means, I don't mind sharing you. But I draw the line when you cause my business to suffer with your temper or anything else."

I did not understand at all what she was talking about. Bewilderment must have splashed across my face.

"She's gone, Longinus! Because of you! She wouldn't take anyone last night, and this morning, she left, saying she couldn't forget the madman."

"Maybe she was speaking of another soldier. After all, if it weren't for the Roman army, you'd probably have scant few customers, my dear," I said in desperation.

"No!" was her emphatic reply. "It was you she spoke of. 'The madman with the spear,' she said."

I forced a smile. "Are you sure she meant my Legion issued spear and not my man-spear?" My feeble attempt at humor only served to incur Irena's wrath all the more.

"No, damn you! You know she meant *this* spear!" She reached for the weapon at my side. Something inside me snapped. Reflexively, I yanked the weapon out of her reach, and violently threw up my other arm to block her from getting to it.

But the force of my block was much more than I had intended, and, for that matter, much greater than I thought I was capable of. With a gush of air from her chest, Irena flew back some ten feet, sprawling and flopping on her back like a child's straw doll. For a moment she lay motionless and I shuddered. *By the gods*, I thought, *what have I done?*

Since the time I had been assigned here, Irena had become much more than just a bed-companion. She had become a friend. No, even more than a friend. In that moment, I suddenly realized that I cared for her on a much deeper level.

My heart leapt into my throat as she lay before me. "Irena!" I yelled, leaping to her side and kneeling before her. Why had my reaction to protect the spear been so strong? And what of my physical strength in that moment? Where had that come from? I was becoming unstrung; like a damaged archer's bow, I was quickly becoming useless.

"It is you, is it not, Longinus?"

Her voice brought me back to myself, and my nearly overwhelming concern for her. "Yes, I'm here. I'm so sorry."

"No, I mean, it is you they speak of," she said, gaining her strength with each word. Her demeanor had completely changed; no longer angry, as if her anger had been used to cover something else. A fear, perhaps? She sat up and fixed her beautiful eyes on mine. "It is you who pierced the side of the Jew-King, I know it now; the way you protect that spear. Does it hold magic now? Some say that it must."

I was speechless. What was she saying? To whom had she spoken? A few moments of silence filled the space between us. Irena smiled, a teardrop rimming her eyes. "I'm…I'm," she stammered. "I'm sorry I yelled at you about the girl. I don't think she was cut out to be as the likes of me anyway."

My heart swelled. "The 'likes' of you? You're, well, I'm proud to be your friend. You're a smart woman, Irena, and more."

It was then that I felt myself opening up to yet another new sensation. It was the inexplicable feeling that I'd known Irena for a very, very long time, long before I was even born. But how could that be? Yet, something deep within my Being recognized that same something deep within hers. I felt myself drifting in a fog, an ethereal mist. What was wrong with me? I had had thoughts like this before: a deeper recognition of someone, but dismissed them, relegating the thoughts to imagination.

Yet somehow, this was different. Somehow, I knew this feeling to be correct. I knew that I was grasping a deeper Truth, a deeper Mystery.

"Oh, Longinus," Irena said, once again pulling my attention back to her. "I am your friend?" she asked tenderly.

"And more," I replied. I gazed at her again, my full awareness coming back to the present; to myself, Longinus, Centurion to Caesar. "Who has told you that it was I who pierced the side of the man on the cross?"

"Two men. And a woman."

"Who were they?"

"I don't know who the men were, but the woman, her name was Mary. She used to work in a house a short distance from here. Then she started to follow the man you crucified."

"Why?" I asked.

"She said his words cleansed her, freed her," replied Irena.

I thought about this for a moment. Then another thought took its place, one with more urgency. "When did you speak to them last?" I asked.

She pondered the question for a moment. "Two hours ago. They were elated over…" Her voice trailed off as a look of understanding and awe crossed her brow.

"Over what?!" I insisted. But a feeling crept over me, an awareness of the answer that had been there all along.

"Over the 'fact,' as they put it, that this crucified 'Jew-King', Jesu, I think they called him, had arisen from the dead early this morning."

Of course. That was it. That's what today was about. "And they saw this feat?"

"Mary did. And then one of the men, later."

"And you believe them?" I asked, somewhat incredulous.

She hesitated. I could tell that she wasn't sure whether she was speaking to Longinus, her friend, or Longinus the Centurion.

"I…no," she said, but her face betrayed her, as it had a moment before.

Deep within my own being, I knew the truth even then. But Centurion Longinus was in command. I had to check into this. By now, rumor, myth or truth, this would be spreading throughout the city. Things could get out of hand very quickly. Was this the real reason that I wanted to delve into this? No. But in that moment, it was the reason I allowed my mind to believe. The spear in my hand seemed to pulsate in that moment, almost as if it were divining, pointing the way to go.

I ran for the door and was out in the street before I knew it. My heart was pounding. A sensation, an urging, was compelling me to go north. It was coming from the spear. Just as I was about to step in that direction, someone was next to me.

"I'm going with you," Irena said, her jaw set in that stoic and defiant way that I'd come to love.

All I could do was smile. "Of course, you are," I said. We set off down the street. We'd gone about a hundred yards when I noticed something odd; the street—indeed, the whole area—was empty. No one was about. Irena and I exchanged a wordless, questioning glance.

One of the men, one who had been at the gathering on the previous day, the old man who had so reverently kissed the spear, suddenly and mysteriously stepped out from behind a tree on the edge of a path, one leading northward off the street. The hood of his tattered robe or cloak was up over his head, but I could still see most of his face and knew it to be the same man. But, he was different, somehow, from that moment of yesterday. I stared in amazement, for his face glowed with a light; a light of the Gods; a light of the divine. His eyes, though filled with depth yesterday, now showed even more profoundness. In those eyes seemed to be the knowledge of creation and the awareness of having seen first-hand the Great Mysteries. Our eyes locked only briefly. I had to avert my own eyes, so deep was his gaze.

"Centurion," he said. "I have seen it, Centurion. I have seen *him*. I have witnessed the Resurrection."

I knew what he said, but feared it. "What say you, man?" I replied.

"The burial chamber lies empty," said the old man.

Again, Irena and I exchanged a look. "Do you speak of the one they call Joshua, or 'Jesu'?," she asked the man before us.

"Yes, I do."

"Take us there," I commanded, the Centurion in me taking control.

The man was about to protest because of my tone, I could tell. But then his demeanor shifted, and he suddenly smiled instead. "Follow me," he said. He turned and headed up a path. Irena and I did as he bade.

III

Several things kept pushing into my mind as we walked to the burial site, the tomb. Most of these things were of a superficial nature, such as thoughts that amounted to justifying why I was making this trek to the burial chamber, not much more than a cave really, of a man who had died on a Roman cross. One of thousands who had perished that way, and certainly not the first I had helped to speed on the way to meeting his gods, or his God, in this case.

I glanced at the spear in my hand. It still seemed to be pointing the way, pulling me along. *Nonsense!* I yelled silently. Yet, along the path I went, Irena at my side, the raggedy old wise-man before us. *I'm going to see this cave, this tomb, for security reasons*, I rationalized to myself. If the body were to be missing, then it could present a reason for the locals to become agitated. Even now, there were those calling this one Joshua, as he was called in his Hebrew language, or Jesu in the Greek, or Jesus in my Latin tongue (I never had been one for the pretentious Greek that the Patrician classes of Rome were so fond of espousing)—even now, there were those calling this Jesus a Savior. But it was not a savior from Rome that he was to be.

I should have checked in with the garrison by now. My men will be wondering about me, I thought. Still, I walked on.

We came to a clearing. The smell of sage and dust hovered in the air. Somewhere in the distance, a sheep bleated frantically, urgently. *Where's her shepherd?* I wondered. Before us, between two sets of ancient cedar trees, was the mouth of a tomb. It was not very impressive, yet it was more than just a cave.

The opening itself was not as high as an average man, and only slightly wider. On the outside entry frame, extending some fifteen feet up the top of the tomb-cave, and off the right and left sides, were carved ornate Kabalic symbols. Set to one side, resting in its carved-out rolling track, was what could only be the Sealing Stone. It was large: approximately my finger-tip to elbow thick, twice the height of a man, and the same width.

The Sealing Stone was not round. Not really. It resembled a severely damaged stone wheel; a huge, broken and largely chipped stone wheel. Thus, it was more square than it was round. It was apparent that it had always been square, and at some point, someone had tried to make it round, unsuccessfully. It would have taken at least four strong men to even budge it, let alone to put it in place to seal the tomb and then remove it again.

As we approached the cave or tomb, the old man spoke. "I assure you, Centurion, the stone *was* in place, the tomb had been closed," said the old man.

I then looked at him, studied him. That feeling I had a while before with Irena—that overwhelming sense of familiarity, of recognition—now hit me with this man.

From over his shoulder, I suddenly noticed two other men. Had they been here when we arrived at the tomb? If so, I had not seen them. Each of them looked on with expressions of fright and awe. They were Legionnaires, but not in my charge. Regardless, I was a commander, a senior officer to them, and thus, was about to question their presence.

But the spear began to vibrate in my hand. I almost dropped it. For an instant, it felt alive. I found that I didn't have the need to question this, however, but was instead compelled to go in the direction that the spear seemed to be insisting I go, into the mouth of the tomb. Slowly I walked forward, Irena right on my heels. She too had seen the spear's demand.

Cold and dank was the tomb. Musk and death were its smell. The coppery smell of old blood lingered as well. And there was something else…Nay, two other things: A tingling charge was in the air, as if the lightning bolt of a god had been thrown through the tomb's air. With it was the unmistakable smell of something burned. Was it an offering that someone had made and left? No, not likely. It smelled more like slightly burnt cloth than anything else, not the incense or wood figure one would burn in an offering such as this.

The burnt smells were faint, wafting on the stale air of this place as an afterthought. If something had burned here, it had only been singed.

"Come, see," said our guide, the old man. I hadn't even noticed that he had walked past me and was standing in the center of the tomb, or more accurately, the center of the burial chamber near a large, rectangular slab. Obviously, this was where *His* body had been placed. But, all that remained there now was a large cloth, a shroud. I approached the slab, and hence the shroud. It almost seemed to glow of its own accord.

I reached out to touch the cloth. Irena's breath caught in her throat. I stopped in mid-reach and looked at the old man. He smiled and nodded his...encouragement, approval—I knew not which—compelling me to pick it up and see. I did, slowly lifting it up for inspection.

"His shroud," I said reverently, to no one in particular. I suddenly dropped the thing, afraid. Why was I doing this? What did I care about this man? As if to answer, I felt the spear vibrate again. Was I imagining it? It did not matter. The message the spear was sending me was clear.

I placed the spear on the slab so that both my hands were free. Gently, I lifted the shroud once again for a better look. Now, *my* breath caught in my throat, for on the cloth, an image appeared. A face. Though its eyes were closed, the face watched me, stared at me, its features connoting a peaceful bliss. I looked even closer, and as I did, the strange odor of singed cloth grew stronger. It was coming from this cloth! How could that be? I held it higher, examining more of the cloth. As I looked further, I saw that the image of an entire body had been...imprinted, singed (however one wished to describe it), onto the shroud.

"That is Holy cloth, touched by God, as an Anointed One was raised from death," said the old man.

I could not deny the feeling that I held something beyond my comprehension, the same type of emotion that the spear had affected upon me for three days past. I was completely overwhelmed; overwhelmed by a number of things that I simply could not fathom. They coalesced into that state of being most prevalent in humans when faced with that which they do not understand: fear. When fear spoke to me, I simply hardened the heart, walling out the threat of the unknown, so that I stayed in control. Invariably, this took the form of my Centurion mantel shining forth. It was always such a nice guise to hide in. Such was the case in that instance. I dropped the shroud and turned to the old man.

"Where is He?" I demanded. The old man's face became taut as he heard the shift in my voice, command bordering on menace.

"But, He is risen," he said.

"Impossible," I stated flatly.

"Longinus," Irena said, "what are you doing?"

"Stay out of this. Go back to the house."

"But—"

"Go!" I barked. I then spun on the two Legionnaires standing dumbfounded at the entrance to the tomb. "What do you know of this?" They looked at each other as if I'd spoken Greek, or some other language their feeble minds were too illiterate to grasp. "Well?"

"I, we, don't know, Centurion," stammered the boldest of the two, a short, dark-haired, middle-aged soldier of about thirty-six summers, with a nasty scar on his left cheek. The other, a light-haired boy of perhaps seventeen, was trembling. This one had something to say.

"You. Out with it!" I demanded.

"I am Legionnaire Gaius. I...we were assigned here by Centurion Cascie, sir, to watch the tomb so no one would steal the body. Mine was the second watch, sir," said the boy. My gaze wandered to the scarred one.

"I am Legionnaire Romi, Commander," he said, saluting me crisply. It is true. I had first watch. When..." he hesitated, looking at his comrade, not wanting to implicate him in anything.

"The tomb was sealed and all was well when I relieved Legionnaire Romi, Centurion," said Gaius, saving his friend from having to continue on. "No one was around. The night was cold and quiet, and after a time...after a time..."

My eyes narrowed, piercing the boy's. His shame-filled gaze dropped from mine.

"It was my fault, sir," spouted Romi. "I should've taken the second watch."

"No," interrupted Gaius. Summoning his courage, he pulled his gaze back up to me. "After a while, I fell asleep. When I awoke, the sealing stone was moved and the corpse was gone." He stopped, waiting for me to respond. I did not.

The truth was that I did not know how to react. As a soldier, this man's severe dereliction of duty had to be punished, even if with his own life and those of some of his company. But I knew that something else had happened in the night; something infinitely bigger than a mere soldier falling asleep.

No, I thought. *Someone must've stolen the body.* I did not want to believe in the alternative. I looked at the ground. Too many feet had trodden over the earth here to yield any evidence of a theft. And the only potential eye-witness had been asleep. But if the body had been stolen, could the thieves have made the image on the cloth? And if they did make it, how'd they do it? Obviously, they'd have made it to bolster their claim that He'd risen, but...

I couldn't think anymore. I was confused. But, I certainly could not let these men see that.

"There was no one around when I awoke," continued the lad, "so I ran to summon help. When Romi and I returned, a woman was near the opening of the tomb."

"What woman?" I asked.

"Don't know, sir."

"You didn't get her name?" I asked, incredulous. The two soldiers exchanged another fearful look. Another transgression. "No wonder you're still just a Legionnaire, soldier," I spat at the middle-aged one.

"Yes, sir," was all he said.

I took a breath to hold my temper in check. "Proceed. The woman…"

"Yes, sir. Well, the young lad here asked her what she was doing. At first, she said nothing. She looked as though her mind were gone, far away, like. When she finally did speak, all she'd kept sayin' was that she'd seen *him*, that He's alive, and that He'd spoke to her."

"I…figure she meant the dead Jew in this cave, sir," said Romi, clearly thinking that I had not grasped the meaning.

I came close to hitting the man.

"But, she never talked right to us," put in Gaius. "More to the air, to the spirits," he said, dreamily, as if he were also talking to the spirits.

"Then she left," offered Romi.

"To, 'spread the news,' she said," added Gaius.

"And neither of you stopped her," I reprimanded. Their faces fell in shame again. "You, Legionnaire Gaius, fell asleep on guard duty. Neither one of you detained a witness, let alone even got her name? What is wrong with you? Especially you, Legionnaire Romi. This is obviously not your first tour of duty!" My anger was beginning to get the better of me.

"But…but that's just it, sir," stammered Gaius. "We both know that we should have done those things, but—"

"But what, soldier?" I exclaimed, almost yelling.

"We weren't really thinking straight. It was as if something was in the air here…" Romi trailed off, his brow crinkling, eyes looking down. He seemed to realize how stupid that must sound.

I became silent, thinking. My anger was getting back under control, and it was because what Legionnaire Romi had just said somehow made sense to me. The two soldiers, however, took my silence as a malicious sign. The younger one began shaking, one of his hobnailed sandals actually clattering on the ground.

"You should be flogged, flayed and executed," I said, then fell silent again for a moment, allowing those images to sink in.

I thought Legionnaire Gaius was going to piss his Carass, or at the very least, burst into tears. Romi, on the other hand, was blank faced, stoically rigid. A lifer, this one, I thought. He's seen many a battle; a true soldier.

"However," I continued aloud, "you are not in my Command. You will have to explain yourselves to Centurion Cascie, and probably to Horse Commander Luctus. I pity you. Right now..."

"Longinus," whispered the voice, interrupting my speech.

I whirled around to see Irena still standing there, near the slab. But, I knew, the whisper had not come from her. Nor had it come from the old man, also still standing near the slab.

Suddenly, a knowing smile splashed onto the old one's face. "You hear *him*, do you not, Centurion? He calls to you."

Shocked by his words, as well as by the voice in my head, I stood there gaping at him.

"I...I do not know what you speak of," I replied lamely. I forced myself to gain back my composure and spun back on the two Legionnaires, intent on reasserting my authority.

"And, you two," I said with inflated gruffness. "Report immediately to your commanding officer and inform him of the events here."

"Yes, Centurion," they said in unison, shocked that I wasn't going to turn them in personally. They both slammed their closed fists to their chests in salute, then spun on their heels, leaving as quickly as they could.

"And send back three others to guard this place," I called after them.

"Yes, Centurion!" Romi yelled as their footfalls receded in the distance.

The inside of the tomb was now utterly silent. Outside, a bird sang a joyful tune, and the distant sheep's mournful bleating drifted to my ears once again. *Still have not found your shepherd, little one?* I thought. Or, was that the voice addressing me again? I began to back out of the tomb.

"Longinus," said Irena.

I stopped and stared at her. There was something different about her entire countenance. My eyes saw it, but my spirit and mind perceived it more. She seemed somehow transformed, and a light emanated from her. She reminded me of the Ones in the stories the Hebrews tell; stories I've heard told around even a Roman soldier's campfire. This region infected us all. What was it they were called? Ah, yes: Angels—a race of Divine beings that helped humans on behalf of the Hebrew God.

We did not really have anything like them in the Roman pantheon of gods and demigods, although, one could argue that local deities filled that role—and, I was certainly not Hebrew. Still, Irena stood there glowing. Was it a trick of my mind? It must have been. Or, perhaps it was a spell.

Ach! I yelled at myself in my head. I had never adhered to such nonsense. I would not journey down that path now.

I glanced at the old man. He had the same glow emanating from him as Irena. An odd thought impinged itself in my brain; I suddenly realized that I did not yet know his name.

"Peace, my friend," he said. "We have all been touched by the Divine this day."

I looked back to Irena, who now appeared normal, though the old one still glowed. He now held the Shroud rolled up and cradled in his arms, with the gentle touch of a doting mother holding her newborn. I was about to say something when my gaze caught sight of the spear still lying on the slab where I had left it. I picked it up and left the tomb, leaving the others looking silently after me.

I did not know why I left so abruptly, other than to say that something was happening to me; something was stirring to life within. And, it was terrifying.

IV

After leaving the tomb that day, I went straight into town. Legionnaires had been sent in to make sure the people stayed more or less in line. Word had spread quickly of the Master Teacher's rising from the dead, or alleged rising. By late afternoon, early evening, all of his followers—his disciples, they called themselves—were found, gathered in one place. Soldiers I encountered on my way through town were only too eager to tell me where the disciples were.

I arrived at the courtyard of this place just in time to see a lieutenant thwacking the one I took to be the owner of the house, the one called Paul, with a standard issue short-club, while the rest of the flock looked on helplessly, including a woman I recognized as one of the locals. I was later told that she, too, had become one of the Teacher's disciples, a questionably close one. Five legionnaires also looked on, nearly salivating with sadistic pleasure at the misplaced and trivial display of Roman power.

"Lieutenant!" I yelled. His arm froze in mid-strike. He turned to see who dared interrupt his fun. Upon seeing that it was a superior officer, he lowered his arm and assumed a look of guilt. But I saw right through that look.

Insincerity cascaded forth from this one. His eyes showed not true guilt, but a cruelness and defiance masked by a veil of good. Hardness and cruelty is all he would understand. So be it. I did not gain Centurion rank by being a pleasant fellow. Before I could speak, however, he spouted off.

"Centurion Longinus," he began arrogantly, summarily losing the facade of guilt.

I did not know this lieutenant. Obviously, though, he knew me. And, judging by his posture, his arrogance, he was probably from a prominent Roman family. But I cared little about that.

"I was merely attempting to…to—" he tried to continue.

"To what, you shit-hole? Were you told to beat him?" I bellowed. My gaze landed on Paul. His lower lip was ripped and bleeding profusely. His nose was smashed on the bridge, and bleeding from that wound and the nostrils. A dark, painful-looking mound was already forming under his left eye. Yet, it was none of those ugly things that stood out about him to me in that moment. It was, instead, the stupid, childlike smile which adorned his face; a smile that seemed to glow and grow in radiance the more I looked at it; to pull me in to a whole other world; nay, a whole other Universe.

But my heart and head had to stay rooted here, in what was happening at this moment. I had to control this entire situation. "I should let this officer hit you once more just to knock that smile off of your face," I caught myself saying to the man, Paul.

"It would not matter," Paul replied through his broken lips. "Nothing can hurt me on this glorious day."

"Your spilt blood bespeaks otherwise," I said.

"'I am in this world, but not of this world'. My Master said that, and on this day, it was shown true to me. You may hurt this corporeal form, but it is not who or what I truly am," said Paul.

"What you are, is a madman," quipped one of the legionnaires, thus inciting a round of laughter from the other soldiers.

"Silence!" I commanded, with the wrath of the gods. "You will stand at attention, all of you." I narrowed my eyes at the lieutenant as I spouted the order. They obeyed.

With them all lined up at crisp attention, I grabbed the short-club from the young officer and hit him upside the helm. His head snapped to one side and his helmet shot off, clattering noisily to the floor.

Slowly, dramatically, almost menacingly, the lieutenant brought his head, and thus his face, back to attention, boring his eyes into mine. Death and malice flashed in those eyes—for half-a-heartbeat only, but they had been there, nonetheless. This one was not only cruel, but dangerous.

To his credit, though, he said nothing. The other legionnaires were stunned and shocked by my violent outburst. The air seemed to be sucked out of the courtyard as they made a collective, shocked intake of breath.

I turned then, and addressed all the soldiers as their clearly superior officer. "Your insubordination and lack of discipline disgusts me! You speak out of turn. And you, lieutenant," I said, rounding on him again, my spittle spraying his face, causing him to blink involuntarily. "I should drop you where you stand."

The legionnaires seemed even more shocked at this. But, it wasn't shock. There was something else beginning to creep into their faces, their countenance. I could see it in her eyes; they were thinking, *Why would a Centurion care if we were beating Jews, especially if they might be hiding something, in this case, possibly a body, a possible rallying point for those civilians wanting to revolt?*

"Do not be angry with them, Centurion," Paul said, intruding upon my thoughts. "They were only doing their duty as they saw it."

I stared into this man's pale-brown eyes. That light was there; the same light that was in the old-man's eyes, the one in the tomb. "Leave us, all of you," I said to the men while still staring into Paul's eyes.

Legionnaires and Paul's flock alike began to file toward the front gate. "No, no. Not you," I said, motioning to the civilians. "Just the soldiers." I turned to the lieutenant. "You wait for me on the road," I commanded, none too gruffly. They marched away. Paul and the others who were left stared at me, waiting.

Paul's eyes, still alight, glanced down at my spear. His face beamed all the more. "That is the instrument, is it not?" he asked.

"Yes."

"May I?" he asked, reaching gently, slowly for the weapon.

I said nothing, but allowed him to touch the shaft, then the blade. He caressed it as if it held the Master himself. My soldier-self wanted to yank the thing away from him. But, I knew he was no threat. I felt a certain inexplicable bond with this man through the instrument.

Finally, he pulled away and looked deep into my eyes. I felt his soul touching mine. "You will go beyond your bounds, my friend. You will leave all this behind," he said indicating my uniform, "to seek and speak the Truth. This will occur soon. Very soon. Of course, it is up to you. You could choose to turn your back on it all. The choice is yours."

I stood speechless. I knew naught of what he spoke. The path before me was dark, save for the knowledge that I was Centurion Longinus, Centurion Gaius Cassius Longinus of the Imperial Roman Legions. Yet, within my being, I was unfolding into much more. I could feel it.

I finally gathered myself back together. "See..." I stammered. I cleared my throat and began again. "See that you stay out of sight for the day."

Paul simply inclined his battered head in response, giving away nothing. Good enough. I turned on my heels and left the courtyard.

V

I had left Paul's home that day, ignored the lieutenant and his soldiers waiting for me on the road, and all but staggered to the Legion base.

In truth, the Legion base was barely an army encampment, save for some stone and concrete dwellings: barracks, that the men had managed to erect since my arrival. That particular day had turned out to be unusually hot and dry. It seemed the gods had sucked all the moisture out of the air.

I rarely came to the base at mid-day. I was usually out in the *field*, as we called it, with only a handful of my soldiers at a time, while the rest stayed behind to attend their assigned duties, so my men were surprised to see me wandering back in alone. At least, that's what I took to be the reason, at first, for the look on their faces. But then, I came to realize what that look truly was: deep uncertainty.

Word had quickly spread throughout the area, including throughout Rome's Legion of the land, that this Jew had supposedly risen on the third day after his death, as He Himself had foretold.

Many of these men were indeed superstitious to a fault, as well as uneducated, and so undoubtedly believed the tripe of a risen body. This, I thought, was their reason for the look of trepidation.

But, that was not the only thing that had them uncertain. Word had indeed traveled fast, for they had already heard that a guard, a fellow legionnaire, had fallen asleep on duty, an offense serious enough in its intensity to invoke the rule of decimation, the rule of one-in-ten. The rule had not been implemented in some time, to my knowledge, but that did not mean it would not be in the future. In fact, somehow, that was the rumor that was floating about: that the rule of decimation was going to be implemented for this offense, which was also why the men were on edge.

Simply put, the rule of decimation states that if a soldier—a legionnaire—committed a grievous error or offense, a gross dereliction of duty, then all one-hundred men in his century, and or his fellow centuries, were lined up by officers. One soldier was selected at random, and executed on the spot. Then, every tenth man in either direction from the first, was also selected, and executed on the spot. Usually, after watching in horrified, bowel-loosening terror, the offending legionnaire was also slaughtered. The remaining legionnaires would never forget the lesson: Obey, or be the cause of death to your comrades and yourself, and the befalling of shame on your family's honor.

Rome ruled by many methods. Not the least among them was fear, in various forms. That was especially true within the ranks of the military.

As if it were not enough, the men were agitated for yet another reason. By now, they all also knew that mine was the spear that had pierced His side. Thus, these soldiers embraced the gods of fear on more than one count.

In my mind, at that moment, however, I dismissed them all, intent only on going to my quarters. I did not know what I was thinking. Or perhaps I would not admit to myself then what I was thinking, but now I must reveal the truth of my mind. I wanted to escape to the familiar: the military, my command, my home.

A soldier's life; it is blessed among all professions for its regimentality. Although, I will admit now that in my case, established structure was the coward's refuge.

As the days, then weeks, passed, I went beyond my usual gruff self, and became an abusive tyrant to those around me, particularly, to the men beneath me in my command. Those closest to me, when in my presence, began to walk as if on burning coals, and if possible, did not subject themselves to my person at all.

Even Irena, my sweet Irena, was loath to venture near me. She tried on several occasions. I found myself enraged by her mere existence. I insulted her profanely each time. She was still effected and affected by that day in His tomb, and simply wanted to enrich her understanding of the experience by talking with the one who had shared it with her, the one she cared about, and the one to whom she was now bound in a most profound and unusual way. In the time since the experience, however, I was of a mind to destroy its reality, or at the very least, push it into the oblivion of the irrational.

"What you think happened, you stupid whore, is the farthest from the truth," I had said at our last meeting. "There are logical explanations for everything that happened that day."

Something in our perceptions of each other shifted in that moment.

Irena was never one to back away from an argument with me. She would turn her back on others in the same context, not caring about them or what they thought or said enough to engage them, but not me—never with me. Yet, now she did. A long silence ensued before she spoke.

"Maybe the girl from that night was right, Longinus. Perhaps demons do possess you," she said.

She was not serious, of course. Was she? She had said it with a smile upon her face. But, it was the smile of pity, of indifference; the kind one might give to another whom they feel is beneath them, or is simply ignorant. I knew in that moment that I had lost her. I realized once again what I had truly shared with Irena. Not just at the cave—the tomb, of course—but what we had shared since my arrival in this desolate place which the gods had forsaken.

We had shared our bodies, for one. On so many, many nights, we satisfied the primal, animal urgings of our bodies. It wasn't mutual at first. It was a business transaction. But, it blossomed into much more. Soon, our spirits and minds began to intertwine as well, profoundly. We would become enveloped as one in spirit, merging together in mind as our sweating, writhing bodies melded together in the climactic ecstasy that was the reflection of the divine, explosive creation of the Universe. Am I exaggerating? Not at all. For that is how I came to view our coupling. In that final moment of climax, I was the Highest of Gods, creator of all. I realize this now.

I acknowledge now, too, that I had never experienced anything like it with another human being. Ever. I knew she felt it, too, though we never spoke of it. I could see it in her eyes, feel it in her embrace. From there, we became very close on all levels. She was a confidant, a partner, a friend.

Appearances, however, were important in my line of work or duty. As a Roman officer, I could not be seen to have a relationship, let alone a serious one, with a woman of her profession and nationality, even if she was part Roman. So, I continued to pay her. At one point, she began to refuse to accept it, even becoming angry when I insisted. But, insist I did, almost becoming belligerent about it. I know I hurt her then. For, I said things I did not mean in order to force her to accept my money. I know this diminished me in her eyes, and caused her to question what was really between us. Yet, our passion for each other only grew. And, yes, I would call it love. Even in argument.

If someone were to see us or hear us arguing, on occasion, they would have sworn that we hated each other. However, the opposite of love is not hate. Love and hate are two sides of the same coin. The opposite of love is indifference.

Such is what I felt from her in that last moment, when she had said that perhaps the girl had been right about demons possessing me. And, it saddened me.

She left me then. I was told that she left the city entirely shortly thereafter. I know not where she went. North, was all that I was told, upon inquiring. I convinced myself that it did not matter at all. I was a Centurion, and thus above such things. How absurd. Nevertheless, it is what I told myself.

I was in the command tent when I received a visitor. It was someone familiar.

A young legionnaire swept into the tent with the self-importance only reserved for the young and naive. "Centurion Longinus," he said with his formal salute.

"Yes," I replied, pretending to ignore him, not looking up from the report I was studying.

Quite apparent was the lad's disappointment in my seeming lack of interest in him, for his voice fell in volume and assertiveness substantially. "There is a man here to see you, Centurion. An old man," he said.

Though my eyes stayed on the report, the writing became a blur. My hand, for some reason, drifted to the spear leaning against the table at my side. I rarely left it more than two feet from my body now. I had no explanation for this, other than that it had become more important to me than my own arm. I was connected to it in a way I could not explain nor understand. Or, perhaps I simply feared to.

"His name is Jacobi. The old man has been waiting since dawn to see you. We thought he was a little...off, so we kept him away until now. He's persistent in saying that he...a...," the lad stammered.

I looked at him then. "He what?" I asked. But I already knew.

"He says he met you before at the...a..."

"Tomb. And, once before that," I finished for him.

Perplexity ran across my legionnaire's face. "Yes," he said. "But the old man said that he never said his name."

"'Tis true," I admitted. "But I know it now." I thought for a moment, not sure whether I wanted to hear anything that the old man had to say. Curiosity got the better of me, though. "Show him in."

"Yes, Centurion." With that and a salute, the lad disappeared and returned a moment later with Jacobi.

The older man's face still had the glow which had descended upon him that day in the tomb. But now, as I looked at him, something within me quickened, as if, for the first time in a decade, I was seeing a dear old friend. His semi-toothless smile beamed when our eyes met, as if to confirm my thoughts.

"Ah, Centurion Longinus. Thank you for seeing me," he said reverently.

"I apologize for not seeing you before now. I was just informed of your presence," I found myself saying. But why? I was a Roman Centurion, and made no apologies for lack or delay of audience with a Jew civilian! Still, as before, for some reason, something compelled me to administer to this one with respect.

"How goes it with you, Centurion Longinus?" he continued. I found the question odd, yet oddly comforting, as if I could unburden myself of anything to him.

"Quite well." I lied.

His eyes left mine for a moment and landed on the spear, then came back to me. My fingers, resting on the spear, now closed, gripping it in a gesture of protection, or more accurately, of coveting. "Jacobi," I said amiably, "an interesting name. Why have you come to see me?"

Again, his eyes drifted to the spear, then back. "Does It speak to you still?"

I brought the spear closer to my body. "Speak to me?" I asked, playing the fool. He simply smiled.

"Come, Centurion. I know The Voice has spoken to you through it. Does it still?"

I pondered for a moment as to how or why I should answer that. Indeed, as I have pointed out, odd voices in and out of my dreams, and one in particular, had plagued me since that day Jesu was hanged and I stabbed His chest. But, as of a while ago, I simply chose to push them aside, ignore them, and they had stopped. Though it had been only a little more than a month, I had convinced myself that the voices—the voice—was gone, and, indeed, had only been a phantom of my mind. Yet, now with Jacobi in front of me again...

Still, I denied it. I did not want to hear It again. "My dear Jacobi, I fear I know naught of what you speak."

He looked at me then with piercing eyes, as if looking into my very essence. "Have you no shame?" he asked. "You deny the greatest gift that could be bestowed upon anyone?"

My anger began to rise. "Take care, old one," I breathed. "Do not forget your place here."

"Do I forget it?" he declared sarcastically. "What difference? You deny your True place," he countered.

His statement was confusing. Yet, there was a part within me where it made perfect sense.

He sighed then, as if letting go of a hope. "I came because I feared this, but had to see for myself. You have turned your back on the gift of Your Self. Alas, it is a shame, but it is also your choice. Yet, know this: It will always be there for you when you are ready."

I looked at the spear. For one of the few times in my life, I was speechless. Yet, part of me wanted to rail at this little old man for his presumption. Part of me grappled with a truth which I knew he was trying to teach me. Before I could find my tongue, however, he was gone. I looked up from my spear and he had vanished.

I ran around the table to where he had been standing, then to the tent flap. Peering out to the area beyond my tent, there he was, walking away. Jacobi was now approximately two-hundred yards from my tent. By the gods, how could he have walked so far so quickly?! Or could I have been staring at the spear that long?

"Sir?" came my guard's voice. I looked at him with what must have been astonishment. "Are you all right, sir?"

"Yes. Yes, of course. Carry on," I said and ducked back into the tent.

I sat down again behind my make-shift desk, piled with reports and maps, when one I seemed to have overlooked caught my eye. I picked it up: A leather-rolled missive with the seal of the Emperor's Guard, the Praetorians. "Guard!" I yelled.

The lad came rushing in as if a demon's teeth were chomping into his ass.

"Yes, Centurion?"

"When did this arrive?" I snapped at him, waving the leather roll.

"I...do not—"

"When, damn it?"

"This afternoon, I presume, sir."

"You presume? Why was I not told? Can you not see the seal? It is from Rome herself!"

"Yes, sir, but it was not accompanied by a royal courier, sir," he said. "It must have come through with other reports. I did not know it was here until just now. Sir."

The boy was right. This should have been accompanied by a high ranking minion of the Emperor's Guard, a glorified courier. "Are you sure, Legionnaire? Are you sure this was not accompanied by anyone?" I asked, with the edge of a razor, challenging him to defy me.

He straightened and lost all fear, exuding the confidence of one who spoke the truth. "Yes, Centurion. I am positive. I have been here since dawn and personally inspected those reports that came in this morning. That message was not there, so it must have arrived after the noon meal without royal escort. I would have seen otherwise."

"Yet, you did not find out if any reports came in after the noon meal, else you would have notified me of this, the only one with the royal seal," I pointed out.

The lad's confidence evaporated, his chin dropping to his chest.

"I do not know the seal of the Emperor's Praetorians. This...this is my first post, sir. I—"

"What? Every soldier knows the Praetorian Seal...," I started. But my heart suddenly went out to the boy. Ignorance. That's all this was. Indeed, I had committed a similar sin in my first year of duty. My slip had cost the life of my Centurion's servant. I had allowed a missive to slip through, containing a powerful poison. Upon opening it, my Centurion's servant spilled some of the foul substance on his skin. Blisters formed on his hands almost immediately. It ate through to the bone and a grizzly death ensued.

Surprisingly, my Centurion had not punished me beyond a month of latrine duty. I never understood that, until now. This lad's transgression of not notifying me of this leather-bound message, was nowhere near my sin.

"Son," I began, "your lack of attentiveness could cost you someone's life, even your own."

His brow crinkled. Clearly, he did not grasp my meaning. "See that you go through the deliveries and arrivals everyday, anytime and every time they come. Understood?

"Yes, Centurion."

"Dismissed." He saluted so hard that I thought his clenched fist might go through his chest-plate. And, he nearly tripped over himself in his hasty retreat.

A smile tickled my lips. Had I ever been that young, that eager, that...green? I must have been.

My eyes dropped to the leather scroll still cradled in my hand. Trepidation crept into my mind. Why had there been no escort accompanying this? Of course, perhaps there had been an escort with the missive, but he had traveled in common civvies instead of the Praetorian uniform. And, perhaps further, he simply got tired of waiting. It was most unusual if that were the case. Then again, the Praetorians could be an arrogant lot.

The escort to this thing, or lack thereof, suddenly became irrelevant as my curiosity to its contents finally got the best of me. There was only one way to find out what it contained. I slipped my finger under the wax seal and pried it from the leather. Expensive parchment greeted my eyes as I unrolled the communication. I read the words, not quite comprehending what I was seeing.

"Come now. The message cannot be that glum."

I was startled by the voice. I looked up to see before me once again the old bright face of Jacobi. Speechless was I again.

"Well, when do we leave?" he continued.

"Leave?" I stammered.

"Is that not what it says? You are being recalled to Rome, are you not? And, I shall be your servant on the journey," he stated flatly, conveying the obvious.

"How could you know that? The message was sealed. It is death to view a royal communication meant for another!" I said. "And, and, I thought you'd left!" I was babbling. Why could this one unnerve me so?

He simply stood there smiling. "As you pointed out, it was sealed. I could not have seen it as you think because I did not open it."

A silence ensued. I was, once again, speechless.

"Well?" he finally said. "Do I speak the truth?"

"Are you a magician?" I asked lamely.

He laughed. In fact, he rolled with laughter. It was actually quite refreshing, that laugh. It immediately put me at ease. I found myself smiling, smiling as much at this little man as I was laughing at myself for my inane question.

"No," said Jacobi at last. "Unless, of course, you consider running into a young, drunk courier, who was blabbing how he was of the Praetorian ranks, though he was dressed plainly, and asking him why a Praetorian was here, an act of a great Magician!" he laughed again, showing a wonderful, toothless grin, full of life and warmth. I could not help but be drawn in by it. He also had graciously explained what had happened to the royal courier.

VI

The heat was oppressive, burning the lungs as it entered, deflating the soul as it left. Overall, I was glad to be leaving this barren place. The gods baked this land and its people, scrambling the brains and creating a ripe environment for one to lose one's mind; actually, for the many to lose their collective balance.

For example, more than a few people were beginning to view me as some kind of demi-god. My spear and my contact with the Anointed One, as many were now calling *him*, had caused this. Ignorant fools. Jacobi was among them. He certainly held me in this reverent light, but, only to a point. He was continually harping on me that my human part, my Roman part, kept getting in the way of the True Gift and Realization which I had been given.

At first, I would simply bellow at him to leave me alone; that he was an old fool. But his deflection of my words and attitude was done with the gentle demeanor of a wise old sage and father-figure. And, with persistence.

Once, I yelled at him with such wrath and violence that I was sure he would piss his robes and lose his bowels. Any of my soldiers would have, and then fled for their lives. But not Jacobi. Dear Jacobi. He simply smiled his toothless grin; that Otherworldly glowing Presence emanating from his whole being. I had tried to drive him away. I failed. I could have had him forcibly removed from my post forever. But I did not. I could not. He was here for me. He was a guide of sorts. I do not know how I knew this. I just did.

Thus, I accepted him into my circle as my "servant." Some of my men snickered at this, behind my back, of course. It was not uncommon for an officer to take a young man-servant into his tent to be part of his staff. Some preferred the sexual pleasures of a young man, as well as those of a woman, or even instead of. Perfectly fine. But not me. I had always preferred the company of women. My men knew this, which made their jokes about the older Jacobi becoming my man-servant all the more humorous. Again, these hilarities were never told to me or in front of me, but I heard them, nonetheless. And, it mattered not.

Even at the time I was leaving this place, I had still received no official word as to why I was being recalled to Rome. My superior officer would only say that in the official missive he received, the reason stated was reassignment. As to where and why, he would not say, if indeed he even knew. My missive said nothing save for recalling me to Rome. The General, my superior officer, was also obviously quite perturbed with the whole thing. There was more going on here than I was being told. For instance, why was I not being allowed to take my men with me, if, in fact, this was simply a reassignment? One hundred of the finest lads I have ever had the honor of commanding were they. Although, it was true that since the great Julius Caesar, or rather, just thereafter, an officer was not allowed to take all his men when transferring—too much loyalty can be a dangerous thing. But, I was only a Centurion in command of a hundred; not a General in command of a Legion of thousands. Besides, when previously I'd been reassigned, my men had always come with me. Why not now? I was told to pick a platoon and support crew only. Why?

No matter. I was a soldier of Rome. I obeyed orders. I told my men I would see them again, and then chose two Decurion officers, seven legionnaires, and four servants to man supplies and domestics. My replacement had arrived the next day, so off we went—me, my nine men, plus four, and supplies. And, of course, Jacobi.

The first two days of the journey were utterly uneventful; hot and boring. We were to stop in a small village on the third day to replenish our food and water, and rest our mounts. Two more days and we'd reach the coast and passage back to Rome herself. Approximately half a mile from the village, my two scouts returned to report that the place seemed empty. Though they had not actually ventured into the village itself, there appeared to be no one about at all. This was somewhat odd, but not that unusual. The sight of Roman soldiers often instilled fear in the locals. Fear enough to stay inside or, out-and-out hide. Still, someone should be around.

"You did not see anyone?" I asked, for clarification.

"Not a soul, sir," the scout replied.

"Any holiday that we know of?"

"Sir?"

"Any observance, holy or otherwise, that would draw the people elsewhere or keep them indoors?" I restated.

"Ah, well, I don't know, Centurion," the scout replied sheepishly.

Then, as one, our gaze turned to Jacobi for an answer. This area was still Jewish, after all. "I do not know the local customs of these parts, but I assure you that in the general sense of the Law of Moses, this is a day of normal enterprise," he said as he casually leaned on his walking staff.

"Can you never speak plainly?!" I retorted.

"This is a normal work day," Jacobi said simply. "But..." he said, eyes narrowing.

"Well, what is it?" asked the scout.

"I...I'm not sure," answered Jacobi. There was a silence. The raspy caw of a vulture sounded in the distance.

"It's the heat, is what it is. It's cooking your brain, old man!" quipped a legionnaire, and the rest laughed.

"All right, enough," I said. "Proceed with caution," I told the scout. "Lead us in."

Indeed, no one was about as we went in. Small plumes of smoke were hovering just above the ground in various places around the village. One of the servants suddenly made a grotesque guttural noise and vomited. In an instant, we realized what had made the poor fellow wretch. It was not smoke hovering above the ground, but dust; the dust surged up from the wings and jostling of dozens of scavenger birds as they vied for their place at a gruesome feast. The heat-filled light breeze suddenly shifted and brought the stench of the slaughtered villagers into our nostrils. My scout had been correct; not a soul was here, not any longer. But their hacked and disemboweled corpses were.

The bodies were in groups. The mutilation was an abomination; a child's arm hacked off and protruding from a woman's vagina; a severed penis and scrotum stuffed into an elderly man's mouth; the hilt of a sword standing out of the anus of both men and women, the blade still up inside the victim; heads and torsos on pikes. There were other atrocities that went beyond the imagination. It was obvious that these horrors were performed on the people while they were still alive. The final look on their faces was beyond unspeakable pain and terror, frozen there forever. That servant was not the only one to lose his breakfast at this point. Even two of my hand-picked, battle-hardened legionnaires did, as well. I could not blame them. The wrath of the gods coursed through my veins in that moment. I knew not these people, cared naught for them. Yet, something inside me wanted to avenge them, if only on the basis of human dignity. There was another reason, too, going through my mind—not quite as lofty; this was a slap in the face to Rome. "You see?" it bespoke. "Rome is nothing! She cannot even protect her subject people!" I looked at Jacobi and was quite surprised to see his reaction. He was calm, almost serene. Though he surveyed the scene with eyes wide open and obviously smelled the rotting stench, he was unaffected, at least in the way the rest of us were. For some reason, I was angered to see him thus.

"Jacobi!" I yelled. "What in the name of the Gods? Are you dead yourself? These are your people, destroyed. Yet, you stand there as if...as if..." I could not finish.

"'As if' what, Longinus? These are not my people alone. All are one People, within the One. Their eternal spark or spirit is not here any longer, but it is not gone. This," he said gesturing to all the death, "is tragic perhaps. Yet, it is what it is; an experience in the Mind of God. There is no judgment."

I was astounded.

"That is not to say," he continued, "that those who are guilty will not meet justice; 'those that live by the sword, shall perish thereby,' it has been said. Again, no judgment. It is simply the way of it, reaping what one sows, the Law of the One."

"Of course, you old shit!" squawked Decurion Demitri, clearly tired of Jacobi's rants. "I *choose* to live a soldier's life. There is no more honorable way to die than by the sword!"

In spite of everything right then, I had to smile. Demitri was the son of a dear friend of mine. He was part of the equestrian class. He was educated. And, he had been my ranking Decurion for some time. He could have left the army the previous year, but chose to stay with me. At times, he over stepped his bounds. But, usually, he was both amusing and insightful.

"As you say," Jacobi said with a bow.

Demitri made a move to strike the old man. Jacobi moved not a muscle.

"Hold, Decurion!" I commanded. "Stand down. We have more important matters here."

"Centurion!" said a legionnaire. "All the water supplies are contaminated. There are corpses down the wells.

"Understood. We'll ration what we have," I said. "Gather any arrows and weapons left behind. I want to know who did this. Dispatch two men to search for any survivors." The soldier opened his mouth to speak. "I know," I cut him off. "It's futile. Do it anyway. Have the rest of the men pile the corpses in the center of the village. Burn them."

The soldier saluted fist to chest and left to fulfill his unpleasant task. There was then a preternatural silence, as if all the air in the immediate vicinity had been sucked away, taking all sound with it. The spear began to vibrate in its harness on my saddle. Jacobi and Demitri both saw it as well.

"They're still here," said Jacobi.

Across the center of the village, one of my men dropped, an arrow protruding from his back. "Form up!" I commanded, my mount dancing nervously beneath me.

A score, plus ten filth-encrusted bandits, poured out of the humble dwellings, screaming with blood-lust. "Shit on Rome!" yelled one. "Kill them all!" yelled others, all waving swords and weapons.

"To the outskirts," I directed my men. I was proud of them at that moment. We were outnumbered three to one. Yet, there was not a hairsbreadth of fear between them. One man had gone down. He would be avenged. There was nothing else to be done. Of the remaining eight, six were legionnaires on foot. Demitri and my other Decurion quickly remounted and moved rapidly, the way we had come. The other servants had remained outside the village with the supplies. Only Jacobi had ventured in with me. He, too, was on foot. But, unlike my well trained young legionnaires, Jacobi could not run in formation to a protected site. He could not even move his sack of bones faster than a brisk walking pace. He was standing next to my horse's flank. Without so much as a "by-your-leave," I bent down and grabbed the scrawny old man below the armpit. I kneed my horse hard in the sides, urging him to a sprint from a standstill. Using Jacobi's own weight and the horse's momentum, I simply swung the old man up behind me on the mount as we galloped off.

"STOP, Longinus!" yelled Jacobi.

"I'll not leave you to these barbarians, Old One!"

"So you would sooner break my old bones this way? I've had a long life. I've seen the One incarnate, and now I see It within myself. I fear not the next life. Now put me down!" demanded Jacobi.

"You'll not venture to that next life just yet, my friend. You belong with me!" I yelled over the pounding hooves and screaming bandits.

My men and I met up where we had left the other servants and the supplies. The servants had already been slaughtered. Seven more bandits awaited us at the bodies. They were easily taken down. Demitri and my two mounted lieutenants sliced their heads off where they stood. I felt bad about the servants. Ordinarily, I would have assigned guards to them and the supplies but I had not the man power. Besides, all the servants I had picked had battle-practice experience. I had used them for skirmish practice when I was short of troops. They were loyal and knew how to fight. But they had been outnumbered and not properly armed.

The remaining murderous scum were running out from the village. They came at us in a rag-tag group, no organized attack formation whatsoever. This would be easy. With a light nudge from me, Jacobi slid gently to the ground. My men and I regrouped, forming a small wedge; a miniature version of a tried and true battle formation that would slice through and divide an enemy horde. The screaming, murderous filth was now running full tilt right at our v-shaped wedge. Our horsemen were at the front of the wedge with myself at the point. I pulled my spear from its harness and lofted it, ready to signal our own charge.

"Hold, Longinus," said the Voice; that same voice, from my dreams. Now, though, it seemed to be coming from the spear—from the blood stain on the spear's blade.

Fear gripped my heart. "You again!" I heard myself whisper. I quickly pushed the fear away and replaced it with anger. "Hold? And what, allow ourselves to be slaughtered?!"

"Sir?" said Demitri from behind me. Apparently, I had answered the Voice a little too loudly.

"Nothing, Decurion," I said.

"Longinus," continued the Voice in my head, "that will not be the way of it."

I watched the oncoming scum. Against my better judgment, I held; did not move a muscle. Though I could not see my men because I was at the point of our little wedge, I sensed their agitation; could almost hear their thoughts. "What in Hades does he wait for?"

"Sir?" Demitri's voice.

"Hold your ground, Decurion," I said.

The horde, if you call them that—thirty or so disgusting, smelly, disorganized, marauders and murderers, a mob, really—were still running at us full speed, still screaming at full throat. But then it began to happen. When they were about forty yards from our position, their voices began to falter, their sword arms began to drop. Some of them began to fall back. By the time they were within fifteen yards of us, the "mob" had dwindled to about ten. The rest had stopped at various points on their charge and were now bent over, hands on knees, panting for their lives. The final ten had also stopped, fatigued. They could not maintain a full sprint to engage us. They had expected to pounce on us in the village. They were not the well-conditioned legionnaires of Rome. Drawing them outside the village at their frenzied pace had fatigued them completely. It was time to destroy them.

"You will not kill them," said the voice.

"Like hell, I won't!" I said through clenched teeth. "Advance!" I yelled. As one, my men and I sprang forward.

"You will not kill them," repeated the voice. I tried to turn a deaf ear. I glanced back at Jacobi. His eyes were closed. I know that he had heard the voice, too. No matter. Our wedge sliced through what was left of the mob and dispersed; no need to keep our formation. Individual fighting broke out. In outright defiance of the voice—I would not obey a phantom!—I made a violent stab down with my spear from horseback at the first enemy I came to. It should have run him through, skewered him where he stood. Instead, to my horror, the spear snapped. The lance shaft broke at the place where it joined the blade, the blade itself falling harmlessly to the ground. The enemy was as stunned as I. He stood there. Frozen. I reigned in and drew my sword. My mount's momentum had taken us a few yards beyond the man I had thought to spear. I turned and spurred my horse to a gallop back at him. Before I could reach him, however, one of his comrades stepped into my path, stabbing his short sword at my horse's legs, but missing. I cleaved the lad in two with my sword, swinging down and slicing through his shoulder, collar bone and ribs. Almost in the same motion, I smashed his face in with my stud-soled boots to dislodge my weapon from his body. I galloped on to the first enemy. To my amazement, he had picked up the spear blade. For some inexplicable reason, I was angered by this beyond comprehension. *How dare this pig even think of touching it!* I thought. Even more amazing was the awe with which he now looked upon it.

I reached him and reigned in, stopping my mount within arm's reach of him. I swear that in that moment, as he looked into my eyes, he knew who I was and what he held. I raised my arm, and severed his head from his body. It dropped off his shoulders and thudded to the ground, its eyes still blinking at me with comprehension. For five heartbeats, his body remained standing, blood spurting in a rhythmic fountain from the neck stump. Then, the truly astounding thing happened: The hands, still holding the spear blade, raised in the air toward me, clearly offering the blade back to me. As soon as I took the blade, the body's legs crumpled in death.

A silence filled the air. Fighting had ceased. I slowly became aware of many eyes being upon me. Everyone had witnessed what had happened. The enemy began withdrawing. The man I had beheaded had apparently been their leader. They had also taken in how I had killed him and his offering up of the blade, the significance of which was not lost on them. *A superstitious lot*, was my first thought.

"You did not heed the voice," said Jacobi from behind me. I turned to see the old man standing there, stern disappointment splashed across his face. At his side, he held the shaft of my spear. I had dropped it when it broke, unaware, to free my sword hand.

I was confused and angry. Why was Jacobi reprimanding me, and how dare he presume? I was also afraid. Why was he hearing the voice, too, yet no one else heard it? To dispel this confusion and fear, I did what I always do; I hid behind my mantel of being a Roman Officer. "Who are you to question me? This man led the killing here," I said. Then I remembered something else said earlier. "Why do you care, old man? You said earlier that, what was it? 'Their eternal spark is not gone...an experience in the mind of God...no judgment...' and yet you stand there in judgment of me? Take care, Jacobi!"

"It is your intent here, your lack of heed to the Higher voice within you that is at issue, not this one," he said, indicating the headless form before me. "He chose his path as we all do."

"I tire of your riddles, old man. I don't know why I keep you around," I said.

"Yes you do. I am one of your inner voices," he retorted with a toothless grin.

I could not tell whether he was serious.

"Sir!" yelled Demitri. "They get away!" All eyes swept to the retreating, more like slinking away, outlaws.

"Take them," I began. I locked eyes with Jacobi. "Alive, if possible."

"But Centurion, there are too many and they are unworthy," continued Decurion Demitri. "They cannot be allowed to escape. It would be simpler to kill them with arrows and—"

"Enough! You will *not* question me thusly! You will follow my orders or end up like this piece of shit," I said, commandingly, pointing to the decapitated corpse. "I don't care whose son you are. Is that clear, Decurion?" My anger, though misplaced, silenced him utterly.

"Yes...yes, sir," he stammered.

VII

We headed for the coast, arriving two days later. I had repaired the spear, reattaching blade to shaft as best I could given the tools at hand. It wasn't pretty, but it would hold solid. Of the murderous raiders that had been left alive, we captured fifteen. The rest fled, eluding us as they ran back into the maze of rock formations in the hills that surrounded the village.

Eluded is perhaps the wrong word. Eluded implies pursuit. I was not about to order my men to pursue them all the way. We had neither the manpower, nor the time for that. So, I settled for capturing a handful as an example. As I had implicitly promised Jacobi, we took them alive. Foolish, that was. Once I turned them over to the Roman regiment at the port to which we were headed, they would all be crucified. It's not as if any of them were of note, from a wealthy family of the occupied territory who could be ransomed back to their people. They were nothing, worthless. Capturing them alive had, in some ways, been crueler then killing them outright. Then again, perhaps one or two of them would make it to the arena to fight for his life and maybe even live, for another day or so. Still, I was of the mind that that would not happen. They would be crucified.

I pointed this out to Jacobi. "'Twas stupid to take these men, Jacobi. You know that. They are going to be executed anyway, in a much more prolonged and brutal fashion than they would have received by our hands."

"Then why did you spare them?"

I felt the flush of anger color my face. "What say you?!" I growled through clenched teeth. "You bid to spare them! *That...*" I lowered my voice to a conspiratorial whisper. "*...That voice*, too. You heard it. I know you did."

"No, I did not, Longinus," he said.

"But?" I began, confused. I was sure by the look on his face, at the time, that he had.

"I knew it was there, however. I knew that *you* were hearing it," he continued. "In that moment, Longinus, it was a lesson for you to learn. It was not about saving those men. Their fate had already been sealed by the choices they had made and believed in. In that moment, it was for you to acknowledge your own conscience, your highest Self through compassion, to step outside of your Roman persona and—"

"Stop!" I pleaded. "Why must *everything* with you be in the form of a riddle?"

"'Tis not a riddle if one understands its point."

"Ach!! I surrender."

*   *   *   *

The port city of Najaffi—as it was now called, at least, perhaps, until the next solstice; it had changed names so many times over the past two decades, that it was somewhat difficult to keep an account of what it might be called at any given time—was as beautiful to the eye as it had been when I first arrived in this region of the Empire. For the most part, however, its beauty ended there.

As we approached the city, we were first met with the smell of the salty sea, the ocean. I always warmed to the smell of the ocean. It bespoke travel, adventure, going home. But this time, there was no opportunity to revel in the feelings that scent conjured. For, no sooner had the ocean smell wafted to us, when it was rudely usurped by the offensive stench of the city itself: stale urine and excrement, thousands of unwashed human bodies, not to mention unprocessed and rotting trash and refuse. As it had been the last time I had come through Najaffi, its waste disposal system was still apparently non-existent. It baffled me as to why the city leaders, who changed almost as frequently as the name of the place itself, did not develop some way of dealing with this problem, or, indeed why the Roman Prefect, the military head of this realm, did not simply implement his own solution. Then again, very few cultures other than that of the Roman people had as an acute sensibility to personal cleanliness and hygiene, which, of course, extended to their surrounding living environment. And, as to the Prefect stepping in, well, when occupying a region, a province, a people, we did try our best to respect their customs and ways of living, even if they were disgusting to us. Such was my train of thought as we approached the city.

That train of thought was all but forgotten, however, when the next wave of smells happened to hit us. Food! Cooking meats and vegetables; that wonderful smell made our mouths water and our taste buds lust for gratification. I had not realized how hungry I was until that moment.

We arrived at the outskirts of the city. I ordered Demitri to stay outside and make a temporary camp with the prisoners. I would send out supplies and food as soon as possible. I was not about to march the filth through a crowded thorough-fare. I took my other mounted Decurion and Jacobi to seek out the local Roman authority. If my information was accurate, then the Prefect, the man in charge here, was still Maximus Centilius, a somewhat brutal lower General turned Prefect for Rome, who thought nothing of flogging and flailing prisoners for entertainment; even those whose crimes were petty: the stealing of bread, for example.

The main thoroughfare into the city was flanked by several Roman Guards as was appropriate. We dismounted and I approached the soldier nearest us. He was obviously a Gaul, a Celt, as evidenced by his mane of red hair and mustache. No Roman-born soldier would be allowed to keep that mustache and that length of hair, though it was tied back to flow out the back of his helm. Certain allowances were beginning to make their way into Rome's military mind with regard to the recruitment of foreign fighters. The Celts from Gaul were among the fiercest fighters in the world, though tough to discipline. A handful of them were starting to make their way into Roman life, including, and especially, the army.

"You there. Where might I find your Prefect, Centilius?" I asked.

The Celt studied me as if I were a fly on shit. Though recognition of my uniform and rank finally dawned on him, he was still clearly unimpressed. His silence dragged on to the point of utter rudeness, not to mention insubordination. My patience by this time was non-existent. Though he was almost a head taller than I, we both stood on uneven ground. By stepping toward him, I actually came eye-to-eye with the brute, as I was on slightly higher ground. As I did this, I could smell his rancid, stale-ale breath, no doubt the result of the previous night's inebriation. My nose was practically on his.

"Take care, soldier. I am Centurion Longinus and I am here to see your Prefect, who is an old acquaintance of mine. You will take me to him now, or I will rip your balls off where you stand and feed them to the hungry prisoners I've dragged here. Is that clear, my ignorant Celtic friend?" There is a point at the beginning of any confrontation where it will explode or snuff. I could see in his eyes that in any other time and place, he would have done the former, attempting to, and probably succeeding in, tearing my head from my body. But, fortunately, his Roman training was paying off; he maintained his discipline. The Celt stepped back from me and eyed my dirty uniform again, then looked over my shoulder at my companions. "My Decurion and servant," I offered.

"Follow me," he said, and turned on his heels without the customary—actually required—salute to a senior officer. So much for discipline.

I started to follow, when I heard the voice. "Do not leave it," It said. I didn't flinch at hearing it. Perhaps I was getting used to the unbidden inner commands. Jacobi was staring right at me. The old fool knew I had heard something. The "it," of course, was the spear. I stepped toward my horse and retrieved it. My Decurion raised an eyebrow, but said nothing. I motioned to my companions to move out. The three of us followed the Celt, leaving our horses with one of the other city guards, a decidedly more Roman-looking soldier.

The Celt led us through the crowded plaza of the city. There were all numbers of merchants, vendors and sellers of everything imaginable, and some quite unimaginable: fine linens and jewelry, cooking wears, meats and other food, spices, soothsayers—everything that one would normally expect to find in a port city. But, then there was the bizarre things; magic potions made from the dung of priests, animals being sold not as food, but as sexual surrogates, and naked humans being led by twine tied to their genitals, being marketed specifically as sexual playthings. I ignored most of what I saw. I turned to see my battle-hardened, yet worldly-naive Decurion's face writhing in disgust. Jacobi, however, was smiling his toothless grin at one and all. My first thought was that the old fart had gone off his nut and didn't realize what some of these people were peddling. But then I looked into his eyes. And, there It was: that other-worldly glaze; the depth that I'd seen many times. He was looking at all these people as equals, distaining none of them. I turned back to look at our Celtic guard as he continued leading us to the Prefect. Clearly, he had been observing me and my little party as we progressed.

His face was difficult to read. There was a mixture of contempt and respect. He turned away as we walked on. Though it mattered not what this one thought, I was curious.

"Speak your mind, soldier," I said.

"Very well. Your officer is puss-food," he said, prompting my Decurion, whose family name was Flavius, to begin to unsheathe his gladius at the insult. A subtle shake of my head and the blade was re-sheathed, much to Flavius' disappointment.

"He is one of the finest soldiers I've fought with," I countered. The Celt simply grunted, but said nothing else. "Well? What else?" He stopped and turned to look at Jacobi who was now quite a few paces behind us. I stopped next to him. Flavius walked on. The Celt and I simply observed the old man for a moment. The Celt's contempt had obviously been for Flavius. The respect was for Jacobi.

"That one. Where I hail from, we would say the he has the look of The Old Ones," the Celt stated with reverence.

"He *is* old," I said, confused.

The big Celt looked at me as if I were a stupid child. "Not 'old' in the man-sense, sir, but as in one of The Old Ones—the God-Men that created all—that my people are descended from."

Now I understood. So, it was not just me who saw this light in Jacobi. I suddenly felt a bit of a kindred spirit with the Celt. I felt that this might be someone, even as obviously barbaric as he was, who might understand some of the things I'd experienced over the past few months. But, the feeling was short-lived. My reason kicked in. He was an ignorant Celt, after all. He was a subordinate, not to mention that I did not know him; not even his name. "As I said, he's simply my servant," I impotently stated.

The red-haired man smiled and said, "Are you sure who is the servant, and who is the master?" He laughed and we walked on.

I had exaggerated a bit to the Celt when I said I was an old acquaintance of Centilius'. In truth, it was an out-and-out lie. I'd never met the man before. I knew him by name and reputation only. His reputation of cruelty was not exaggerated. We heard the squealing pleas for mercy as we approached the huge wooden doors. The door-guard obviously recognized the Celt. But, to my surprise, he did not give me, Decurion Flavius, or Jacobi a second look; he opened the doors right away, as if we had been expected. An uneasy feeling began to wrap itself around me. Before I could give any thought to it, however, my uneasiness gave way to nausea. As we entered the great hall behind the doors, we were greeted by the sight of a man stretched on some kind of wooden device. He was lying on his back, the contraption at an angle so that the man was leaned back, but not quite lying flat. His arms were outstretched on wooded planks, his head tied back to a post from which extended the two planks holding his arms. No, his head was not tied back. The post had an indentation which cradled the back of his head. His head was being held there by his ears; his ears had been nailed to the post with two very large nails—spikes, really—to help keep his head back. If he lifted his head too much, his ears would rip off his head. His hands were also nailed to the planks. The source of his screaming pain, however, quickly became apparent: His scrotum had been nailed to a separate piece of wood and was being twisted in the hands of another man in a black robe.

A short distance away, across the plush black marble floor, reclined several well-dressed men, their togas rimmed with gold. They were eating what appeared to be a very sumptuous lunch. A couple of the men were obviously as disgusted by the sight of the man being tortured during their meal as I was. I am all for disciplining someone, flogging, even. But I have never been one to torture, especially in the context of what is clearly nothing but entertainment. Yet, I stomached it; made no indication that I was bothered by it. The Prefect, after all, who was apparently the man in the middle of the rest—as he seemed to be the one enjoying the display the most—far outranked me. Besides I needed him. I looked to my Decurion and subtly shook my head; not a word, my thoughts were to him.

Slowly, the spear's tip began to glow softly. I looked from the spear to Jacobi. The old man had stopped in his tracks, eyes closed as if in some kind of trance. The tortured man began to become still, his screams turned to simpering moans. Finally, he was silent, as if asleep. My spear returned to normal, Jacobi opened his eyes and came to stand beside me. The Celt smiled and looked at Jacobi with revered awe. He then looked at me, eyebrow raised, silently telling me that Jacobi was indeed one of the Old Ones.

Prefect Centilius, however, was not so reverent. "What is this?" he bellowed, looking from the racked prisoner to myself, then to Jacobi. A most awkward silence ensued, during which Jacobi made his way to my side. The Prefect's gaze was intense, almost demonic. But, Jacobi merely yawned.

Prefect Centilius was a short, stocky, petty little man, with the brains to match his stature. It was widely rumored that in addition to his cruel nature, he had a taste for young boys. The latter is ultimately what had forced him out of the military; he allegedly had raped a senator's thirteen year old son. The only reason he didn't lose his life, so I'd heard, was that there had been no direct evidence; no witnesses, just the boy's sketchy accusation—his word—against the then second-rate General. Glancing around at the young man-servants doling out the food and wine, I had no doubt that the General's lust for the youthful male was true. Looking at his ugly, almost demonic, expression at that moment, I felt certain that the charge of rape also had been true. I suddenly hated and distrusted this fecal excuse of a man, this putrid example of a Roman.

Fortunately, our Celtic friend spoke up, breaking my thoughts and the silence. "Noble Prefect. Please forgive the intrusion, but this is Centurion Longinus. He has been escorted to your presence as requested," he said, rather too formally and with a sarcastic edge.

Escorted to his presence as per request? I was stunned. Perhaps we had been spotted on the road, but to know my name and for someone to be commanded to be escorted to the Prefect immediately was something else. The uneasy feeling in my gut tripled. "What is the meaning of this?" I demanded. "I am simply on my way to Rome as ordered."

There, behind a partition, near the couches where the diners were reclining, appeared a Praetorian Guard, then another, then another, and yet one more.

"It appears that you have something the Emperor desires," giggled the Prefect.

"Shut-up, Centilius!" barked the lead Praetorian, a General by rank. That, too, was quite odd. Why was such a high-ranking officer in the Emperor's Guard here? And what could I have that they, or the Emperor, wanted—if indeed the whore-spawn Prefect was correct? Then it became clear. All of their eyes simultaneously drifted to the spear in my hand. I should have known. It was strange that no one questioned me about it coming in to a Prefect's court hall. True, I was an officer of Rome, and thus, a side arm gladius was permitted on my person. But, bringing in a weapon such as a spear was simply not permitted. It had not even dawned on me that I still carried it until that moment.

"You let quite a few of the murderers from that small village get away," continued the Praetorian. "That was a mistake."

How could he have known? Spies? Some of the escapees made their way here, told their stories, perhaps? But what of it? "I had not the man power to capture them all," I said, defensively.

"You could have, should have, killed them. 'Twas your duty. But we saw what we needed to see, on more than one level."

I was outraged. "You've had spies watching me?"

"Of course. And then some. You and your weapon performed most admirably. It even speaks to you, does it not?"

There was much more going on here than just espionage. Though he outranked me, I had gone beyond caring about the consequences. "Explain yourself!" I commanded.

"Why, Centurion, you forget your place."

"I don't care who you are anymore. Something is happening here, and I want to know what it is."

"Very well. Your village raiders were hired thugs; a chance for us to see the spear in action. It's becoming the stuff of legend, you know," confessed the Praetorian.

I was utterly confused. My rational mind could not get itself around the notion that my own beloved Rome would stoop to such a feat simply to watch a meaningless piece of wood "in action." I had seen many atrocities during various campaigns, most of them displayed by the cruelty that human nature can turn to when allowed. Yet, most had been products of a confused circumstance of the moment, or of desperation. But this..."I don't know what you're talking about," I replied. "The spear did nothing."

"The man it hit, his headless corpse handed it back to you."

I said nothing.

"And, it glows while in your grasp, then it speaks to you, does it not?" he reiterated.

Glows. Yes, it has, but usually not before I hear the voice. It shakes, or vibrates, and even then, sometimes the voice is simply there, in my head. How could he know even a twisted version of these things. Perhaps...enough. This had gone on long enough. I held the spear aloft, over my head, but in a non-threatening manner. "This is nothing but wood, metal and—"

"And magic," interrupted a burgundy-robed wisp of a man. Obviously, he was one of the court soothsayers or Apollo Temple priests.

"You're a fool if you truly believe that," I said.

"But it soothed and silenced the prisoner," he said, indicating the motionless wretch on the rack. Had that too been planned?

"I, the spear had nothing to do with that," I said, holding the spear by my side and turning to Jacobi. Why was he not saying anything? It certainly was not for fear of offending a superior. That had never stopped him before.

Before I could say anything to Jacobi, the Praetorian mistook my glance at the old man and stepped forward to get a better look at Jacobi. "Yes. This one, too. This one silenced the prisoner, but in conjunction with the spear's tip glowing. He will come with us too."

"Too?" was all I could stammer.

"Yes. The spear, you and this old man. You see, Centurion, rumors have been infiltrating the palace in Rome. And, as I said, the priests convinced our emperor that the spear must have powers beyond this world, and therefore, his highness should be in possession of it, being that he is a living god and the most powerful man on earth. The thought was to have you simply bring it to Rome on a recall mission. But then, our sources," he continued, as he made the subtlest of head nods to Flavius, "indicated that you'd die rather than part with it. So, we organized the assault on the village to test it, and you."

I turned and glared at Decurion Flavius, hatred spilling from every one of my pores. The spear began to shake in my hand violently. The movement was not lost on the Praetorian, nor on anyone else in the room.

"There! See there! It responds to you. You know now that Flavius was our man and that angers you. The sense of betrayal, and so forth. We came here to take the weapon from you. But I think now that you must come."

VIII

I was now completely ignoring the purple robed figure, seething in my anger at Flavius. Betrayed, yes. Though I hadn't known this one all that long, it was long enough to believe that I could trust him. "How much did they pay you, Flavius? You have disgraced yourself and your family forever."

"Quite the contrary, Longinus," answered the Praetorian. "He has done his patriotic duty, as I expect you to."

I said nothing.

"Come, come, Longinus," the Praetorian said at last.

"No," I said, burning my disgust into the bastard's eyes.

"Do not look at me like that, Centurion. It is not I who demands this, but the Caesar himself.

"He has no idea what this is," I said, holding up the spear.

"Exactly why you must come with us—to show us."

For a moment, I faltered. Could I go to Rome and presume to show them…show them *what*? I had not the faintest idea myself what this…thing was all about. I had been denying it all along. And, it was only just in that moment that I fully acknowledged to myself that there was something here; something larger than myself happening to me, through me, and the spear was a part of that, but certainly not the thing itself. In truth, it was only a very small part of the overall story that was beginning to take shape within my mind's eye, my soul. The fools in Rome would never understand this. "If it's such a small part, then simply give it to us," they would say. Never!

"My patience is done," said the Praetorian, interrupting my thoughts. With the snap of his fingers, all became chaos.

Purple-robed figures descended on us from all sides. I spun, and the spear caught two of them with barely a touch, yet both crumpled to the floor as if scalded by hot oil. Spinning again, I caught another Praetorian's sword with the blade of my spear. It did not parry his weapon, but sliced through it as though it were lard. Stunned, he stepped back, afraid, that dumb look of the superstitious splashed across his face.

"Take him!" the General Praetorian commanded, pointing to Jacobi.

I could not get to him fast enough. The four remaining Praetorians pounced on him like lions on a rabbit. But, they were in for a huge surprise. The butt of Jacobi's walking staff stabbed into the balls of the first Praetorian to reach him, the head of it under the jaw of the second, drawing the first up off his feet in excruciating pain, shattering the teeth and jaw of the second.

Two other Praetorians wrapped themselves around Jacobi, though, smothering him with their bulk. The spear left my hand before I even realized that I had hurled it. It slammed into the side of the Praetorian on Jacobi's front, sending the guard screaming to the ground in a crumpled heap of fury and burning pain. The stench of searing flesh filled the air. He yanked the spear from his side and a wisp of smoke trailed from the wound.

For an instant, no one moved; frozen, stunned by what we had just witnessed. In that moment, I covered most of the floor between me and the spear, now resting at Jacobi's feet. I stopped short, though. The last Praetorian now had Jacobi in a choke-hold from behind, jewel-encrusted knife at his throat. In contrast to his burst of heroic fighting a moment ago, Jacobi was now quite relaxed and, so it seemed, almost limp in the guard's arms, with that odd smile upon his face. Then my eyes met the Praetorian's. I saw fear there. Hesitation, indecision. He would not slice the old man's throat. Not because he was afraid to, but because he saw the prize on the floor: The spear, the Lance, the supposed Magical Staff of the gods, the blade of which carried the blood of the Powerful Prophet.

I could see the dilemma play out in his eyes; to grab the spear, he must release Jacobi and face me—hence, the fear in his eyes. *Is this Centurion a powerful prophet of some kind as well?* he would be thinking. *It is he who wields the spear, after all.* The fool was giving his own power away to me with such thoughts, because it paralyzed him. He could not decide.

Then I would. I had to.

The Praetorian General was still there, and no doubt, more Palace Guards would enter at any moment.

"Guards!" squealed the snake-of-a-Prefect. Indeed, I would not have long to wait at all before his reinforcements came.

I saw movement out of the corner of my eye. The Praetorian General had started to move toward the spear. And then it happened: The act, the deed, that would forever change my career, my path, my very life. Although, one could argue that my path, my life, had already *been* forever changed back on a lonely hill many months before, where three souls had hanged on lonely crosses.

His sword drawn, the General lunged toward me and the spear. I could not draw my gladius quickly enough. The General's sword was almost upon me. Suddenly, there was a flash of metal from another sword, and the General's sword arm was lopped off in a spray of blood, arm flopping to the floor, his sword clattering some eight feet away. The General fell to his knees as the death thrust came into his side. My Celtic friend now stood next to the fallen Praetorian General, bloodied sword in hand, his mustache tugging upward at the corners, framing his grinning mouth.

A hand and dagger suddenly appeared from behind the Celt, moving toward the center of his back, unseen by the big man. My instinct took over, unfortunately. That is when, without conscious thought on my part, my short-sword gladius left my hand. I had become adept at throwing this weapon many years before. There was quite an art to it, or, at least, to doing it well. The trick was to flick the arm, so to speak, from the elbow down—not from the wrist, as so many assume—at precisely the right moment, so that the blade, which is lighter in weight than the hilt, will fly lead and land true in the target. Within a fraction of an instant, it was done. Within a quarter of a heartbeat, I had become an enemy of the state, an enemy of Rome. The hilt of my gladius protruded from the chest of the Prefect.

The Celt had seen my eyes, my body language, assessed my intent, or what he thought to be my intent, in a split second, and ducked as I knew he would, thus exposing the Prefect behind him. The big man looked at me, amazed. "I thought," he began with the awe of one whose life had just been spared, "I thought that you were aiming for me."

The Prefect now lay on the floor, gasping for breath, gurgling air escaping from the bloody hole in his chest.

"No," was all I could manage to say. I had instinctively come to the aid of a comrade-in-arms, a man who had just defended my life against one who was not supposed to be an enemy. But the man I had defended was a Celt! Not even a true Roman. Obviously, though, that didn't matter. In the inferno of battle, your comrades are those you fight with as one, each an extension of the other. Personal origin, individuality itself, was rendered meaningless in that instant.

And yet...and yet...By the Gods, what had I done? This Prefect—Maximus Centilius—was a piss-ant. All of Rome knew that. But, he was still, or rather, had been, a Prefect of Rome, appointed by Rome to govern here. My life in the Roman military machine was over; the only life I had ever really known. Certainly, the only one I had ever loved.

"Centurion!" It was the Celt, shattering my self-loathing. I simply looked at him, dazed with disbelief. "Where is your officer?"

He was right. Flavius was gone. No doubt he had slithered off when the commotion started. Aside from the Celt and myself, the only ones left alive in the large room were the dancing girls-prostitutes, and the men—so-called dignitaries—cowering behind the reclining cushions. And, of course, Jacobi, who was still being held by a Praetorian.

I managed to come out of my daze, and saw that the Praetorian was still in a bit of daze himself. Indecision is the worst of enemies. It is paralyzing, allowing the depth of fear to swell up within one's being, bubbling to the surface in heretofore unimagined ways. I could see it in his eyes. The problem was, he still held his arm around Jacobi, knife at the old man's throat.

Then, to my amazement, Jacobi calmly lifted his free hand to the sharp blade under his chin, and gently pushed it away. The Praetorian complied as if he were in a dream, slowly backing away, eyes betraying a glazed, trance-like stare, probably in disbelief over all that had just happened. Reverently, Jacobi, leaning on his staff, bent down and picked up the spear, handing it to me as he stood once again. I accepted it back with the same respect and reverence with which it had been retrieved and offered.

"It is not yours, Longinus," began the old man, "but It has been entrusted to you for a goodly amount of time. It is nothing in and of Itself; wood, metal. But, It has His blood, and will aid those who Know and are on the Path. You are not only on this Path, but are a leader on it. You may not accept this yet, but your higher-self—that part of you that is Truly Eternal, and that is *him*—says it is so. And so it is."

For the first time since I'd known the old man, I was consciously aware that he was making sense. Sort of.

But there was no time to dwell on it. The large doors crashed open and a half-century of legionaries and local palace guards poured in, led by Flavius and a Tribune.

"Centurion Longinus, in the name of the Emperor, you will cease hostilities and surrender your weapons and person!" ordered the Tribune.

"This way!" yelled the Celt, before I had a moment to think. I grabbed Jacobi by the wrist and half-dragged him as we began to run to the back of the large room. I let go of him long enough to yank my gladius out of the now dead Prefect, never breaking my stride or pace as I did so. I now had no free hands with which to pull Jacobi along. Yet, to my surprise, when I looked to Jacobi, he was right there with me, keeping up with the Celt and myself, step for step. For the second time that day, I was amazed at his youthful bursts of energy.

We had been heading toward a rear door that led to a balcony. At least, it appeared to lead to a balcony as I glanced out its adjacent window. Suddenly, a platoon of soldiers barged through the door and into the room. We stopped in our tracks. I looked to the Celt. He was unsure. Obviously, he did not know the palace as well as I thought. No matter. They were coming for us; for me, in particular. I had been branded an enemy of Rome—though those in power now had scarcely ever exhibited the ideals of Rome, twisted and perverted power-mongers that they were, and therefore, in my eyes, were not true representatives of what Rome is, or was. That was the only idea that made me feel that I was in the right. And, as such, I had to turn and fight, then and there, and die the only honorable death left to me. But then I heard Jacobi's words echoing in my head, "...It has been entrusted to you for a goodly amount of time."

"My lady," came Jacobi's live voice. Yet I paid no heed, thinking that it was still the one in my head. Until, that is, I heard the other voice in reply; a decidedly feminine one. And, familiar. Lovingly familiar.

"Yes! It's me, Longinus!" it said in a loud, urgent whisper. She was standing in the shadows, dressed in the bright colored silk and satin of a palace mistress. I could barely see her face. But I knew her. Irena. My Irena. My heart leapt. "This way, quickly!" She disappeared down a dark narrow hallway off to our left.

"Seems you have a friend," observed the Celt. Jacobi simply smiled. We ran into the dark hallway without hesitation.

Light spilled from four open doorways, two on either side of the hallway, approximately fifty paces or yards down the otherwise dark corridor. We stopped momentarily, not wanting to cross the doorways. Shadows played frantically in the light. More soldiers massing, I assumed. Though I knew not what lay beyond these doorways—the outside, more rooms—one thing was certain: we were not entering them. Irena, still in shadow, was already well beyond them.

"Hurry!" she called.

We were at a full run in an instant, passing through the light as quickly as possible. Still, I stole a glance through the first doorway on my right as we darted past. What I glimpsed confirmed what I had suspected; soldiers. They were scrambling up the stone steps leading up to the balcony off the main room we had just come from. Apparently, this doorway also had a side-landing for the steps, before they continued on the balcony. But it had been just a glance and I had seen no more.

The corridor remained dark, but my eyes had adjusted and told me that the way was becoming narrow. Something else, too: our flight was becoming easier. We were heading down, the path becoming a steep downward gradient with every step.

We reached a circle, a point where the corridor we were in emptied into a room or anteroom, and halted. Off of this anteroom were three other corridors—one directly ahead, which seemed to be a continuation of the one we had just come from, one to our right, one to our left. Irena paused just long enough to make sure we were all together, then headed off to the corridor on our left.

"This way," she said.

"Wait!" I said, grabbing her arm and stopping her for a moment. "Irena," I breathed, almost panting, partly from our pounding flight and partly from my disbelief at seeing her, the not so buried feelings for her still pining within me. My eyes washed over her, taking in every bit of her. "It really is you! But how? What are you...?"

"There's no time, Longinus. Please, this way," she pleaded.

"Where are you taking us, woman?" the Celt demanded gruffly, before Irena could move.

Having been insulted by his tone—when she was trying to help us, after all—and in her typical defiant way, she shook off my grasp and stepped fearlessly up to the Celt, the top of her head barely reaching his ribs, and locked eyes with him. "This passageway," she pointed, indicating the corridor to our left, "leads to a cave that's partly under water. It's an underground dock. The underground canal to which it's attached leads to the harbor. There is a boat mastered by a countryman of yours named Ventrix. He's a trader and is set to leave for Gaul on the evening tide. He will take you."

"Why? Why would he do that?" I asked. "We've just killed a Prefect and the Emperor's guards."

Irena spun back to me, fire in her eyes. "It's because of that! He hates Rome. Yes, Rome has made him a rich trader. But he hates what Rome has done to your people." She said this last bit to the Celt, then turned back to me. "More than he likes being a successful trader. Besides, he's…a friend. He'll do it because I ask him to."

My heart began to race, my emotions wavered, and a hundred different questions came to mind. But there was no time. The spear began to glow. We could hear faint voices and see the distant flicker of torches from back down the corridor from which we had just come. They would be upon us soon.

"Quickly now! No more questions!" commanded Irena as she ran down the new corridor.

As we all entered the narrow stone passageway in single file, Irena suddenly stopped and jumped up, attempting to grab a dangling leather strap that protruded from the ceiling. She jumped once, twice, thrice, and missed. The strap was just out of her reach.

"Allow me," offered the giant Celt. Casually, he reached up, wrapped his large hand around the leather and looked to Irena.

"Pull hard!" she ordered.

He did.

The crash of iron made us all jump. Then there was another, and another and another. An iron gate now blocked the entrance to the corridor we were in; another blocked the corridor across the ante room, and still another blocked the one next to it, and finally, an iron gate blocked the opening of the passageway we had originally come down.

"But," I lamely began.

"The royal family had built these for their escape, but never got the chance to use them," she called over her shoulder as she continued on the run, and we followed. "There's a separate pulley system to open them all up again."

"Who else knows about the passages?" asked the Celt.

"The Prefect and a few of the palace staff."

"And you?" I had to ask.

Before she could answer, we were upon a set of steep stone stairs leading what seemed to be straight down.

"Watch your footing. These steps crumble easily."

Down and down we went. It seemed an eternity as we descended into the bowels of the palace. It certainly smelled like bowels. The air became musty, moist, rotting—rank. It smelled of wet death. Yet, we pushed on.

I began to hear the sound of trickling water. It became louder and was suddenly accompanied by a larger, subtle rumbling sound—the ocean. Our staircase turned right, then left and we were standing on the edge of water, with a seven man boat in front of us, tied to a short wooden dock. The area was lit by the daylight coming in at the small mouth of the cave off to our left. It was about 80 yards away, but allowed enough sunlight in to reflect off of the water and the sparkling shards of crystals in the cave.

"It is beautiful," intoned Jacobi, who had remained silent up until now. I had assumed he had been conserving his energy. But perhaps he simply had had nothing to say. He was fearless, it seemed, even now; placing his energy not in complaining of our plight, but instead, using it to praise the beauty of our immediate surroundings. "Is not our creator wondrous?" he asked, to no one in particular.

"Yes, Rabbi. The Creator truly is. But now you must go. Into the boat with you," Irena said, as she gently helped the old man into the craft. The Celt climbed in and helped settle him. I handed the spear to Jacobi, and put my gladius in its scabbard.

"I must get back before it's too late" said Irena.

"What?" I said, still standing on the dock. "You must come! You can't go back!"

"I have no intention of going back. There's another way that leads out and off the palace grounds."

I didn't move.

"Please, Longinus. There's...there's someone. Someone I need to go to."

I was crushed. I felt my face flush with anger and embarrassment. "But," I stammered.

"There's no time to explain. But I will. I will find you. There's another ship taking your same route in a few days. If all goes as planned, I will be on it."

"And if it doesn't?" I asked.

She was silent.

"How are we to know which is Ven...Vent..."

"Ventrix. Master Ventrix. He flies the Boar. Here," she said removing an onyx and diamond necklace. *And what Cretan gave this to you?* I thought, but said nothing. She placed it in my hands and folded my hands in hers. "Give this to Ventrix. He will know it's from me and it will more then pay for your passage."

There was an awkward pause. We looked into each other's eyes, deeply. It was still there; that old spark, the ethereal connections that had been there since time began. "Irena," I started. "When you left..."

"I know, Longinus. I know. Much has happened since then. I have much to tell you and I will. But you must go now. Please."

She released me and guided me into the boat as she had with Jacobi. I complied. It was all I could do. The Celt had untied the little boat and we slowly began to drift toward the cave opening. A short oar was thrust into my hand. I looked at it, then back to where Irena had been standing. She was gone.

"Come, Roman," the Celt said gently. "Let's go find the Boar ship."

IX

The ship rocked gently as it cut through the small waves on its way to the gods knew where. Actually, I did know—more or less—where we were headed. But it might as well have been the end of the world. I had been informed that we were going to a specific "outland" region of Gaul, a place where Romans had come years earlier, conquered, and then essentially, moved on. Our captain, for want of a better title—these people did not really have organized military or naval rankings as did we Romans; Owner and Master of the ship would be more accurate—declared that we would go to this region for goods which he could only procure there: exotic wines, herbs, certain leather goods, for example. But he was not very convincing. Obviously, at least to me, he was attempting to display his authority. I believed that the real reason for our specific destination was that my Celtic friend had convinced him to take us there. Whatever the reason for our destination, I was not a man at peace.

I sat huddled in the prow, my back against the rail, legs tucked up under me, chin upon my knees; a ball of sunken humanity. The sun had set an hour earlier, and darkness enshrouded me except for the occasional light from a sliver of a waxing moon somewhat obscured by clouds. How in Hades did I get to this point? Only a matter of days before, I had been a proud Centurion of Rome. And then it was all gone. So, this was despair. There was no other word for what I felt in that moment. But I would not let it consume me. I swore it. And yet...and yet...

Finding the vessel with the flying boar had been easy enough. The Celt knew exactly where in the harbor to look, as all ships landing from Gaul were quartered in a specific region of the docks. There had been several ships moored that hailed from various parts of Gaul, but the banner/flag with the boar insignia had been the largest of them all. In fact, some of the ships or vessels had no identifying flag or insignia at all; an illegality in a Roman port. But the boar flew on the largest flag, on the largest ship.

Her captain, a man named Ventrix, had been dubious at first when I addressed him. But when the Celt spoke to him in their guttural tongue, and then instructed me to hand him the necklace, Ventrix immediately warmed to us, inviting us onto his boat without further delay. Our eyes locked as I passed him and boarded his vessel, and I saw no hostility there.

"Yah, Irena," he suddenly said, with an indefinable smile. I was not sure what he meant. Was it meant for us—he and I—as if we shared some lecherous bond through the favors of Irena? Or, did he simply mean to say, "Irena. She is quite a woman, is she not?," as in a simple statement of respect. I chose to believe the latter. Otherwise, I would have killed the man right then and there, and I had killed enough for one day. Besides, he was our only chance of getting out of this place alive.

Master Ventrix ushered us into the hold immediately. Or, rather, he tried to. Something possessed Jacobi just then, and he took it upon himself to walk to the prow of the boat, which faced the open sea, stood on the forward gunwale and began blessing the boat and all aboard in a none-too-quiet voice. His Hebrew tongue grated on many of those on deck and even a few close by on the docks. More than one person made the hand gesture, the sign against the evil eye.

"Jacobi!" I barked for him to stop, more out of fear for his safety from fellow Romans on shore, than out of embarrassment. He made no sign that he had even heard me. I looked to the Celt with a silent command. He simply sighed and stepped up to Jacobi.

"Forgive me, old one," he said, and gently picked up the old man, who, oblivious, kept speaking his blessing as he was carried into the hold.

There was cargo already locked down and ready for transport back to Gaul. Ventrix said something to my Celtic friend and they had a brief conversation, after which the ship's master looked at me with a new respect, even bowing at one point. He then disappeared across the hold.

"What was that?" I asked.

"I will tell you later. We must hide now. The Romans will be all over every ship looking for us," answered the Celt.

"I know that, but where are we supposed to hide? There's a lot of cargo here. And what space there is left, is too open," I said as I looked around. Indeed, there was a lot of cargo, but the hold was not completely full.

"I believe the captain wants us to follow him," came Jacobi's voice from underneath the Celt's arm. We had both forgotten about the old man, still gently slung through the big man's arm.

"I am sorry!" said the Celt, flushing redder than his beard as he placed Jacobi on his feet.

"Bless you, my son. I enjoyed the ride, though I was not quite finished on deck," Jacobi scolded gently.

"Yes, well," stammered the Celt.

Just then, we heard Ventrix call us. We made our way through the labyrinth of crates and boxes and bundles of goods to the far wall of the hold. The ship's master stood by the wall, beaming with pride. He had pushed aside a huge crate to expose a section of wall; a wall, on the other side of which, I thought was the ocean. What was he so proud of? And then he showed us.

He placed a chubby, grimy finger on a wooden knot in one of the planks and pushed. A section of the wall slid open, but instead of revealing the ocean, it exposed a very slim passageway with very narrow steps leading down. His face exploded into a huge grin, then into an opened-mouth laugh at our astonishment. Ventrix motioned for us to follow as he led us down the steps, all eight of them, and into a cramped little room beneath the hold. Obviously, he dealt in human cargo as well, probably smuggling escaped slaves back into Gaul. Is this what Irena had been planning for herself? Is that how she had known about Ventrix and his ship? She had been a free woman when I had known her in Jerusalem; a business woman—albeit, the owner of a brothel. But here...

Ventrix and the Celt began talking to one another again, interrupting my thoughts. When they finished, the big Celt turned to me and Jacobi. "We are to stay in here no matter what we hear going on up above. He will come for us when we are safely away."

"You mean we are to be locked in here," I stated flatly.

"He must seal us in for a time, yes. But he *will* come for us when all is clear."

No, I thought. *I should end this now; go up and onto the docks. Fight them and end it. Honor dictated...*

"He will," asserted the Celt, obviously misreading the expression on my face. "I trust him. He will come for us when the time is right. We are distant cousins, it turns out," he added, as if that meant Ventrix was the definition of trustworthiness.

I looked at Jacobi, who simply nodded toward the spear in my hand, reminding me of my new charge. "Fine," I said. "We wait."

The Celt turned and said something to Ventrix. They then quickly embraced and the Ship's Master was gone, up the steps, sealing us in behind him.

Three-and-a-half days, we spent in that room. We ate old bread and dried meat and drank water. The Celt pulled them from a box in a cabinet, obviously having been told of their presence by his cousin. There was even a piss-pot.

A few hours after our sort-of imprisonment, if you will, we heard thumps and raised voices outside. The Romans had come. But, the thumps and voices were gone soon enough. And then we and the ship waited, and waited and waited. We lost track of time. Two days later, we were eventually told, the ship left the harbor. The three of us felt the ship's movement at the time and expected to be released within the hour. We were not. I hoped it was to make sure that no ship followed us. It was. I was assured by Ventrix.

"Centurion Longinus," the Celt broke into my thoughts. His face was silhouetted against the dark sky, the waxing, small crescent moon behind and above his head. "We are free," he declared.

"Are we?" I asked rhetorically. I began to formulate other questions in my mind. But before I could put these questions into words, my thoughts changed again, and I suddenly realized something for the first time. "What is your name?" I asked. "I've no idea what it is."

Although his face was mainly in darkness, his white teeth shined with his smile. "Thought you'd n'er ask, you bein' a high Roman and all," he said in mock submissiveness, bowing his head once.

Obviously, in his mind, because of my fall from Roman favor, we were now more or less equals. Unlike Roman society, where one was almost always born to position, the Celts could move "up" or "down" in their culture's structure. Some of the Kings or Chiefs of the various tribes were even chosen by the people, changing every so often to ensure balance. Oh, true enough that many stayed King by force throughout Celtic history, but even that was usually relatively short-lived. No wonder we thought of them as inferior; what society could survive by electing their own Kings? Not all are equal. And, their women; I had heard that their women could even lead men into battle. Madness! The only branch of their society that seemed to always be above everyone else was the Druidic priesthood.

Yet, Rome was once a Republic, her leaders, senators, elected by her citizens—albeit, the Patrician class—and then sometimes, two overall Councils, Leaders or rulers, elected by the Senate. I could hardly fathom allowing a commoner, an uneducated peasant, to be allowed to vote for a leader. Yet, *I* was from that humble class, I reminded myself. Within Roman society, there was only one way to better one's allotted place in life: the military. And, I had done so. I had, through intelligent deeds and uncommon soldiery and valor, risen from common foot-soldier through the legionnaire ranks, at least as high as Centurion. But now it was all gone. There would never be another way to redeem myself in the eyes of Rome. I envied this Celt and his free ways.

"Dosameenor," he said. "My name is Dosameenor. 'The Seer,' it means."

I gave him a quizzical look.

"When I was young," he continued, "I glimpsed certain future things on occasion. I was going to enter the sacred brotherhood, even took preliminary studies for a year."

"A Druid. You were to become a Druid?" I asked, surprised.

"You know of them?" asked Dosameenor, with none-too-little pride.

"Yes, I have heard. I have heard your Druids burn folks alive for your gods; enemies, displeasers…"

"We did. But, most were given the sacred potion of the mistletoe made by the Druids. It dulled their senses from much pain, enabling the spirit to soar free in the flames."

"Oh, well of course! That makes it all perfectly fine then!" I retorted sarcastically. "Barbaric."

"All things not of Rome are barbaric to you people. But it matters not. That ritual practice ended a long time ago. Banned, actually. 'Tis no longer performed."

"Hmph," I grunted, not quite believing him.

"'Tis not. It was a complex ritual having to do with releasing the spirit, the soul, as a Roman would say." He paused, reflecting, I presumed, on what he had just said. Then he went on, "Not important anyway. The Brotherhood is much more than one ritual," he said in a far-off tone. "They hold secrets—secrets that are ancient. Secrets of the workings of *all* things."

"Hmm," I grunted again, doubtfully. "You speak as if your Druids are still around. They were disbanded, even outlawed when Gaius Julius Caesar swept through Gaul and beyond."

"Perhaps. But they thrive still, as you shall well see," he replied.

I simply stared at the silhouette before me, the eyes sparkling, the teeth glinting in the moonlight. There was something about this man, this Celt named Dosameenor, The Seer. There was a depth there beyond what the eyes could see. The spear quivered ever so slightly as if to confirm my feeling. I glanced to my left and saw a figure sitting, not far off, leaning against the railing as I was, but asleep. Or, perhaps he was in a meditation. The figure was Jacobi.

I looked back to my Celtic friend, and was about to ask him if he still "saw" future things on occasion. I thought better of it, however—though I wasn't quite sure why—and simply said, "Yes, we shall, Dosameenor. We shall see." He smiled again and left me.

Daylight finally dawned and I sat where I had through the night. At sea, one has only his own thoughts for company, in spite of the occasional interruptions by other souls traveling on board. My thoughts were becoming darker by the league; my self-loathing more profound by the breath. I had destroyed everything in my life; all I had known; all I had achieved. Gone.

"Let go, my friend," came Jacobi's soft voice. He sat next to me, apparently having moved closer during the night. Dosameenor was nowhere to be seen. "Trouble not over what is done, what is passed," he finished.

"Easy for you to say, Jacobi," I replied. The spear, the lance, lying across my lap, grew slightly heated for a moment, as if to accentuate what Jacobi had just said. I peered at the thing. I still was not convinced that its quiverings and heatings and doings were simply not the product of my imagination. But I could not deny the now permanent dark red stain on the blade. I had cleaned the fresh blood off when we were in our tiny hovel-hideout in the bowel of the ship as a way of passing the time; cleaned it easily of the traces of killings in the palace. But *his* blood remained, as it always had, regardless of how many times I cleaned it. My life was changed completely and forever, inexplicably wound and bound to a power, a mystery beyond my comprehension.

We traveled for several days. After the third rotation of the sun, I stopped counting. The further we sailed from the port city, the more despondent I became. I was lifted only briefly. Not because of the clear skies and smooth waters, both of which were our constant companions, but because, for a time, I believed that we had sailed only miles from Rome. The area felt of home, the air smelled of it too. Indeed, when I asked Ventrix, he confirmed my belief.

"You made for seas," he said in his broken Latin, meaning, I assumed, that I should have been in the Roman navy instead of the army. Perhaps. My senses on the water told me we were close to my home—well, somewhat close to my home—and my stomach had been stable, unlike even a couple of the more "seasoned" ocean farers on board. Although, I suppose I should not make too much of my stable stomach. As I said, we had traveled through fairly mild conditions. No matter. I belonged on Terra Firma, in the army, leading men to glory on the battle field! But, alas.

We had passed about six miles off the coast near Rome because of the ocean currents, Ventrix said, which were aiding us on our journey to Gaul. His boat had sails, but his Celtic crew was not the most adept at using them. Most of the men were rowers, but they could not row all the way to Gaul, Ventrix said.

"Why not?" I inquired of the ship's master. "They can be pushed, forced to," I said, assuming the rowers to be slaves, as they were aboard Roman Triremes.

His face crinkled at my ignorance. "Deese men are free men. Some serve me for debt. Dat iss all," he explained.

"You mean, they're indentured," I offered. His brow crinkled again, but this time in confusion at the new word. "Indentured," I began. "One who becomes a slave to someone to pay a debt to that person," I explained.

"Dey *not* be slaves!" he insisted.

"No, no. At least, not forever. Only until they pay the debt." Ventrix's face showed near malice. It was useless. "Never mind. Yes, they are freemen, free Celts," I acquiesced.

I had taken to sleeping and spending much time in what had been our locked room. It offered the isolation I desired. I did, though, make brief visits on deck to take fresh air and to see where we were. On these occasions, I usually would observe Jacobi holding court with two or more crew mates, discussing philosophy, religion, God. God. His One God. The God of all things, including, or rather especially, man. What a strange concept. I had heard this only once before; from this Jesu—The One God, The One "Father" concept.

Most of the time when I saw Jacobi speaking, Dosameenor was also there listening, absorbing. Invariably, Jacobi would see me, and with a slight head nod, or the raise of an eyebrow, beckon me to join them. Always, I would decline, gently shaking my head "no," and move on. Until one day...

I awoke at dawn on what was to be the final day of our journey at sea. There was a tentative knock on the door.

"Enter," I said groggily.

The door slowly creaked open, and a boy stepped in, bearing a tray with an offering of fresh bread, cheese and wine.

"Master says we land at dusk," said the boy, unsolicited, in perfect Latin.

"You are Roman?" I asked, astonished. I had not seen the lad at all, let alone heard him speak, on this trip. He was about fourteen summers with short brown hair that curled about his forehead. His eyes were blue, his frame was thin; too thin.

"Roman, yes. Well, Spanish," he answered.

"Your Latin is flawless," I said.

"My father was of the Horse-class, my mother was a mistress to my father—a whore. She died when I was very young and my father took me in. He had had only daughters with his wife," he explained, matter-of-factly. "My father declared me his son. Thus, I began my studies, Latin, Greek, among others. I even now speak several dialects of the Celtic language."

"I see," I said contemplatively. "Unusual. Bastards are rarely acknowledged publicly."

"Yes, but as I said, he had no other sons. And, once acknowledged publicly by the father, then a bastard is a true son of Rome. Was this not so of Caesarian, Julius Caesar's bastard with Egypt's queen?" he questioned pointedly.

I laughed out loud. "Indeed! And you are quite educated. And bold. But we know what happened to young Caesarian, don't we?"

The lad was silent, assessing whether my last statement was a veiled threat or a simple statement of fact. I changed the subject. "So, how came you to be Ventrix's slave?"

The young lad bristled with indignation. "I am no one's slave! Master Ventrix saved my father's life—twice." He lowered his gaze and plunged ahead. "My father's—my family's—money was almost gone. My father drank and gambled and dumped his seed in anything female," he said, clearly ashamed of his father. "Master Ventrix and my father became friends after the first time he rescued my father. He offered to help pay father's debts."

"In exchange for you."

"And my older half-sister. She's in Gaul."

"I see," was all I could manage.

"That was two years ago, and I have served Master Ventrix well. I mainly served in his quarters and the galley," he finished.

"Which explains why I've not seen you until now," I said.

"Yes, sir. That and the fact that you have remained down here during much of our trip."

I cocked an eyebrow at the lad's impertinence, but let it go. I tore off a piece of the fresh bread and placed it in my mouth. It seemed to melt there. For some reason, in that moment, nothing had ever tasted so good. "Why…" I started, then swallowed the bread, "…are you telling me all this?"

"When we land, I am free to go. I am ill aboard the ship more often than not and therefore, inefficient. Master Ventrix loves my sister. He truly does and she asked him to release me. He has, as of the end of this trip," he explained.

"Again, lad, why are you telling me all this?" I asked.

"I wish to accompany you when we leave this vessel," he declared, as if it were the most obvious thing in the world.

The look of utter surprise on my face must have been quite comical. The boy simply smiled and hurriedly said, before I could speak, "You will need a translator, you will need a guide, you will need someone to prepare your meals, you will need someone to carry your belongings." His eyes drifted to the lance on this last point.

Possessively, I placed a hand on it for a couple of moments. But it was unnecessary. I sensed that there was nothing malicious about the boy; nothing hidden or dark. He was a servant and a seeker. His eyes glazed over as he continued to stare at the Lance. He had that same awed, reverent expression on his face as Jacobi had when <u>he</u> had first seen the spear.

"What is your name, lad?" I asked.

"Paulonius. Paulonius Renius," he replied, finally taking his eyes off the weapon.

"I thank you for your offer, but I travel light and I already have a translator and guide in Dosameenor," I patiently explained.

"The Celt you travel with is a good man, according to Master Ventrix. But he intends to find his family and be with them for a time," the lad imperiously informed me.

"Then I will move on."

"To where?" asked Paulonius.

"You're impertinent, boy. Take care," I said between somewhat pursed lips. Obviously, he knew everything.

His tone abruptly changed, realizing that he'd overstepped himself. "I'm sorry, sir. I did not mean to offend. It's just…" he trailed off, eyes downcast in a gesture of respect. "The rabbi says that you are an instrument of God. That you are to help spread the word of an anointed One, the Word of…of God's true nature, and—"

"Rabbi?" I interrupted. "What rabbi? You mean Jacobi? Most of the time Pauli…Paulo…"

"Paulonius."

"Most of the time, boy, Jacobi rants like a lunatic!" I nearly shouted.

A long silence ensued.

Finally, Paulonius began to back out of the small room.

"Wait," I said. I paused in thought before I continued. "I did not know you listened to his . . . sermons on deck."

"No, sir. Well, a couple. He has frequently visited Master Ventrix, even taken meals with him on occasion," explained Paulonius. "The Master and the Rabbi both wanted you to come too, but . . . but it was seen that you preferred, um, solitude," said Paulonius, timidly.

"Hmm. And who 'saw' that?" As if I did not know.

"The Rabbi, Centurion," replied Paulonius.

"The question was rhetorical! And, he's not a rabbi! He's . . . he's Jacobi!"

"He is a knowledgeable Teacher. The One God, the One Source of All, clearly speaks through him. A Master Teacher in his tongue is called a Rabbi," stated the lad quietly, firmly, factually.

"Well, I'll see about that," I said, and nudged past Paulonius to head up to deck.

Jacobi was in his element. I saw him at the stern as I arrived up on deck, Paulonius at my heels.

"How? I hear nothing," said a quizzical-faced, grizzled shipmate in broken Latin. He was sitting on the deck with a handful of others, Dosameenor among them, at the old man's feet. Jacobi himself was seated on a crate, facing the little group. His aged-pruned hands were wrapped around the neck of his walking staff, the tip of which was firmly on the deck; a King's scepter to a King and his court. Well, not exactly a King was Jacobi, but he did look like he was holding court.

"It is not a hearing with the physical senses, good man," answered Jacobi. "To say that, 'all are called, but few are chosen,' is to say that one simply feels, knows, that God calls him. It is this inner feeling, this inner urging, this inner knowing that is God's voice. To acknowledge this feeling or knowing is to 'hear' the call."

"But," began another man seated in the group, "I never had that thing; a feelin' or knowin', like you talkin' 'bout."

"Yeah," another put in.

"But you are here, my good fellows, listening to what I'm saying, to what the God says," explained Jacobi. "Something moved you to be in this moment with our little group. That something is the One God in you, the Voice, calling you, moving you. Do you understand?"

They both nodded duly understanding, but not fully grasping.

"How can *all* be called? Many, maybe. But look around. Not everybody every-where, not possible," said yet another man, an old man. This shipmate had to be even older than Jacobi. His thin, withered features betrayed a hard life. Yet, his eyes were still stark-green, bright, youthful, intelligent. Several of the others nod-ded their agreement with his sentiment.

Jacobi became silent for a moment, his body still, his eyes closed. He was deep in thought, or waiting for that Knowing voice from within. His stillness dragged on, and his listeners began to wonder if he was not actually asleep. They looked to one another, not quite able to make sense of the awkward silence.

"All," Jacobi suddenly said, eyes popping open, startling everyone and gaining their full attention once again. "All is possible with the One, and the One is all there is! Master Jesu knew this. And, therefore, all of us, every one, without exception, is from and of the One God, and thus, the One is in all of us. Now, not all choose to 'hear' the call, or rather, at their deepest levels, choose not to recognize it," Jacobi finished, to blank looks of confusion.

"You see?" Paulonius whispered from behind me. "He is a great rabbi."

I looked at the boy with a cocked eyebrow, sardonically conveying my disbe-lief that he had actually understood what Jacobi had said.

Jacobi observed the faces in front of him. "Ah..." he finally said to their blank stares. "I see that I get ahead of myself." His gaze swept the rear deck and landed on the boy and myself. "Hello, Centurion Longinus," he greeted me.

I was no longer worthy of the title or rank of Centurion and cringed inside as he said it. "Jacobi," I stated simply.

"And my boy, Paulonius. Are you both to join us?" asked Jacobi, clearly delighted at the prospect.

"No," I said flatly, before the light of excitement in Paulonius' eyes could reach his mouth. "I need to speak with you and Dosameenor."

"Ah, well then," he said, and then turned back to his listeners. "Shall we con-tinue this another time?"

"But we land tonight," protested the bright-eyed, wrinkled old man.

"Yes, we land tonight," echoed another of the listeners.

"We will find a way, my friends," declared Jacobi. "We will find a way either on board or on land." With that, Jacobi stood and the others followed suit, dis-persing to their various posts or duties. All, except of course, Dosameenor.

I approached my two companions with Paulonius again at my heels. I wheeled around on the lad with more intensity than I meant to. "Are you now my shadow, boy?!" I barked. "I would speak to my friends alone."

Paulonius looked as if I had slapped him. He flushed red with embarrassment at the public rejection. With downcast eyes he mumbled, "Yes, sir," before skulking off toward the bow. He glanced back once, an expectant look on his face. He opened his mouth to speak, no doubt wanting to remind me of his request. But then, wisely, he thought better of it, closed his mouth, turned and was gone.

Dosameenor, Jacobi and I were left alone. I waited until I was sure no one would overhear.

"I need to know your intentions," I said, addressing both men.

"Our intentions?" asked Dosameenor, as if buying time to phrase his answer.

"Yes. When we land, what will you do?" I then looked to Jacobi. "I am asking you both."

Dosameenor looked away, seeing something far off in his mind. Jacobi simply looked confused.

"Why, I go where you go, of course. I serve God within and you without," Jacobi answered. "Why would you even ask?"

"One might say you serve two masters," I said somewhat facetiously.

"We all serve the One. And I serve you to remind you of that fact," said Jacobi.

"You're a clever one," I said with a chuckle. I quickly turned serious again, though, and looked to my Celtic friend. "And you, Dosameenor?" I asked. He had become very quiet.

Finally, he looked me in the eyes, his brow somewhat crinkled. "Who do I serve?"

"No," I said. "What will you do when we land?" I repeated. "I thought you were going to be with me, guide me, help me in this land of yours, until I determine what I am to do."

"And so I shall. But..." he hesitated, stiffening almost to attention, as if what he was about to confess would earn him a reprimand from his superior officer.

"Speak your mind, my friend," I said reassuringly. "I certainly won't judge you."

"I have," Dosameenor continued, "been away from my family, my wives, my children, for three years. Soon after I was 'recruited,'" he nearly spat the last word, "conscripted, into the legions, my clan...left the regions which had been our ancestral home for centuries." His eyes narrowed, anger brimming to the surface. "Actually, we were forced out, to put it mildly," he said, his tone laced with bitterness. He took a moment to release the anger before he continued, breathing steadily, as a legionnaire is trained to do in any tense situation. "I have had no word on their whereabouts for quite some time," he continued. "I have been wanting to go and find them."

"Why have you not done so before now? Surely you've had opportunity."

He thought for a moment before going ahead. "Legionnaires watch each other. Sometimes, they inform superiors about each other. Especially those of us not Roman born, we in particular are scrutinized. Deserters are hunted and killed. I had to be sure I could make it all the way back. You were the catalyst and all the conditions were right," explained the big Celt.

"Hmm," was all I could manage. In truth, I felt for the man.

"Please come with me. My people will welcome you."

"Your people will hate me! I epitomize Rome. I represent those who drove your people out of your homeland, raping and killing and enslaving in the process," I said. There was no point putting a sweet glaze on it. We both knew how the Roman Military machine worked.

He frowned. It was a hard, sad look. "No," he said at last, his frown leaving, confidence in his people replacing it. "When they know the truth, they will embrace you," Dosemeenor assured me.

"Which truth, Dosameenor? That I've been a soldier of Rome all my life, or that I am a fugitive of Rome?"

"Yes!" he said, laughing.

We were still at the stern and I looked out to sea, to where we had already passed, back toward Rome. In every way, I was going farther and farther away from her. "Your people," I finally said, "are noble. You have proven that. But then I think I always knew it. Still, not all of your folk will embrace me. Some never will."

"Perhaps," he said, after a moment of thought. They are of no consequence, though."

I said nothing to that. My thoughts drifted to something else. "We are bound to run into Roman patrols," I finally said.

"Maybe," Jacobi put in, "and you will know what to do then."

"I suppose I will," I admitted. I looked the old man in the eyes. "You are not my servant, Jacobi. You never really were."

"Oh, but I am!" Jacobi declared. "I serve those who truly serve the One. And that you do, or will quite soon," he insisted.

There was nothing I could say to that. I had tried before to deny those types of statements from him. It was futile.

He could see my thoughts. "Think of me as a guide for your soul. For now," he offered with a toothless grin.

"A teacher?" I asked, smiling back.

"Of sorts," he said.

"Then, so it is…Rabbi." With that, I turned to Dosameenor. I placed a hand on his shoulder and nodded. We would stick together. For now. I had a sudden urge to go back down to the room; to hold the lance. I left my friends then to do just that.

X

We first heard the drums a few miles out, when it was still daylight. It was daylight no more. Trudging through the wilderness at night was disturbing enough. But, to have the rhythmic, primal percussion piercing the darkness as well, was to have the demons of Hades gnawing at your bowels. Dosameenor, on the other hand, was elated.

"We are close to home!" he said.

His home, or rather, his people. Not mine. I still questioned why I had come. But there I was. Where *there* was, however, I was not certain.

We had landed and disembarked from the ship during a busy evening at the port. The Celtic celebration of Samhein—the fall celebration of the harvest and fertility, among other things—was in preparation by the locals. We found a stable in which to spend the night. It smelled. Horribly. The fodder was rotted, but at least it was dry. A light rain had begun to fall earlier and was continuing still. Every other lodging option was already taken. Even camp space outside the port city was non-existent unless one went quite a ways out. Many folks were coming and going for the celebration, which was four days off.

Dosameenor did not spend that night with us, at least not most of it. He left us to secure supplies for our journey on foot and verify, as much as he could, the information he had on the whereabouts of his clan, his family. It took almost all of the coinage we had between us, which was not much. Yet, apparently, it had been worth it. For, upon his return, late into the night, he not only had secured ample supplies, but was himself light of being and happy as a child whose wish had just been granted; his information had been correct.

We left the following dawn. Our group was eight: Dosameenor, leading the way, Paulonius—against my better judgment—Jacobi and myself, and four men from the ship who were also heading to their families, part of a neighboring clan to Dosameenor's. One half-lame, half-blind old mare, which cost us the last of our coins, carried most of our supplies.

"We could all carry the supplies on our backs. Why did you waste our silver on this thing?" I demanded, upon seeing the decrepit pack-beast the night before.

"What difference does it make?" asked the Celt. "She'll do for the journey and save our backs. We don't really need the coin where we're going."

"And after? I am not staying in this land forever," I retorted.

"Then we will trust that a way will be revealed at that time. Live in the moment, Longinus. Tomorrow will take care of itself," replied Dosameenor.

"You've been listening to Jacobi too much. You sound just like him," I said, irritated.

"Perhaps. But maybe it's just my way of thinking, too. A Celtic way."

I said nothing for a moment. We were getting off the point. I said, "Well, the money was partly mine. You should have asked before buying that mare."

"Ah," interjected Jacobi, who, as always, stood close by, almost invisible until he spoke. "That's it then, is it not? You are used to being consulted on matters, Centurion Longinus, yes? But here, you know as well as I, you must defer to Dosameenor. Besides, truthfully speaking, you are no longer a Roman officer, so do not expect everyone to act as if you still are."

"What?" I said, almost yelling in anger. The old man had struck the most tender of spots.

"What I mean, is that you are no longer an honorable one in Rome's eyes," Jacobi continued. "But that is not to say they are right, Longinus, or that you are not a most capable leader. You simply are no longer an officer of Rome. You must trust in those around you now. Equals, one and all. Your time to lead will come again very soon, though probably not in the way you are expecting."

As usual, he spoke in riddles. I was silent. Perhaps that was the best tact to take; be silent and let it go. I retreated back to the corner of the stable where I had been sleeping, lay down and blanketed myself in the comfort of self-pity, the reassuring presence of the lance by my side. All that had happened, and whatever was to come, was inextricably linked with this instrument.

As I said, we left the following dawn, walking by day, camping by night. Four days had past. The land was beautiful and rugged. I had never seen so much dense greenery; untamed and intimidating, yet exhilarating and inspiring. The giant oak, or the "Sacred Oaks," as I quickly learned was the proper and respectful way to speak of these majestic trees, were much more than just trees to the Celts. They were beings, housing the divine, in service to humans. A lot of Celtic society's belief system revolved around the sacred oaks and the rituals the Druid caste performed around the trees on behalf of the people.

The weather had been mild: fairly warm days, cool nights. There was no rain as on the night we landed in the port, but there was a perpetual dampness in the air, which, I supposed, helped to account for the lush greenness throughout most of the region. It was wonderful! Nothing like the hot, arid, dust-plate I had been serving in.

On the fourth morning, we had set off again. This time, however, we did not stop when the sun disk went down, but pushed on, because we had begun to hear the drums.

Jacobi heard them first. At an age when most men are at least half-blind and half-deaf, Jacobi's senses were seemingly more acute than one a third his age.

"How is that possible?" I asked him.

"It is not that my ears are better. It is that I use them more. It is not that I hear better. It is that I truly listen."

"Yes, yes!" squawked the young voice behind us. "I understand."

Jacobi and I both stopped and looked back to see Paulonius trailing us closely on the narrow forest path. I should have known. He had barely left the old man's side since we left the boat.

"Paulonius," I reprimanded, "you shouldn't eavesdrop on others' conversations. 'Tis a good way to lose an ear."

"Yet," Jacobi said, "he exemplifies my point. How will he learn if he does not truly listen, regardless of where the instruction comes from or when?"

I looked at Paulonius. "All right, then. What did he mean, boy?"

"Rabbi Jacobi meant that his hearing is no better than anyone else's, simply that he better turns his *attention* and full awareness to that which he is listening to, thereby completely drawing it in and discerning it," the lad said.

Jacobi threw back his head and released a guttural, cackling laugh. The noise sounded like a chicken being strangled; a happy strangled chicken, but still a chicken. "That, my boy, is precisely right," Jacobi said, tears of mirth streaming down his cheeks.

"By the gods, I give up!" I said, rolling my eyes in resignation to the absurd. I turned and resumed my trundling walk, Jacobi and Paulonius in tow. I caught up to Dosameenor, who was leading the way on the path. "Do you mean to push on through the night?" I asked him. The shadows were long and it was getting gloomy on the forest path.

"If necessary," he said with an amiable smile. "You hear the drums? We are not far off. Besides, I do not believe it will take us through the night to get there.

But then, his smile faded. He suddenly stopped on the path, all of our little party doing the same. Dosameenor's initial excitement was now tempered by something else: concern. He was listening. Truly listening. Something in the sound of the drums had caught his attention. He took a few more paces on the trail and stopped again, peering over the ridge into a valley. We had been marching on a path through a tree-filled area, up on a ridge. The path or trail had begun a slow descent about a mile back.

I caught up to Dosameenor again and followed his gaze over the ridge and into the valley, both of which had been off to our right. My gaze landed on our apparent destination. The valley was lit up by fires; huge controlled bonfires. The ridge opposite our position was also lit up. "The Samhein fires you spoke of. We are close," I said. But there were two fires in the center of the valley that were larger than any others. It was almost dark and they stood out like two moons on earth.

The lines in Dosameenor's face became deeper, etched with concern, almost fear.

"Not just celebration fires," observed Jacobi.

"Then what are they?" I asked, confused.

"We must make haste," spat Dosameenor as he broke into a legionnaire's trot down the path. We all followed suit.

"Answer me!" I demanded as we ran down the trail, which was now partially lit by the glow of fires. I looked down at the fires, my breathing in rhythm with my jogging steps. "The fires in the center; they're too large to be celebration fires," I observed. "Are your people under attack?"

"No. No attack. They are all celebration fires—of Samhein, yes. But those two are more. Celebrations of victory in battle," he replied, pausing briefly for his own breath to fall back into rhythm. "Only they," he continued "could make flames as big."

"You mean...you mean victory over Romans?" My stomach lurched at the thought. It made sense. We had not seen one Roman patrol since leaving the port. We had noticed two patrols within the port city itself—only two—which now struck me as odd. It did not at the time because I was too preoccupied with avoiding them, which had been easy. That ease meant there were very few patrols within the port, probably only the two we saw. When I thought about it, I remembered that the patrols had seemed oddly agitated, almost fearful. You could see it in their eyes, the stiffness of their bodies. They were alone, but trying not to show it. But, as I said, at the time, I must have taken note of these things, though they hadn't sunk in 'til now.

I had changed my clothing to avoid the patrol's attention. Even now as we trotted through the forest, I looked down at my Celtic garb: leather breeches, drab gray woolen tunic, green cape pinned back over my shoulder with a copper broach. The shoes, however, were my Roman-issued laced, hob-nailed sandal boots. They were too comfortable not to wear. I had packed the rest of the Centurion uniform, which was now being carried by Paulonius. My gladius, however, was at my side, and the spear, of course, was in my hand.

I shivered just then. I suddenly felt an overwhelming, oppressive weight from within tugging at my bowels. Then the realization hit. Oh, Mithras, god of the warrior, god of the soldier, no! I held my tongue, did not voice my fear, willing it to leave my mind. But for naught.

We finally came off the forest path, down off the ridge and into a clearing. We began to run, to sprint, following Dosameenor to the largest of the central fires. And there I had my nightmare confirmed.

XI

We were on the valley floor. Knee-high grass now replaced the huge trees that had been our constant companions; flowers dotted the whole area, a variety of colors twinkling in the light of the fires and the crescent moon.

We ran, urgency feeding our steps. The din of the drums was nearly deafening. Their tempo was frenetic, building to a climax that we could yet discern. But then, another sound took over; agonized, feral shrieks and screams. Animals. The sound could only be coming from animals in searing, unearthly pain. In the next moment, yet another sense took over—smell. A grotesque stench filled our nostrils. Burning flesh.

Dosameenor stopped in his tracks, staring. The rest of us did the same and I, too, stared at the most unholy sight I had ever beheld: The Wickerman: a big, wooden cage in the shape of a man, with arms and legs and chest and head filled with prisoners.

There were three Wickermen. The two outer ones, about twenty-five feet high, were aflame. These were the two larger flames or fires we had seen from the ridge. The center one, the biggest of the three at around forty-feet high, was not yet lit. But it was full of the doomed: those awaiting the same fate as the occupants of the other two Wickermen. The screams were not from animals. They were from men. They were from the men trapped in the burning Wickermen.

And they were Romans. Romans being burned alive and screaming in agony as the skin boiled off their bones.

We were so frozen with the shock of what we were witnessing, that it took a moment to realize the drums had stopped.

I was the first to come out of my stupor, throwing Dosameenor a look of disgust and revulsion. So much for this ritual being banned. A group of shaggy-looking Celts were coming towards us, weapons out, yelling some primal battle cry, ready to destroy the newcomers who dared to intrude upon their sacred rituals. Their fierce battle-cry was rendered rather impotent, however; all but drowned out by the shrieks of the fire victims.

"Dosameenor!" I yelled in alert, ready to command evasive, defensive maneuvers. I stopped short of that, though, remembering who my cohorts were, and where I was. Old habits do not die. "Dosameenor!" I yelled again.

He looked at me, then at the oncoming warriors, locking eyes with the apparent leader. Again, I assessed the odds and hence battle tactics. As I said, old habits do not die. Or, perhaps I should say, loved habits do not die. We were eight against thirty, with dozens, no, probably hundreds, more warriors and defenders behind them if needed.

But apparently, they would not be necessary.

The leader and his band halted not ten feet in front of Dosameenor. I thought it was to address the intruders. But it was not, for they said nothing. A soft glow from the fires and waxing moon cast an eerie light on both Dosameenor's face and that of the warrior leader. It was then quite apparent why they had stopped. Their leader's face; his nose, his forehead, his eyes, even his mane of hair was almost identical to Dosameenor's.

"Dosameenor," smiled the warrior. "My brother! Is that truly you?" he said in Celt. I had obviously picked up the language since boarding the Flying Boar in Najaffi; at least, in the hearing of it. I could understand most of what was being said.

"Aye, Renaulus. 'Tis I," replied Dosameenor.

The one thing the brothers did not share was their smile. While Dosameenor's was pleasant, his brother's was rot: missing teeth and dark, broken ones adorned Renaulus' mouth. He gave a belching laugh and stepped forward to embrace his brother.

Dosameenor's response was chilly at best, returning his brother's embrace only to the degree that custom apparently dictated so as not to offend.

Just then, a tremendous crash of wood and debris was heard, startling us all, as one of the burning Wickermen collapsed into the pit where its foundation lay. Burning bodies and limbs flailed as the structure fell in upon itself. Once again, the drums beat on and the screams from the other still burning Wickerman continued to fill the night. Then suddenly, the second one collapsed as well. It did so in a hail of embers and death-throw shrieks. It sobered us back to the horrendous event taking place before us. It was all I could do to keep myself rooted, waiting to see how Dosameenor's unscheduled reunion would play out.

Finally, Renaulus spoke. "I regret that your homecoming is in the middle of this madness," he said sincerely.

Dosameenor exuded genuine warmth then, seeing that his brother was apparently not a part of the human sacrifice before us. "Why is this happening?" he asked.

"They are Roman?" I interjected in broken Celt. I was sick from the thought and would not be silent, even if it meant giving away my Romaness by my clear mangling of the Celtic language.

Renaulus' demeanor changed. He was once again the guarded warrior, ready to pounce on the enemy. He stared hatefully into my eyes, my soul, but spoke to his brother. "Who is this?" he demanded of Dosameenor as if I were a worthless pile of horse shit.

"Peace, brother," replied Dosameenor. "He is my friend. His name is Longinus, Centurion, or former Centurion of Rome. He is no longer favored with Rome."

"Why?" asked Renaulus suspiciously.

"Later. Just know that he is my honored guest. He will be treated accordingly," answered Dosameenor forcefully.

Renaulus paused. He clearly did not like the answer, but accepted it as custom dictated.

I took advantage of his momentary silence. "Why are you burning Romans?" I blurted out as I involuntarily stepped toward him. His men, three of them, immediately stepped to his flanks to protect him. At the same time, Dosameenor extended an arm to my chest to halt my progress.

The shrieks of terror and anger from those in the center Wickerman, the only one left, rose to a deafening volume, as they knew they were next to be put to the flame. I looked even closer at them to be doubly sure. They were Romans. Even the naked ones had the short cropped hair and relatively clean-shaven faces of the legionnaire, but most still wore their wool army issued tunics. These were light-blue or gray when new. They were still their original colors—so it seemed in the available light—but battered. The garments were torn and stained with the blood and mud of battle, and with the shame and guilt of utter defeat. "Who are they?" I demanded.

"'Who are they,' you ask?" repeated Renaulus as if I were a stupid child. "As you see, Centurion," he continued sarcastically, "they are legionnaires of Rome."

"No! Which legion?" I shouted in bitterness, wanting nothing more than to strangle this hairy, ignorant fool where he stood. On my arm, I suddenly felt the calming touch of Jacobi's hand. At the same time as Jacobi's touch, came that inner voice again; His voice. "All is well," He whispered in my head. It had been awhile since last the Voice, He, had spoken to me. "All is well," He said again. "Their spirit, their soul, is freed this night. It matters not how."

"Stop!" I hissed between clenched teeth. Only Jacobi heard me. Only Jacobi knew that I was hearing something in my mind. I could tell by his touch.

"Your spirits are Free. They have always been and always will be Free. You imprison your spirits, your souls, yourselves, by your thoughts, your beliefs, your actions. Almost all must be freed eventually because you believe so. When you come to truly understand, to remember your Truth, you will no longer need even death," the Voice whispered.

I was speechless. The absurdity and madness of the evening had been punctuated by the voice in my head. I looked at Jacobi. The old man simply smiled calmly.

"I do not know," Renaulus declared, breaking the spell I had been under.

In that moment, I chose to ignore the voice in my mind. At least for now. So, I pulled my attention to Renaulus, gently taking my arm away from Jacobi's touch.

"I don't know what legions they're from, Centurion," continued Renaulus, condescension dripping from his words. "The battle went on for three nights."

"How could you see?" Paulonius chimed in.

Renaulus scowled at the insolent lad, truly confused by the boy's ignorant question.

"I'm sure my brother means that the battles were fought in the light of day. We Celts measure time by nights, not days. I would think you'd know that by now, boy," Dosameenor answered for his stupefied brother.

Renaulus, ignoring the boy entirely, said to me, "These were the legionnaires left after our victory." He spoke almost as if it were nothing. "Their leaders, their officers, were allowed to fall upon their swords. Then we took their heads and—"

"You did what?" I exclaimed, appalled.

"We took their heads for only a while. They were placed with their bodies in the cages, the Wickermen, as you call them," spat Renaulus contemptuously, as if he had no cause to explain this to an inferior such as me.

"The head is the seat of the soul. Possess your enemy's head and you have his soul," Dosameenor said offhandedly. "I'll explain more at another time."

Enough. I had had enough. "There's one of those things left not yet aflame. There's still time to stop this," I said, trying to sound firm, not wanting to reveal my own terror.

"No," Renaulus said flatly, arrogantly, regrettably.

"It is the Druids' doing. Their word is Law," Dosameenor explained. "But why, this is beyond me."

"An evil one has seized control," said Renaulus, bitterly. "For now."

Dosameenor suddenly had a glazed look in his eyes. But it quickly turned to one of hostility. "Draco," he stated, disgustedly.

"The only Druid in recent memory to revive all of the old rites of sacrifice. You remember him, eh brother?"

"Yes. But how? How is it that he is in control? When I left, he was still only an apprentice on the council. How could he have risen so quickly? I haven't been away that long." Dosameenor said.

"How'd you know it was him I meant, then?"

"A feeling. You forget, Renaulus, I was one of them for a time." Dosameenor then paused reflectively. "Actually, who else would it be?" he asked rhetorically. "Draco tortured animals when he was young, when we were all young, remember? He said he was driving out demons! Of all the stupid..." he said, caught up in that moment in the past. "Then the time that he insisted a boy caught stealing pelts in winter—for his mother, no less—should be burned alive for the crime. Thank Dana the elders didn't listen then."

"Aye. I remember that," replied Renaulus.

"Please!" I interrupted. "We must stop this," I said, as the spear vibrated again. "We must stop them from lighting the third Wickerman! No matter who's responsible."

"No, Roman," said Renaulus, "As my brother said, 'Tis the Druid's doing. One does not defy the Druids." But, Renaulus' tone was edged with sarcasm. He, too, hated what was happening this night, but certainly could not admit that to the likes of me.

"Are the Elders agreed, or is Draco alone in this? asked Dosameenor.

Renaulus' eyes narrowed, "What do you think, my brother?" he queried. "Draco seized the head of the Druid body, it is true. And, most of the Elder Council of Druids, so I've heard, are against him—at least in private. But they fear him. And he does have supporters. I know you were a Druid once, Dosameenor, but that was a long time ago. There is much under-handing and back-knifing amongst them in these times."

Dosameenor thought for a moment. I was almost jumping out of my skin. Much more talk and I would stop the last Wickerman from burning, myself. Or die trying. The latter, of course, being the more probable outcome. Then Dosameenor's face changed. "What of Detrom?" he asked, slightly smiling, clearly reliving a fond memory in his mind.

"Your teacher, yes?" said Jacobi.

Dosameenor smiled. The old man's perception was amazing. "Yes," he said. "My Druid Mentor, Teacher, Rabbi, if you will."

"Gone. Driven off by Draco," Renaulus said grimly.

Dosameenor's face lost all ease, ripping him back into the present moment. Anger filled his being. "Then, by Dana, I will put a stop to this and find out the meaning of all of Draco's doings."

"Could be suicide, brother," Renaulus smiled, gritty maliciousness showing through. Obviously, Renaulus hated this Draco as much as Dosameenor. "Forget what I said, Roman," Renaulus said to me, then turned back to his brother, "I'm with you Dosameenor. To the end." Both men embraced, then turned as one and sprinted toward the center of the crowded festivities, toward the large Wickerman.

We all followed, Paulonius aiding Jacobi. I ran faster than all. I may have been a fallen Roman officer in the eyes of Rome, but I was still a Roman. And, those were my people stuck in the cage.

Yet, we were too late. As we sprinted toward the midst of the barbarity, the third Wickerman burst into flames.

"No!!" I howled like an angry, wounded beast. It was useless. I could hardly hear my own voice. The screams from within the Wickerman were horrifically loud, as were the still pounding drums. Adding to the cacophony was the noise of the Celts around it. Madness reigned this night.

There was a throng about the wooden structure. Closest to it were many white-robed, hooded figures. They formed a loose circle around the Wickerman and were chanting. The chant itself was a rhythmic and morose, yet, lilting melody. The robed, hooded figures—whom I took to be Druids—were repeating the chant over and over again, holding their arms spread wide toward the Wickerman as they chanted, as if to embrace the souls agonizing within. (Indeed, I was later to find out that they were doing something quite like that. They believed they were mentally and spiritually aiding the souls of the doomed to cross over to the Otherworld into complete freedom through the purity of the flames.) The rest of the throng seemed to be regular Celts; ordinary folks. There were hundreds of them: men, women and children. They were all there bearing witness to the sacrifice, the archaic rite, the macabre spectacle.

None of them, however, were celebrating Samhein, as I understood it. Most were simply staring blankly, numbly, at the Wickerman. Until, that is, the stench of burning flesh again reached their nostrils. At that point, most had a look of utter disgust splashed across their face. Many turned away, or covered their face in a vain attempt to hide from the horror. Some could not take it at all and vomited at their own feet. Mothers pulled their children into the folds of their clothes, attempting to shield them from the terrible deaths before them. But, alas. This was also in vain; they could not be hidden from the sounds and smells of grizzly death this night.

Yet, as shocked and disgusted as most of the people were, none of them left. No one turned and walked away. No one backed out of the crowd and ran home. *No one.* It was as if they were all anchored there by some unseen force, or rather, perhaps, by some unseen threat.

Our group came to an abrupt halt at the outer edge of the crowd. We then pushed our way through to the inner circle, to the Druids. Once there, Dosameenor's brother pulled out a hollowed beast's horn, placed his lips on the small end, tilted his head back and blew.

The sound of the horn blasted through the valley, drowning out even the drums and screams of the victims. Those closest to it slammed their hands over their ears lest their insides burst and bleed. When the single note blast trailed off, all became silent. Even the screams in the burning Wickerman had become whimpers, though that was probably more because of death and the final throws there-of than because of any herald. Most of the Druids, too, had ceased their chanting, and some had even thrown off their hoods to gaze at the intruders. Others, however, continued their vocalizations, oblivious, obviously deep in a trance.

One, the tallest of them, and the only one wearing a light blue robe, turned slowly to face us. Looking into his face, though, was like trying to look into the mouth of a cave. For, his hood was more of a cowl: long and tubular in the front, thereby completely obscuring the wearer's face, and thus, invoking in the viewer a sense of awe mixed with fear—as if some demigod from the Otherworld stood before them, not simply a man.

"Who dares disturb this sacred rite?" boomed the deep voice from within the cowl.

All at once, the spear began to vibrate in my hand.

"Who?" he demanded again, anger and hatred and darkness seething from his being.

"Dosameer dares, Draco!" answered my Celtic friend with the power and authority of a god.

The spear continued to vibrate in my hand, though subtly, as if growling. Or, more accurately, as if warming up for a release of power. I pulled it closer to my side, hoping no one would see it.

The blue-robed figure before us pulled back his cowl, revealing the head and face beneath. Draco.

He had long black hair that reached down to the center of his back. It was slicked flat and back with lard. His eyes were an unearthly ice-blue, which contrasted intensely with the pasty-white skin. He was not ugly, but rather had a comeliness that struck from the Otherworld, as the spawn of a demon may be glamoured (glamoured being a magically induced spell or veil), with beauty.

There was something else.

I thought at first they were dirt smudges and shadows playing upon his features. But then he stepped closer and into the light. They were not dirt and shadows, but tattoos and scars. Obviously, the tattoos had been tapped into the skin purposely, but to my surprise, the scars appeared to be self-inflicted, as well; they both—scars and tattoos—wove together in intricate circular knot-patterns on his face.

I admit that in that moment, looking into those eyes—that face—I knew a jolt of fear. But then I felt the spear in my hand, still quivering and thought of *him*, the One on the cross, and heard the Voice in my mind saying, "Fear not, for I am ever a part of you. Fear not, for I am ever your-Self." As usual, I did not completely understand the statement, the riddle. But, this time, rather than thinking about it with my head, I let it seep into my being—deeply. The result was profound; I was instantly soothed at the deepest level of my soul. I lost all fear—of anything—because I had a sudden realization of my own eternalness, not of the flesh, but...

"Dosameenor," Draco hissed between clenched teeth, thus interrupting my split-second of contemplative, spiritual awareness and snapping me back into the moment. Draco was surprised to see Dosameenor, but hid it well.

"What is this?" bellowed Dosameenor. "These rites were banned generations ago."

"They have been revived, and you of all people know that it is death to disrupt them," replied Draco, threateningly.

Several of the Druids threw off their hoods and withdrew swords from beneath their robes. From shadows close by, we heard the unmistakable smooth-sliding sound of blades being removed from scabbards and belts.

"Since when do Druids carry weapons during rituals?" demanded Dosameenor,

"Prisoners may escape," Draco replied casually, dismissively, deceptively. He then smiled maliciously. "Also, because your coming was foretold, though we did not really expect you so soon. I did not think you would be in agreement with us on our...revival." He said this last bit with an arm gesture to the Wickermen, or what was left of them.

Dosameenor, his brother, and his men drew into a tighter group, forcing the rest of us into it, as well. My soldier instinct fought this; we were too close together to function in a fight. But it didn't really matter. We were hopelessly outnumbered.

Suddenly, the spear began to vibrate violently in my hand, the tip—its blade—to glow. Those closest to me quickly moved away, clearly afraid of what they were seeing the lance do. I spun to Jacobi, silently questioning him, imploring him to advise me. He smiled and nodded toward the spear. I understood. *Let It guide you*, he was silently saying. I had no choice. But how? Was I simply supposed to ask It for guidance? I closed my eyes for a moment to think. And then it hit me: *Do not think. Do not think at all. Let go.*

So, mentally, I did just that; I let go of any and all thoughts, of any and all feeling; of any and all attachment to a given outcome to this madness and turned my entire being over to the spear or to that which was working through the spear: to *him*, the Voice, the Power within.

I felt a complete change in my perception of the moment. I was detached, but present; an observer and a participant. I realized in that instance that I was infinitely more than the present situation, yet at the same time, an integral part of it.

I opened my eyes and was compelled to step forward, raising the glowing, quivering lance as I went. All could see It, the Lance. Fear and awe came into their eyes. They parted for me as I walked toward Draco and the remaining Wickerman. The latter, amazingly, was still standing, but raging ever more intensely with angry flames.

I was being guided, for I knew not what I was going to do. I was not in control of my actions; yet I was in complete control, for I allowed it all to unfold: An Infinite Power, an Infinite Intelligence was working through me, as me, because It *was* me. I do not mean to paint this a mystery. It is not. When one has the experience I speak of, he or she knows It for what It is: the Infinite Mind—or God, or call It what you will—working through him, as him, period.

Draco stood stalk-still, eyes glinting in the firelight and moonlight. There was a hint of fear in those eyes as he watched me approach. None of his followers moved to flank him. I stopped five feet in front of the dark Druid. His eyes suddenly darted to the lance's tip, the blade now pulsating with an intense bright glow. Somewhere in the back of my finite, human mind, I dismissed the glow as reflective light from both moon and fire.

But then it happened. The Lance's tip, the spear's blade, continued its pulsating glow as the entire field and valley grew dim by nearly half as the moon was suddenly shrouded by dark clouds. I quickly realized that I had been thinking of something, imagining it in my mind's eye for quite a few moments. Rain. Rain is what I desired to end the mad fires of this night. But how, I had asked myself, could that happen on an apparently clear night with a bright crescent moon? I had doubted.

But right then, it was as if the conditions surrounding me were responding to my intensely doubtless desire to end the torture. *Rain!* I commanded in my mind.

The Lance, as if to amplify my thought, glowed brighter. "Rain!" It was my own voice this time, yelling, commanding the desire into reality. I felt detached, in a trance. I simply allowed what was happening to flow through me, to channel through.

Now, some have said that what occurred next was perhaps coincidence. I know otherwise.

I turned my face skyward and the deluge began.

The first drops hit Draco on the head. He turned his face skyward as well. He began to mutter something: a spell, an incantation, perhaps, or a counter-spell. Whatever he was saying, though, was useless. Sheets of water from the heavens fell. The mass of people began to murmur in awe and confusion. The noise was drowned out briefly by the sudden loud hissing of the fires being extinguished. The hissing died away and the crowd's noises became louder, near panicked as darkness completely engulfed us.

The fires were out. Smoke enshrouded the last standing skeleton of a Wicker-man, but the rain rapidly cleared it as if it had never been there.

Then, it stopped. The rain suddenly stopped as if someone had closed a valve. The spear tip no longer glowed. The people became silent, awed once again. The only sounds were the pathetic moans coming from within the last Wickerman. Some of the sacrifices still lived.

Soft light began to blanket the valley. We all looked upward and saw the clouds peeling back from the moon. The sight inspired more murmurs from the throng. Then, all eyes fell upon me.

Some of the people made a gesture with their hands and arm—the sign against evil. Most, however, looked at me reverently; a few even dropped to their knees worshipfully. More than one began to whisper a name—"Grosgon". "Grosgon," Dosameenor later told me, was their clan's name for the Elemental God. I was he, incarnate, they believed. Others called me "Merlanco"—their word for a master magician, a master wizard; one who through years of study and many blessings by the gods is able to command the elements. Still in a trance-state, I looked at Draco then—who was rigid with fury—and back to the Celtic tribe around me.

Jacobi stepped up to me smiling. "You have taken a large step tonight, Longinus," he said.

I came back to my senses just then. I was in a state of peace I had never known. Yet, my normal Roman self began to quickly reassert its position in my mind. I found I had many questions about what had just happened. And, as usual, I wasn't entirely sure of what Jacobi was talking about. *A step to what?* I thought.

But before I could ask him, I saw movement out of the corner of my eye. From the edge of the tree line, from the edge of the darkness, they came. A new murmur arose from the people as everyone saw the figures approach like spirits from the night mist.

XII

The murmur rose from the crowd, panic laced within. The figures appeared like spirits. They seemed to materialize out of the mists as they came rushing from the edge of darkness.

"Antewonc!" *The Ancient Ones!*—the people whispered fearfully. *Ghosts*, they thought. I could almost agree with them. Even my heart pounded with apprehension as the strange apparitions approached. But it quickly became apparent that they were neither spirits, nor ghosts, nor strange apparitions of the night, but flesh and bone and blood.

Dosameenor was the first to recognize one of them. "Detrom?" he said in breathless disbelief.

Detrom was the one leading the group from the darkness. He wore a heather-colored robe, torn, tattered and stained from living in the wild. In his right hand was a tall, intricately carved walking staff. Something on the top of it gave off a greenish, pulsating glow, though I could not tell exactly what it was.

His aged face peered out from a shawl of dark blue, equally as torn and worn as his robe. There were dirt smudges and wrinkles of time on that face. But beneath those was a look of intensity and determination of one who could not be denied. His dark brown eyes were portals to the Otherworld, allowing one to glimpse the Infinite, as well as the mundane. There was a depth of Kindness in those eyes, as well. Intriguing, was this one; one of infinite strength and courage, yet also of eternal patience and goodness. And Knowledge. In those eyes and in that face was pantheistic Knowledge; the Knowledge of the gods; the Knowledge of the Universe—True Knowledge. There was something else there, too: familiarity. I suddenly had the overwhelming sense that I knew this man. Or rather, had known him in some way, some form, in a distant past. That was impossible, of course. At least, that's what I professed to myself then.

He was immediately flanked by several others who were similarly clothed. Holy ones. Druids, they were. But many in the group were clearly warriors. Some of them wore short battle tunics. Some, nothing at all, but the colored wode smeared and painted on their skin. They had weapons brandished, their bodies rigid and flexed, ready to fight. Detrom and the others halted near us. As with Dosameenor, the people began to recognize loved ones and kin within Detrom's ranks.

"Ronas!" someone called to a face near Detrom.

"Tramon!" a woman squealed to someone else as she ran forward, falling into the man's arms. Happiness swirled around us as spontaneous reunions took place. Dosameenor embraced his mentor, the former High Druid Detrom.

But the reunions were over quickly. A multitude of questions abounded. I listened and observed, and was able to piece together that most of the returning folk, nearly a century in all, had been driven off by Draco and his followers under threat of death. Others from the community had run off to join Detrom, despising Draco and his new regime. Later, still others had urgently left the tribe to find Detrom, and alert him and the outcasts, about Draco's plans for the Wickerman fires. It was hoped that this news would spur Detrom and his group to retaliate against Draco and stop the abominable ritual sacrifice. Yet, even with skilled trackers, it had taken many, many days to find Detrom. Draco had chased them far and away, 'tis true. However, Detrom, being the powerful High Druid he was, had caused himself and his group to magically disappear for a time. Or, at least it seemed that way. They reappeared when Detrom had a vision of the impending sacrifice and literally bumped into those searching for them while on the way to stop the evil proceedings. But alas, the vision had come too late for those being fed to the flames.

The questions and talk died down and all turned to confront the instigator of the night's madness. Draco was pensive, to say the least. He had the demeanor of a snake, cornered and coiled, ready to strike at a threat. The number of his followers had dwindled, substantially. During the brief, spontaneous reunions and the delightful ensuing chaos of such things, most of Draco's people had put down their weapons or shed their robes and drifted back into the populous, absorbing into the throng when it became obvious which way the wind had blown. Others had slunk back beyond the burnt Wickermen.

Confronting a Druid is no easy thing. The Celtic people revered their Druids; indeed, their whole Druid class, and stood in utter respect, awe and even fear of their knowledge and power. No one wished a dark hex cast upon himself by any Druid, let alone a mad, dark one. Yet there is strength and courage in numbers; there is power and movement with like thought. A palpable change in the atmosphere took place. Anger charged the air. Almost as one, the people advanced a step toward Draco. He backed away three paces, angling toward the edge of the clearing, toward the edge of darkness. Fear was in his eyes. But he cloaked it with empty arrogance, draping Druidic power, or more accurately, Druidic status, over his being, preying on the people's fear of that status. He attempted to glamour his person with power; attempted to create the illusion that he was larger than life, powerful as a god. Indeed, for an instant, a dark glow of deep magenta pulsed around his body, expanding to twice the size of his form.

"Cease and obey me or be cursed! All of you!" he hissed.

For a brief instant, all were still. I knew not if others saw the evil glow about him. Perhaps not. It was clear, however, that for a moment those present warred within their mind as to whether or not Draco's statement rang true. But their single-mindedness—their anger—led them to see through the dark Druid. Draco's 'power' was naught but a shallow understanding of true workings of the Universe and hence, any strength derived from that understanding was depthless, a perversion of Truth. As such, it was only as powerful as people believed it to be, allowed it to be.

"Kill him!" someone shouted.

"Burn him!" demanded another.

Draco backed away, impotent against this onslaught of hostility. The mob took another step toward the dark one. Any farther and a murderous riot would add to the night's insanity.

"Stop!" boomed Detrom's voice as he stepped between the people and Draco. Detrom was glamoured with power, too. But, unlike Draco's paltry aura, all could see Detrom's Otherworldly glow. The look of awe on their faces told of that. Detrom's Power was True. He seemed larger than any mortal; truly, a god among men. Then, his aura decreased in size somewhat. He appeared a man once more. "There has been enough killing this night, enough death," he said with heart-penetrating sincerity.

Silence reigned for a moment. The fact was, Detrom did not have to glamour himself with power. His people revered him, even adored him. That was clear.

"But…but," someone tentatively began, "he deceived us all." The man, a medium-sized, balding Celt in his middle years, gestured toward the carnage in the wreckage of Wickermen. "These were not rites to be brought forth again. These were not Romans deserving of this burning death!"

"'Tis true!" shouted someone else. "They were withdrawing, going elsewhere in their Empire. 'Twas Draco who spelled us with his dark magic to hunt the Romans down, High Druid Detrom. You know this to be so. He drove you off before we went to battle with these Romans," he said, again gesturing angrily toward the charred corpses. The man paused then. His head bent forward and a shock of thick, curly, red-blonde hair fell across the left side of his face, only partly obscuring his eyes as he began to weep. "I lost my son, my only son, that day in the fighting. And for what? 'Twas not an honorable battle." He paused again until he gained control of himself. Then, in true Celt fashion, he looked straight into Detrom's eyes, straight into his soul, speaking to the gods through the once and future High Druid, and said with controlled rage, "'Tis my right. I want revenge."

"Yes!" cried a voice in the crowd.

"Vengeance for Draco's deceptions and evil!" yelled another.

Others quickly joined in the call for Draco's blood.

Detrom let them rant on for a moment; let them vent their frustration and anger. But, only for a moment. "Peace!" he finally said once again, in that booming voice of the gods.

"Peace," he said again.

A silence filled the air. The anger abated momentarily as all heeded Detrom. He had garnered their attention. But it lingered not long. It was broken by the dawning realization that moans and groans of pain and agony came from the half-dead.

"Oh, Dana!" exclaimed a woman. She stood staring into one of the burned Wickermen, or what remained of it; looking at the charred carnage. "A few still live!"

Tortured and guttural sounds emanated from black, smoldering forms. Yes, some still lived; if it could be called living. The agonized noises had been drifting around us for several minutes, along with the crackling of the dying fires. We had all been too preoccupied with Draco to hear them—until now.

We turned our attention to the victims of Draco's twisted plans, the Dark One himself forgotten for the moment.

A tribesman, a warrior by the look of him, began to gently pull apart the frame of a Wickerman. He yelped with pain and quickly yanked his hand away, causing that section of the now fragile wooden cage to crumble into sizzling embers. The wood in the Wickerman's frame was black and wet and only barely smoking. Deceiving that was. Beneath the damp, blackened outer layer, the wood still burned at the core. Fire can be a warm and gentle lover; a servant sent from the gods. Or, it can be an evil, deceptive monster, bent on torturous destruction. Someone tended to the man's scorched hand while others, following his initial attempt, but with a bit more caution, made their way through the first two dilapidating cages to the remnants of burnt and twitching Romans. My people. My stomach churned yet again.

"Please!" someone yelled in crisp Latin.

The last Wickerman's flames had also been put out by the rains. But, having been lit the very last, only moments before the mysterious deluge from above began, for the most part, it still held strong. Most of its occupants were either lying on the cage's floor, or dangling limply from where on the cage they had been tied; unconscious, but hardly burned. Hardly burned, perhaps, yet most were still dead, nonetheless. If the flames do not engulf the victim, then the smoke will usually destroy him from within, filling his lungs with poisonous breath. There were only two men standing on their feet, their lower appendages precariously perched on a rung of the frame, ankles tied to the frame itself. Their hands clung white knuckled on higher wooden bars. Except for the second fellow: one of his arms was hooked round a bar at a strange angle.

"Please," said the first one again. His blue eyes were piercing, his tunic barely singed.

"Help us," croaked the other, a pair of blood-shot eyes looking at me wildly, beseeching me from a dark, sooty face.

They were both speaking to me directly, begging for liberation. The second one did indeed have something wrong with his left arm; it was bent at a backward angle at the elbow. It wasn't a fresh break—no swelling where it was bent abnormally. And, its bend to the wrong angle was slight. But its appearance just accentuated the gruesomeness of the evening.

"Sir," said the first man. "Centurion Longinus," he addressed in a tone of familiarity.

Did I know this man? I took a closer look at him, stepping up to the cage. He was a legionnaire, but not a young one. His tunic though filthy, was clearly a Roman soldier's, as was his crooked-armed friend's. And yes, he did seem familiar. But then again, I have commanded so many. After a time, their faces all blend together. Plus, it was hard to tell with this one; his face was dirty and swollen in places from battle. Or abuse. Still...

"How do you know me?" I asked without suspicion, and not without compassion.

"From…" his voice cracked and broke. He swallowed hard, his throat obviously damaged and painful from the fire's heat and smoke. He gingerly swallowed more and tried again to speak, attempting to sound as crisp as a moment before when first he'd captured my attention. "From the cave," he rasped, not sounding at all crisp. "The Prophet's tomb, the day he had risen. We," he continued, indicating his bent-arm comrade, "had been guarding the tomb and…and…" The man's voice gave way again.

"Yes," interjected Jacobi. The old man apparently had been shadowing me the whole time. "Yes," he repeated. "You were so instrumental that day and the night preceding. Bless you. Both of you. Longinus," he said turning to me, "free them from their cage."

I felt my left eyebrow cock up out of indignation. Jacobi was ordering *me* about? "I was about to, Master Jacobi," I snapped at him. I immediately felt embarrassed at having done so.

Jacobi simply smiled and gave me a slight nod.

I looked again at the soldier who had spoken. "What is your name?" I asked. "Romi, sir. Romi Romanus. This is Gaius Hentapas," he replied, indicating his friend.

I stepped closer still to the cage, this time searching for a weak spot in the wood.

"We are in your debt from that night, sir. We…fell asleep…somehow—though I assure you, it'd never happened before, as I think I—well anyway, we fell asleep at the tomb, but were never reprimanded because of you, though it was common knowledge what had happened there. He had risen, they said…a woman was there and saw *him*, and us asleep…I think. You said nothing, but even our superiors didn't want to scold us…" Romi went on, now on the verge of babbling with fatigue, trauma, injury.

I did remember him now, and his friend, though they were hazy in my memory; there had been a more important event that day. Although, I was quickly realizing, as Jacobi had pointed out, these two were also a part of that event in one form or another. I still was not totally convinced that the Prophet had indeed risen that day. Well, actually, I simply hadn't thought much about it since then. Fear, I suppose. "And you'll owe me twice-over after tonight," I said, more to snap me back to the present than allow myself to stay in thoughts about the past.

I and several others began to break open the cage near the legionnaires. We had to use large stones to smash through. The Wickerman was a sturdy prison.

Hard, urgent whispers clumped from behind me. I turned to see the big Celt engaged in heated, but low-toned, conversation with a few fellow tribesmen. "What is it?" I called to him.

He broke from the others and approached. "Draco has vanished. We must pursue him," he replied.

"No," said Detrom.

"But," began Dosameenor.

"He is gone, Dosameenor," Detrom continued. "You will not find him now."

"But he must be punished!" cried Renaulus, now standing next to his brother.

"And so he shall," Jacobi said calmly, "In his own way, in his own time."

"Indeed," agreed Detrom smiling sagely at Jacobi. "Indeed!"

Dosameenor grunted, clearly not happy, but let it go.

"Come," I said. "Plenty of time to get that piece of shite. Right now, I need your help."

He paused, looked over the cage in front of us, then at the remnants of the other two and nodded. He turned and yelled orders in Celt. The mass of people formed into several loose groups around the Wickerman. The rescue and recovery effort thus began in earnest.

XIII

And so it was that twenty-two men—twenty-two Romans—were pulled from the ashes and timber that night. Of the twenty-two, thirteen succumbed to burns or smoke inhalation by the next morning, crossing the river of the dead to the next world. A blessing that was. One of them in particular was so badly charred that he was more skeleton than flesh. How he had remained among the living for even the night was beyond any of us. His strong spirit finally knew it was time to move on, though, when morning came. Five more were balancing between this life and the next come mid-afternoon, with no one expecting them to make nightfall.

We did what we could for them. Detrom and his Druid physicians had a salve for burns concocted from plant extracts and oak sap and crushed mistletoe. It was laced with herbs that gave the salve a vaporous quality, thus allowing those with severely afflicted lungs to inhale temporary relief. These same herbs also gave the salve a numbing agent. When rubbed on the burned area of skin, the victim often felt a temporary relief from the pain. But, ultimately, it did not matter what we did. These five would not make it for long.

The remaining four, however, were another matter. Amazingly, for the most part, they were unscathed. This included Romi and Gauis.

We had not yet moved from the site of the Wickermen. I insisted on cremation of the Roman remains—an honor usually reserved for officers and nobles and heroes. But in this case, they were all heroes to me, thus cremation was totally appropriate.

We could also not move the more severely injured until they left us or healed a bit, the latter being very unlikely.

I was resting my eyes, my mind, my soul, my heart, in a make-shift sheepskin lean-to shelter the Dosameenor had erected. He and some men had erected several, three of which had been used for survivors. This one was now empty. Jacobi was off helping Detrom. I was alone. The stench of the burned and dead still filled the air. I tried not to dwell on that or my own circumstances. What now?

The shelter's flap whipped open, spilling light from the late afternoon sun into the space. A figure was silhouetted at the opening. "Yes?" I said.

"Sorry, sir," said Romi as he stepped into the dimly lit shelter. "Mr. Jacobi wished you to know that three more have . . . have died," he managed to croak out, as much from emotion as from a ravaged throat. "Just within the past hour." Romi was cleaned up, but his face was still bruised and that scar—yes, I definitely now remembered this one from the cave.

"Not at all unexpected. And the other two?"

"One is dead to this world, but still breathes. Barely. The other, well, uh, the other has awakened and asked for death, for someone to send him on his way," said Romi sadly.

"And no one has yet obliged him," I stated.

"No, sir. You are now my senior officer. I'll do it if you order, but . . ."

"Make no mistake, soldier," I interrupted. "I am not your officer or anyone else's. In fact, Rome hunts me."

"Yes, sir."

"Mind you, boy. Stop addressing me as your superior."

Romi paused then, and simply looked at me, unflinchingly. There was no fear in his eyes. "I meant that as an agreement with your statement. I know Rome hunts you," he said. He then nodded at the spear, which leaned blade-up against a wall of the shelter. "You, It, is what brought several of us here, searching for you."

"Ah, yes. You and your crooked arm friend thought to cash me in. Me and this thing I carry. I see how it is," I snapped.

"No, no," he bristled at the misunderstanding. "You do not see how it is, sir. We came to find you, to join with you, to help you. You are helping to create a new world, and we wish to be a part of it."

"What are you talking about?" I asked, stupefied.

He looked at me as if I were daft. "That day at the tomb, He rose from death. Your spear has his blood on it. It, he, speaks to you, guides you . . ."

"You know naught of what you speak," I interrupted, anger momentarily seeping into my being.

Romi ignored that, pressing on. "And last night, out there," he said, pointing to the killing field where the Wickermen had stood the night before. "You called rain from a nearly clear night's sky with the spear's aid, I believe."

I said nothing.

"Something is happening," he continued, "the likes of which has not been seen before. It's bigger than me or you alone, bigger than Rome. Yes, even that. I am no traitor to pursue this in spite of Rome. But I have heard a call. So has Gauis."

Again, I said nothing. *By the gods,* I thought, *I should just throw the spear away.* But it would not help; it would make no difference. The change surrounding me was actually from within. Something infinite, profound—even magical—had opened deep within my being and there was no closing it. And, yes, the spear was guiding me in all of it, or something divine was working through It. I could feel the power that coursed through It. Rome did not pursue me. She wanted the lance and Its power.

I suddenly became aware of a head poking through the shelter's front flap just behind Romi. It was quite still. The eavesdropper had probably been there awhile, listening. I needed only one guess at who it was, since I knew Jacobi simply would have burst in, and no one else would have dared listen in on my private conversations.

"Gauis, I presume?" I said. "You might as well come in, too." He entered slowly, cautiously. "Come on, man. I won't bite you."

He obeyed, stepping in fully. He stood five-feet in front of me. He was only slightly older than when I met him at the tomb—perhaps eighteen summers now. But his demeanor had aged considerably. He had obviously been through a lot since last I saw him. And, indeed, his left arm was slightly bent in the wrong direction at the elbow. It looked to be from an old injury. How could he be a legionnaire? Even if the wound was from battle, he would not be allowed to remain a soldier as a cripple. His arm made me look at him more closely. He was not Roman born. He had darkish skin, but light brown hair and grayish eyes. Then I remembered his family name. Hentapas. Definitely not Roman. I noticed that he wore something around his neck. It was an Ankh, the key of life, an Egyptian symbol that dated back thousands of years. It was an elongated crucifix or cross, somewhat like those Rome used to hang prisoners. But instead of a vertical top bar, there was an oblong vertical loop, almost like a head. Rome's cross meant death. This cross meant life and resurrection into the afterlife. This boy, Gauis, was Egyptian. I had not seen it on the previous night; it had been dark and he had been covered with ash and soot—not to mention all the other distractions of the evening. But now it was obvious; his skin color, noble lined face, grey eyes and name. "Egyptian," I said aloud.

"Yes. Gauis Hentapas is Egyptian," answered Romi.

"What happened to your arm? I do not believe that you had a crippled arm at the cave, the tomb." I said.

"No, sir," Hentapas began, his voice also still scratchy. I am from a noble Egyptian family near Aswan. When I arrived back there on leave, one month after the day at the tomb, the military governor there ordered me to his presence. It was almost as if he'd ordered my leave from duty and waited for me." He said this last part shuddering, the revelation still fresh. "He tortured me for information about you and the day at the tomb, I think to make an advance for himself, or maybe to get the…that," he said pointing to the spear. He paused then and stared at it.

"Go on," I prompted.

"Yes: He did this to me," he continued, holding up his bent arm. "It was on the first night, and then he threw me in an isolation cell for two weeks when I could not give him any useful information. It healed wrongly because it was never reset properly." He paused then, looking at the arm. A proud, defiant look came into his eyes after a moment. "But I can do anything a normal legionnaire can do. I have hidden the defect from my superiors. It's simple," he insisted.

"I'm sure," I said. "Aswan, Egypt. That would be Prefect Murius. Molonus Murius. A Spaniard. He is a pig, a sadistic fuck-hole by reputation. I'm sorry he did this to you," I told him. I was indeed changing. In my past, I never would have apologized for the actions of a superior officer to a legionnaire, especially to the face of the legionnaire in question. "Why didn't you report it?" I found myself saying. I knew it was a stupid question before it was even out. No one would ever take the word of a legionnaire over that of a Prefect. "Never mind," I amended.

"Sir," said Romi, ignoring my demand not to address me so. "The survivor wishes an honorable death," he said, bringing us back to the reason he was here.

"Yes. We will see," I replied, rising and picking up the lance.

"I wish to clarify…I want to…" the Egyptian began.

"Spit it out, Hentapas," I said, without patience.

"Romi misspoke last night. I was the one who fell asleep at the tomb, not Romi. Remember?" confessed Hentapas.

I softened. Something about this lad was touching, calming.

"It does not matter now, my young friend. As Jacobi said, you were instrumental in the happenings that night. All was as it was supposed to be. Now, let's go aid our fellow legionnaire." I clapped the young man on the shoulder and led us out of the concealment of the shelter.

The day was beautiful, despite the horror of the previous night. It was bright and crisp, affirming the promise that life moves on, always changes, quite often to newer and better things.

Romi, Hentapas, the Egyptian and I made our way across the field to another hastily erected shelter. (Although Hentapas was also known as Gaius—a common Roman family name which he no doubt adopted when he became a Roman citizen—I now preferred to call him by his birth name, though I didn't quite understand why, at the time—it simply felt more honorable somehow.) The field itself was mainly clear now. Scorched earth was all that remained where the Wickermen had been. Off in the distance, some three hundred yards away, smoke still rose from the pyre we had lit to cremate the dead. I had refused to honor the deed by cremating their remains in the same spot where they had been tortured by flame. We had lit the funeral pyre earlier in the day. Bones took long for fire to consume.

Not many of the tribes people remained. Most of them had finished with their helping tasks and returned to their respective clan villages a mile or two away.

We entered the shelter, which was open-walled on two sides, and consisted of several animal skins sewn together for the other walls and roof. The whole thing was held up by the strong oak branches of an adjacent tree.

I have seen horrible things in battle. But what I saw before me now shocked me to a new stomach-churning height: a living corpse. Over most of his entire body, his skeleton showed through the thinnest of blackened-pink tissue. There was barely any skin or muscle on his head. There was no face; only a blackened skull and shreds of flesh clinging to it here and there. But his eyes! His eyes were more than intact. They were huge in their lidless, hollowed-out sockets, but they were bright and clear and could see. Yet, it was more than that. They were bright with their light-brown coloring, yes, but they were bright with something else as well. I was hard-pressed to figure out what it was—love, happiness, peace, all of them? He stared off, seeing something. But it was not something on the outside; it was something within and beyond this world.

The pallet the man was lying on held him approximately six inches off the ground. Cowled Druids stood silently, near it with Jacobi and Detrom at the foot on either side. They both of them were silent as well; solemn, but not at all downcast. In fact, I began to feel a lightness in the atmosphere of the shelter, and my shock at the man's appearance suddenly abated. The form on the pallet slowly shifted his gaze to me, then to the spear, as if to say, "I'm ready for you." But, I stood impotent with indecision.

"Longinus", came Jacobi's soothing voice. "Open yourself. Let it wash over you and you will know what to do."

I looked into the eyes of the man who lay before me, and breathed deeply. I focused on my breathing for a moment, then shifted my attention to the spear, silently asking for guidance from It, from the power that coursed through It. After several breaths, I knew what I was supposed to do; I was to ease this man's spirit through its transition. I was not there as an officer who had been requested to perform an honor killing. I was there to aid his soul with its journey, as a guide of sorts, to the next world. The spear, the lance, began to vibrate ever so slightly; its blade aglow. I knelt next to the pallet and touched the lance's tip to the man's charred forehead. His eyes shined with joy.

He should not have been able to speak. But he could and he did. "I...I see a palace. A glass—no, a crystal, palace!" he rasped. "And...and..."

"Shhh," I gently hushed. I closed my eyes and continued to focus on my breathing; *inhale deeply, hold for a beat, exhale thoroughly, repeat.* I was in the flow and rhythm of my breath when I suddenly felt a floating sensation. In the next moment, I was there; in front of the palace. I controlled my awe at what was happening, what I was seeing, by simply allowing it to happen without censor, without judgment. The palace did indeed seem to be made of crystal. The bright light that hit the structure from a brilliantly blue sky was bent and split into an infinite variety of beautiful colors within its walls and within its endless number of rooms. Mere glass, at least in the world of men, could not do this: reflect and refract the light of the heavens into an infinite variety of colors, thus reflecting the infiniteness of creation itself.

In the palace, in all the rooms that I could see and sense, there were people; many, many, many people. They were all looking at me, including, and especially, one in particular. He was standing quite close, not far in front of me. It was *him*; Jesu, the one whom I had pierced while on the cross. Instinctively, I looked at my hands. I held a shadow of the lance, but not the thing Itself. I did not panic, but knew this to be the way of it in this realm. There were several others who stood close to Jesu, shoulder to shoulder. They, including Master Jesu, seemed to be their own clan—not separate or above any of the other people in the palace, but somehow special. Though I did not recognize any of those surrounding Jesu, I knew in my heart that when these individuals had been alive in the world, they had all been anointed ones in their own cultures. Curiously, too, at least as they appeared to me, they all had similar facial features to Jesu—or he to them—even the heavier, far-eastern Asian looking sage who was standing just to Jesu's right.

Someone stepped from behind me and stood next to me on my left. I turned my head and looked him in the eyes. It was the man from the pallet. He was whole. Not burned. I had not known this man in life and certainly could not tell what his features had been like, given his charred condition back on the pallet. But I knew it to be him. I knew those eyes.

"Thank you," he said to me in a whisper. He then faced the anointed ones and the crystal palace, and walked forward.

I started to follow, taking a tentative step forward, as well. But Jesu held up a hand and stopped me. "No, Longinus," he said in a familiar voice. "This way is not for you."

I paused. Of course this way was not for me. At least for now, it was not. There were so many things I wanted to ask. But one question stood out above all. "What am I to do?" I asked.

"You already know. You are here, helping one in need to cross, are you not? You breathed and opened and asked, and the way was made known to you. That is all you ever need do to know an answer."

"The spear guided me and…"

"No. *You* guided you. The lance is simply a tool, a point of focus just as your breath is."

"And you. You guided me."

"I am your-Self. All that I am is within you," he said.

"I don't understand," I replied.

"I believe you do in your heart, in your soul. There is a part of you, Longinus, that you know is eternal. It is your true, infinite self, that part of you that can never be separate from the source of all things. And it has been awakened within you and is ever expanding. You are here because on some level, you know this, you feel this, you are listening to this. Continue to listen and to trust and you will be guided every step of your path," he concluded.

His words, his thoughts, infused my entire being. They cleansed my mind, my body, my soul. I found myself crumpling at his feet in emotional and spiritual awe and humility. I touched the ground with my face. I stayed that way for what seemed a long while. When I finally looked up, I was back in the shelter, on the floor. I stood and looked once again into the eyes of the man on the pallet. Those eyes now stared blankly into space. The charred shell remained. The soul had made the transition.

A soft white light surrounded me and the man's body, Jacobi and Detrom. The other Druids were also attuned to the holiness of the moment. With eyes closed, they chanted softly in prayer. Hentapas too was chanting rhythmically, softly in Egyptian. Their prayers and chants had helped me, had sustained me and aided our burnt patient on the journey to the Otherworld. The light, the aura, which surrounded us gently began to fade. The chanting of the Druids and Hentapas quietly faded, as well, and ceased. They all stared at me.

"I...saw..." I began.

"We know," Jacobi smiled.

Detrom smiled as well and simply nodded.

How they could know where I had been and to whom I had spoken, I knew not. But it mattered not. They had sensed, or somehow seen, what had transpired and were in reverent awe. Though not nearly as much as I.

XIV

It had rained during the previous night. Vapor appeared before my eyes as I took in and then released my first conscious breath of the day. Cold it was this morning. My lodge, my quarters, in the village was small, but sturdy; a mud-brick hut with a thatched roof. It was large enough for a sleeping pallet made of rushes, a stool, and a small fire-pit which was in the center. The structure was round, the roof conical with a hole in the top-center for the fire-pit smoke to escape. It had belonged to Detrom's second, the High Druid Malard. He had been among the first killed during Draco's insurrection. Word had spread of my "participation" in the burned legionnaire's "Journey of Spirit," as the people were calling it. I was now truly being hailed as some kind of Roman healer and magician, equal to a powerful Druid. Appropriate, the people thought (indeed, even insisted), for me to have the Malard's dwelling.

I could smell freshly cooked oatcakes and hot mead. That and cheese had been left for me every morning at the stooped doorway entrance to the lodge since I had come to the village nearly three weeks ago, two days after the night of the Wickermen. I had kept to myself since arriving in the village. Much of that time had been spent in quiet reflection; reflection upon the experience with the burned soldier, my own soul's journey to the crystal palace (What was the crystal palace?); the experience of the rains that seemingly came at my will to dowse the flames of the Wickermen, and all of the experiences profound and otherwise, that I'd had since that day on the hill of crosses. And Irena. I even thought of Irena. What had become of her? But mainly, I thought about the spear, the words that had come to me, the guidance in times of need, and the attunement I was feeling with all creation because of It.

Jacobi said I was in meditation and prayer. He and Detrom would visit me once a day, to check on me. They both seemed immensely pleased with my desire for solitude, the opposite of how I thought they would feel. But then again, I was probably putting that opposite attitude on them myself. In my past, I would have interpreted someone's desire for solitude simply as laziness, a rouse to shirk a duty. Not anymore. At least, not in this context.

Perhaps Jacobi was right; I was in a sort of period of meditation and prayer. I simply thought about my experiences in the recent past and asked the Gods, the God, the Universe, for guidance. No concrete answers came, but intuitive feelings abounded as to what was to come. Of course, my reasoning mind asked for more details. But they would not come from the intellect. Patience and trust of my intuitive faculties had to be allowed to grow. Just this last thought alone made me realize for certain that I was truly a changed man. A passion had bloomed within me; a passion to know the truth behind all that had happened—which seemed to inevitably include knowing the truth of my own nature and the powerful source within.

I threw back the stag-skin blanket and rolled off the pallet. Groggily, I staggered to the entrance to retrieve my meal. I pulled back the entrance's flap to reveal the platter of cheese, oatcakes and mead, and the three pair of feet just next to it. I looked up and there stood Jacobi, Detrom and surprisingly, Hentapas, who stood next to them shoulder-to-shoulder as an equal. They had plans of a sort; that much was obvious. "You are early today," I said somewhat annoyed.

"Forgive the intrusion, Longinus," said Jacobi, his usually light demeanor slightly heavier.

"Longinus," began Detrom, "tonight marks Luna Prima. It is the rise of the awakened mother. It is an extremely powerful time. It is the perfect time for one to be initiated, formally, into The Mysteries. You have been chosen by the Gods and God. Your abilities are raw, but they will grow. The ritual we will perform will help you immensely."

I stood there stunned. "What? You want me to be part of your Pagan rite?" I said a little too harshly. Yet, images of the last ritual of theirs I had witnessed still lingered.

"That's unfair of you," replied Jacobi, reading my thoughts as usual.

"Yes. I apologize, Detrom. You are no Draco. I know that," I said.

"No, I am not," said Detrom. "But make no mistake; Draco and I wield the same infinite power—as we all do. We just use it for different purposes.

"This rite, the Luna Prima. What is it?"

"That it has to do with the full cast moon on its first night, I'm sure you've already surmised. As to its exact meaning and ritual aspect, well, you will see," was all Detrom would say.

"Hmm," I grunted. "And you, Hentapas? Are you here with these two or do you disturb me this early as well, but for another reason?"

"I am with Master Jacobi and Arch Druid Detrom, sir," he stated in a manner that did indeed indicate equality with the other two.

I was not sure what to make of this and it must have shown on my face.

"As it turns out," offered Detrom, "Hentapas was raised in Thebes, Egypt, at Karnack Temple. He was a priest of the old religion there; a strong priest, powerful, despite his young age. He will be joining us tonight, assisting in the rite, which is not unlike those he's performed in his homeland. He has demonstrated much power, and much knowledge of the sacred arts."

A part of me was a bit stunned by this, although the larger part of me was not surprised at all. There had been something about the lad...Still, the old religion of Egypt?

"I left the temple to become a legionnaire only because I had been conscribed to," said Hentapas.

"I thought," I began, "that all the temples of Egypt had long since been abandoned and left for ruin, or at the very least, rededicated to Roman gods. And your land's old religions, aren't they long dead, too?"

"Appearances. Do not always trust appearances, sir," answered Hentapas. "The old ways thrive, though not in the open, nor exactly as they once were. But they are there, nonetheless."

"Hmm. I never really...I never gave it much thought," I confessed.

"Someone will come near midnight to escort you, Longinus," Jacobi said, somewhat abruptly.

"Jacobi," I said, "are you assisting in this too? Is it not an unclean thing for you?"

"I am an observer. And no, I don't believe it to be the unclean, undivine thing you may think it is. I have seen that all power, as Detrom pointed out a moment ago, is from the same place and source. It is simply seen in different ways and in different things by different peoples. It is all of God," he concluded.

"Until tonight, then," stated Detrom. "Forgive the intrusion this morning and forgive us for rushing off, but there is much to do."

I said nothing. It was time for me to move to the next part of my life. Rome was nearly dead inside of me. She would always be a part of me, but that part was shrinking. I looked at all three of them, one by one. "As you wish," I said, and slipped back inside with the food to break my fast.

I went for a walk after my morning meal. The village itself was a simple place. Twenty-five or so, small, circular wood and mud structures—huts, really—sat on either side of a narrow main thoroughfare. All this was surrounded by small oak trees and pine trees. I had been out and about several times since my arrival in the village, but I still received glances of curiosity mixed with reverence as I strolled along. The spear received as many of these looks as I did. I took It with me everywhere. As the people looked my way, I would simply smile and walk on.

I left the village and walked a short way down a path which wound through a stand of trees and ended at a lake. The lake was a fairly small body of water, only about a-hundred yards in diameter, and fed by an abundant fresh water stream. On its tiny beach, I removed my tunic, folded it and placed it on top of the spear, which I had already put under a nearby bush, along with my hob-nailed sandals. I turned and plunged into the cold water. Oh, how I missed the hot Roman baths. Hot baths were the gods' gift to civilized man. I could have asked the locals to heat some water for me in one of their large cisterns, but the lake was much simpler. Besides, a part of me did not like the thought of the Celts laughing at the tough Roman's prissiness, his delicate sensitivity to cold water. But, as it turned out, it only took a few minutes to get used to the lake's temperature. I scrubbed and cleaned myself, then simply enjoyed a relaxing, gentle swim, all the while contemplating the coming night's ritual.

Half an hour went by. Or, maybe it was an hour. I lost track of time. I was floating on my back, basking in the peaceful surroundings: the serenity of the lake, the brilliance of the clear blue sky. And then, I became aware that I was not alone. I saw movement out of the corner of my eye. I turned and clumsily stood in the somewhat shallow water, leaving barely my head above the surface. A distance away, a naked female form entered the lake with a splash. Did she not realize I was there? I could not believe that she did. Why would she jump into the water naked, knowing a strange man was there? But, then again, these Celts were a very open people.

Still, courtesy dictated that I make my presence known to the woman, and the sooner, the better. But I did not. I was enthralled with the sight of her and did not want to break the spell. Seeing her long brown hair, full breasts, round buttocks and small, but shapely feminine form, made me realize just how long it had been since I had laid with a woman. Once again, Irena came into my mind. I missed Irena. I missed our love making, certainly. But I also missed her, the person. Yet, the truth was that probably, I would never see her again. That thought made me sad. But I had known that I'd probably not see her again for some time. I was resigning myself to the fact. Life moves on. And there I was, in the present moment, with a nude woman swimming about. I was quite aroused by her and her nakedness as she glided through the water. My immediate desire was to stay silent and simply enjoy the sight of her. Yet, I knew I could not do that. I had to let her know that she was not alone.

The lake's shore was only about seventy feet from my position. The woman was now much closer, leisurely swimming right toward me. I cleared my throat aloud. It was a feeble and cowardly attempt at declaring my presence, and did not work. I had not made the sound at all loud enough, especially since I'd made it at a moment when her head was submerged. Her upper body sprang above the surface for an instant before going under again. I opened my mouth to speak, but was too slow. I stood there, my toes barely touching the lake's bottom, open-mouthed, as her snow-white buttocks broke the surface briefly, as well, before disappearing as she dove under the water. She continued her underwater sojourn, swimming right at me. Gently, I swam a few feet to my right to avoid her. But she veered to her left in the same instant. I tried to reverse my course, but it was too late. I bumped right into her—or she into me. She broke the surface in a gasp, her face contorted with what appeared to be mock surprise and anger. She stood there, seemingly on higher ground than I, or on an underwater rock or something, for she stood almost a third of the way out of the water. There in the water, I could not tell exactly how tall she was, but I refused to believe that she was taller than I, let alone by almost a third! Yet, there she stood, her bottom two-thirds in the water, top third above. Her breasts floated, or appeared to, her dark, wet hair clung seductively to her shoulders.

"I'm sorry," I said stupidly, not sure whether I was apologizing for bumping into her or for staring at her bobbing breasts. She still looked angry, but there was something not quite sincere about the look. However, I did not know this woman. Perhaps this was her look of genuine anger.

She studied me with bewitching hazel eyes and then said quizzically, "You are not as tall as I thought."

"I...what?" I stammered, caught completely off guard.

"And you are older too. I am twenty-eight summers. You are obviously much, much older."

"I am not!" I blurted out defensively, feeling like an awkward schoolboy. "Well, I am older than twenty-eight summers for certain—by eleven, in fact—but..." I stopped myself in mid-sentence as a thought occurred to me. I found my own bearings again and looked to where I had put my clothes and more importantly, the spear. The area was undisturbed. I looked back at the woman, studying her for a moment. Her eyes were actually more green than hazel. A small nose and mouth adorned her face. Her lips were full and curled up at the ends on both sides, giving the impression that she had a perpetual smile. She was beautiful. But that was irrelevant. "Are you spying on me? What is your name," I demanded.

"Camaroon," she replied, with a bit of playful haughtiness. "And no, I am not spying. I simply wanted to see you up close."

"So, you waited 'til I was naked in a lake?" I asked. "You're an odd one."

"Not really."

"Does your husband know where you are?" I asked, with an air of superiority. At twenty-eight summers, she would be, should be, married.

"Husband or no, I do as I please," she answered.

"Really!" I said with mock arrogance. "He must be very understanding," I said sarcastically.

"*He*? I never said I was married to one man. Nor even to a man," she said mischievously. "In fact, I never said I was married at all."

"Camaroon!" came a child's yell from shore. A girl of about ten, dressed in a long white hemp gown, stood waving at us, or rather, at Camaroon. "You are needed!" the girl said, not urgently, but leaving no doubt that the woman before me was about to get back to shore.

"I am coming," Camaroon replied.

"Your daughter?" I asked playfully. She gave me that quizzical look again. "Well, you never said you weren't married either."

"Silly Roman. You needn't be married to have a child. But no, she is not my daughter. She is what you Romans might call a Vestal."

A Vestal Virgin? I asked myself. Vestal Virgins were young virgin girls who were keepers of the eternal flame in the temples of Rome, and priestesses in waiting and training. They were very highly regarded. Before I could ask anything, though, Camaroon spun in the water and swam back to shore.

"Wait," I said. She stopped for a moment and looked back at me. "Just like that, you're off? You swim out here to view me, then leave?" Again, I felt like an awkward schoolboy.

"You heard the lass. I'm needed. Goodbye for now, Centurion Longinus." She swam the rest of the way to shore, got out of the water and dressed. With a wave to me, she and the girl headed off hand in hand.

"I'm no longer a Centurion!" I called to her, receding back for no particular reason. No response. She and the girl disappeared into the stand of trees, headed back to the vicinity of the village.

XV

The full moon was bright and clear, nearly at its zenith. After returning from the lake, I spent the rest of the day and evening in solitude. But this solitude felt different. Something compelled me to mentally prepare for that night's activity, not just to reflect upon it, as I had been doing in the lake, but to open my mind and soul and spirit to it. I knew not from where the compelling came; whether from my own instinct or a higher power or a higher voice guiding me. But then, much of the time, in essence, instinct and a higher power's guidance are one in the same thing.

The flames in my shelter's fire pit were flickering, dwindling, dying. No point in feeding them. The spear stood near the entrance, waiting as I was. I couldn't tell completely in the dim light, but it looked as if the tip, the blade, was glowing slightly.

"Centurion Longinus," came the voice from outside. How I wished they would stop using my former rank. "We bid you join us." The voice was feminine. I stepped to the lodge's entrance and pulled back the flap, hooking it from above so it would stay open. Ten robed figures stood just outside. Six of them were in white robes. All of them were hooded with large cowls; all of them had their faces obscured. The leader, however, the one closest to me, the one who had called me out, pulled back the cowl of her white robe just enough for me to see part of a face splashed with moonlight. I could also see one bright green eye peering at me from beneath the cowl's edge.

It was Camaroon from the lake; I was sure of it. And, she was indeed a tall woman. We were eye to eye, at least. She may have even been slightly taller. I chuckled to myself; it was now apparent that she had indeed been standing on something in the water earlier in the day. "You are…" I began.

"We are the guardians and keepers of the Mysteries," she interrupted. "We have no names but Guardian or Keeper. You will address those of us in white as such. Those in blue, you will address as Guide. But you will only address any of us if asked to do so. Do you understand?"

I hesitated briefly. I had questions to ask her. But, obviously, that would not be acceptable. I gave in to the moment. "I do, Guardian," I replied.

"Good. For now, you will be known only as the Seeker or the Neophyte. Come with us now to be initiated into the ranks of the Mysteries. Do you accept this invitation, Neophyte?" she asked.

"Yes, Guardian."

"Excellent." With a nod of her head, two blue-robed Guides stepped forward and stopped in front of me. One of them ceremoniously held out a small white sack made of linen and a neutral colored robe. "You will wear this robe and the sack, the ritual hood, over your head, for you are not yet worthy to behold the path to the place of enlightenment," Guardian Camaroon continued. I started to protest, but thought better of it. "It is also so that you may learn trust—trust in your guides and Guardians, in no matter what form they appear. Do you object to this?"

I picked up the spear, holding it at parade rest. I could see that my white-hooded Guardian was about to say something. Obviously, no one was allowed to bring a weapon to ritual ceremonies, except for the High Priest or the one performing a sacrifice, if indeed there was one. However, for every rule, there are exceptions. This was no ordinary lance, and she knew it. "I do not object," I said, and stepped over the threshold of my dwelling and between the two blue-robes.

My Guardian looked at the spear's tip, which was indeed aglow. "So be it," she said.

The linen bag or hood was placed over my head, blinding me to the night. I felt hands on either side of me gently grasp my arms and guide me. I walked and knew that we were all walking in unison. And so, with the rank precision of a small military unit, we silently and reverently marched out of the village.

The ground beneath my feet was smooth and packed. No doubt it was a well-worn path. I was a bit nervous. It seemed as though we had walked for some time, but it had probably not been more than a few minutes. I assumed we were going to the sacred grove of oak trees. It was the Holiest place in the area, where many a ritual had been performed over the centuries. Supposedly, it was quite close to the village. Yet, it was a risk. By now, once again, Roman patrols and military would be coming into the area. Dangerous it was, then, to hold a ritual in a grove of trees, regardless of how sacred they were. Caesar had shown this when he burned down the sacred groves of oak to the east and north of us a few decades before. It had been the largest and most sacred grove of all; a place where all the continent's Druids and those from beyond as well, would flock once a year. It was there no more. Although, amazingly enough, I had heard that it had already begun to grow again.

We came to a halt and I stood in blind silence. Faintly, I could hear extremely muffled voices chanting in slow, rhythmic unison. Why were they so muffled? I wondered. It wasn't because of distance, for they did not sound far off. Nor was it because of dense tree growth. That would have merely filtered the sound. The chanting voices sounded as if they were coming from beneath thickly packed wet blankets. Then it dawned on me.

The guides released me. The hood which had blinded me, was removed. I was not in a grove of trees. I stood at the threshold, the entrance to a passageway that led into a hillside. The stone frame of the threshold was intricately carved with many Celtic symbols. The bright moonlight lit the hill well. I studied it for a moment. There was something not quite right about the hill; something not quite natural. And then I realized what it was. It was a hill made by the hand of men and women. A King's Burial Mound. Roman historians had written about these mounds. They were intricate structures built by the people for their dead king or leader, not unlike the great pyramids of Egypt, except for the fact that these structures were then covered with earth, rather than built upon. The end result was that from the outside they looked like a formation of the earth itself, a hill. But inside, they were the resting place for a king and much, much more. They had even been constructed to display astronomical events on specific days, or nights, of the year. That they were used for rituals, however, I was not aware. But, nor was I surprised.

"Neophyte," said Guardian Camaroon, whose face was once again completely obscured. "You stand at the threshold of the Temple Mound. Within is sacred and holy ground, and this is a sacred and holy night. Do you still wish to proceed?" she asked. I opened my mouth to respond, but she quickly held up a hand to silence me before I could speak. "Know before you answer," she said ominously, "that if you choose to proceed, there is no turning back." She let this hang in the air for a moment. "What say you, Neophyte?"

I was not quite sure what would happen if I changed my mind once inside the Mound, but it mattered not. "With heart and soul, I wish to proceed," I replied.

"So be it," she said. She turned and entered the Mound, followed by three of the other Guardians, Keepers or white-robes, then two Guides, myself, the other two Guides, and finally the last two Guardians. The spear tip glowed, and my heart beat quickened, but not from fear; from ecstatic anticipation of the divine. For the intensity and the importance of the moment was becoming more palpable with every step I took.

From there on, the night was a blur. Upon entering the Temple Mound, I began to slip into a trance-like state of being. I thought at first that perhaps someone had slipped a mind-altering substance to my food. I had not eaten anything since that morning—which in and of itself shows that no one had slipped me anything. It would have taken effect long before midnight. Or, perhaps it was the smoke from all the torches lighting the inside of the mound. But that was unlikely, as well. My lungs felt no discomfort, whatsoever. My mind, my soul, were simply surrendering to what was happening. A strange sensation was that. I was unaccustomed to giving in or surrendering in any circumstances. But this was much bigger than just me.

I remember winding through a maze of tunnels to the heart of the mound. Soon, though, I found myself in the center of the structure, deep inside the earth. I was surrounded by all manner of hooded figures, whose faces and identities were hidden by cowls. There was some kind of large stone altar in the center of the room we now occupied. Someone, it sounded like Detrom, began speaking in an ancient Celtic tongue. I understood not a word of it. I stood before the altar for quite a few minutes, listening to the voice drone on in the ancient language. Though I could not understand what was being said, there was something calming and soothing about the words, the voice. It was an incantation invoking the divine presence of the Universe, I decided: a calling forth of the blessings of the gods; of the One God. The trance I felt myself drifting into now became profound. I experienced that floating sensation again; the same one I felt when I was in front of the burned legionnaire. Strangely, I welcomed it. It was beginning to feel familiar; almost like I was about to go home. I don't mean the kind of home that we all might abide in here on earth. I mean the Home of all; a remerging with my soul's Source, the way a drop of water falling from the sky into the ocean is remerging with its source.

Two hands gently touched my sleeves. A slight tugging ensued. I sensed all this, more then actually felt it. And then it happened: I was outside my body, floating above all who were there, looking down on the proceedings as if I were an observer. Panic began to seep into my mind.

"Fear not," the voice said. His voice. Jesu was next to me. We were not float-ing, exactly. But we weren't standing, either. We simply were there, above the heads of all the others, who were now shrouded in a thin, mysterious type of fog. "The world they are in now appears as it does because you see it through a veil," He said.

"Are we in the Otherworld?" I asked.

"No. All are in the Mind Of The One. There is no separation, only gradations of form and phases of existence. But all swirl in and through each other."

We watched the rite continue, as the two robed figures pulled on my sleeves and helped me to disrobe. My earthly form stood before the congregation, still holding the spear, but naked. My awareness, my consciousness, though in astral form felt a twinge of embarrassment. I looked down at my ethereal body hover-ing there with Jesu. It was robed. "For a minute there…" I started.

"You are only clothed in the form of Longinus now because it is familiar to you, to your human self. But, of course, there are no forms to your True Nature. You simply are. Consciousness. An Individualized point in Mind—as mind," said Jesu.

My earth self handed the spear off to someone, Camaroon, I believe, who, in turn, handed it to the Head Druid standing before the Altar, Detrom. I was sur-prised at my actions, but knew all was unfolding as it should. My naked form was then led to the altar, and aided in climbing onto it and lying down.

The chanting continued. It now sounded more like a dirge, but was not mournful. It was full of depth, aiding me on this leg of the journey. I felt my astral form beginning to fade. I looked back at my earthly body lying on the stone altar, and noticed something for the first time: a white cord extending from the navel area of my body on the stone to the navel area of my soul-body. I was about to ask Jesu about it, when I noticed something else even more intriguing. Some-one else was disrobing. It was Camaroon. She proceeded to step up to the altar. The scene continued to fade.

"It is time to go, Longinus," said Jesu. "Come. I have much to show you."

The interior of the Temple mound faded entirely. In its place, appeared the Crystal Palace.

XVI

My head ached. My legs felt tangled, as if I were wrapped in a cocoon. A brief flash of panic ensued, but was quickly quelled as I opened my eyes to see the familiar surroundings of my own lodge. I started to disentangle myself from the skins on the pallet, but bumped into a form lying next to me: Camaroon. Her naked body was next to my equally nude self.

"Hello, Longinus," she said. "How do you feel?"

I was somewhat at a loss. "I...feel fine. Head hurts a bit," I said. "Why...uh..."

"Why am I here? To watch over you and keep you warm."

My brow crinkled in question.

"You were not entirely yourself after the ceremony," she continued. "You were shivering and chanting and conversing with...Jesu, I believe?"

Bits and fragments came into my mind. Jesu. "I don't remember much of the actual ritual," I said. "But, yes, Jesu came to me." I thought more about it and decided that was not quite the way of it. "Actually, *I* went to *him*." More of the whole night was coming back, and excitement grew within me at the memory. "Yes! I felt myself lift out of my body and float upwards. I could see all of you from above, performing the rite, and we, Jesu and I, went away, to the Crystal Palace, the same one that was there when I aided the legionnaire to the other side, and..."

"Longinus," Camaroon interrupted, "it is best to keep the actual events or happenings of your vision, or your journey, private. They were meant for you and you alone. What you learned from it may be shared with a chosen few, but the fine points of the experience are yours alone."

I understood what she meant, but was a bit disappointed. I felt a strange connection with this woman. I was excited about the experiences and wanted to share them with her. I fell silent for a moment. I threw the skins off both of us and truly took in her naked form. "Did we?" I began. There was that school boy feeling again.

"No," she smiled. "You had trouble coming out of your trance. Your body was cold to the touch. I came into your bed to keep you warm. As you can see," she said, indicating the healthy fire in the fire pit.

'*Tis true*, I thought. I would have let the fire die out in the night. Plus, it was indeed stiflingly hot in the lodge. Another thought occurred to me; another memory from the previous evening. "When I was watching from...above," I began tentatively, "I saw my...self, my physical self, being disrobed and laid upon the stone slab or altar."

"Yes."

"Then I remember seeing you disrobe and...well, I don't know exactly, but it seemed that you were led to the altar too. What happened?"

"You don't remember?" she asked, in a tone of mock disappointment."

"I'm afraid not."

"Well, let's just say that the two halves of the Universe were joined to completion."

"Hmm. Sounds fairly pagan to me," I said, only half-joking.

"Those that look down upon our rites look from a place of ignorance and their own unfettered lust. They have no understanding of the balance of the Universe and the need to keep that balance in check. Besides, what was accomplished on the altar last night was only one aspect of the night's ritual. There were many other facets to it." She paused then, and I thought about it all. "You really do not remember much of it, do you?" she continued.

"No. I do not. At least, not the ritual part of it. It seems I was in a trance from the time we walked into the Mound."

"Well, that's not unheard of, but it's very unusual. You are powerful, Centurion Longinus, or, should I say, Master Longinus."

"Master? What does that mean?"

"It means that you gave quite a demonstration of your ability last night. You and the spear, that is. Twice you drifted into prophesy. Twice you healed individuals in the rites who were infirmed. One of them was the Egyptian, Hentapas.

You straightened his arm perfectly without pain. It was as if it had never been crooked."

"What are you talking about?"

Before she could respond, though, there was a rustling sound from outside. Someone began to mumble. We both strained to hear the conversation, and suddenly realized what it was. Whoever was outside was mumbling to himself, rehearsing a prepared speech for me. I looked at Camaroon, and she at me, and we both burst into laughter. 'Twas time to let the person off the point of the sword, so to speak. "Who is there?" I called out.

"I, um, it is me, Centurion Longinus."

The voice was definitely familiar. "Who is 'me'"? I asked.

"Paulonius, sir."

Paulonius! I had not seen nor heard from the lad since the night after the Wickermen. Jacobi had sent the lad away on an errand when I took my recluse upon arriving in the village. The errand, I believe, was to scout the surrounding countryside with some warriors, for Roman patrols.

"I have your meal, sir," he continued.

My thoughts were still on what Camaroon had just told me, but I quickly realized how hungry I was. And, it would be good to speak with Paulonius. So I pushed the previous night's events out of my mind for the moment. Camaroon and I would talk more later. "Excellent!" I said, as I jumped up and threw on a robe. I motioned for Camaroon to do the same. "Come in, lad."

He entered the lodge with a tray of delectable foods—oat cakes and mead, cheese and smoked fish, dried venison and herbs. He placed it on the table near the fire pit. I stepped up to him and embraced the boy. "It is good to see you," I said.

"And you," he replied, keeping his eyes lowered as Camaroon finished placing the robe about her.

"Please join us. Help us break our fast," I said.

"Oh, I do not wish to intrude."

"Nonsense," said Camaroon.

"Indeed, I insist," I added. "We've much catching up to do."

"I would be honored, sir," he said timidly.

And so, we sat together and feasted on the morning meal.

From then on, I spent a lot of time in a haze of study and duty: study with the Druid sect; duty to the people of the community. It seemed that my status had indeed changed to that of a "Master," at least in the eyes of the villagers. Many came to me with various ailments and, much to my surprise at first, and after much prompting by Camaroon, I found that I could help them. Or, more accurately, I found that some kind of healing energy, ability, was coming through me and the spear.

I reached a point where I could nearly always call upon the trance state that I had found myself in on the night of the ritual. I would then concentrate on the individual in question, seeing in my mind's eye that this person was whole and perfect on a spiritual/physical level, regardless of the present appearance of his or her physical state of being. It simply was a knowing, left over from the enlightenment I had received on the night of the ritual: There is only One Mind, One Source, and all, *everything*, is from this One Source. Spirit, the Gods, The One, God, whatever name it is called by, is knowing and experiencing Itself through that which it creates; the good *and* the bad. Good and bad are mainly just human points of view. Everything simply Is in the Mind Of the One, because everything Is the Mind of the One. Therefore, there can be no separation from something of which we are all intrinsically a part.

It is this perception of separateness on a very deep level of the individual's human mind that causes the disease or unhealthy conditions.

Hmm. That sounded a lot like Jacobi. Well, I finally understood a lot of what the old man had been saying.

The spear was the focal point through which the healing power seemed to come. And, admittedly, much of the healing that took place was due to the strong belief on the part of the person involved. In fact, their belief in the healing was at least as important as anything I could do. That was the first step in healing oneself. Change the core beliefs at those deeper levels of the human mind and one would indeed go very far in the healing. But aiding in the belief that they could be healed was the spear. I doubted that many of them would have come to me for help if I were without it. No matter.

Camaroon was instrumental in my studies. She mentored me in the use of herbs and other medicinal aids in the realm of nature. I was also under the tutelage of the High Druid Detrom, as well as Jacobi. Though Jacobi was not a Druid, he was given the unofficial title of Merlin, for he had become somewhat of a Grand Master of the natural laws of the universe. He had been busy with his own studies and had developed a particular ability that was quite astonishing.

One day, as Camaroon and I were sitting under an oak, plying at the great tree's roots and slicing up the mistletoe we had gathered earlier, Jacobi, Paulonius, Romi and Hentapas—whose once crooked arm was now perfectly normal—approached us.

The younger lads were grinning from ear to ear. Romi was stoic as always, but there was a twinkle in his eyes. Jacobi's face was adorned with his usual friendly, toothless grin.

"Show him, Merlin Jacobi!" exclaimed an excited Paulonius. "You have never seen the likes!" he said to me.

"Boys, this is simply a tool. It is not a plaything," Jacobi reprimanded, more, I thought, for show than for any other reason.

"Please," Romi said, maintaining his stoicism, yet lighting the area with a flash of excitement from his eyes.

"Very well," said Jacobi.

"That was an easy battle," I observed. "What are you to show me, Merlin Jacobi?"

"Watch," he said.

He lifted a hand toward a large ceramic bowl next to my leg. It was nearly empty, not yet filled with the root stuff we had been extracting. The old man's face contorted with concentration. I looked at the bowl. "What are you—" I began.

"Shhh!" Hentapas, Romi and Paulonius responded in unison.

The look on Jacobi's face became calmer, detached. Suddenly, a tingling sensation filled the space around us. Camaroon's hair, which had been hanging loosely over her shoulders, began to lift into the air. And, the bowl next to me began to shake, rattling on the hard-packed ground. And then it shattered, fragmenting into a hundred pieces. I quickly covered my face to protect it from the flying shards of clay, as we all did, but only for a brief moment. Within an instant, the tingling sensation in the air was gone, and Camaroon's hair was resting on her shoulder as if nothing had happened. All was back to normal, except, of course, for the shattered bowl.

For a moment, all were silent.

"What...what have you done?" I asked in disbelief.

"The bowl is easily replaced, Longinus," said Paulonius.

"I don't give a goat's ass about the bowl. I mean, what have you learned, Jacobi? Doesn't this seem...I don't know...violent? Even dark?" I asked the old one.

"Longinus, my boy," the old man began, "what have I told you? What has Detrom told you? Hmm? It is not the power itself that is dark. It is the use to which it is put. It is in the heart of those that wield the power as to whether it be dark or light. What I just demonstrated is the use of a law of the Universe—a mental, spiritual law that responds to my mind when my mind is aligned with it properly, because it is Mind Itself, and must respond by its own law. Is an arrow, or a spear, light or dark when it finds its target? Can it be blamed for an evil wound or death? No, Longinus. The arrow and spear are subject to certain laws of nature set in motion by the one who wields them, and the arrow or spear cannot help but abide by those laws once set in motion. It is the same with the power I just demonstrated, but on a much larger, universal scale. You know this to be so."

"All right, all right," I said, throwing up my hands in mock surrender. "I understand the point. And, yes, you and Detrom have certainly said that before! I get it!"

Camaroon laughed at my discomfort, and the others joined her. Obviously, some things were never going to change between Jacobi and me. Thank the gods, or God, for that.

After a moment, one by one, we all became silent, soberly pondering the significance of what we had just witnessed. Truly, all things are possible with the One when the workings are understood properly.

"You are an amazing talent, a powerful Merlin indeed, Jacobi," said Camaroon, the first to speak again.

"No, I am just attuned to the laws of the Universal Mind. We all have The Merlin inside of us, all of us."

Much time passed. I reached a point where I tapered back on the healing work and became more of a Monachus, a sort of Monk, or Ascetic, than anything else. I loved nothing more than to spend days on end studying and meditating, sometimes with the others, but most of the time alone. I felt most connected with the All in the state of meditation, for it was in such a state that I was truly at one with my eternal nature. The feeling or experience itself is difficult to describe; to put into words. The spoken or written word is by its very nature finite and, therefore, limiting, and how is one to use a finite medium to describe something that touches on the infinite? While in the meditative state, I was truly myself; at one with creation; seeing my human self as just a small dot on the map of expression; a blink of God's eye, even as the Eye Itself.

But as profound as that sounds, I was also still Longinus the man, and Camaroon had become my wife. At least, that was what everyone was saying. We had shared my lodge ever since the initiation ritual. And, of course, we shared the bed, as well. We devoured each other's bodies nightly. Our parts were as made for each other. Exploding inside of her brought me a momentary oneness with the

Source of All akin to that which I felt during deep meditations. Sexual climax can be fragmentary enlightenment.

I was still Longinus, the soldier, as well. Paulonius had briefed me that morning over the meal, and continued to do so. Many Roman patrols were in the land. Many of the other villages had been hit. Some of the lads from our village rallied to their aid, and had never been heard from again. Our village was safe for a number of reasons. Rome still hunted me and the spear, so a plan of deception had been implemented to lead them off in different directions. We were also located in a valley that was dense with oaks, forested from prying eyes. Finally, Detrom and the other powerful Druids had placed an immense Glamour of protection and obscurity over the valley, concealing us and rendering us invisible to those who meant us harm.

I had been part of the ritual to invoke the Glamour. Was it working? We had been left alone, after all, for well over a year now. Actually, it had been much longer, two years or more. I had lost track of time, for awhile. Ever since the night of the Glam ritual, a mysterious fog or mist hung over the valley, veiling us from the rest of the world and, it seemed, from time itself, for a year felt as only a month. But I think I might have been the only one who felt this way about the time passing; a carryover from my Roman sensibilities and training, perhaps. The Celts didn't seem to notice or care. But then again, they wouldn't; they've always had their own sense, definition, of time.

It was indeed a strange thing, this mist. In addition to invoking a feeling of time-lapse, the mist was also thin enough during the day to let sunshine through normally, and thick enough at night to prevent our cooking fires from being seen from afar, as reported to us by our scouts that were sent out nightly.

Then, one day, a group of strangers arrived—peaceful travelers who were fleeing Rome.

They came into the village in the early afternoon, escorted by two of our perimeter guards. As I stepped out of the lodge, I saw that Camaroon was talking with one of the new strangers, a woman, who appeared to be cradling a child in her arms. Hentapas was standing with Romi and a group of our people. The local folks were curious and excited about the newcomers.

"They made it through the mists," a villager whispered. "Obviously, they mean us no harm then!" observed another.

The former legionaries, however, were white as ghosts. They stared at the newly-arrived entourage.

"What is the matter with you two?" I asked. "Have you not seen travelers before?"

"It's *her*," Romi said, as if I'd not said a word.

"Who?" I demanded.

"It *is* her. The woman holding the child," answered Hentapas, as if I should know her.

I looked at the travelers. They all looked weary, about fifteen in number; more men than women, and mostly on foot. Many of them were in the shade of one of the big oaks, so it was difficult to see all their faces. The woman whom Romi and Hentapas were talking about, though, stood in the light. She was the one speaking with Camaroon. Through the dirty face and travel ravaged clothing, I could still tell that she was attractive, probably twenty-nine to thirty-three summers. The child, asleep in her arms, appeared to be a girl of about three.

"All right," I said. "I see her. Now tell me who she is."

"She...is the woman from the tomb that day. *His* Tomb," Romi stated tonelessly.

"What woman?"

Hentapas turned to me slowly and looked directly into my eyes. There was intensity in his gaze, a kind that I had never seen before. It conveyed the seriousness of what he was about to say.

"She is the woman who was first to find the tomb opened when Romi and I had fallen asleep, sir. The one who said she had seen Jesu risen from the dead," he stammered.

I stared at the woman and my heart began to pound. I thought at first the pounding was due to what the lad had just told me. But it was not; at least not entirely, for I began to sense something else—something else altogether. I could feel it in the air; it rode on the mists.

Then I saw her.

Another woman stepped out from the shadows and stood next to the one holding the child, and Camaroon, and I knew my life was once again changed.

XVII

Dosameenor, who had escorted the outlanders into the village, ordered his troops, which amounted to several platoons of men and women warriors, to gather food for the newly arrived contingent of travelers. It took me a moment to get over the shock of seeing Irena standing with Camaroon and the other woman, before I realized that Jacobi was speaking to me. He was standing next to me. I had not heard nor seen his approach.

"Did you hear me, Longinus?" Jacobi asked. "Of course, you didn't. How could you? You are clearly in a state of disbelief, are you not? Yes, it is her, Longinus. And the other is Mary of Magdalene."

"She, Mary, was the one at…" began Romi.

"I know," Jacobi interrupted. He looked closer at Mary, and then especially closely at the child in her arms. The child; the little one sparked something in the old man. That light, that brilliant other-worldly glow that I'd seen on Jacobi before, began to project from his entire being, but this time, it had an intensity to it that I'd never seen before. "Is that…could it be?" he asked with reverent awe, more to himself than to anyone else.

And, just like that, he was off, shuffling toward the group.

"He may be somewhat of a Merlin now," observed Romi, "but he is still odd."

"He knows things that you and I may never understand," said Hentapas sagely.

"Hmph," was Romi's skeptical response.

I watched as Jacobi approached the group of travelers slowly. Irena took notice of him and released a squeal of delight. Tears filled her eyes as she embraced the old man, nearly crushing the life out of his seemingly frail body in her excitement.

They conversed then. I was not close enough to hear them speak, but I watched intently and could see words tumble from their mouths. The words, combined with an animated flurry of hand gestures, told each in a moment, the basic journey of life for the other, as it had unfolded over the past years since last they'd seen one another. Jacobi kept looking at Mary and the child, clearly wanting to speak with the woman. Finally, Irena placed her hand lovingly on Jacobi's cheek, drawing his full attention back to her. I saw her mouth the words, *where is he?*

Jacobi turned to me, smiled from ear to ear, and pointed.

I thought my heart would leap out of my chest.

Tentatively, on wobbling legs of anticipation, I stepped forward to meet my past, my destiny.

She wiped the tears from her eyes as she walked toward me. We approached each other slowly at first, as if in a fragile dream whose world would dissolve with a sigh. But the reality was that she was here; I was here. Our steps picked up as we got closer to each other, until we were covering the ground in a flying run. We slammed into each others' body with the force of a long-exile-ended. Our arms wrapped tightly around one-another, as if we wished to never again be separated. After a moment, I pulled back, cupping her dirty, but still lovely face in my hands.

"Where have you been? I thought you were going to follow us. You never came. I thought I'd never see you again. Why didn't you come?" The words just shot out of me. I couldn't help myself. I had not realized until that moment how much this woman had meant to me.

She simply smiled. A solitary tear rolled delicately and meanderingly down her cheek, leaving a streak of contentment on her face. "Oh, Longinus," she said. "I have sorely missed you, too."

We stood there and stared at each other for a moment. I looked over her shoulder and could see that most of the villagers had come out and were now watching Irena and me. Irena's fellow travelers were also gazing at the odd reunion here in the middle of a glamour-affected valley. Then there were the others who were watching us with even more curiosity; Jacobi stood with them. Mary looked at me, with what thoughts, I could not say. Her child, too, gazed at me, but with eyes as old as time itself. And, Camaroon—there was something forlorn in her face as she stared at me; a resignation, perhaps.

Jacobi shuffled his way toward us, motioning Mary to follow him. Camaroon hung back for a moment, but quickly caught up.

"All right, then!" boomed Dosameenor's commanding voice to the rest of the villagers. "Come on now. Let's get busy and make our guests feel at home!" The other villagers quickly obeyed and scurried about their work.

Hentapas and Romi still stood close by. They wanted to stay—I could feel it—but they both began to step back, believing that it was not their place to be present for this meeting. "Remain here!" I ordered. "We are all a part of this."

Hentapas nodded, clearly pleased.

The little group arrived and halted before Irena, myself and the other two men. An awkward silence filled the space around us. Or, perhaps it was only I who felt the awkwardness. For a brief instant, I focused on other things; I heard birds singing, the chatter of the villagers around us and my own breath going in and out. I stared at the woman, Mary. Yes, thirty-three summers at the most, wavy brown hair with shades of auburn. Dark, dark brown eyes accented with long dark lashes; a beautiful woman. But she was much more than just a woman. Her countenance seemed to radiate a depth and a wisdom that transcended all the knowledge of the Universe. It reminded me of the power I had felt from Detrom the first time I saw him. This, however, felt even more powerful. So much so, that a sudden feeling of complete unworthiness at being in her presence swept over me. I almost felt compelled to drop to my knees in awe. I stopped myself from dropping, though, and stood my ground in front of her, but with eyes lowered.

Other thoughts then began to gnaw at me. In spite of all the training and enlightenment I had received over the past couple of years or so, I was still very, very much human. I felt guilt, tremendous guilt, over what I had done to Jesu, her Master and Teacher…and…and…

I looked at the child and suddenly realized who the father was, or had been. The babe, the girl-child, stared at me with *his*, Jesu's, eternal eyes.

"Longinus," said Jacobi, interrupting my thoughts, "none of it matters. It all took place as it was supposed to, as Master Jesu wanted it to," he explained, reading most of my thoughts as always. "Detach yourself, as you have been taught, and look at it all from the true perspective of your Higher, Eternal Self. You will see that what I say is true."

I closed my eyes briefly, willing Jacobi's words into my mind, attempting to shove out all other thoughts. I opened them at the sound of her voice.

"Centurion Longinus," Mary's sweet voice intoned, as but a whisper. She smiled a radiant smile of forgiveness and Love, the Love of God.

"I...am just Longinus now, please," was all I could manage to say.

She inclined her head in acknowledgement, stepped up to me and touched my face with her free hand. A feeling of divine warmth and comfort coursed through my entire being. "Let it go now, my friend," she soothed. "I know that *he* speaks to you, for *he* speaks to me, as well. You think that it's through the spear, but it is not. But you know that, too, don't you?" She laughed, a sweet, tinkling sound. "I think we all have crutches that we must let go of." She stepped back then.

I had the inane thought that perhaps she would like to see the spear, which I now kept, some of the time, at least, well hidden in the lodge. A stupid thought, that. Why would she care to see that thing? It had been a thought born of my own insecurities; a juvenile need on my part for her to accept me and forgive me, or for me to forgive myself. But all I had to do was to open my heart and mind and spirit, and hear what she was saying to know that there was nothing to forgive.

Irena spoke then. "Mary is the reason I could not come to you when I said would, or rather, my vow to help Mary was the reason," she explained. "When you left on the boat that day from Najaffi, Mary was due to give birth at any time. Sara here," Irena said, gently tousling the child's hair, "was longer in coming than we thought she would be and there were complications with Mary afterwards."

"I was in a fever for a very, very long time, Longinus," Mary said. She smiled, recalling the memory. "While I was in the fever, I spent all that time with Jesu, you see, learning so that I could teach and carry on his work, too, when I was well again. Oh, I had been his disciple when he walked among us, but the teachings he taught me while I was with him on the *Other Side* for a time were even more infinite in their scope." She studied me for a moment. "But I think you know what I speak of, Longinus, or you soon will." Adjusting the child in her arms, Mary held Sara so that I could see her face more clearly. "Can you say hello, Sara?"

The child said nothing, but stared at me until a smile to light up the world splashed across her little face. The smile quickly grew until it burst forth into peels of glorious giggles of happiness, which, in turn, rapidly infected us all. We burst into laughter of our own.

"Camaroon?" sounded a young female voice. It was Rintinau, the young girl who had come to the lake, calling for Camaroon. She was no longer a little girl, but blossoming into a young woman. She had been Camaroon's shadow and student for some time now, "Guardian of the Temple Mound Flame" and "Apprentice Priestess of the Mist", she was called.

"Grand Master Detrom asks for your council," Rintinau said.

"Yes, of course," Camaroon replied.

We looked at each other then, Camaroon and I. She had not been laughing with the rest of us. Her face was smiling but I saw emptiness there.

"Excuse me," she said, and walked off with Rintinau.

XVIII

The rest of the day was spent helping our guests to clean up, settle in and generally shake off the road. As it turned out, the group was not going to be here for all that long; they were headed to a community up in the northern region: a community of Jews. Mary would be safest there, according to Irena and Thomas, the leader and Rabbi of the group. Mary was being hunted by Rome for a couple of different reasons, the most obvious of which she had been carrying in her arms. I was quite disappointed, for Irena was going with them. I tried to talk to her about it at the feasting that evening, but could not. Every time I tried to corner her, it seemed that someone else needed her attention, thus thwarting my effort to speak to her. No matter for now. They would probably not be leaving for many days. Surely, I could change her mind by then.

The cooking fires remained stoked, and the feasting and celebration around them went on into the night. It was mostly our people of the village who carried it on. Not all of the group of newcomers were Jewish, however, and those who weren't stayed out celebrating and regaling the village folk with their tales of travel. But most were Jewish, as it turned out, and had their own strict guidelines on food and drink. Most of them retired when their appetites had been at least partly satiated.

Irena had merely smiled at me when the time came for her to take leave of the celebration. Mary wanted to go, as well, so Irena escorted the woman and her child to their lodgings. I sought out Jacobi then, but could not find him near the cooking fires. Nor could I find Dosameenor, nor Hentapas, nor Romi, nor

Detrom, nor even Camaroon. So, I left the cooking fires and their celebratory congregants and headed back to my own lodge.

Pulling back the flap and entering my living space answered one question, at least: where Camaroon had gone. She was not lying on the sleeping pallet, though. She had not retired. Quite the contrary. She was piling her belongings in a stack near the entrance. Obviously, she was leaving.

"What is this?" I inquired.

She stopped what she was doing and stared at me as if drinking me in for the last time. She smiled then. "What does it look like?" There was no anger in her voice, no sarcasm, no hostility of any kind. She was leaving, and that was that.

"You are going somewhere, without even discussing it or a courtesy goodbye or explanation?" I asked, feeling both angry and guilty. I found that a part of me actually wanted this: a confrontation with her—perhaps, even for her to leave me all together.

Camaroon put down the fire tools she was packing away and came face-to-face with me, looking me straight in the eyes, soul-to-soul. She gently touched my cheek then, stroking it lightly. "My Longinus," she began. "Yet, mine no more. Nor ever really, were you, I suppose. Do you remember the night of your ritual, how, the next morning, I told you that you had made prophecies?"

The question caught me off guard. "What does that have to do with anything?" She waited patiently while I thought about it. "All right, yes. I recall that you said I had babbled a couple of prophetic phrases or something or other, but I couldn't remember anything about them and you certainly wouldn't tell me no matter how many times I asked, nor would anyone else who was there."

"That's right and do you remember why I wouldn't tell you what you said that night?"

I could feel my face blushing. She had always retained that ability to make me feel like a school boy. "Something about that they were meant for me and that I'd remember eventually. Well, guess by the gods what? I still haven't remembered them. So, I imagine they weren't altogether such important prophecies after all, eh?" I was becoming flustered, though I was not sure why.

"They were meant—" she began.

"I know," I interrupted. "They were meant for me. They came through me, so were for me to interpret, and so on."

"No," she stated so abruptly that I was utterly silenced. "They were meant for you because they were *about you*."

The air was still. A piece of wood cracked and popped on the fire in the pit, spitting an ember onto the surrounding dirt floor. I simply stared at it, as it harmlessly cooled and died. "What do you mean? I thought I had said things that concerned everyone."

"Oh, you said a couple of things that pertained to the Romans destroying our culture and so forth. But the main things you said concerned yourself and the future." Camaroon looked away then. She sat on the edge of the sleeping pallet and caressed the cover, the place where we had relished each other's bodies night after night. "I kept hoping that it was a false-prophesy. I even began to believe so," she continued, "until *they* arrived: Irena and the others," she finished, a tear glistening in one eye.

I went to her then and knelt in front of her. I placed a hand on her chin and lifted it, thus looking again into her eyes. "I am sorry. I do not want to cause any pain. But I don't understand what you say. Please. Please explain it to me. What did I say that night? What does it have to do with you, with her?"

She gazed back at me, surprise subtly drifting across her face. "You truly do not remember any of it, do you?"

I gently shook my head.

"Very well, then." She took a breath, released it with a sigh, and plunged in. "You...said that your bloodline, 'a descendent of Longinus', is going to found a new nation, one based on truth and justice—one where the weaker are defended and treated well. This is to be in a place, on an island, where the last of the Celts live, some three-hundred years hence. The other thing you stated was that your spirit will incarnate during that time and in that place as the greatest of all wizards, the Merlin of Merlins. So powerful will you be, that the title 'Merlin' will lose all meaning, for it will be your name: a name that you will pass on to a son who will crown a true High King of that land. You said you will do this—incarnate as this being—to aid in the birth of this new country and her King, her King being the descendent of Centurion Gauis Cassius Longinus," she finished.

The crackling of the fire was all I heard for a moment. I remembered nothing of these prophesies. But they rang true, completely true, resonating with every fiber of my being. I could hardly speak.

"Reincarnate as a Master Merlin?" was all I managed to say.

"Not just a Master Merlin, THE Greatest Merlin, and father to the final Merlin," she added.

I didn't know what she was talking about, so I focused on the generality. "I know the Druids convey the belief in reincarnation, but I've never really thought about it."

"Why do you think our warriors are so fearless? It's one of the reasons anyway. They know they will be born again, into this life, to continue their schooling, to advance to a point spiritually where they will choose not to come back here. Even your Jesu alluded to it," she said.

"I don't know about that," I said. I thought about it for a moment. "I don't remember anything about that in our...I should ask Jacobi."

She smiled sagely. "I believe Jacobi would say that with an Infinite God, all things are possible, and must be—by the definition of what it is to be infinite—truly possible. But you are placing attention on only one part of the prophecies."

"Yes, my descendent. I don't understand that part."

"Oh, Longinus, stop it!" she blurted out in frustration. "You are not daft! Figure it out. You will have a child that carries on your bloodline."

"I know what it implies," I said, staring deeply into her eyes.

"Do you?" She cupped my face with her hands and stared right back into my eyes. "Yes, it means that you *will* have a child. But not with me, if that's what you're thinking, and you know that in your heart."

It is in part what I was thinking. I thought that perhaps she was pregnant, but she had just dashed that idea. Several years we had been together and she had never become pregnant with my child. The subject was never brought up. I never questioned why. I know now that it was never brought up, by me, at least, because I had other priorities embedded deep in my mind. Since she never talked about having children together, I, consciously or not, or for whatever reason, did not want to, either.

"I *cannot*, Longinus, not any longer," she continued, the tear now rolling down her face. "I had a child many summers ago, a girl child. The birthing was very difficult for me and left my insides ravaged. I am barren."

I did not know what to say. You can never know someone fully, no matter how intimate you become; no matter how long you are with that person.

An awkward laugh escaped her lips. "You never knew? Why do you think I never became pregnant with you?"

"I...assumed you knew of a special way of controlling it. You are a powerful herbalist and Druidess," I said.

"Is that all you assumed?"

I paused in silence for a moment. "I don't know what else to say, Camaroon. But I never thought that you were barren." A gulf of awkwardness yawned between us. "What of your child?" I finally asked.

"What of her? You've seen her a thousand times, spoken to her almost as many."

My brow crinkled in confusion.

"'Tis Rintinau, Longinus."

My mouth must have dropped agape, for she laughed again.

"You never suspected?" she asked astonished.

"Why should I? That first day at the lake with you, I asked you directly if she was your daughter. You said 'no,'" I answered, feeling utterly foolish. I thought about both of them. On some level, I suppose I knew. "Why did you lie? Why did you never tell me?"

"As I believe I told you then, she is what you call a Vestal. 'A Vestal Virgin,' as a Roman would call her. She was chosen at birth by the Druids. Once a girl-child enters into the service of The Light, The Temple, she is no longer the child of a man and a woman, but a divine child-being of the Goddess. From that point on, we neither speak nor think of her in terms of 'our child'. That is the way of it." explained Camaroon. "So, I told you the truth."

"I see," I said. "And her father. Her *human* father?" I asked, trying to smile.

"He was killed in the battles preceding your arrival. We were never close. In fact, Rintinau was begotten in a ritual designed solely for the purpose of bringing into being a new 'Vestal' servant to the Great Goddess."

"How...that is, why the two of you?" I couldn't help asking.

"We had both been servants to the Goddess in the Temple. Rintun, that was his name, was a powerful Druid, but equally, a powerful warrior. A rare combination. There were several other factors, too—our ancestral paths and so on," she finished, rising from the sleeping pallet. She stared back at the pallet for a moment, letting go, I could feel, of her distant past, and shifting her thoughts to us once again. "So you see, Longinus, it is not with me you will beget a child to continue your bloodline. And it is obvious the time has come for me to move forward so that you may move forward." With that, she turned and resumed gathering her things.

I still knelt at the pallet. I came partially to my feet, turned and sat down on the pallet where Camaroon had been a moment before. "Where will you go?" I asked.

"To Rintun's family's lodge," she said matter-of-factly.

"I thought you said you and he were never close?"

"We were not. But his sisters and I were. Besides, Celts take care of their own. You don't have to be blood to be sheltered for a time or taken in as family. We foster out our children all the time, for instance, allowing them to be raised by another member of the community, and not just in the sense of service to the Goddess as with Rintinau, but ordinary folks do it. They foster their children with some other member of the village. Almost all of our children are raised by the whole community. You've seen that. I could stay with Rintun's sisters forever, but I'll build my own dwelling soon enough." Obviously she'd thought this through.

"I see," I replied. She continued to gather things and I continued to watch in silence. In silence, that is, until I began to hear a slight, quiet rattling, as if something close by were vibrating against a piece of wood. I knew what it was. I went to a spot against the wall near the pallet, pulled back the long vertical panel of wood I'd carved out, and saw that the spear was indeed vibrating slightly, its tip aglow. I took it out of its hiding place and headed for the entrance, knowing full well that it was indeed time for me to move on into the future.

I stopped before leaving and faced Camaroon one last time. "I wish you well. I wish you prosperity in all things. I wish you long life and happiness. Thank you for all that you've given me: your mind, your knowledge, your love. I will always remember you. Please remember me, too," I finished.

"I will, Longinus. How could I ever forget you," she said smiling.

We kissed then; a final, passionate embrace; a remembrance of that which once was, but would be no more.

I left my lodge then. When I came back three hours later, all traces of her were gone. I never saw her again.

XIX

I spent the next few weeks in contemplation, and service to the village. The travelers had made themselves at home, joining in, for the most part, with the community's daily activities. The day finally came, though, when Thomas announced that the group would be leaving the next morning.

Irena and I had hardly spoken to each other during the whole time she had been here. We had exchanged pleasantries and courtesies, pretensions more accurately, but that was all.

Instead of going to the lodge of her ex-sister-by-marriage, Camaroon had left the village entirely. She had told no one of her plans, not even Rintinau. As a result of that and the gossipers of the community, some of the folks in the village cast a disapproving eye at me, and more subtly, so as not to offend our guests outright, at Irena. I believed this was why Irena had kept her distance from me; she was merely being diplomatic, not wanting to give offense overtly to any of the villagers.

But the time for her leave-taking had come. She made it clear that she was going to fulfill her promise and see Mary and Sara all the way to their destination. I had made a decision as well: I was going with them.

The evening meal was being held in the Great Hall, as it had come to be known. It was a fairly large round wooden structure, complete with a beamed roof. The Hall had been used for feasts and celebrations, as well as village meetings, for as long as most folks could remember. The villagers had not used it for a long, long time, however; for it had been the sight of bloody executions by Draco at the time of his short-lived rise to power. Many had wanted it burned to the ground, but Detrom convinced all to let it stand. With a ritual for cleansing and a rite aiding the remaining tormented spirits of those who had been killed there, the Hall was purified, and once again became a lively place for the people. What better way to counteract death in a place than to celebrate life there.

The meal turned into a feast to celebrate the group that would be leaving. Most of the villagers were in attendance. I, too, made my way there.

The sun had long set by the time I went to the Hall. The night was calm, cool and bright with a rising full moon, but the Hall inside was noisy, hot and slightly dim with smoke. The cooking fires were in the center of the large room, and smoke was doing its best to escape out the small hole in the center of the roof, but for the moment, more of the cloudy substance appeared to be staying in the Hall than not. The celebrants didn't seem to mind, though, for they were boisterously oblivious to it.

In Rome, for meals such as this, it was customary for everyone to be seated on cushions on the ground in front of several low tables piled with food and drink. Such was the way in the Great Hall. Jacobi and Irena sat with Mary and the child, Sara, Detrom and Thomas sat with Dosameenor and Dosameenor's brother Renaulus, and several of the Hebrew guards the group had traveled with. The guards were not armed; no one was allowed weapons in the Hall—not even Dosameenor and Renaulus—but they still wore their military-type tunics denoting their station in the group.

The Hebrew guards eyed me curiously, with a twinge of anticipation as I approached the table. They glanced periodically at my side. Clearly, they were hoping to see the spear. I probably could have brought it; the spear would be the only *weapon* exempt from the rule concerning arms in the Hall, but I had not. It was back at the lodge in its paneled hiding spot. The guards took note that they probably would not see the famed lance that evening and went back to their meal, albeit, obviously disappointed.

"Longinus, my good man," Detrom said, as I stopped in front of the table. "You've come out to join us. Please, sit." He moved over slightly on his cushion to make room.

"Yes, my friend!" exclaimed a slightly inebriated Dosameenor.

I was about to decline. I simply wanted to announce my intent to travel with the group. I thought better of it, however. "Thank you," I said and sat between Detrom and Jacobi, the old man smiling at me in that knowing way of his, probably reading my mind, my intentions.

A goblet of mead was placed in front of me, then a platter of meat and cheese. I drank the mead and nibbled on the cheese, somewhat lost in my own thoughts.

"You have something to tell us, do you not?" asked Jacobi.

I looked at him and smiled. "Indeed," I began, and turned my attention to Thomas, The Learned, as many of his people called him. This was my first face-to-face meeting with the man. I had only seen him from a distance these past weeks. A handsome face, he had. An ample shock of red-brown hair mixed with grey waved from atop his head, and a bright red beard, somewhat trimmed, adorned his cheeks and neck. Topping off his facial hair was a not-so-red mustache. It was dark brown, also with streaks of grey. His eyes were a piercing watery brown. They had that same type of depth as did Jacobi's eyes and Detrom's and Mary's, though the latter's were definitely in a class alone. "I intend to accompany your group on the morrow," I stated flatly.

The table fell silent. The sounds of the feasting impinged themselves on us with deafening loudness. The faces of those in my company seemed to be frozen, though why or with what I could not tell. No one really expected me to stay here forever. Perhaps it was because of the way I said it; as a matter-of-fact, no negotiation on the subject. I saw Dosameenor and Renaulus exchange a glance.

Thomas, though, was the first to recover. "Delightful!" he exclaimed. "Yes, indeed, you would be most welcome. Is that not so, ladies?" he inquired, directing his attention to Mary and Irena.

Mary smiled. "Why, certainly. How wonderful."

Irena smiled, too. She looked deeply into my eyes, deep into my soul; the deepest since our reunion on the day of her arrival.

And I looked deeply into her soul, as well. There was something there that she was attempting to conceal. Was it joy? Yes, I believe it was.

"But you have made a home here, Longinus," Mary continued. "The people will surely want you to stay. Are you sure that journeying with us is what you wish, that you do it for the reasons of your spirit?"

What she was really asking was whether or not I was doing it for reasons of the flesh, for Irena. My heart, certainly, and my body, perhaps, belonged with Irena, 'twas true. Yet, it was my higher soul that was telling me that I must go with them. Whatever awaited, whatever my ultimate destiny, it was much bigger than just Irena and I. I had given much thought to what Camaroon had told me the night she left; what she had said about my Prophecies. I had even tried to ask Detrom about them; about exactly what I said the night of my Initiation. He would not speak of it, echoing part of what Camaroon had said: that it was for me and me alone.

My thoughts had drifted on the topic for a few days, but in the end, I let it go. If I were going to have a child eventually, that would carry my blood to far away lands and change the world, then the event of my coming together with this child's mother would play out in its own time and with whom it was supposed to. The only conclusion I had come to in the past weeks was that it was time to leave the village, and it was appropriate to do so with Irena's group.

"Yes," I finally said. "I've thought much and meditated much. It is time to go. Besides, I was once a Centurion. You could use an extra man at arms.

"Ah, but I thought you were more Druid now, a priestly man, a man of peace," commented Thomas.

"Aye, 'tis true, he is that" interjected Renaulus, slurring his words slightly. "But once a warrior, always a warrior. Besides, a man of peace is only at peace when all agree to be at peace. But one must always be on guard. Is that not so my friend?" he inquired, addressing the question to me.

"Well," I began, but stopped. I had come to respect Dosameenor's brother. I even had feelings of fondness for him. But he was a simple man. He was a warrior and thought like a warrior and only a warrior. "'Tis true that one must always practice awareness, Renaulus," I answered vaguely, which only seemed to confuse the man. I glanced quickly at Dosameenor and saw him hide a smile at his brother's puzzled expression.

I then turned my attention back to Thomas. "I am many things, as are we all, and I practice many things. Yes, I practice healing, meditation, the elevation of my soul to salvation and enlightenment. And, I also still practice the art of war. It is a necessary evil," I finished. I had indeed kept up my skills with sword and spear, drilling with Dosameenor and his brother and their men on a semi-regular basis. My body was not, however, in the type of military shape that it had been in the past. No matter.

"I understand," replied Thomas. "We all have many layers, and I, too, practice salvation even in turbulent and violent situations."

"What does that mean—salvation?" Renaulus interrupted. "Salvation from what? I'm no sinner like you people believe."

"That is not what *we* believe, my friend," Thomas said gently.

"But you are Jews, are you not?" Renaulus asked harshly, yet with sincerity, not contempt. Anyone just joining us would have thought that Renaulus was becoming belligerent with Thomas. But he wasn't. Renaulus' way was simply gruff, even when he was not angry. It could be frightening at first until one got to know this bear of a man.

"Most of us in the group are Hebrew, yes, but many of us practice what is becoming known as a 'Philosophy of Knowing' or a 'Gnostic Philosophy,' as it is called in Greek," explained Thomas. "Part of the philosophy is the belief that the only definition of sin is that it is a *missing of the mark*, so to speak. That to not heed to one's higher soul is the only sin; that there is nothing intrinsically wrong with drawing all one's attention to things of this world, it just means that one will stay in this physical realm longer. That in and of itself is the punishment, if you really must label something as a punishment," finished Thomas.

"But I love it here! I love women! I love battle! I love food and drink!" countered Renaulus, hoisting his goblet of mead, slopping some of its contents onto the table.

"So you do," put in Detrom. We all laughed. "Our friend is merely saying that that is fine and good and garners no such thing as punishment in and of itself. But the greater *joy* and higher purpose of your soul is to realize its divine nature and turn to it to lift you to your highest possibilities. I believe your Jesu conveyed this belief," continued Detrom, glancing at Thomas.

Thomas nodded sagely.

"And that can only happen," Detrom went on, speaking again to Renaulus, "through your own awareness and learning and contemplation, not by any set of rules which are imposed from without by someone else."

"Precisely," added Thomas.

Poor Renaulus fell silent. A new and much more profound expression of confusion furrowed his brow.

Dosameenor clapped him on the shoulder. "Fear not, my brother. These things will come to you in time. If not in this life, in the next one, then, or the one after that, or the one after that!" he laughed. He then looked at me in all seriousness. "I go with you, Longinus."

I did not know what to say. I thought for sure that he would want to stay with his people. I looked to Mary and Thomas almost expecting a negative response. But they were simply smiling, awaiting my reply to my friend. I then looked at Jacobi.

"Yes, Longinus. I go with you, too. I am, by the One God, still your servant." He smiled affectionately.

"You are no such thing. You may do as you please and you know it," I replied.

"And I please to go with you. Besides, someone has to watch out for you. And, as always, that duty falls to me," he said jestingly in the manner of a frustrated parent, inciting another round of laughter.

"So be it," I said, looking from him to Dosameenor.

"Good," replied Thomas.

Mary began to rise. "Please excuse us, but Sara and I must retire. It is good to have you with us, Longinus," she said.

Irena also rose to leave. "I will say good night, as well."

"We will see you all at the dawn," said Mary to those of us remaining at the table.

"To the dawn," toasted Dosameenor. We all raised our goblets as the women nodded in acknowledgement and retreated from the hall.

XX

The morning came quickly. I was up with the Druids performing a rite to welcome the returning sun, the "Disc Of Life," as they called it, or "Amon Ra," as Hentapas called it, and to secure blessings for safe travels. The morning ritual was performed outside of the mists enshrouding the village, on the eastern high ridge of the valley. This was only one of a handful of times I had participated in the dawn rite. I don't really know why I had not joined in more often. Perhaps I simply was not an early riser, although, my military career would argue otherwise.

Looking down toward the valley floor and the village, the protective mists enshrouding the community seemed thinner this day than they usually did. A feeling of foreboding passed through my being at the thought, though I could not put my finger on what caused it. Detrom and the others would surely keep the mists strong after I had gone. Reports now came back with every scout sent out; the Romans were everywhere.

For the journey, I wore my Centurion cuirass, but I wore it underneath the robes and cape of a Celtic elder. I abandoned my Roman sandals, something I was loath to do, and donned traditional Celtic warrior footwear: sturdy leather boots. They bit into my feet, but would do for the time being.

To further cover my Romanness, I even allowed my beard to come in a little. I had been doing that for several weeks, since Irena and the others had arrived. I suppose that a part of me knew I'd be going with them when they left, even before I actually realized it, and thus started to conceal my identity as Centurion Longinus. I kept it quite trimmed, however. I refused to give up all semblances of being civilized.

Detrom and some others had given me a horse, a large and magnificent beast by the name of Macha, the Celtic Goddess of War. The horse was indeed powerful and full of life and rage, traits usually reserved for steeds of war, yes, but steeds of war were also usually male. She warmed to my touch from the first, though. A good match we were.

Mounted on Macha, I came to the center of the village after breaking my fast with some of my fellow travelers. There were many people there, and much activity had been underway; seeing to last minute provisions by the men and so forth. Irena, Mary and Sara, however, were nowhere to be seen.

Jacobi was mounted on a horse of his own, an ancient mare about half the size of Macha. "It appears your mount has seen the light of a few summers," I couldn't help but tease.

"Yes, yes, she has indeed. But let not the wrinkles of time fool you, or the fool you will become!" he quipped. "She has many summers and miles left in her."

"No doubt, no doubt," I said, standing corrected. "Have you seen Irena?"

"She was here mere moments ago. That is her chariot and provisions there," he said, pointing to the large four-wheeled wagon-type vehicle some twenty-feet away. It had the appearance of a large, extended chariot and was drawn by two strong horses who waited patiently, already harnessed to the wagon. The vehicle was laden with provisions and covered. The covering was over a frame that rose a few feet into the air to conceal contents and to comfortably, more or less, seat passengers. It almost reminded me of some wagons I had seen Roman royalty transported in across vast distances, except without all the pretentious accoutrements and silk trappings, and refinements in drapery.

Just then, I saw the child, Sara, crawl out from the covered portion onto the back of the wagon. "Please stay with me, Sara," came Mary's calm, tinkling voice as she, too, appeared at the back to retrieve the errant child. Sara simply giggled at the game as her mother wrapped her arms about the babe and pulled Sara to her body.

"It would appear that Sara is anxious to go," I observed to Mary.

"Good morning, Longinus. Yes, I believe most of us are," she replied. She glanced down at my horse's side. There, in its sheathing, was the spear. The blade itself was well hidden. Only the shaft protruded out of its nest. Nonetheless, she knew what it was. Her eyes lingered only for the briefest of instances before returning to me. "And you, are you anxious to be away?"

"It's time, yes."

"You've much history here. And, you've learned much and progressed much to know the Truth, have you not?" she asked, as she looked into my eyes.

Sara was staring intently at me as well, as if she too awaited my response; as if she, too, would weigh my answer.

Foolish, Longinus, I thought. No one was waiting to judge me, but me. "Yes, to all. But, as I said, it is time for me to move on."

"Indeed it is," said a familiar voice. I looked down to see Detrom standing beside Macha, patting her flanks with affection. Behind Detrom, sitting atop their mounts were Dosameenor, Romi and Hentapas. Paulonius, too, was with them, but on foot, holding a small shaggy horse of the hills, by its long mane. Most Celts did not ride with stirrups or reigns, and only rarely with saddles, preferring instead to ride bareback and using the animal's mane as the main control and command device. Paulonius had taken to this form of riding. There was another animal behind Paulonius' little horse that looked just like the first one. The latter was loaded up with supplies. I simply took note of the lad, his horses and the others, then turned my attention back to the High Druid.

"Detrom. I'm so glad to see you," I said as I dismounted. Truth was, I was glad to see all of them. Though Detrom was staying, I was not sure until that moment if the others—Romi, Hentapas and Paulonius—were actually going to come with me. I had given them all leave to stay if they wished it. More than one of them had become involved with the local women over the course of our stay here. Paulonius, in particular, had become attached to a fetching lass with the most beautiful emerald eyes and flowing auburn hair I had ever seen.

That same fetching lass suddenly appeared, stepping out from the other side of Paulonius' horse. She was in full travel attire. Obviously, she was coming, too. I looked from the lass to Paulonius, who was turning all shades of red, and seemed completely at a loss for words. Ah, the idealistic impulsiveness of youth! Would that we all retain that quality as time marched on. But then again, perhaps that would not be such a good idea.

"He was too afraid to speak to you last night," said the lass.

Sixteen summers, I judged her to be, and brash, but in a cute and charming way. Hopefully, that would not turn to a sour way as she aged. "I see," I replied, in a non committal tone.

"So, I will speak in his stead," she said with nervous determination.

I put my hands up in mock surrender. "Wait," I said. "There is no need to speak of anything. You already have made your decision to accompany us as evidenced by your clothing. There are no restrictions as far as I'm concerned, as to who comes with us. Thomas voiced the same. So, there is nothing to say. Paulonius has leave to do as he wishes. If that is to bring you along, then so be it. The rest is up to your people."

"Yes, sir," she said looking surprised. She obviously had been expecting to meet with resistance.

"But," I continued, "you will serve the needs of the group. What can you offer?"

"I make and repair weapons: arrows, bows, lances," she said, looking at my spear shaft on Macha as she stated this last information. She glanced back at a pair of proud people, a man and woman, standing just beyond our group. "My mother and father taught me," she said, indicating the two. "They have been the village's armorers for many, many summers."

"We hope not to need those services."

"Even so, we may. But, I can also cook and…"

"All right," I said, laughing. "We are glad to have you, as I know Paulonius is."

"Thank you, sir," she said.

"Just one more thing. Your name?" I asked.

Paulonius opened his mouth to speak, but was beaten to it by the lass.

"My name is Genevieves, The Seventh," she replied.

"Carry on, Genevieves, The Seventh. You too, Paulonius," I said, and smiled. They both darted away with their beasts of burden before I could change my mind.

I looked at Detrom and we both laughed.

Jacobi sided up to us then.

"Ah, I am going to miss you, my friends," Detrom said, looking from Jacobi to me.

"And we you, High Druid Detrom," replied Jacobi.

"Yes, indeed," I said.

"Yes. I will, however, look in on you from time to time in the waters of the lake, Master Longinus, and in the light of the sacred flame. In that way, I will still be with you. Open your heart to me. Open your mind and spirit to me, always, both of you, and I will commune with you on the planes of the Otherworld, and impart any information to you that I can, whether of the mundane or of tantamount import," Detrom finished.

"So be it," I replied.

"So it is," said Jacobi.

"And, one more parting gift for you both," Detrom said, handing Jacobi and me each a beautiful and intricately carved gold broach. On the circular portion was the image of the mighty oak tree surrounded by the swirling knot-work which represented the eternal journey of spirit. In the center of the tree was a delicately carved image that looked like a snake, a serpent, which symbolized the Highest Wisdom, as well as the office of the High Druid. Even the pin that went through the middle of the broach to fasten it to one's cloak was intricately carved with the knot-swirls.

"Detrom..." I began, astounded by the gift, even more so than the gift of Macha.

Jacobi had dismounted and was embracing the High Druid. "Thank you, my friend, but I also sense that there is a practicality to this as well," said the old one.

"Indeed," smiled Detrom. "I know not what you will find, how many of us, the Druids, there are truly left throughout Gallia. But we are here and always will be. These will show that you come from and represent the office of the Highest Druidic authority in the land, should you need to show it. But beware, for it may also be your undoing should the wrong eyes land upon it."

"Thank you," I said.

"Yes. Thank you. And your warning is duly noted," said Jacobi, gingerly remounting his mare.

Thomas and Irena and Dosameenor finally arrived then, arms loaded with the last of the supplies.

I caught Irena's eye and smiled.

She smiled back, a loving glint in her eye.

So began our trek out of the village and out of the valley of the mists.

XXI

Our first three days of travel were relatively uneventful. The worst thing that happened was that one of the mares pulling Mary's chariot-wagon broke an ankle and had to be killed. The poor beast simply took a bad step, lodging a fore hoof in a forest rodent's large hole. She panicked and began to buck wildly in her harness, kicking the wooden panel behind her: the panel in front of the driver's platform. It splintered the panel and knocked the driver to the floorboards, unhurt, thankfully.

But the mare was not so lucky. The force from her hind leg kicks against the panel completely shifted her whole body weight to her front legs and beyond, toppling her over onto her muzzle. Of course, the stuck fore leg could not budge, and with the beast's momentum hurtling forward, it snapped at the ankle.

Howling sheiks of pain tore from the animal, causing all of us within earshot to grimace in sympathy. I had witnessed the whole incident and instantly gave the order to slash the mare's throat. I hated to do that, but allowing it to suffer was crueler.

It was strange; watching one of Thomas' guards carry out my order; I caught myself looking away. Was I squeamish just then? No, mournful is more accurate. I had come to fully appreciate life in all its forms. This horse had been a faithful servant. She had worked unconditionally, yet met with a tragic end.

Some would say that I was attaching too much value to the beast. It was, after all, simply an animal; a dumb beast of burden. But I had come to believe that all of life was sacred. All of life was sacred, and all of life carried on after this existence in some form. Detrom and Jacobi believed that we come back here again and again to learn and learn, until our souls have learned enough and move on. I was still not sure if I held with them in that thought. But if it were so, would this animal also come back here again? Did that mean it, too, had a soul? On that point, as well, I still debated with myself. I did believe that something of the animal's spirit carried on, though, so better to release it from its suffering here and now.

I do not think that I would wax so philosophical over killing a man again, however. I had killed many in the past under the guise of duty and, I confess, simply out of the blood-lust of battle frenzy, even enjoying the act at the time. I was different now, 'twas true. As I said, I now valued all life; saw the God-Spirit in all men and women. We are all brothers and sisters in The Great Light, as the Druids call it.

But men make choices. Quite often, they are choices that consciously and purposely bring harmful consequences upon others. They must be met with equally harmful, even savage, repercussions. But I did not believe that I would seek out battle and death, any longer, as a matter of stately duty or war, or for some other idealistic reasons.

I would, however, brutally defend myself and those close to me, and in that context, I would have no inhibitions whatsoever in killing a man. In spite of my Druidic studies of natural laws and spiritual principles and Godly Truths, I was still a soldier on many levels. I did not believe, as many did, and more were coming to believe, that a path of spiritual study and practice, and a soldier's life were incompatible. How could they be if everything came from the One?

We left the mare for the forest beasts and carrion animals to feast upon. Life's circle. We thought briefly about cutting up the carcass and taking it with us, but decided against it. We had not the time or inclination to prepare the meat properly for travel: to dry it and salt it for preservation, not to mention storing it. Besides, no one really wanted to eat horse meat when we had plenty of venison, goat meat and beef on hand.

Toward the end of the third day, a short while before we stopped to make camp, I was hailed from behind by a familiar voice. "Longinus," she said, approaching me on foot.

I halted, and spun my mount around, not because of any urgency in Irena's voice, but because I was at last, apparently, going to get the chance to speak with her. I confess to resentment in minute proportions directed toward Mary for her coveting of Irena's time and services. Of course, it was all by Irena's choice. She did nothing against her will and took orders from no one.

I dismounted and stood stiffly at Macha's side, nervously stroking her flank as Irena came to stand before me. Although, Camaroon had had the ability to make me feel like a school boy on occasion, that paled as compared to what I was feeling now: sweaty palms and an eagle's wings flapping in my stomach. Even the spear in its sheathing was vibrating slightly, not as a sign of danger, but simply in empathy with my state of being at Irena's appearance. Macha, too, sensed my nervousness, for she craned her neck and looked back at me as if to say, "silly man."

Control yourself, Longinus, I thought.

Irena stood silently before me.

"Hello," I finally managed.

"Hello," she replied, her own nervousness evident in her voice.

Awkward silence filled the space around us for a moment. I took that time to simply drink in her beauty. I had almost forgotten how lovely she was. Oh, I had seen her at the village, of course, but it was only now that I allowed myself to take her in without inhibition, without censure of myself.

"I..." we both said simultaneously.

The shell had been cracked. We laughed together with the ease of two souls a long time attached, all the awkwardness fallen away. I reached out and touched her hand, caressing it gently. I then pulled her close, embracing her, while looking into her eyes, as she looked into mine. After a moment, we both became aware of other eyes; some of the others in our traveling train were watching us, smiles on their faces as they hiked along.

"Come," I said as I took Irena by the hand and stepped away from the horse. Macha would stay in place, nibbling on the green grass at her hooves. I led Irena into a nearby stand of trees. We stepped behind an oak, out of view.

Pent-up passion spewed forth from our beings; our bodies intertwined as if we could mold ourselves into one person. Our mouths found their counterpart; our tongues also intertwining in a dance of love, lust, longing and spirit. Just kissing her made me feel a oneness with creation that I had never known. I think it had always been that way with her. I was simply just now realizing it.

I wanted her, right then and there; body, mind and spirit. A soft moan escaped her lips as my hand drifted down and over her breasts to her hips, searching, in part, for the opening to her mantle.

She pulled away slightly, but I continued the search with my hand, as well as kissing her neck. "Longinus," she whispered out of breath.

I stopped and looked at her.

"We must wait 'til tonight at least, when we're at camp. I'm sorry I've waited so long to come to you," she said, "but we can wait a little longer. I...I actually wanted to find you just now to ask your help in securing another horse for Mary's wagon."

I looked at her, dumbfounded. She could not be serious.

We both suddenly burst into laughter.

"Well," Irena continued when our laughter subsided, "that's what I told myself and Mary. Mary just smiled and nodded. She knew." Irena paused then, and looked at me lovingly. "Oh, Longinus," she said. "My Longinus, my Gaius."

"Yes, my love. I am yours. But you've never used my family name, so don't start now," I admonished teasingly. "And you're right. We will wait 'til tonight. But no longer!" I added, only half joking.

I took her hand once more and we walked out of the stand of oaks back to Macha. The others had moved off up the road.

I mounted Macha and held my hand out to Irena. "Come," I said. "Ride with me."

Hesitation splashed across her face. I knew that it was not Macha she feared, but what others might think upon seeing us together. Ultimately, though, it mattered not what anyone else thought and she knew it. Besides, most of those who traveled with us knew that Irena and I had a history, so why would they be surprised to see us together? She took my hand and leapt up as I pulled and swung her onto Macha's back behind me. We trotted up the road to catch the others.

Irena's arms were wrapped around my waist and after a moment, she playfully tickled my ribs. "Mary's wagon really does need another horse, you know," she said.

We caught up to the others in no time. Once again, smiles greeted us as we rode through the group to catch Mary's vehicle. The group overall had a couple of supply wagons, but Mary's was easy to spot. In addition to the fine draperies covering it, one solitary mare now labored to pull the laden chariot-wagon. Mary and Thomas both walked beside the vehicle, in an attempt to help ease the animal's burden. The effort only produced a minimal relief for the beast.

I was still unsure of what exactly was being carried in Mary's wagon; supplies for Mary, Sara, Thomas and a few others, certainly. But it was too large for just supplies. Something else was in there, too. I gathered, from overhearing bits of conversations, that it was a fairly sizable item, significant in a personal, mystical sense. Neither Mary nor Thomas would reveal precisely what it was, and I don't believe Irena knew any more than I did. It was a genuine curiosity, but I left it at that and respected their wish for privacy on the matter.

We arrived at the chariot-wagon and I halted Macha briefly, so that Irena could slide off and rejoin Mary and Thomas as the entire company kept moving.

"Well, well," Thomas began playfully.

He was prevented from continuing the thought, however, by a none-too-light elbow jab to the ribs. Mary retracted her elbow quickly and gave Thomas a look which said, *That's enough out of you!* She turned to Irena and said, "Sara sleeps. You needn't have come back so soon, you know."

Irena paused for a moment, not quite sure how to respond to that. "Thank you," she finally said with slight embarrassment. "If that's the case," she said turning to me, "perhaps we could find that other horse now."

"Uh…oh, yes," I stammered, caught off guard. "Let's go find Paulonius. I think he and—Genevieves, isn't it? I think they would spare one of their animals for a time."

"Splendid!" exclaimed Mary.

I turned and addressed Thomas. "We should make camp soon," I said, glad to change subjects. 'Twas true, though. The sun was dropping quickly. The road we had followed thus far was surrounded by green grasses and meadows interspersed with stands and groves of pines and oaks. But aside from the small stand of oaks that Irena and I had ducked into briefly, we had not seen many clumps of trees this day. 'Tis better to make camp hidden among trees than exposed in an open meadow. But either way, we needed to stop soon.

"Agreed," replied Thomas, his tone all business this time. "The scouts have just reported a large grove about two miles up the road. We'll stop there. We should reach Alesia by midday on the morrow."

"So be it," I said. Turning to Irena, I held out my hand for her to once again vault onto Macha's back; then we trotted off in search of Paulonius and Genevieves.

"Has Thomas or Mary revealed to you why we must first go to Alesia?" I asked after a moment.

"No," she answered. "But it's something to do with what they carry. That much I'm sure of."

The community that Mary and Thomas wanted to eventually reach was well west of the village we had left, just outside of Jubionyus. The community, which apparently did not have a name as of yet, was comprised of Hebrew outcasts, as well as others, who had formed a growing sect called Gnostics; the same sect, at least in thought, that Thomas, himself, belonged to. Yet, for shrouded reasons, we were first heading north to Alesia—the famed location in which Vercingretorix (the first and last unifier of Gaul) surrendered to the great Caesar—then traveling west, southwest to Jubionyus.

An hour and a half later, and with the mighty sun disk just sinking over the horizon, we came to the grove of trees and made camp. I helped many put their shelters together. I had shown them how to put together a quick, temporary one in the manner of a legionnaire, but some were a bit slow to grasp it. I then set up my own, making it clean and spacious in the hopes that Irena would indeed be able to join me later.

We had found Paulonius quickly enough before making camp. He was quite amiable to giving up one of his horses for Mary's use when I asked him to. I think there was a part of him that was still grateful to me for allowing Genevieves to join us. Then again, seeing the way they interacted now, I was not sure that he should be grateful; she was quite the bossy one.

Irena had taken the beast back to Mary. I had not seen her since. Paulonius had come by my shelter to see if I needed anything, which I did not, and a while later, Jacobi brought me food: oatcakes and venison. He stayed while I ate and we chatted. I brought out the spear at one point during our conversation, as we were talking of the healings and seemingly magical energies that came through this weapon, this instrument. As if it knew we were speaking of it, its blade began to glow, pulsating ever so slightly.

But that was incorrect, for I began to sense that there was another reason it vibrated. An ominous wave of foreboding washed over me. It was momentary, brief, and then it was gone at the same instant the blade stopped glowing.

Jacobi, too, had seen the blade glow and observed my reaction. "Longinus, what did you see?" he queried. "What did you *feel?*"

"I...I know not," I replied, still trying to decipher what I *had* sensed.

"Be still. Breathe deeply. Let the feelings, the images, whatever, come through unfiltered, uncensored," Jacobi said, guiding me to that higher place within.

I did as the old man bade. I stilled my mind, breathed in and released and then saw it in my mind's eye: fire, violence death, all in the near future, and two figures that I took to be nemeses, though I could not tell whether they were foes of ours or someone else's. Such is the nature of visions; clarity is illusive at best. I conveyed what I'd seen to Jacobi.

"We must be vigilant," he said.

"We are always vigilant. Besides, I did not sense that the victims were of our group," I replied.

"Regardless, we must be especially watchful. I will speak to Thomas." Jacobi stood up gradually, his old bones slowing of late, and walked out.

I sat in silence for a moment. Then, I thought about seeking out Irena, but decided against it. If she were busy with Mary and Sara, then I would be intruding. So, I sat on my sleeping pallet with the spear, the lance, across my lap, closed my eyes and began to meditate on the vision I'd just had, as well as my own place in the vision and everything else.

I was drifting in an ethereal realm of the mind. *The Mind* in which all creation is one. During this meditation, no new information on the vision I had came through. Nothing. So, I instead focused on achieving a deeper connection with my Inner Self. In the process, many Divine Masters, so to speak, Jesu among them, appeared to me, spoke with me, imparting knowledge to me, to my soul.

Perhaps it was all just my imagination, these visions of Divine Masters and the conversations with them; a way of escaping. Sometimes, I had trouble believing in all of the mysterious and mystical experiences I had since the night of the Wickermen. I had not doubted them while I was still in the village and near Detrom and the Druids. But now that I was away from them all, back in the *real* world, all of those experiences just seemed a bit...unreal. I had even voiced my feelings to Jacobi. But he had just laughed and called my doubting natural and good.

"'Tis only natural. Questioning things is always good. But you know in your soul what the truth of it is," he had said.

Another figure came into my mind during this meditation: Irena. She was suddenly floating with me in this realm of Mind. It was her spirit, her soul.

This did not feel as though it was a conjuring of my imagination. Her soul was there with me in that moment; I knew it, I felt it. Our minds, our beings suddenly merged as one; two souls, one mind. The sensation was overwhelming. I welled up with emotion, with happiness, with, with...

My eyes flew open. I was back in my shelter, sitting on the pallet with the lance still lying across my lap. Five feet in front of me, sitting on a stool, was Irena in the flesh. I had no awareness of her coming in. Her eyes were closed, so I simply watched her for a moment.

Her eyes came open. A smile slowly grew on her face; a smile to melt a snow-capped peak.

"That was simply..." I stammered.

"...Wondrous," she finished.

"Yes. You *were* with me in my meditation, on the..." I wasn't sure how to say it; how to put into words where it was we had been; what had happened.

"I was." She paused for a moment. "I...came in, to your shelter, I mean, a while ago," she continued. I was going to call to you from outside, but something told me not to; to just come in and join you."

"I'm glad you listened to that 'something,'" I replied.

We stared at each other then, each silently reliving that moment of disembodied oneness. As we did this, a connection began to reveal itself; a tugging sensation began in my chest. I physically reached out to Irena and drew her to me. We lay on the sleeping pallet, she atop me, chest to chest. The tugging sensation grew. It was as if a rope, a line of energy, connected our hearts and the sacred energy center there; the most powerful of the seven in the body as taught by the Druids.

She moaned slightly. "Do you feel that, Longinus?" she asked nearly breathless.

"Yes," I replied, equally breathless.

Our chests were touching. In addition to the tugging, I could feel her heartbeat. It was my heartbeat. Our pulse was exactly the same. As in the meditation, suddenly, there was no Irena. There was no Longinus. We were one being.

Soon, our oneness of spirit broadened to include oneness of body. We loved; our bodies joined together in one explosion after another. Then we talked. She told me everything that had happened to her since last we saw each one another, and I shared all of my experiences with her. Then, we made love again, and again, 'til almost dawn.

Shortly before the sun rose, we finally collapsed from exhaustion, falling into each other's arms. Our eyes grew heavy, but sleep would not come. For, it was then that we heard the first screams of terror.

XXII

Irena and I bolted awake and out of my shelter as soon as we heard the first scream, our night of passion all but forgotten for the moment.

The camp was in chaos. Animals were running in panic, their owners doing their best to control them. But the chaos was not caused directly by any outside source; we were not being overrun by an enemy. The chaos apparently had been caused by the panic of the animals, mainly horses, and the screams of terror had come from two women who had been trampled in the process.

One had a partially crushed leg; the other, surprisingly, only a single cracked rib. Dosameenor had the men already about, gathering the animals back together and aiding in the restoring of calm. Thomas was in the midst of it all as well, lending whatever help he could. Jacobi was tending to the wounded women near a fire pit—who apparently had been trampled while piling wood for the morning cooking fires—and waved me over. Irena and I ran to where he was and I knelt next to him.

"These woman need your healing touch, Longinus," said Jacobi.

I hesitated. In my desire to get out of the shelter, I had forgotten the spear, something I had not often done. I was about to voice the fact that I needed to get the lance when Irena suddenly held it out to me.

"Thought you might want this," she said slyly. She had come out of the tent-shelter right behind me, right on my heels, yet had the presence of mind to grab the spear on the way out. Seeing her there holding the spear, I was instantly catapulted back to the time when I had nearly knocked her out when she attempted to touch the thing. Guilt flashed briefly though my mind over that. But that was then, and now it was more than appropriate that she held it.

"Thank you," I managed. I took it from her and turned to Jacobi. "I can't heal a smashed bone, Jacobi." The woman's leg was nearly flattened at the shin of her left leg. A mass of blood, skin, tissue and splintered bone.

"Of course you can't, because you believe that you can't. And you don't need that to heal," he said, pointing to the lance. "Never mind. Come. Help me get them both back into their tent. We will set the bones or whatever needs to be done. You will ease their pain with your skill."

"How are you going to set that mess?" I asked, indicating the leg.

Jacobi clucked like a disappointed old hen. "Master Longinus, you really have begun to doubt things, haven't you?"

The question was rhetorical, so I didn't answer him. Instead, I gently picked up the woman, balancing her against the spear, as Irena helped the other injured woman, and took her into the nearby shelter-tent, where I placed her on a sleeping pallet.

We had just set the women down when a voice hailed me from outside. "Longinus," called Dosameenor.

I stepped back out of the tent and came face-to-face with the big Celt. "Yes, my friend."

"Don't be long. We must be under way soon," he said with a warrior's intensity. Something was happening.

"What is it?" I asked, and then realized it for myself. The smell of smoke permeated my nostrils: fire. I could see the smoke just through the trees; too much of it to be from any cooking fire. In fact, the women who were injured had not even had the chance to start our cooking fires. This was coming from somewhere well outside the grove of trees we were camped in; probably from over the next hill.

Dosameenor saw the realization dawning on my face. "Yes. The horses sensed the fires before we did and panicked. Those fires are not from anything natural. A village or town burning, if you ask me. Romans," he spat with disgust. Almost in the same instant he had said it, he became aware of the insult. "Agh, Longinus, I'm sorry. I did not mean you. And, I know I was once a legionnaire. It's just..."

I smiled and put a hand up in friendship to silence him. "Please, I take no offense. You know that."

"Very well," replied the big Celt. "As I said, we must leave soon."

"We will. Jacobi and I will help the wounded while you ready the camp to leave."

"Done," he said, and walked off to do just that.

We took care of the women's wounds. Jacobi was simply amazing. Truly a Merlin, as it were, for he seemed to have learned a great deal in the art of healing from the Druids; much more than I. He nearly reshaped the crushed part of the one woman's leg with the ease of a magician. The other one, with naught but a cracked rib, was simple enough to bind. For my part, I had simply used a calming spell or prayer—however one prefers to think of it—on the women by holding the spear's blade tip over the first woman's leg and muttering the incantation of healing and calming that Camaroon had taught me.

The incantation itself was nothing but words aimed at putting me in the right state of mind to allow certain healing energies to come through. They did. The spear tip began to glow and a warmth of energy went through my body, down the spear and into the leg. The woman winced at first, having barely maintained consciousness to begin with, but soon relaxed with her eyes closed, the pain subsiding, which allowed Jacobi to do his work. All that remained was to secure adequately comfortable transport for them, for which Mary volunteered her wagon.

The whole company, several dozen of us, were on the move again within an hour. Scouts reported back to Thomas, Dosameenor, and myself that it was indeed a village on the road to Alesia that Romans had sacked and burned. It appeared to have happened at some point deep in the night. We had not detected any smoke until dawn because the winds had been blowing in the opposite direction. I had no doubt that whatever legion was responsible for destroying the village, they were still in the area and knew of our presence. They probably were watching our every move.

Why they had not approached us was the mystery. We were a fairly sizable contingent of men, women and guards; not an army, granted, but any Roman patrol coming upon us would have stopped us, at the very least. Why then had they not done so?

Another mystery to me was why Thomas insisted that we stay on the road to Alesia. Both Dosameenor and I counseled him to go around the village and off the main road if he still wanted to take us to Alesia. But he would have none of it.

"Staying on the main road shows that we're not hiding anything," he argued.

He did have a point, but it was not a point that I shared; stealth was more of the ally that I wanted in situations like this, not trusting a potential enemy to believe my innocent intentions. But in the end, we stayed on the main road.

Irena was with Mary in her wagon helping with Sara and the two injured women. I would not see her much the rest of that day. We passed the burned village about an hour after leaving our encampment of the previous night. Many in our group turned their faces away, covering their noses and mouths to keep them from gagging at what they saw.

Perhaps it was my jadedness as soldier, but the sight was not nearly as bad as what I had been expecting. True, there were a few charred corpses on the ground, but for the most part, the village was empty. No doubt, most of the inhabitants had either been driven off or taken as slaves.

Still, my heart and soul went out to those who were slaughtered here, and whose lives had been forever altered by Romans. I was ashamed, perhaps for the first time in my life, that I was Roman-born.

Suddenly, a sound permeated the air. It was a high-pitched, rhythmic whirring sound. I thought at first it was the wind. But there was no wind. I realized that the sound was coming from within the village. I scanned the village remains for the source of the sound. There, about fifty yards in toward what looked like the center of the place, or what had been the center, was a toddler wailing with all its might.

It—she, by the looks of it—was standing next to an unburned adult female corpse. Dosameenor had been quiet, maintaining a discipline in passing by the village. But at the child's cry, he lost control of that discipline. He turned his mount toward the sound and bolted into the shell of a village.

"Dosameenor!" I called. But it was no use. The people in this village had been Celts, and Dosameenor was taking their destruction personally.

Hentapas and Romi came up next to me on their mounts. Macha was skittish under me because of the smoke and stench of death and the sudden approach of Romi and Hentapas, but stood her ground, maintaining her own discipline.

"What should we do, sir?" asked Romi.

"We shall stop and bury the dead," interjected Thomas from behind me.

I turned to see Mary and Thomas riding at the front of the chariot wagon, and pulling up to a stop next to me.

"I thought you wanted to move through this place," I said.

"I was wrong," he said, deferring to Mary.

"We cannot leave these people this way," she said, clearly having been the one to convince Thomas to have a change of heart.

But I did not agree for a couple of reasons. "I'm not sure we have the time. Also, these are Celts. They have several different customs of disposition of the dead depending on the region. You should consult Dosameenor. Furthermore, whoever did this is still in the area." I paused while she thought about that. "Besides, didn't Jesu say 'let the dead bury the dead?'" I added.

"Not the same context, Longinus," Mary said, in a near scolding tone.

"Perhaps, but you get my point."

"I do and I will ask Dosameenor, nonetheless," she replied.

We all looked in the direction of Dosameenor. He was kneeling in front of the little one. She seemed to grow calm at his presence. A moment later, she held out her arms to be hugged, and he scooped her up as if she were a feathered pillow. The little girl clutched his beard as he leaped onto his horse. The child would surely squall from fright at any moment I thought. I was wrong. Instead, she giggled, her troubles forgotten for the moment.

Mary had a smile on her face. Even in the midst of death, life can seem to magically assert itself.

Dosameenor rode straight up to us. "The other men searched the place. I fear only this one lived," he stated flatly.

"We will find a place for her," said Mary.

"No, I will care for her," Dosameenor asserted powerfully.

We were all shocked by the statement. How in the world was this man going to care for a girl of about two summers? Why would he want to?

"But…" Mary started. She stopped when she saw the look in Dosameenor's eyes. It wasn't hostility, just finality; there was no arguing the point. It would have been absurd to try. When the big Celt made up his mind about something and stated that something was a certain way, then that was it. No room for negotiation.

"So be it," Mary said. "We must bury the dead left here," she continued on, changing subjects.

"No," Dosameenor said in that tone of finality again.

"Burn them?" asked Hentapas. "Will that not alert the Romans?"

"Are we sure it was Romans?" asked Thomas.

"Who else?" answered Dosameenor. "Your own patrols have seen them.

"Yes, Hentapas. They would probably be alerted, if they aren't already watching us. I still say we leave the dead to bury the dead," I said, looking from Dosameenor to Jacobi, the latter just joining us, his old mare hobbling up to our group very slowly, even under the old man's slight weight. I made a mental note then and there to secure a new beast for Jacobi. The poor thing he was on now looked as though it would collapse at any moment.

"Agreed," said Dosameenor.

Again, we were all left speechless at his decision. I expected Jacobi to agree with me; he had said as much in the past in similar situations. But I did not expect it from the big Celt.

"If you still wish to make it to Alesia with your precious cargo—whatever it is—without interruption," Dosameenor continued to Thomas and Mary a little gruffly, "then we leave this place now and do not stop."

So, I thought dryly, I was not the only one who was curious about the contents of Mary's wagon.

Mary bowed her head.

Thomas stared at the big man. "So be it," he finally said.

Thomas' calculations had been off. We did not make Alesia by midday. Nor by dark fall. We made camp in a small stand of pines under a near full moon. My senses were peaked. The spear tip was even at a constant but slight glow. We were being watched. I could feel it.

I sat at the campfire. No shelters tonight. We needed to be mobile fast. All would sleep in the open, near the central fire. Even the horses pulling the wagons would remain harnessed. Hentapas, Romi, and several of Thomas' guards were at the perimeter of the camp. Dosameenor was with me, awake at the fire, the babe asleep in his arms.

"What do you call her?" I asked in a hushed tone so as not to wake the others.

"Mattea," he replied fondly.

"Mattea," I repeated. "What does it mean?"

"'Beloved,'" answered Dosameenor.

To my surprise, the big Celt was near tears. I said nothing. If he wanted to tell his tale, he would.

"I..." he began. "When we got back to my village, after the dust settled from the night of the Wickermen, I found my wife and family, or what was left of them. My wife had been raped by one of Draco's worthless followers. She had born him a bastard boy that my wife had drowned when the lad had been born.

"When Draco's man found out what she'd done, he took my only daughter, raped her and drowned her," he paused, his face crinkling with renewed agony, as if it had just happened, muffled sobs shuddering into his beard. "She was only three summers," he said when he was in full control again. "Her name had been Matteoua. It means 'Beloved of my soul.'" He paused a long while then before continuing. "You see, this little one," he said brightly, looking at Mattea, "looks a great deal like her. Same hair, same eyes..."

Yet again on this day, I was fully surprised by the man before me. I had known nothing about this. Nothing. I looked at Mattea then. She could easily pass as Dosameenor's daughter. But she wasn't. "You," I started delicately, "you know that it's not Matteoua, right?"

"Of course, you stupid Roman," laughed Dosameenor. But then he turned serious. "It is her spirit, though," he said as a matter of fact. "Her soul, you know."

I must have looked confused.

"Mattea is two summers," Dosameenor went on. "She barely walks or speaks. Matteoua was killed at three, over three summers ago."

I thought for a moment. I would not argue against the man's belief, though I could not fathom it.

"You want proof, don't you?" he challenged.

I could not deny it.

"This little one called me 'Frap-Frap,'" he said.

I shook my head, not understanding.

"So did Matteoua."

"Your first daughter called you that, too? What does it mean?" I asked, trying desperately to get my tired mind to accept what he was saying.

"That's just it. Nothing. It means nothing. It's a nonsensical pet word—a pet name Matteoua had made up. At the village today when Mattea looked right at me and said it..." he trailed off.

I could see why he would believe this little girl was the reincarnation of Matteoua. Indeed, I could almost believe it, too. I wanted to. Very well. For him, I would accept it; the little one in his lap was his daughter. Period.

We sat in silence for a few moments. I was about to ask him about the rest of his family.

He was reading my thoughts, as he spoke of it before I could ask. "My wife went mad. Demons took over her mind. She ran off into the hills two days after I had arrived home. My oldest boy had already run off to another tribe. My youngest son blamed me for it all. I had not been there to protect them, you see," he said.

"Dosameenor, you can't believe that," I offered lamely.

"I don't," he said, not very convincingly.

"Why am I just now hearing of this?" I asked. Truly, I could not understand how he had kept it quiet.

"You must understand that in our culture, if one turns his back on something, then that is *all*. It is *never* spoken of again. To do so would bring shame on your family and clan, and possible exile. Besides," he smiled, "you were...busy when we first arrived. You had exiled yourself to the quarters you'd been given, remember? This was something I dealt with and tried to put out of my mind forever. Until today."

"You are one of the bravest men I've ever known," I declared. "I'm proud to be your friend."

"And I, you," he said.

"Even though I'm Roman?" I quipped.

"Even so. Besides, you're more Druid, which is decidedly *not* Roman."

Silence again fell between us.

After a few minutes, I began to drift. My eyes closed. I did not sleep, but my mind calmed and I saw things within the mind's eye—the same things, the same vision, that I had had in Jacobi's presence. Only now, I was in the middle of the visionary mayhem; a future event that I would be a part of?

Suddenly, the spear, which had been resting next to me, began to vibrate, snapping me out of my semi-trance state. After less than a minute, it stopped as suddenly as it had started. Dosameenor had also seen it.

Silence again. We both sat for a moment, trying to deduce the spear's meaning.

Then, off in the near distance, at the perimeter of the encampment, we heard a dull thump, a grunt and a thud.

They were unmistakable sounds to the trained ear; an arrow finding its mark in a man's chest, the grunt of the victim upon the arrow's impact, and the landing of the body on the ground. Our perimeter had been breached.

Dosameenor and I wasted no time. We jumped up and shouted for all to awaken at the same moment Romi was yelling from halfway between the perimeter and my location near the fire.

"To arms! To—" he called.

He was close enough that I could see the whites of his eyes and the enemy just behind him.

His call was cut short when a gladius blade pierced him from behind, the point protruding grotesquely through his front ribs. Shocked, but not frozen, Romi turned and sliced the neck of his assailant: a pimply-faced legionnaire, who crumpled to the ground like a whimpering dog, his life's blood saturating the ground. Romi turned back to me, saluted fist to chest, then fell to the ground, dead.

There was no time to think about him. Chaos was overtaking us again, this time perpetrated by a definite enemy. Legionnaires poured into the stand of trees, rapidly approaching the campfire.

But our chaos was short-lived, for everyone in our company was armed, including the women, producing weapons from within their bedding as they came awake. I was shouting orders, but it was not necessary; they all began defending themselves, fighting as a cohesive unit. It was amazing to behold. I looked to Dosameenor, who simply smiled proudly.

"You were busy before we left," I said to him.

"Indeed I was," he said, laughing. He ran with Mattea to Mary's wagon a short distance away, handing his daughter to Irena.

I caught her eye briefly before she popped back in with the child. She looked at me. *Be careful*, her eyes said.

Something was off. There were not as many Romans as I had thought. The group did not comprise a Century, barely a platoon. I saw no officers. All of the legionnaires were in single combat here and there. They also seemed to be fighting for an objective other than killing everyone. Many of the legionnaires were fighting to incapacitate their opponent, but not delivering a death blow. Instead, they would shake off the one they were fighting and move toward one objective: Mary's wagon.

"Rally to me!" I shouted as I ran to the vehicle.

Then I saw their leader atop a black stallion. Draco.

What in Hades was happening here? Why were Roman soldiers following a Dark Lord of The Druids?

The answer to those questions could wait. Right now, we were under attack. For the most part, our people were gallantly holding their own, but that wasn't going to last long. The Romans were a few less in number than we, but much greater in skill, despite Dosameenor's training of those in our group.

"Form up to me!" I commanded, as I arrived at the wagon.

The men in the group, Thomas' guards and others, did just that, as did Dosameenor and his men. The women bounded to the wagon as well.

The Romans ceased their fighting when our people disengaged, but began to encircle us. I looked about, trying to find the rest of the guards who had been manning the perimeter. I only saw Hentapas, kneeling next to Romi's body.

He looked up. We made eye contact and I motioned my head for him to join us. He was loath to leave his comrade's body, but knew the greater good of the moment demanded it, and ran over to me.

"Thank the gods you made it," I said.

He said nothing but his face was a mask of angry grimness.

Next, I saw Paulonius and Geneveives coming from behind the wagon, the latter just finishing a last violent hack with her short sword into an attacking legionnaire. They came toward our group.

We were all near the fire and Mary's wagon, with the enemy closing around us. Irena, Thomas, and Mary descended from the chariot wagon. The two wounded women's heads poked from the curtains. I could only assume that the babes, Sara and Mattea, were tucked safely inside.

But was that safe? As I said from the start, the invaders seemed to be after the wagon. More than one of them had been cut down in their path to it.

Jacobi? Where was Jacobi? Dread began to creep over me. I looked around frantically. He was nowhere to be seen.

XXIII

"Halt!" came a booming voice. It was a glamoured voice, infused with more power, false power, than was actually there. And it came from the Dark Druid atop his horse.

"Draco," hissed Dosameenor under his breath, vengeance and murderous intent seeping from every pore.

I placed a hand on his arm, silencing him.

Then my own blood boiled as I looked up and saw that the Dark One had something lying across his lap, a human form draped across his legs: Jacobi, unconscious, or worse. He looked dead, his skin was pasty-white. I covered the fact that all I wanted to do was rush to the old man's aid. To do that at that particular moment would have ensured the death of us all. So, I endeavored to remain calm and in control. At least, in appearance.

"I should have killed you the night of the Wickerman," spat Dosameenor.

"But you did not, did you? And here we are," gloated Draco.

I glared at him and at the lifeless Jacobi.

Draco looked down at the old man. "Fear not, Longinus. He merely...sleeps. For now."

"Release him!" I demanded.

"No. We must talk first. Then perhaps I'll think about it," Draco said, toying with me.

"Why are *you* with Roman soldiers?" I demanded.

"That is none of your concern," retorted the Dark One.

"Now, now, Arch Druid Draco," said another voice. "He should know that Rome and you have reached...an agreement, shall we say?"

The owner of the voice came forward into the light on a brown bay and stopped next to Draco. He was dressed as a Roman Tribune.

"Detrom is Arch Druid—not that piece of shite!" said Dosameenor.

"Who are you?" I asked the apparent Tribune.

"You don't remember me, do you? Pity. I remember you," he said, in a mock hurt tone.

I looked at him carefully. Yes. There was something familiar about him, but I did not voice that.

"I'll help you remember then. You reprimanded me, chastised me in front of my men," the Tribune said, anger exuding from his being. "'Twas a long time ago, but I never forgot. Or forgave. Remember?"

I did not remember any of what he was saying.

"No? It was at a man's house by the name of Paul, a follower of that pathetic false Messiah, Jesu. Do you remember yet? I was giving the man a well-deserved beating for speaking against Rome, and you, the mighty Centurion Longinus, interrupted me and belittled me in front of my men!" he shouted, nearly losing his control.

This one's whole demeanor was off; not normal. Demons had him, or he was simply insane. Either condition was unpredictably dangerous.

"Of course, I was just a young lieutenant then. Green, was I then, or I would have killed you for that insult. I was from a prominent Roman family, after all, and you, you were from...what, a whore's ass?"

I had been born into the plebian class. That much was true. But both my parents had been honorable citizens. My father, a legionnaire, had been killed in a street-brawl outside of an Egyptian beer house in Thebes, while trying to drag a drunk comrade away from a fight with some locals. It was a pointless death. But it happened before I was born, so I never knew the man. My mother had been a well-paid servant in a senator's household, as her mother before her. She certainly had not been a prostitute. She died shortly after I first became a legionnaire. One day, her heart simply stopped.

Obviously, this Tribune was trying to inflame my anger. He was failing. But I did remember him now, and the incident he was talking about. However, I would never give him the pleasure of knowing that. "No. I do not remember you. Apparently, you were not worthy of remembering."

That struck a nerve, I could tell. He fumed at it, but to his credit, maintained control.

I glanced at Jacobi. His motionless form still showed no sign of life.

"Get to it, Draco," the Tribune said to the Dark Lord. "The General will not wait long for these things. But leave that one to me," he said, pointing to me.

Draco turned to Mary first. "You and your brat will come with me. The contents of your wagon will go with the Tribune, as will your spear, Longinus."

He lied. I could see it in his eyes, sense it in my soul. He had no intention of giving my lance to Rome. Nor the contents of Mary's chariot wagon, either.

"Draco lies," I said to the Tribune. "If you think I wronged you in the past, then you must understand that it was in the context of my duty. But believe me now. This one lies to you. He may have led you to the items Rome seeks, but he will not part with them and you're a fool to think otherwise."

"Shut up, Longinus," said the Tribune, drawing his gladius, "or I will drop you here and now. I'll not do permanent damage to you, though. Did you know that there's a bounty on your head? You're an enemy of the State—deserter, among other things. Much gold awaits the one who captures you. I stand to become even richer." He then turned to Draco and made the biggest mistake of his life, and the last. "Seize the wagon, seize the spear!" he yelled to his men as he struck the sword tip out at Draco's throat.

But the Dark One was much faster; Otherworldly fast. He was also Otherworldly strong. In the blink of an eye, he grabbed the Tribune's sword wrist and snapped it like a twig, even before the sword really got close to his neck.

In the next instant, Draco's free hand had clamped onto the Tribune's face, crushing the facial bones like a dried-up egg shell.

The legionnaires were oblivious to the Tribune's plight. They had their orders and were already beginning to slash in earnest at everyone in their way.

Draco pushed the dying Tribune, now screaming in muffled agony, from his mount to the cold ground.

Then Jacobi slipped to the ground. I rushed over to him, scooping his fragile frame into one arm, and at the same time, hurtling the spear with the other.

It found its mark, landing with a loud thud into Draco's shoulder. He howled, not with pain, but delight. *What had I done?* I had all but given him the lance!

But then its imbedded blade began to smoke. The smell of burning flesh permeated the air. Draco's howls of delight now turned to cries of tormented pain as the lance and its power burned him from within. It was more than he could stand. He yanked out the weapon, letting it fall to the ground, smoking and glowing with heat at the blade tip. I snatched it up before Draco could recover himself, Jacobi still in my arms.

"Leave us!" commanded Dosameenor to Thomas and myself, "I will deal with this, me and my men. Go! Take Mary and the wagon and go!"

I was about to protest, but did not. Instead, I turned to Thomas. "Go," I said as I loaded Jacobi into the chariot wagon under a side flap. I wanted nothing more than to examine the old man right then and there. If he were not dead, then I would heal him and bring him back to full consciousness. Yet, there was no time. We had to leave this place immediately, but the soldiers who came with Draco and the Tribune must not be allowed to follow.

"But—" he said.

"No, go."

"Longinus, you must come," Irena implored.

For the first time that I could remember, I saw genuine fear in her eyes; fear for me. "It's all right, my love. I will be right along."

"You better be!" she commanded.

Mary jumped into the back of the wagon as did Irena. Thomas took the driver's place and they were off, rolling quickly through fighting bodies and dead ones. A minor contingent of Thomas' guards went with them. But many brave ones stayed to fight alongside Dosameenor.

I wanted to, as well. But something was compelling me to go with the wagon. They would need my protection, true, but...

I ran to Macha, still tethered to a tree, dancing nervously at all the activity. "Shhh, girl."

I mounted Macha and took one last look at Dosameenor, who was in the throws of battle, and loving it. I turned in time to see Hentapas joining the fray. "No! Hentapas, come with me!" I barked.

"Romi must be avenged, sir!" he countered, tears of rage and anguish in his eyes.

Paulonius and his young lady had jumped upon one of their horses, Paulonius in the front. They were now next to Hentapas, clearly unsure of what they should do. "All three of you—I need you with me! Hentapas, you are not mine to command, but I tell you, I need you with me. Romi is gone, lad. Nothing you do here will change that. You both said you came to find me, to join me. Well then, come with me now! It's what he'd have wanted."

Hentapas thought about it for a brief moment. Then, with a shout of rage, he turned and threw his drawn sword at a nearby Legionnaire. It landed true, catching the man in the chest, splitting him open. The legionnaire was dead before he hit the ground.

Paulonius kicked his horse's ribs. He and Geneveives galloped past me, following the chariot wagon.

I held out my hand and Hentapas ran to me, leaping onto Macha's back behind me without my aid. I dug my heels into Macha's side and we were off to catch up to Mary's wagon.

We caught up to them quickly. They were moving as swiftly as possible, but even with two horses now pulling the wagon, it was quite a burden with two injured women, two children, Jacobi, Irena and Mary, supplies and the item, whatever it was, all inside.

Irena looked out from the back of the vehicle, poking her head through the drapery coverings. She simply nodded her head in acknowledgement that I was once again with her. There were only seven guards escorting the chariot wagon and about twelve civilians, all running on foot, who had been traveling with Mary and Thomas from the start, back in Palestine. The rest had stayed to fight Draco and the Romans.

There was no sign of pursuit. Still, I urged them on. "Keep moving! Do not stop 'til I give the order!"

We traveled the rest of the night, which wasn't very long. An hour and a half later, just after sunrise, we had to stop briefly, to rest the horses and the folks on foot. There was no other source of water, so we let the animals drink from our own water supplies.

Still, there was no sign of pursuit by Draco. I had no illusions that the spear had killed him. It would take much more than just that to send him to the Otherworld. Perhaps the legionnaires had turned on him when they saw that he had killed their Tribune?

Not likely. I don't believe that any of them had witnessed the Tribune's death, having been preoccupied with carrying out their orders of slaughter and theft. Besides, Draco could easily blame one of us, who were resisting them, for killing the Roman officer. Or, if a young legionnaire *had* witnessed the event, Draco could use his Dark power upon the mind of the impressionable legionnaire, steering him in a completely different direction. The point is, Draco was alive, no doubt, and would continue his Dark quest at all costs.

But, for the moment, we seemed to be relatively safe.

We were tucked into a hillside just inside a stand of trees. I did not like having our flank being drawn up against a mound of earth, no retreat for us on that side. But the animals, and especially the people, were too tired to continue on.

We had only been there a few minutes, everyone trying to catch their breath and satiate the need for water, when Irena came forward and threw herself into my arms. "Damn it, Longinus!" she declared. "You scared me. I thought you were going to stay and fight them."

"I wanted to, but I couldn't," I said, not quite knowing what I meant.

She obviously saw confusion in my face over the matter, for she looked at me quizzically. "You mean, you didn't come just for me?" she asked only half in jest.

"Of course, but there was something else. Something was telling me that I had to stay with the wagon and you, and..." I was starting to babble.

"Shh, Longinus. As much as I love you and want you with me, you must always follow that inner voice of yours. It guides you for the highest good," she replied. "Trust me when I say I understand."

Just then, Thomas stood on top of a tree stump where all could see him. He had a frantic look on his face, a fearful look. "We've been going east! We must go back northwest, to Alesia. We must get to Alesia!" he declared.

I would have none of it. I was not going to let him lead any longer. "Are you mad? The roads will be scoured by the Romans. A Tribune of theirs is dead, and one way or another, we will be blamed for that. We will never get close to Alesia.

"And what you carry in that wagon is not remotely worth the risk."

"You have no idea what you say, Longinus," countered Thomas.

"Then show me! I demand it! Show me what it is and explain to me why it is so important that it go to Alesia!" I said, my anger boiling up inside at the man's impudence.

"You would not understand," was all he said.

"Thomas," said Mary, "for one who has been given an inner knowledge and enlightenment, you can still be a fearful doubter. This is Longinus. He possesses the other great treasure touched by *him*—the other great relic that has on it His sacred blood. Who else to better understand what we carry?"

Thomas was silent for a moment. He collected himself, and seemed once again to be in control. "Yes, you are right," he said to Mary. He then turned to me. "Forgive me, Longinus."

I simply bowed my head slightly in acknowledgment of his apology. "What is it that you have that could possibly be related to my spear, which is, I assume, what you're referring to?"

"Come, Longinus," Mary said.

Irena took me by the hand. Did she now know what it was? Together, we followed Mary and Thomas to the wagon. Mary lifted the back flap, hooking it open, and I climbed in, the rest remaining outside the back of the vehicle, but looking in, watching me.

The interior of the wagon was spacious, nearly enough for me to stand up in, even with the arched covering. Deceiving, that was, from the outside. Despite the ornate drapery that clung over the outer frame of the raised portion of the wagon, the inside was plain, a pallet to one side for lying on, a stool on one end, and, surprisingly, only two small boxes of supplies at the very rear. I had thought there to be much more in the way of supplies. Those folks who were occupying the inside had moved to the front. Jacobi was sitting up on the pallet, smiling, as was the woman with the injured leg, which now seemed to be miraculously better, almost completely healed. Not even a bandage on it.

The old man also looked invigorated. "Jacobi!" I said, surprised, but grateful, to see him looking so well. He said nothing, but looked at the item which took up most of the rest of the space in the wagon.

I looked down at the item in question. At first, I was not sure of what I was looking at. It simply looked like a few pieces of large, squared lengths of wood, darkly stained by time. But then I noticed that some of the darkest stains were not from age, per se, but from a liquid substance in a time past. There was something familiar about the shape of this thing. I stared at it for a moment. And then it hit me: it was a crucifix cut into several large pieces.

But it was no ordinary cross. By all the gods! By *the* God! My heart began to race, my breathing to quicken. I reached out to the thing and, closing my eyes, I touched it.

Blinding white light flashed before my inner sight. I was transported in spirit and mind to a hundred years in the future, two hundred years into the future, a thousand, and back again, in less than a moment. Then I found myself in a holy place, though I knew not where that was, with all manner of strange beings before me; some of the flesh; others of a form that I cannot begin to describe. Divine Masters, one and all I knew them to be.

"Longinus," came His voice. "You have come far."

He was standing before me. "Jesu," I breathed.

"The cross that your earthly form now touches, and the spear that you carry, are touchstones for all who believe in me. But I fear they may not understand the Truths of themselves and what I taught, and instead will rely on the power of these things to venerate the Man and not the lessons and knowledge. You must help them see the way, Longinus. You and the others," Jesu said.

"But how? I am wanted for worse by many. Anywhere I go, I will be captured or killed," I replied.

"You will do what you can in this life, but will not finish, 'tis true. You will continue in your next life upon returning here."

"You believe in rebirth to this place?" I asked, astonished.

"*All* things are possible with the Infinite Mind of the Universe. *Never* forget that. But it is up to the individual soul when, or even if, to return. Not all come back to the earthly form. But you will. You are the Teacher, The Merlin, for the ages. Go now and take these things away so that those who mean evil do not get them, and those who do not understand the Truth, fall to worship of me through them. Get them not to Alesia, but to the land of your next birth—to the island in the west," he finished.

The vision, the place I was in, began to fade.

"Wait!" I pleaded. "I know naught of where you speak!"

I suddenly found myself back in the wagon, slumped over the Rood, the wooden cross that Jesu had been crucified on.

Tears filled my eyes. My body felt weak, as if I'd had been on a hundred-mile forced march. The others were staring at me, waiting to hear what had happened; what I had *seen*.

"We...I...spoke to Jesu. He said I...we are to take the Rood not to Alesia, but to the Island in the west," I managed to say.

"What?" asked Thomas, his tone laced with disbelief. "That is rather a coincidence, isn't it? After you were just saying we shan't go to Alesia?"

"Do not doubt what Longinus says he saw or heard in the vision, Thomas," said Irena. "He speaks the truth and you know it."

Thomas fell silent.

"What island, Longinus?" asked Mary.

"I don't yet know. But I will find out," I said.

"What else? What else did the Master say?" queried Thomas.

I simply shook my head, still trying to grapple with the vision myself.

"That's enough for now," said Irena, fending the others off.

Sara giggled then, and Mattea followed with peels of laughter, reminding us of their presence, and Jacobi and the wounded women were smiling in a way that conveyed they knew what the wood was before us. Perhaps that is what accounted for Jacobi's rejuvenated condition and the woman's leg healing so fast and well. I trusted the other woman's ribs were just as healed.

"Come and rest for a few minutes, Longinus," Irena said, beckoning me to come out of the chariot wagon.

"Rest in here on the pallet," offered Mary.

"Thank you," I said, climbing over to it. I put my head down and slipped into a deep sleep.

The sleep was short-lived. I awoke two hours later to commotion outside in our makeshift camp. I thrust my head outside the wagon. Irena was a few feet away, talking to Jacobi. "What is it?" I asked them.

Irena ran over to the wagon; Jacobi hobbled. "Thomas sent two of the men back the way we came to see if Draco was following," she said.

"And?" I questioned impatiently.

"They are about an hour behind us," said the old man.

"They are numerous. One of the scouts said two Centuries strong at least," added Irena. "What are we to do?"

"We cannot outrun them," I said, trying to think of something. Anything. I looked up to the steep hillside next to us. "I knew we never should have stopped where we did. A death trap, it is," I railed under my breath.

"Or...a help in concealing us," Jacobi countered.

"What are you talking about?" I asked him, incredulous.

The old man simply spread his arms wide as if to say, *Look around, my friend.*

I looked about me, searching for his meaning. The morning had dawned cloudy, foggy, misty. And then I realized what he was trying to say. The fog, the mists, somewhat buttressed up against the hillside, could be amplified to conceal us. But could we do it? Could we veil ourselves in a glamoured mist the way Detrom had? Even if we could, would we be able to maintain it? Perhaps it would only be necessary for a short time, until we figured out our next move.

"Jacobi," I said with awe and respect, "can we do it?"

"Not if you have to ask! Of course we can! The mists are already here. We need only grasp their element, their essence, and create them anew!" he exclaimed with delight.

"Do it!" I commanded.

"Oh, not me. You," he said.

"Me?"

"From a clear sky, you brought down the rains the night of the Wickermen, and you think you'd have problems with this? This is child's play for you!" he said.

Thomas and Mary approached us then, and Jacobi and Irena explained what we intended to do, as I thought about how to go about it. Mary and Thomas went off to gather everyone together to be near the wagon, so we might all share in the calling of our only hope.

As if it knew our minds, the foggy mist began to become thicker in our general area, not lesser as it would seem it should normally be as the morning wore on. Within a few moments, each person in our dwindled party had gathered near the wagon awaiting further instructions. They understood in general that Draco and the Romans were coming, and that we were going to attempt to—no, not attempt to, but *do*—shroud ourselves in a mist. Some had fear in their eyes; not from the pursuing Romans, but from the thought of a *conjuring*, as one of them put it, that I was going to perform.

"'Tis demons' work," said a woman, an older woman with white hair and stark grey eyes. She was one of our group, but I had not heard her speak until now.

"No, it is not," Mary said, gently, going on to explain in abbreviated terms, that there are natural laws that govern the universe, and how these laws respond to everyone according to one's mind and thoughts. The higher the training in such things, the more adept one can be at controlling or using these natural laws.

The woman—whose name was Leona, I was to later find out—looked doubtful. But she trusted Mary, so she agreed to at least be passive in the proceedings. Negative thoughts in the group during the *ritual*, for want of a better term, could adversely affect the outcome.

Hentapas offered to help in the proceedings and I gratefully accepted. "Please sit," he said to all gathered. They did as he bade and sat on the ground. Hentapas remained standing near me.

I, too, remained standing, breathed deeply and pushed all doubt from my mind. "We will do this quickly, and well," I declared. "All of you close your eyes and breathe deeply and steadily," I continued, "holding in your mind only the following thoughts: The power of the Universe flows effortlessly through us, protecting us in the Veil Of Mists. We command this to be so! So be it!" I said.

"So be it!" echoed Hentapas, Jacobi and several others.

The others all had their eyes closed and breathed steadily, focusing on my words. But words are just empty shells without the thoughts and images behind them, and the thoughts and images come from the mind. Thus, the real work of making the mists mask us was done in the mind.

I had the lance in my hand and held it aloft with one hand, blade tip pointing to the Heavens. I closed my own eyes and created in my mind the image of the mists presently surrounding our physical forms becoming thicker, enshrouding us and the entire immediate area. But we needed more. I felt the spear begin to quiver in my hand, and then I felt myself, my mind, my spirit, exit my body.

I traveled to the smallest level imaginable within the mist itself. Down and down within it I went, until I felt as if I *were* the mist; its fundamental essence. I stayed there for what seemed liked a long time, all the while *knowing* that I, the mist, was infused with Divine power and protection, and that no one, no-thing, could penetrate it to see our group's sanctuary unless they meant us only good.

Then something amazing happened. Where I was with my mind, with my spirit, in and as essence of the mist, all the others suddenly were too, with Jacobi and Hentapas leading them. We all merged as one in the protective mist. The combined power of all of our spirits as one was almost overwhelming. We sustained this feeling for a while, etching solidly our desires for protection into the mists core.

Slowly, very slowly, the others faded from my awareness. I, too, began to withdraw from the mist, having completed the work needed.

I opened my eyes and was back in body, holding the spear tightly at my side. I looked around at the awe-struck faces. They were, no doubt, astonished by their experience. But equally, I think, they were astonished by the appearance of our immediate area, for many of them were looking around with wide eyes.

The area we were in was now fairly bright with the sun. As with Detrom's valley village, a slight layer of mist covered us like a ceiling—like a sheer, nearly transparent dome made of wispy threads of cloud. It was thin enough to allow ample sun in, but, I trusted, that as with Detrom's mist, no one could see in from above it; from on top of the hill.

Off in the distance, some one-hundred yards or so in all directions, through the surrounding trees, was a wall of mist extending up from the ground to meet the dome mist. The wall mist was thick as honey and marked the perimeter of the forested side of our sanctuary. From where we stood, to the wall mist, was bright and clear.

My eyes met Leona's. There was no fear there at all, only awe. Her eyes said, *Perhaps this was not demons' work, after all.* "Master Longinus," she said aloud, "I was there with you, with everyone, there in the mists. I felt the Goodness all around!"

"Quiet!" ordered Thomas suddenly. "Listen!"

We could hear them, off in the distance: horses trotting and men tramping at a forced march pace, which amounted to a half-run in unison, for miles and miles at a time. Panic started to rise in our midst; I could feel it. It was palpable. Murmurs began to filter among the people.

"No," I said. "Fear not."

I did not know whether my words would sit with them. But Jacobi backed me, saying in a hushed voice, "Yes! Do not concern yourself. They will pass us by."

All of them became silent once more, waiting patiently to see what would transpire.

The noise grew louder. We could hear voices now, commands and responses. "You there! Tighten the flank! We should be upon them at any moment!" barked an officer to a subordinate.

"Trying to, sir! Can't see shite for this fog, Centurion!" came the answer.

It was strange: We could hear the commands and responses, and the scuffles of feet and hooves, and shouts of confusion. They all sounded as if they were right next to us, not more than a few feet away. But they were not. We could *see* no one; no origin whatsoever for the sounds. It was as though we had suddenly entered an unseen land parallel to the normal earthly world.

I heard the voice of Draco. "This is a mist of Glamour. Curse you, Longinus!" he shouted from outside the mists. "Curse all of you. I will find you. You will not escape me!"

Soon, however, the noises and voices receded; moved off to continue their futile search for us elsewhere.

"God of Abraham!" exclaimed the woman. "'Tis truly magic, what ye've done, Master Longinus."

"*Merlin* Longinus, or, just Merlin, I think. He's earned that title with this bit 'o 'magic,' don't ya think?" said the familiar voice.

I turned and saw a sight for weary eyes: Dosameenor and ten men who had stayed to fight Draco and the Romans. I stepped forward and embraced the man as my brother. "I thought...I didn't know what to think," I stammered.

"Aye, the fight was hard, but we held our own and then some. After an hour, they broke off and ran. We began to follow your trail. We'd just come to the outer portion of this small grove when the mists descended. I knew it was more than natural. More than the gods' work. I knew it was you!" exclaimed Dosameenor. "You are surpassing even the Arch Druid himself! I therefore declare you to be a Merlin, my friend!" He paused for a brief instant, then added, "I *can* declare that, you know."

Before I could say anything else to Dosameenor, Leona looked at him and threw him a question of her own. "But, you came through the fog, I mean the mists. The Romans could not. Why?" asked the woman, now utterly intrigued.

"Only those who mean us harm are repelled by the mists. Those who mean us no harm will pass through, which means we can pass in and out," I explained.

"But, how? How does it know?" she inquired.

"It has to do with the state of mind or kind of Thought with which we infused in it, and the state of mind of those who come upon it," I answered.

She looked at me, trying very hard to understand.

"Simply trust that *It knows*, my good woman," said Dosameenor.

She nodded and said, "*It* has its own spirit, then."

That sounded as reasonable as any other explanation. "As you say," I replied.

Dosameenor then turned to the group in general. "Is there no food with which to break our fast? I could eat a horse," he joked.

Macha, tethered a short distance away, seemed not only to have heard and understood the comment, but to have taken offense. She *whinnied* very loudly in protest.

"Sorry, girl!" said Dosameenor.

Several laughed, albeit nervously. Dosameenor's words, though, made everyone realize how hungry we all were. None of us had eaten since the previous day.

We quickly set about to remedy that.

XXIV

The first days spent in the misty sanctuary consisted of regaining our strength and, for the most part, planning our next move.

Dosameenor organized hunting parties while I organized the perimeter guards and their shift roster, though I was confident that a guard posting was unnecessary as long as I reinforced the protective mist regularly. The guards, however, made everyone else feel better.

We had decided to stay for only a few days, a week at most. Enough time, we thought, to allow those pursuing us to move on. At the end of that time, we would split up into small groups and trickle slowly out of the mists one group at a time over several nights.

The hunters had no problem going out and coming back through the vaporous clouds. The game was plentiful, and a source for water, a stream, was found a short distance away. Surprisingly, they encountered no search parties, no Roman patrols, no one at all. Many attributed this good fortune to the mists, as well as to *my magic powers*. I was not so sure. I was sure that the hunters would have seen someone.

We rested and ate, and ate and rested. Temporary shelters were put up around the area, and we came to feel a sense of security for a bit. Deceiving, was that, for we found ourselves lulled into a feeling of being at home.

As with the mists that Detrom and his Druids manifested, time seemed to stand still for those within these mists, or simply didn't exist at all. I was aware of that fact, as were Jacobi and Mary and Thomas, and I determined not to let it influence me or any one of us.

But some of the others in our party seemed oblivious to the lack of a time definition, even going so far as to sight that here in the mists, we might establish a whole new community free of religious persecution, free of the political oppression, free of any constraints or conventions at all. A nice thought, perhaps. But dangerous. No one really wanted to stay here forever.

For the moment, it did not matter. When the time was right, I would convince them that we should leave. If I had to, I would lift the mists altogether, and then we would have no choice but to go. But, I let the matter rest for now.

Irena and I put up our own shelter, a large tent of skins given to us by the two women who had been injured the morning we saw the smoke. They were grateful for the healing and the protection of the Rood and mists. Irena and I fell into a comfortable routine; we were up in the morning to break our fast with a morning meal, which usually consisted of bread, cheese, apple mead and sometimes venison, with the whole company and then attend to the needs of the people. Then we would share the evening meal with everyone in the communal center of the encampment, and afterwards, Jacobi and a few others would tell tales in the bardic tradition, shortly after which Irena and I would retire to our sleeping pallet for anything but sleep.

One morning, Irena could not get up from the pallet. After a bit of fussing, and at Irena's insistence, I left to attend to the camp. By the noon meal, she was still not off the pallet, so I asked Jacobi to look in on her.

When I returned later in the afternoon to check on her, I saw not only Jacobi, but Leona, as well, just exiting my tent. Why were they both there? Panic struck me suddenly. I ran up to them. "What's wrong?! Is she ill?"

Leona burst into laughter and Jacobi just smiled his toothless grin.

"Irena is quite fine. Perfect, in fact," offered the old man. "Leona, as it turns out, is a midwife. I asked for her expert opinion."

They were both silent for while, allowing me to absorb what they had just said.

Finally, the implications of what they were telling me sunk in. "By the gods!" I said. "You mean…I'm to be a father?"

"Yes," replied Leona in a sarcastic tone which meant, *why is it men never grasp the obvious when it comes to these things?*

"You're sure?" I asked.

"Yes," she stated in a hard, matter of fact tone. But her tone softened as she went on. "I have been a midwife for a very long time. On many occasions I know these things even before the mother-to-be does."

I was at once excited beyond belief and nervous beyond comprehension. "Can I see her?" I asked.

"Of course, Merlin Longinus," said Leona.

I started to head into the tent, but Jacobi placed a hand on my arm, halting me before I could enter. His whole countenance had shifted. "After you see to Irena, please come see me, Longinus," he said, in all seriousness.

"What's wrong, my friend? Why so grave?" I asked, fear for Irena again gripping my heart.

"No, no, nothing grave. Do not be alarmed. Just come and see me."

"I will," I said, clapping him on the shoulder. I then turned and entered the tent.

Irena still lay on the sleeping pallet. Though she looked a bit peaked, the mother-to-be of my child now wore a bright smile. "You beam," I said.

"'Tis because of you, you know," she replied sleepily.

"No, it is not. 'Tis because of what you carry," I pointed out.

"Which you implanted in me," she countered. "And thus it is because of you that I beam."

"You sound like a logician," I said teasingly. I walked over to the pallet and sat on the edge. Tenderly, I reached out and placed my hand on her belly. "It's a marvel," I said after a moment, with more than a little awe.

She saw the contemplativeness in my eyes; heard it in my tone. "Are you all right, Longinus?"

"Yes, of course. This changes everything, doesn't it?" I said. "Perhaps we should stay here, make this place our home."

"Permanently?" she asked with distaste.

"Well, I don't know."

"No, Longinus. You know we cannot. You have too much of a destiny. We," she said, placing her hand on mine, which was still on her belly, "have too much of a destiny. Your son is to carry our bloodlines to an island world, a new world, remember?"

I was shocked. How did she know of the prophecy I had uttered during my Druidic initiation? "How...how did...?" I let the thought dangle without completing the sentence.

She sat up on the bedding. "That is not important, my love. Really. The important thing here is that I believe our son will help to create a new people in a new land. I feel it in my heart, in my very soul. But it is not going to happen if we stay here."

I thought about what Irena had said. I thought about all that Camaroon had said on the last night that I saw her. It appeared that the prophecy was about to come true, or at least part of it: my bloodline was about to be carried on. "Well," I finally said, "you can't go anywhere for awhile. We'll take it a day at a time, at least until your sick feeling passes. Then again, we could travel when you do feel better, but we'll have to stop again before too long, for you to give birth. I will not let my child be born on the road. But where is that to happen? We're without a country right now. I could be arrested almost anywhere. Maybe—"

"Longinus," interrupted Irena, "you're starting to sound like a whiney old man!"

I smiled and fell silent, and lost myself in thought again for a moment. Something Irena had said finally hit me. "A son, you say?"

"Yes. I know it."

"So be it," I said, smiling. I stood up and took the spear from its secured place. "I must see Jacobi. I'll bring food back when I return."

I bent down and kissed her forehead as she slid back under the skin covers, closing her eyes. With a last stroke of her hair, I slipped out to find Jacobi.

I found Jacobi with Dosameenor, Thomas, Hentapas and Paulonius near the central cooking fire. Mary and Genevieves were there, too, but excused themselves to pay a visit to Irena as soon as I arrived. I was going to tell them that she was resting, but they looked too excited to be dissuaded from the visit.

"She is well, as I said. Is she not?" Jacobi asked.

"'Twas as you said," I replied, lightheartedly. The lightness of my mood shifted, though, when I felt the concern in the air. "What is it, my friends?"

"We have been here a very long time, Longinus," said Dosameenor.

"Couldn't be," I said, dismissively. "A few weeks perhaps, but—"

"Actually, it's been more than a few months," Jacobi interrupted.

I thought about it for a moment. It was inconceivable. "That can't be so. Irena and I, we just put up our shelter last week. We..." I stopped. No. That had actually been...how long ago? More than a week; perhaps, but not by much.

"Several of the hunters just got back. They'd not been out for at least a week, by their reckoning. They killed plenty 'o game last time, so no reason to venture out again for a bit, save for reconnaissance, which is what they did today," explained Dosameenor. "When last they were out, the air was a bit crisp. But this time, blankets of snow were everywhere, freezing conditions. Dead of winter it is out there right now."

Impossible, I thought. It was still mild here in the mists. It had not been close to winter when we came in here.

. "I knew there'd be a bit of a time distortion from the last misty place we'd been in," I said. "It did not seem all that bad back there, though—barely perceptible."

"Not so here," said Hentapas. "I've been calculating our stay here as it pertains to the outside world; I went out briefly myself to measure the amount of snowfall in the surrounding area. I've talked to two of our people who grew up about five miles from our present location.

"The amount of snow fall I measured on the ground is normal for the month of March, late March at that. Which means we've been here in this misty sanctuary for approximately ten moons," Hentapas finished.

I was astounded. "But, it can't have been more than four or five weeks," I said.

"Indeed, for us, that's about right," admitted Jacobi. "But when invoking the laws that govern the mists, we are also invoking other laws of the Universe that we don't yet comprehend."

This put a wrinkle into things that I'd not anticipated.

Jacobi saw my apprehension. "Longinus, ultimately it matters not. But we need to be aware and more vigilant about the time difference. That's all. I suggest that it is time for some of us to leave."

He was looking at me when he said that, but I was not ready to go yet. I would not leave without Irena, and there was no way that I would force her to travel just then.

"Not you," Jacobi said, reading my thoughts, as usual. He looked then to the Egyptian. "Hentapas has volunteered."

I looked at Hentapas. He had come a long way since the day I had first seen him at the tomb, in more ways than one. He'd been but a boy then. He was more than a man now. He was a mystic-warrior with no equal.

But, I could see something else in him now, too: purpose. I could see it in his eyes. "What else is there to it?" I asked. "It's not just about the leave-taking."

Hentapas looked at Thomas, who stepped forward. "We—Mary, Jacobi and myself—thought that perhaps it would be best to take the Rood out and away in pieces so as not to jeopardize losing it all to the Romans, or worse, to Draco, if some of us are eventually caught or stopped," he explained, clearly not happy about the decision. "I'm loath to do it that way, but hopefully, all the pieces can eventually find their way back to us in Jerusalem."

"That's where you're going?" I asked.

"Yes. Well, eventually. Hentapas will go first. Then we'll send more out later, with more of the Rood," said Thomas.

"I will try to send word back as to what is happening in the outside world as often as I can," added Hentapas.

We were all silent then. I was particularly reflective.

Thomas took my silence, at least in part, to mean something else. "Forgive us for not consulting you, Longinus, but this all just came up this morning, and you were, well, a little busy. Congratulations, by the way."

"Thank you, and I do not take any offense whatsoever by your 'not consulting me,' as you put it," I said. Then I turned to Hentapas, clasping him on the shoulder with my free hand. "When do you leave, my friend?"

"Within the hour, sir," he stated as a matter of fact.

"So be it," I said, embracing the lad.

And, true to his word, within the hour, Hentapas was packed, saddled and ready to go, with one-thirteenth of the Rood hidden in a bag tucked into a larger wrap all stuffed into a fairly large backpack. The number 13 was an ancient mystical number. We had thought of cutting the Rood into more pieces but, any more than thirteen would have been too many, so thirteen pieces was perfect, on more than one level.

Four others were to travel with Hentapas: two from Thomas' original group, who had come from Palestine, and two who had come with us from Dosameenor's home. Hentapas, as it turned out, wanted to go back to Egypt, and one of the Palestinians, a beautiful young woman with silky black hair and deep brown eyes, clearly wanted to go with him wherever he went. The two from Dosameenor's home were his own fighting men and volunteered to go with Hentapas. They had voiced an interest in seeing the land where Jesu had walked, dangerous as it might be.

"Protection of the gods, protection of the God, goes with you, Hentapas," I said.

"The One Mind blesses your way, know that to be so, my lad," said Jacobi.

"Thank you. We will see each other again," Hentapas declared.

"Indeed, we will," I said, smiling. "Irena sends her regards, apologizes for not seeing you off in person."

"Please, sir, I wish only that the lady Irena be healthy and deliver you a fine, strong son, which I know she will," he said. "Goodbye one and all!"

With that, he and his small group, all on foot, turned and hiked out of our sanctuary, disappearing into the mists.

*   *   *   *

We, Irena and I, were going to go next; leave in a week or so with a thirteenth of the Rood. I thought she would get better, well enough to travel for awhile at least. But, it was not to be. She was to have a very difficult time of it throughout the whole of her pregnancy. Extreme fatigue and nausea plagued her constantly. I was concerned at first, but was assured by Leona, the midwife, and Mary, as well, that it was not uncommon for one to have a difficult time of it. "She's strong and no doubt will weather this just fine," Leona asserted.

I had my doubts, but left it at that.

It was many weeks before she could get out of bed, and even then, she could only go for very short walks before the need to lie down struck again. Obviously, we were not going to make it out of the camp any time soon.

But group by group, by twos, fours, and sixes, we watched the occupants of our little sanctuary dwindle, each group taking with it a part of the Rood and heading off in a different direction about two to three weeks apart. Two to three weeks apart by our figuring, anyway.

Paulonius and Genevieves left, Genevieves with child as well, as it turned out, but seemingly completely unaffected by her pregnancy. "You'll be a fine father," I told Paulonius. He was quite frightened by the prospect, as his father had been ill-suited to the role.

"Thank you," said Paulonius. "I'd like to stay here with you, but..." he trailed off.

"You must consider what is best for you, your lady and the little one to come," I pointed out. "Thank you for your service to me."

"Yes, sir, and you for the honor of it," he replied.

Dosameenor and Mattea also left for his home with two of his men. They would stay there for an indeterminate amount of time before then getting the portion of the Rood they would carry to its final destination.

The rest of his men, six more, were instructed to stay with me until I saw fit to give them leave to go, no matter how long that might be, and no matter what corner of the world I dragged them to. I told Dosameenor that it was greatly appreciated but not really necessary; however, he insisted. Truthfully, I was relieved at his insistence; very grateful for the added men at arms. Of the six, four seemed more or less ambivalent about the order. But it didn't sit very well with two of the men, who had wives and families back in Dosameenor's village. In the end, however, I won them over to the cause of hiding the Rood and Spear from

Rome, and by the promise to release them of their duty to me sooner, rather than later, despite what Dosameenor might say.

The day of Dosameenor's leave-taking was difficult. We had been through a lot together and I had not realized how much I loved this big Celt. "My friend," I said with tears brimming my eyes.

He made a show of bringing his hand to his face and bowing his head as if to show respect. But we both knew that it was to conceal his emotions more than anything else. "I will miss you my brother," he said, as he embraced me in a squeezing bear hug. He then held me at arms' length and said, "I look forward to the time when we will hoist mead together again."

But as soon as the words were out of his mouth, my stomach lurched and fell, and I knew that it would not be so; I would never again see this man—in this life, anyway. I knew not how I knew, nor how each of our lives would play out. I only knew that our paths would not cross again.

"Yes, I look forward to that as well," I said feebly, trying to hide the additional emotion I was now feeling over this latest revelation.

I remained silent as he said goodbye to Thomas and Mary and Irena, who, having one of her better days, made it out of the tent to say farewell to the big Celt. "Thank you for being with him, for protecting him, for being his 'brother' in so many ways and for being my friend, too."

I had never in all my years seen anyone turn so many shades of red as did Dosameenor in that moment. "Th...thank you, me lady," he stammered, then added, "I only wish I could see your son born."

"Well," said Irena, "we'll just have to make a point of coming to you eventually so that you and Mattea may meet him."

He nodded. After a moment, he stepped away and turned to Jacobi. He looked at the old man and finally genuinely burst into tears. "You are revered in my eyes. You are a Druid of old, truly one of the Ancient Ones," he said once he gained control of himself again.

"'Tis you, Dosameenor, who have honored me by being my friend, listening to the ravings of an old man," Jacobi said.

"Even when I've been less than gentle with you?" the big Celt quipped, probably referring to the time he had carried Jacobi under his arm aboard the ship shortly after our first meeting.

"Even so!" laughed the old man.

Slowly, Dosameenor turned and looked at us all one more time, drinking in the sight of us. Something told me that he also felt deep inside that this would be the last time he would see any of us. Finally, he mounted his horse, a large pack behind the saddle, which I assumed to contain the Rood piece. He gave us all one last nod goodbye, turned with his traveling companions and trotted off into the mists.

I looked at Irena, belly now swelling with about eight moons of child. Had it been that long already? What was the outside world doing? Had it advanced in time by the same amount of time as first calculated by Hentapas, or had that changed? Perhaps time had slowed in comparison to us. Perhaps it had sped up. It was mind-numbing to contemplate.

We had heard nothing from any of those who had already left; no word from the outside world at all. A bit troubling was that, but not too much so. At least not yet.

Then, one day, something happened that shook me to the core. Jacobi took ill. Age was part of it to be sure, but something else afflicted him that we could not define; something within his lungs.

His breathing became extremely labored to the point that he, too, was confined to his sleeping pallet.

I was beside myself. Nothing I tried seemed to work in healing him. I enlisted Leona's help, as well as Mary's. Nothing worked.

For some time, he faded in and out of consciousness. I meditated, prayed and conjured healing energy over him night and day, seeing in my mind's eye that I merged with his spirit, his body; going to the deepest levels imaginable of his lungs to aid and cure his breathing. I used the spear in conjunction with these treatments. I used what remained of the Rood, hoping beyond hope that it would aid in healing as it had miraculously done in the past. Nothing. He was indeed dying. There was no other way to put it.

Finally, one day when I was sitting by his side, on his pallet, he inexplicably awakened into one of his more lucid moments, and managed to rasp out more than a few words. "Longinus, Longinus! I was dreaming just now," he began with a cough, but was excited, nonetheless.

I motioned for him to be still and not spend the energy on speech, but of course, he wouldn't hear of it.

"I dreamt that I was young, oh so young. Just a small lad. Not as I had been in this life, but in a life anew. You and Irena were there, too." His brow became furled, trying to figure out what he had experienced in the dream. "Though I'm not sure as to..." he coughed violently. It took a moment before he could continue. "Though I'm not sure as to the capacity...I mean, why you were in it."

"Please, Jacobi. Rest. Save your strength. Speak no more," I pleaded.

"Save..." he coughed, "...my strength for what? It's time for me to leave, Longinus."

I felt this to be so, but to hear him say it stunned me terribly; it confirmed my worst fear.

"I need you to aid my journey."

"What do you mean?" I asked suspiciously.

He gave a retched, liquid-lunged laugh which turned into a fit of coughing. "No, no, lad!" he finally managed. "I need no help in bodily demise. I would like you to bury me here, in this misty sanctuary, and cast a spell, or a blessing, whatever you wish to call it, of rebirth for me upon the grave. There is magic here. Who knows what may happen, eh?"

I remained silent. Of course, I would honor his wish. For a moment, though, I had thought he was going to ask me to burn his remains in the Celtic manner to release his soul.

"I'd thought about that, you know," he said, reading my thoughts.

I smiled. Even in death, I could keep nothing from him.

"But, I'd rather be buried," he finished, with a cough.

I was silent for a moment, and then said, "Certainly, I'll honor your wishes." Profound sadness overcame me and I wept.

"Stop, my son," said Jacobi. "I will see you again and again for many lifetimes to come." He paused briefly in thought. Then a gleeful look of realization suddenly donned on his face. "And the very next life, I believe, will be much sooner than you think!"

I wasn't sure what to make of that, but did not question it. Instead, I fell quiet, reflecting again on the loss I was about to experience.

"Longinus," he said coughing. "Longinus, be not sad for me, or for yourself. You know I go simply to my Source, merging with God as One, as one can never do completely while in the body. 'Tis a thing to be celebrated, not mourned."

"You know you will be missed. Very deeply, Jacobi. You've," I had to stop briefly. Tears stung my eyes. Though I knew what he said about merging with the Source to be true, that did not take the absolute pain away from losing him in this life. And that loss deserved the honor and solemness of mourning, regardless of his words to the contrary. "You have been more a father and mentor to me. More than you'll ever know. So whether you like it or not, you will be mourned."

"So be it," he said after a moment. "But always keep in mind where I am truly. My Highest, Truest Self—your Highest, Truest Self—lives forever. You seem to lose sight of that fact quite often. Focus on that, always," he said, before breaking into another round of rattling coughs. "Always heed the voice within, always!

Because, whether you think it's Jesu or your own inner Self matters not, for…" he struggled for breath, "…they are one in the same."

I simply nodded my head.

"One more thing," he whispered with labor. "Would you bring the spear to me? I should like to kiss His blood one more time."

I thought it a strange request. He had kissed the lance's blade the first time I met him, but I considered him to have grown, evolved, beyond that sort of thing now. Still, if that was his choice for his final moments, then I would indeed comply. "Yes."

I had brought the spear with me each time I visited these past days in the hopes that it would eventually aid in his healing. This day was no different. I held the lance horizontally over him, blade near his face.

The blade was dark with age, stained with years of trials and service; stained still, too, with Jesu's blood. It had never come off. I had stopped trying to remove it a long time ago.

A tear rolled down Jacobi's cheek as he looked at the Holy stain.

Instinctively, I moved the blade closer to his mouth so that he would not have to strain to reach it.

He lifted a frail hand and pulled the spear the last couple of inches, placing the flat of the blade, the stain Itself, on his lips with reverence.

I bowed my head respectfully and stayed that way until I felt the spear's weight shift in my hand, indicating that Jacobi had released it.

I then placed the spear on the pallet, laying it alongside my friend.

He closed his eyes and we both fell silent.

Thirty minutes later, Jacobi was gone.

I wrapped his body in some of the fine draperies that had hung over Mary's chariot wagon, torn and cut specifically for Jacobi's burial shroud. I dug the grave myself and tenderly laid him to rest. All those left in the encampment attended the funeral.

I spoke of my love for him and the teachings he had passed on to me. Then, I asked everyone to leave, and I laid the dirt back over him, planting a sapling on the spot. I then spoke the words of power that would aid him on his journey to and through the Otherworld, and then the words of power that would help him to pick the rebirth that suited him perfectly, though I knew he had somehow already picked that even before leaving here.

I went back to my shelter a hollow man. It would take a long time for me to let him go completely. In spite of my *enlightenment*, I was still human and would grieve for him. But I knew in my soul that the rites I had performed at the grave would aid him. Perhaps that sounds contradictory. But as I said, I was human, and as such, I could know that my friend was in a wonderful place, even help him to it, and still grieve for him profoundly.

I carried on as best I could. There were many things around the camp that needed my attention, not the least of which was taking care of Irena, whose time was near.

Mary was a constant figure in our lives, looking after Irena as much as I did. Though they never said it, I believed that she and Thomas stayed in camp to make sure the child was born healthy before leaving. I also felt that Mary wanted Thomas and herself to stay with Irena and me until *we* decided to leave.

But Thomas would not wait much beyond the birth. I had no doubt that they would go on without us. It was not prudent for us to leave right after the child was born. Given Irena's frail state during pregnancy, she would need time to recover. In addition to that, traveling with a newborn is ill-advised even during the best of times, so we would wait before we left the encampment, even if it meant that Irena and I would be the last to leave.

I awoke one morning when the mists around the encampment seemed particularly thick. Despite that, a musical, joyous chorus of bird songs could be heard coming from all directions. The air was light and smelled of...happiness. That seemed to be the best way to describe it. 'Twas true that birds could often be heard in the forest near us. On this particular day, however, they were louder and more musical that I'd ever heard.

I was searching for a reason for the profundity of bird songs, and the other things I felt in the air, when Irena stirred next to me.

She moaned slightly and rolled onto her back. I lay motionless next to her, on my back, as well, and with the covers off. I was about to say good morning when her hand suddenly clamped onto my bare stomach, nearly clawing out a handful of flesh.

Before I had the chance to yell in pain, she shrieked in agony.

"What? What is it?" I cried frantically.

"Aghhhhh!" was all she managed to say as she arched her back in the throws of pain. She had let go of my stomach and now clutched my hand, nearly crushing the bones.

I did not feel any pain, though, as I was too intent on her. *What the devil is happening to you?* was all I could think.

Then, quite unexpectedly, I felt a warm liquid spreading on the sleeping pallet and knew what was happening.

"Get Leona and Mary," she hissed through clenched teeth.

"Yes, yes," I said, partly horrified and partly ecstatic with joy; my child was about to be born!

It took the whole of the day. She labored for over twelve hours. I was crazed for a while, but Mary came out for a breath of fresh air at midday, and assured me that a long labor was not unusual, particularly for a first birth. Irena seemed to be weathering it as well as could be expected.

I had been exiled to the outside, where I spent the better part of the day with Thomas and a couple of the other men, who found my nervousness most amusing.

Then, well into the thirteenth hour, as quickly as it had begun, it was over. The sudden squalling spilled out of our shelter, announcing the arrival.

Mary poked her head out of the tent flap. "Longinus, you have a strong son, just as Irena had predicted!" she said.

I laughed out loud and received a round of claps on the back. But I was not relieved yet. "And Irena?" I queried.

Mary's hesitation said much. "She will fair well in the days to come," she finally replied.

"And now?" I demanded.

"She's very weak, but she will get better. I'm sure of it," she said with sincerity.

I believed her, but I needed to see for myself. I entered the tent and crossed over to the sleeping pallet.

The whole of the place smelled of musk and copper—blood. Leona looked at me from the bedside, a scowl of ridicule splashing across her face. "Here now," she spat at me in hushed tones. "You shouldn't be in here."

Mary entered just then and stood next to me.

"Irena?" I said, ignoring the other women.

"Longinus," she said, in utter exhaustion. She was drenched in perspiration, her beautiful hair plastered to her head. And she had the bloodless coloring of a corpse. For a moment, my heart fell to the floor. "Do not worry. I am fine. Have you seen your son?" she asked, speaking in slow and slurred speech.

Slowly, I became aware of a cooing sound coming from a blanketed bundle on the pallet next to Irena. Leona, having dispensed with her initial wrath at my intrusion to the birthing chamber, picked up the bundle and brought it over to me.

I ever so gently took it from her and placed it in the crook of my left arm. Then, with my free hand, I pulled back the part covering his little head.

I was humbled by the little life before me. As with all newborns, his eyes were still closed, but he seemed to be smiling at me with a familiar, toothless grin. I stared at the babe for a few moments.

"We," Irena began, "we never decided on a name."

I thought for a moment, but the name was obvious. "Jacobi," I said.

"Yes," she said smiling. "Gaius Longinus Jacobi Arturius," she added.

"Arturius? Wasn't that your father's name?" I asked. She had never mentioned naming our child after her father.

"Yes. I loved him very much, you know." she said, reminiscing, almost deliriously, through the haze of fatigue.

Her father had become a legionnaire, was conscripted as one to be more precise, when Irena had been a lass. He had gone off to Britain with a legion and was never heard from again.

"Jacobi Arturius it is," I agreed.

XXV

He was a healthy boy, Jacobi Arturius. He had thick, dark hair and lashes, and bright green eyes. A curious and infectious smile seemed to always play on his face, which instantly garnered gushing attention for him and his parents.

As I predicted, Thomas insisted on leaving shortly after Jacobi Arturius was born, three weeks to be exact. Mary did not wish to, but deferred to Thomas. They left with a portion of the Rood on a morning when the protective mists seemed to be especially thin.

"Be sure and shore up the barrier," said Thomas as we all stood next to the chariot wagon, which was loaded and ready for the journey. "I could help you do it right now if you wish."

I looked around at the mists. I thought about taking him up on the offer and performing the rite then and there. We had been able to hear passersby a few days before. That hadn't happened since the first day we called the misty barrier into being, when we heard Draco and the others on the outside. I did not think, though, that it would be difficult to reinforce the mists on my own. "Thank you, Thomas, but I think I can manage it. You two are ready?"

"Yes," Mary said with a touch of sadness. Sara, her thumb in her mouth, stood next to her mother. She was getting big, Sara. *Perhaps one day, in a different land, she and Jacobi Arturius will be able to grow up together in peace and safety. I pray it will be so*, I said silently.

"Well then," Thomas said, interrupting my thoughts. "We should be off."

He ushered Mary and Sara into the back of the wagon, and gave a couple of last minute orders to the people going with them; the rest of Thomas' guards and three women. That left Irena, me, Jacobi Arturius, Dosameenor's men, Leona and Jenus—the woman who had been injured in the ribs that day along with Leona. Leona and Jenus had both wanted to stay to help with Irena and Jacobi Arturius.

On the previous evening, we, all those who were left in the camp, met to discuss the present and future. The two women insisted on staying with us and Dosameenor's men. Everyone else felt that it was time to leave. We discussed plans and strategies well beyond that, too, one of which was that at a point two years hence, on the Ides of October, Irena and I and Jacobi Arturius would meet up with Thomas and hopefully Mary and Sara, to give them the Rood. The place we would meet would be Antiochia or Antioch. Irena had family there. It was where we decided to go when she was better and our baby boy was fit to travel. At last accounting, Rome was certainly an occupier there, but not in full force.

"Goodbye," said Thomas from the driver's platform, standing alongside the driver.

"Farewell!" called Mary from the wagon's back, tears brimming her eyes.

"Byeeee," squealed Sara with delight, beside her mother.

We stood and waved as the entourage disappeared into the mists.

Time created a void into which we seemed to fall. Or, more accurately, we simply lost track of time. Caring for an infant is an all-encompassing job in the best of times. Yes, we had the help of Leona and Jenus, but even so, Jacobi Arturius kept us extremely busy.

He grew rapidly and we had the time of our lives with him. But before we knew it, he was near his first natal day. Almost a full year had passed. Irena and I were astounded when we stopped to think about it.

Then we awoke one morning to something surprising and quite frightening. The mists were gone.

We had stopped posting a guard through the night a long time ago. The mists had always been a solid presence since the time we first came to this place. Of course, it needed to be shored up on occasion with a ritual similar to the initial one used to create it, but that was simple enough. Yet, nothing had happened to indicate that the mists might vanish outright.

Leona was the first to find it so. She had risen early just before full dawn, as she always did, to prepare the breaking of the fast. We all rose quickly when we heard her cry out.

"What is it?" I called, as I bolted headlong out of the tent, the lance in one hand, my gladius in the other.

Then I saw it: Nothing but green and open forest surrounded us, except for the hill on one side. No mists. Birds were singing their morning tune and a slight breeze was soughing through the trees. But there was no other noise. One could see beyond the trees now, nearly out to the main road.

One by one, all came out of their shelters to greet the new day, and one by one, had expressions of surprise and fear on their faces.

Jenus was the first to regain her voice. "Merlin Longinus, what has happened?"

"I do not know," was all I could manage. I quickly regained my senses, though, and barked orders to the warrior guards who remained with us. "Go out to the road. Scout the area quickly, but thoroughly. Report back to me within the hour."

"Aye, sir," said the eldest, a grizzled old bear of a fighter, named Fracix, who had barely said three words since we all arrived here.

He and the others left at once. The women looked to me for more guidance. "Leona, prepare to break fast as you usually would. If someone was here and meant us harm, they would have already attacked," I reasoned.

Leona gave a curt nod, took the younger Jenus by the wrist and went about her business.

I heard coughing and turned to see Irena, looking a bit pale, holding Jacobi Arturius in her arms, both still in their sleeping wraps and rubbing sleep from their eyes.

The coughing was coming from Irena. It had taken her quite some time to get back to resembling the normal, healthy woman I had always known. Even when she got back to that point, she still tired easily. Now she seemed to have something happening in her chest. "You're coughing. Are you all right?" I asked, trying not to sound overly concerned.

"I'm quite fine, my love. Just a bit of a chill, that is all," she replied.

"Sorry, but I'll take no chances with you," I said.

"Thank you, Longinus, but your doting isn't necessary. What happened to the mist?" she asked, tactfully changing the subject.

"I don't know," I said.

Longinus, said the voice in my head. *Heed the signs.*

"Yes," I said out loud.

"What, my love?" asked Irena, looking at me with a mixture of fear and awe. "You swooned."

"What?" I asked, and then noticed that I was sitting on the ground. "How—"

"You went into a trance mumbling something and then went to the ground," said Irena.

I said nothing, but tried to recall what she said I'd done. All I could remember was the voice in my head.

"Longinus? What is it you saw?" Irena prompted.

"Not what I saw—what I was told: 'Heed the signs,' is what I remember."

"'Heed the signs?'" she repeated.

"Yes. I believe that it means it is time for us to leave here," I stated flatly.

"Yes," Irena said after a moment. "Yes, I agree. It is past time for us to do so."

An hour later, with the morning meal nearly done, the scouts came back to report that no one was in the immediate area. Not a soul. We could easily venture out and probably not run into anyone until the morrow at least. That settled it then. It was indeed time to leave our sanctuary. I felt it in my heart, in my soul. The vanishing mists and the fact that we were alone were the signs.

I thanked the men and dismissed them to eat, but urged them to be ready to leave when the sun was at her zenith. The day was warm and bright and we would have much time to travel. I then informed the rest of our party of the plan.

"Where are we to go?" asked Jenus.

"To Antioch," I replied.

"I have family there," Irena put in as she cleaned up the meal dishes. "You are all welcome to stay with us there."

A slight frown crossed Leona's face.

"Or we will make other arrangements for you to go wherever you wish," added Irena.

"No. It is not that," said Leona. "I really have nothing to go back to. I was just trying to figure out where Antioch is. I've never heard of it."

Jenus laughed. "You tain't never heard of any other place, either, have you?! You never been anywhere outside 'o home but here!"

"And you have?" the older woman countered.

"Not what I'm sayin'—"

"All right," I said, interrupting the little feud. "It is quite some ways south, southeast of us right now."

"Is Romans there?" asked Jenus.

"Yes, but I don't think many," I replied.

Irena coughed several times then.

I waited patiently until she finished and cocked an eyebrow at her that said, *Are you sure you're all right?*

She simply gave me a look of annoyance.

I would take her at her word then. I turned my attention back to the others. "Please be ready to leave by noon. We will eat an afternoon meal on the road, so prepare something and pack it," I ordered.

"Yes, sir," said Leona and Jenus in unison and left us.

Irena, Jacobi Arturius and I also went to prepare for the leave-taking.

We entered our tent. Irena yanked the sleeping skins off the pallet with her free hand and put the boy down on the bare pallet. She gave him the warrior-doll that Fracix had made for him, a toy that was not exactly a favorite of hers because of what it represented. But Jacobi Arturius loved the doll and it had been a very pleasant gesture from the old warrior. It was something that displayed his loyalty, albeit in an abstract way.

Jacobi Arturius babbled incoherently with excitement as he shook the doll. His mother kissed his head and tried to comb the lad's unruly dark locks to the left so they were out of his eyes.

"No," he frowned, as he pushed away his mother's hand.

I had never heard him speak beyond a baby's gibberish. "Well," I said in surprise. "That's wonderful!"

"Not really. 'No' is all he seems to want to say thus far," answered Irena.

"It's a start," I countered.

She coughed again. The bout only went on for a few seconds, but it did not sound good.

"Irena," I started.

"Longinus, don't," she said. "I tell you it is a slight chest cold, nothing more. It will pass in a matter of days. Right now, we must leave as you said. Come, we must ready ourselves."

I stood there, lost in thought. Despite the trance voice, and the signs, we could easily stay a while longer. True the mists were no more, but I could put them back or try. And even if they never came back, we seemed to be alone in this little forested valley.

Yet, I knew that the voice had been right; knew it deep within.

"So be it," I said. "You're right. Let's get ready."

Irena started to roll up the bedding.

An urge suddenly hit me. "Wait," I said, taking her by the hand.

I pulled her close, kissing her on the mouth passionately, rubbing my hands through her hair. She returned my kiss with equal passion, opening her mouth invitingly.

After a moment, we simply held each other, her head resting against my shoulder. As it happened so many other times, I could feel her heartbeat through my chest, my own heartbeat matching hers in rhythm, our souls merging as one. We stayed that way for a few minutes, savoring the feeling of exquisite closeness.

Finally, she looked at me and crinkled her brow. "Longinus, are you trying to become ill?" she teased.

"I would have whatever ails you as long as we could be together," I replied. I truly loved this woman with all of my being.

We continued holding each other and I became aware of something: a fire was burning within me. I wanted her then and there.

And then I looked at Jacobi Arturius, staring at his silly mother and father with that grin of his. He was innocence personified, and I knew that my fire must cool for the time being.

I pulled away then, gently stroking Irena's lovely cheek with the back of my fingers.

I thought of something then; something that had crossed my mind several times of late. "Irena, my love. I have to ask you something."

She must have seen a shift in my countenance; seen a seriousness come into my eyes. "What is it?" she asked, a look of fear in her eyes.

"Nothing, nothing," I answered soothingly, reassuringly. "It's just…it's just that, if something befalls me, if something happens while we're on the road, I want you and Jacobi Arturius to take the spear and go with Mary and Thomas. Stay with them even if it means going somewhere far away."

"What are you saying? What have you *seen*?" she pleaded.

"No, nothing. I am just saying…I want you to be prepared just in case," I replied.

She didn't answer right away. "You assure me you have had no vision to prompt this…this request?" she finally asked suspiciously.

I laughed. "Yes, my love. I promise. 'Tis pure precaution."

"All right then. You have my word. We will go with Mary and Thomas even if it means going to the ends of the earth," she said.

"I thank you," I said, embracing her once again. For some reason, I felt relief at this; relief at having voiced my desire for this type of arrangement.

While it was true that I had not had a vision or dream, something in my being had compelled me to get Irena to make the promise. Whatever it was, it was not in the forefront of my consciousness, my mind—at least, not yet.

XXVI

We left one half hour after the sun had reached its zenith. One of Fracix's men questioned why we didn't just wait until the following morning.

"'Tis foolish. Won't get far this day. May as well wait 'til the morning. More time to supply up, too," he had said.

Ironically, this was also one of the men who had complained bitterly at being ordered by Dosameenor to stay. I would have thought him anxious to leave at any time. But I think in the end, he was just the complaining type.

His comments this time, however, earned the young man three sharp cuffs on the side of his head, administered by Fracix himself. "You show respect to Merlin Longinus and do as he says, you damned whelp, or I'll gut you and leave you here for carrion!" yelled Fracix for all to hear.

As with most bellowers, the young complainer was full of naught but air when confronted with firm authority.

The first few hours on the road were spent marveling at the sights and smells from the surrounding woods. The greenery was beautiful and lush; yews, pines, and oaks abounded. The smells were astonishing. For the first time in quite a while, we all realized that we had been missing a lot of smells altogether. The mists had dampened our surrounding environment at the encampment, laying a type of blanket on the trees, shrubs and ground. The result was that not much in the way of scents escaped for our detection. We had simply become accustomed to it to the point that we didn't notice a lack of forest smells.

Now, out in the open once again, the scent of pine, mistletoe-laden oaks, and the musk of damp dirt—the skin of the earth—wafted to our nostrils. It was delightful.

Most everyone seemed to be in a jovial mood, probably due to the fact that we were once again in the world of men and not hiding in a secluded, misty, hillside glen. We were all quite grateful for the protection of that enchanted place. But a gilded cage is still a cage, even if it's of one's own making. We should have left the misty glen a long time before. But then, from atop Macha, I looked into the small open wagon that Irena and Jacobi Arturius were riding in and I remembered the reason that I had refused to leave sooner.

Irena caught me looking at her, smiled seductively and winked, then coughed. I couldn't help but laugh. The cough rather shattered the alluring seduction of the moment she'd created. I sobered quickly and silently prayed that her cough was indeed just a chill of the chest and did not portend something more serious. Though Jacobi had been an old man even when I'd first met him, his final demise had been due to the lung disease. I could not help having that in my mind when I heard my love cough.

For the time being, however, I respected her wishes and paid no mind to her cough; at least outwardly.

The first day was short. We got our bearings and traveled south, by southeast, enjoying the environment as we went along. As Fracix and the scouts had reported before we left the encampment, we had not seen another soul that first day. We halted at sunset and made camp for the night.

I sent two of the men out to scout in the direction we were headed. Still, they saw no one. But they did see definite signs of people; the road we were on came to an intersection with three other roads, all of which headed in very different directions. There was no one at the intersection, but there was ample evidence to suggest that vendors had carts set up there on occasion, and heavily-laden wagons rolled through. There were many deep wheel grooves in the wet dirt of the roads to support their belief. The road we were on curved a bit at this intersection, but clearly continued in a southeasterly direction, which is what I required. My objective was to reach one of the ports along the border of Gaul and Italy, and secure passage on a boat for myself, Irena, Jacobi Arturius and the two women.

It was not likely that we would find a boat going directly to Antioch. In fact, that would probably be impossible. Antioch was many, many leagues from where we were now. To reach it by sea would be an arduous journey. But, the alternative was a combination of a very difficult journey over both land and sea. Besides, if we stuck to the ocean ways, there would be much less of a chance of being stopped by a Roman patrol.

Whichever port we reached, and once our passage was secured, I would then release Fracix and his men from their obligation of service to me. If one or more wanted to come with us, then they would be most welcome to do so. But, I'd not hold a man any longer than necessary. I thought about some kind of gift or reward for them. I even thought of giving Macha to Fracix. As much as I would have liked to, I was not going to take her all the way to Antioch. Upon rethinking it, though, it would not be fair to the other men to give Fracix such a fine gift when I could not match it for the others. Macha would also fetch a handsome price in the market; money was something we'd certainly need for the rest of the trip.

But securing the boat trip and saying farewell to our escorts was still a few days away at best. For now, it was enough to enjoy our first night out of the mists; our first night of freedom in many moons.

We sat on the ground around the cooking fire and I explained my plan for the rest of the trip. At one point, Jacobi Arturius crawled onto my lap, gurgling what sounded like "Da!" He settled quickly enough and seemed to quietly observe everyone and listen to everything that was being said, as if he were taking mental notes.

The spear lay by my side and began to give off a perpetual soft white glow which remained the entire time the lad was on my lap. The energy I sensed from the glow was that of protection; protection for the boy. Others around the fire periodically looked at it, some with a bit of awe on their faces; others with unmasked curiosity. I finally pushed it under my leg as much as possible, out of sight, to minimize the distraction.

"...And once we've obtained passage," I said, continuing what I had been saying to Fracix and the men, "you and your men are free to go home."

The men murmured. Five of them were obviously overjoyed that their tour of duty with me would be coming to an end soon. A couple of them even began to boast in explicit detail of the sexual pleasures they would experience with their wives the moment they got back home.

This banter proved very entertaining to Leona and Jenus, who were sitting with us around the fire, and who, in turn, seemed to delight in this change in conversation. Celtic women were anything but prudish when it came to the subject of sex. To the Celts, sex was the most natural and wonderful thing that Dana, the Mother Goddess of all things, bestowed upon earth. It balanced the Universe.

Irena was not present, having excused herself after the meal to wash up, which I was glad for since young Jacobi Arturius was sitting on my lap and his father was almost as entertained by the conversation as the two women.

"All right, you animals," interjected Fracix. "Can't you see there's a little one here, too young to be hearin' such shite from the likes of you?"

One of the men looked at me, fear in his eyes. "Sorry, Merlin Longinus. We meant no offense. It's just…we're excited to be going home is all."

"No offense taken," I said quickly. "And, I'm sure the boy's a little too young to comprehend most of what we say on any given subject, let alone the topic you were just in."

"Thank you, sir," said the lad whom Fracix had cuffed earlier.

"No. **Thank** *you*. Thank you for your service and devotion. You do Dosameenor proud," I said. "Now, I suggest we all retire. I would like to leave at first light.

"Aye, sir," said three of the men in unison. Everyone got up to gather their bedding. Most were sleeping by the fire. Irena and I were the only ones who put up a small shelter for the night. She had started to almost argue with me about it, but I insisted on putting it up both for her sake and Jacobi Arturius', and I was not going to take no for an answer.

I was about to walk to the shelter to be with my family when I saw Fracix unrolling his sleeping skins near the fire and I approached him.

"Yes, Merlin Longinus?" he said with respect.

"Please, Fracix, you needn't be so formal with me. Longinus will do," I said.

"How 'bout Merlin?" he offered.

"I'd prefer Longinus."

"As you wish," he said sincerely, but with some distance, and continued to unroll his bedding.

"Why did you not celebrate as your men did when I said you'd soon be released of your obligation?" I asked.

"No reason, really. Just not my way," he answered vaguely.

"Have you a family to return to?" I asked. But as soon as I asked it, I realized that perhaps I'd overstepped my bounds. "I'm sorry. It's none of my business."

"No," he replied. He stopped fussing with his bedding and faced me. "No. I've no family. I had a boy and a wife. And a dog. They were all killed by Draco."

I sank inside. Draco had destroyed so many lives. "I'm sorry. I'm so sorry."

"Thank you, Mer—I mean, Longinus, sir. It's just…well, I have nothing to return to."

"You are more than welcome to come with us, you know," I said. "In fact, I would like it very much, and I know Irena would, too."

"That's very kind," he said. He paused then, thinking about my offer.

"Besides, Leona's coming with us. I've seen the way she looks at you," I added, trying to make things a little lighter.

His lined faced creased a bit into a smile. "Leona aside, I *would* like to accompany you to Antioch. From there, who knows."

I clapped him on the shoulder. "Excellent. Very good. I'll see you in the morning, then."

"Yes, sir."

"Again, please call me Longinus and not sir or Merlin. All right?" I asked.

"All right," he said, chuckling.

With that I bid him to rest well and retired to my shelter.

Irena and I were up before the new day was lighted. Jacobi Arturius slept on. He was wrapped in skins and laid underneath an oak while his mother and I took down the tent and prepared a small meal. By the time the sun's light was cresting the horizon, our little company was once again on the move.

We had traveled the better part of the morning. I was on Macha, riding at a gentle pace alongside the tiny wagon which carried Irena, Jacobi Arturius and the two women, when Fracix and one of the other men I'd sent with him to scout ahead came back at a trot, halting their mounts in front of me.

"What is it?" I asked apprehensively.

"Nothing to worry about, I think. There is a very small village, maybe a couple families, about three miles ahead," answered Fracix.

"Any Romans?"

"No, sir," he replied.

"All right. We'll pass through, maybe garner a few more supplies, some information," I said.

We pressed on, coming to the village a while later. Indeed, the village was tiny: three small mud buildings and a fourth structure made of grass and branches.

At the edge of the road, just on the outskirts of the village, a small, filth-encrusted child of about six summers, whose gender was indeterminable, yelled out at our arrival. The little one's eyes lit up as he or she turned and ran back to the structures, yelling something which seemed to be in a regional form of the Celtic dialect, which I could not understand.

I assumed it was an alarm of some kind. Yet, I halted in drawing a weapon. Something stayed my hand, my intuition saying that it was fine. I turned to Fracix, "What is the child saying?"

Fracix looked perplexed, apparently at what the child was saying. "She says, 'More are coming! More are coming!'"

That was indeed perplexing. What did she mean? Even more interesting, I thought, smiling to myself, was how Fracix could tell it was a girl. I gave voice to that thought, "You can tell it's a girl?"

"Of course," he said as if it were the most obvious thing in the world. "But, what does she mean by 'more are coming?'" he added, drawing his sword.

"No," I said. "That won't be necessary."

"But—"

"Trust me. I feel it," I said.

"As you wish," he said, sheathing his weapon.

We proceeded into the village. A small, hobbled old man came out to greet us, the rest of the clan waiting cautiously behind him.

"Greetings, friends," said the elder in a heavily accented dialect that sounded similar to Dosameenor's. I understood him, though. His voice had a high-pitched quality to it, and his breath and words whistled through his lips as he spoke. His tone and demeanor were quite friendly, yet not pretentiously so. There was no fear in him.

I dismounted and faced him, allowing him to clearly see that my weapons were not drawn. "Greetings," I said. "We are simply traveling through and wonder if we could barter for some supplies and perhaps some news."

"Supplies we can help with. News is rather short. We don't really go to the outside world. All we need is here, don't you know," he said smiling, and holding his hands out, gesturing to the plush greenness and beauty surrounding us.

Though I could understand the man's love for his home, I was very disappointed. I wanted to know what year it was, how long we had spent in the mists as compared to the real world of men, and did Tiberius Caesar still rule Rome?

"I must say you are the second visitor we've received in two days!" the elder added excitedly. "Perhaps our other guest can give you news."

My years as a Centurion pricked my skin. Who was this other visitor? But then the inner voice calmed me again and I knew that there was nothing to fear from this other visitor.

I was about to ask about the guest when a familiar voice hailed me from a short distance away. "Longinus, sir!"

I spun around to see Paulonius standing there. He looked weary from travel and thinner. But he was wonderful to behold. There was something else about him, too; there was a bearing about him now. It dawned on me that he was no longer the young lad whom I remembered. He was a man now. "Paulonius!" I exclaimed. I rushed up to him and embraced him as a brother. "'Tis good to see you!"

"Yes, and you," he said.

Irena called out from the wagon. "Paulonius!" she exclaimed joyfully, Jacobi Arturius giggling in her arms.

"Miss Irena!" he said. "And who is the strapping young one?"

"That is my son, Jacobi Arturius," I said proudly.

"A son. How wonderful," replied Paulonius, smiling like a proud uncle.

We stayed in the tiny village for the rest of the day, and that night, too. I did not intend it so, but after a midday meal, Paulonius took to filling us in on the events of the outside world, after which we found the day to be rapidly waning. I decided that it would serve no purpose to be on the road again for only a couple of hours. Besides, Irena's cough seemed to be particularly acute that day, and thus the rest would do her well.

Five years had passed while we had been in the misty sanctuary. *Five* years. Though that did not equal the pace originally put forth by Hentapas' calculations, it was, nonetheless, nearly impossible to comprehend; my thinking had us in the mists only two to three years at the most. No matter; the whys of that mystery could be left for someone else more adept at deciphering the mechanical workings of the Universe, perhaps to some philosopher/mystic/mathematician of the future.

Five years, though, was a long time. I had apparently become the stuff of legends. Me and the spear, that is. Rumors had started some years before that the spear and I had performed miracles of healing and divine magic that, somehow, allegedly proved the divinity of Jesu the Christ, the Son Of God, as many now called *him*. The spear and I, according to these stories, had been called to Heaven by God, Himself (which is why I had not been seen all these years) after I had been preaching the so-called word of God to the *heathens* and barbarians of Gaul and beyond. I had become, according to these misguided folks, the next messenger of God and Jesu.

It was apparent that there was a whole new religious movement growing. Christians, they were being called, for they purportedly followed the teachings of the Christ or Jesu. Unfortunately, from what Paulonius told me, it sounded more like most of them were worshipers of the man, Jesu, looking to *him* for *salvation*, for the *Kingdom Of Heaven*, rather than following His teachings of turning within oneself to seek God and the Kingdom.

Many of these so-called Christians were counting me among their numbers, based solely on the rumors and interpretations of certain events that they chose to call miracles of God, instead of understanding them for what they were: conscious workings with, and of, the natural Laws of the Universe. Adding to the perception that I was one of them was the fact that I had left the Roman military machine and indeed had turned my back on Rome altogether. In other words, I was still a fugitive of Rome which added more to my mystique for them.

But I was *not* one of them. I had experienced enough events and manipulations of the Universal laws that led me to know that a potential Christ existed within each one of us; that A Master Druid, a Merlin of the highest order, is within every one of us. There is no reason to look to the outside for anything of this nature save for a certain amount of guidance in unlocking these inner mysteries; these eternal secrets that are housed at the core of our beings.

Toward the end of the day, the village elder who had first greeted us—Rhetter, was his name—led me to a pile of supplies that his people had put together for us. There were dried meats, furs for warmth, skins filled with water; even a few filled with mead.

I was overwhelmed by his generosity. "I thank you from the bottom of my heart. But, I fear I cannot pay for such riches," I said.

"Pay?" he queried, obviously having no concept of the word.

"Trade, barter," I clarified. "We really have nothing to trade you for these riches."

"No trade," he insisted.

It seemed to me that especially with the meats, these were indeed riches for the villagers. I got the feeling that they were part of their winter stores. But in the end, it would have been much more of an insult to turn down the gifts. "Thank you," I said again.

"Please to take this, too," he said, handing me a ceramic jar about the size of a small goblet. "It is salve from our Shaman," he said. "Even a great healer such as you can use help sometimes, no?" he said in his whistling manner of speech.

"What is this for?" I asked.

"Your wife," Rhetter said. "For her lungs. Rub it on her chest and under her nose before she sleeps. The spirits in the salve work to help her breathe."

I opened the jar and sniffed the contents. Tears came to my eyes as a vapor, *the spirits*, from the salve wafted into my nostrils. The immediate effect was amazing;

even I, who was not at all ill, could breath clearer than I could moments before. "Thank you!" I said excitedly. Perhaps this would indeed help Irena.

I asked Fracix and two of his men to help secure the supplies before retiring. The sun was sinking and we would leave early the next morning. I embraced Rhetter in another gesture of thanks and excused myself to go back to the central fire where Paulonius was waiting for me.

"They are generous people, are they not?" he observed of Rhetter and his people.

"They are indeed. They are indeed!" I replied. I paused briefly, wondering at the lad. "Are you coming with us?"

"Of course," he replied, clearly surprised by the question.

"I mean, are you coming with us all the way to Antioch, which is to be our final destination?" I clarified.

"I know it is and well, yes."

"You knew about Antioch?" I asked, intrigued.

"Yes. I found Mary in Jerusalem. She told me of your plans to meet in Antioch. I thought you'd stay on or at least near the main road when you left the mists, so I was confident I'd find you even if you'd already left that place," he said.

"Mary and Thomas are well, then?" I asked, not meaning to change subjects, but still interested in my other friends.

"Uh, Mary, yes. I suppose Thomas, too, but he was in Egypt. Mary was with a man named Joseph. He seemed kind enough. Quiet sort, though. He owned the tomb in which Jesu had been laid to rest, you know. Joseph of Arimathea, that's it," Paulonius said.

Interesting turn of events, I thought to myself.

"Anyway," Paulonius continued, clearly becoming excited at what he was about to tell me, "before starting on my journey to find you, I took the liberty of securing passage for us all from the Port city of Nicxa. It's just over the border into Italia from Gaul," Paulonius explained. "It's not a straight trip, mind you. There'll be several stops at ports of call along the way. But I think you'll be pleased with the accommodations, providing it all goes as planned."

I was quite surprised and pleased by the lad's initiative. "What...how—"

"You'll see," he said, putting up a hand to silence me, clearly quite pleased with himself.

I trusted Paulonius implicitly and looked forward to seeing what he had procured for us. Another thought occurred to me then. "What of Genevieves and your child?" I asked. "Last I saw you two, she was expecting."

"Twins, we had! Can you believe it?" he said. "Two girls. They're just like their mum. Bossy little things! It's all I can do to get words in on the edge!" he said, laughing with affection. "They, and my two brothers, will meet us in Antioch—if that's all right with you," he added tentatively.

"Of course it's all right! Congratulations!" I said, embracing him. "Irena will be thrilled."

"Thank you," he said timidly, shying from the acclaim.

"All right then," I said. Let's get some rest. I'll see you at first light.

"Yes, sir," he said, giving me a playful legionnaire salute.

The whole of the little village came out to see us off at first light. A couple of the children, one of whom was the filth-encrusted little girl who had first announced our coming, chased our traveling party with delight for nearly a quarter of a mile or so. She finally stopped when her mother called for her. The little one stood and waved to us until we had gone too far and could see her no more.

We headed south, following a trail that somewhat paralleled the main road we had been on.

Paulonius led the way. I was still very interested in how he had secured passage for us and on what kind of vessel, but he remained tightlipped about it until, as he put it, "all things were confirmed," just in case the captain of the vessel was unable to make it after all. "That's very unlikely, though," he added.

The day progressed uneventfully. Irena seemed much better from the use of the salve. She was hardly coughing at all. Still there, however, was the ever present rattling in her chest. I was truly beginning to fear that it actually was more than just a chill. It just seemed to linger. She remained strong, though, even if she tired easily. She had been gracious enough when I presented the salve to her the previous night, if not a bit dubious about it. But, in the end, she tried it and it gave her some relief almost instantly.

The surrounding area was, for the most part, quite lush and green. Patches of dried foliage and leaves were only here and there. There was a slight bite of cold to the air, but nothing intolerable. According to Paulonius, it was actually late fall. Winter would be upon us before long. But, he assured us, we would be at the port city of Nicxa well before the onset of winter; in just a matter of a couple of weeks or less.

Late in the afternoon, I sidled up to Paulonius. "We need to stop soon for the night. Fracix spotted a secluded glen about three miles from here that will do."

"Yes, good. I think we've made good progress for the day," he said.

"Indeed." A silence fell between us for a few moments; the horses' hooves and the chirping of birds were the only sounds to be heard. "So," I finally said, "what of Mary and this Joseph fellow? How did you meet up with them? And Thomas is in Egypt you say?" I asked.

"Well," began Paulonius, "Genevieves and I just kept traveling. Oh, we stopped for a bit when her birthing time came, but not for long, even with twins. We originally had planned to stop and make a home somewhere near her village, near Dosameenor's clan-hold. But I wanted to keep going. Something in me, as it turned out, just wanted to see where you had first met...*him*; you know...Jesu," he said a bit timidly.

"No reason to be shy about it, lad. None at all," I said.

"Anyway," he continued, "We ended up there and heard about a woman speaking in public, talking about the teachings of Jesu. We went to hear for ourselves and lo and behold, it was Mary. Joseph was with her then. Still not sure how they met. She was quite pleased to see me and asked after you and the lady and the little one, of course. She said Thomas was in Egypt establishing a community of his Gnostic types. They were going to join him at a later time. She even talked of going with him, Joseph, I mean, back into Gaul at some point in the not too distant future, maybe even to a large island in the west called Briton or Britain or something."

My heart suddenly thumped in my chest. I felt the world around me close into darkness. A vision came upon me: one of a brilliantly green land surrounded by the sea. It was a place that abounded in beauty: a place that had within it a large lake that contained a small island that was always shrouded in mystical mists. It was a place with giant stones standing in circles that were once places of worship, but now stood as ancient sentinels to a long-forgotten race of peoples whose descendants presently inhabited the marshes and nearby hills of the land, rather than the entire island.

I saw the land as from the air; as if I were a bird. As if I were a powerful Merlin who had taken on the form of my namesake and was flying over the land, and I knew unequivocally that my descendants, too, would thrive in this land. I even saw Irena there and Jacobi Arturius as a grown man and...

"Longinus," called the voice from far away. "Sir!" It was Paulonius' voice.

I came back to myself, still mounted atop Macha, but slumped over in the saddle. Our whole party had halted. The vision had been strong, so real. I ached all over, as if I had actually been flapping my arms, my wings, on the journey over the island in the vision. "Yes," I said.

"Longinus, are you all right?" This was Irena. She had apparently jumped from the wagon the moment she saw the trance state assert itself on me. She turned to Paulonius. "What did you say to him?"

"I was speaking of Mary and Joseph and Thomas and—"

"And the island of Britain," I said, interrupting Paulonius.

I knew the moment I said the words *Island of Britain* that it had been a vision of truth; my immediate descendants would indeed thrive in that place, would become native Britons. But I would never live to see the land. At least, not in this life. That thought saddened me, yet excited me, too, for it made the future clearer.

"Longinus?" Irena repeated.

"I'm fine, my love. I'm fine." I answered.

"You're sure?" asked Paulonius. "I did not mean to—"

"Stop right there, my friend. These things come upon me as they will," I said. "No need to worry. Now, let's proceed before we lose daylight altogether."

"Let's go then," Irena said, coughing slightly.

The company began to move down the trail once again.

XXVII

I was floating, floating above the Isle of Mists in the lake, the lake that was in the middle of the strange land, the large Isle of Britain, it was. Ruins of standing stones dotted the landscape of the small isle as well as its mother, the larger one.

The image changed. I was part of a large circle of white-robed figures. We were a smaller circle inside the circle of ruined stones. A ritual to welcome the full moon is what we were doing.

That image faded and was replaced by another one; another ritual, another night. Many robed figures were in a circle, just as before. This ritual was different, though, an important event: the conjuring of the unifier of Britain. A priest and priestess were naked, performing the essence of the rite atop the center stone altar. All were chanting, including the two on the center altar.

I was there—not just in the vision, but in physical form as one of the participants. Longinus was not who I was here in this place. I was who I would be in that life. This was a distant future. I knew this to be so. The naked priest upon the altar was me.

That image faded, too, replaced this time by a horrific scene in the present, but still yet to come; the not so distant future of this life. Roman soldiers. They were crucifying someone, but I could not see who. The prisoner was being crucified upside down.

Smoke filled the image. I struggled to see more, but could not.

I began to shake. Or rather, someone began to shake me. "Longinus?" Irena said, coughing. "Wake up! Wake up!"

I left the realm of dreams and visions and returned fully to the present moment, opening my eyes to see her beautiful face hovering above me, filled with concern.

"I'm here, my love," I said.

"You were dreaming. What did you see?" she asked.

"The Island realm," I answered, still in the fog of sleep and dreams.

"You were...chanting, too. In a foreign tongue," she added.

"Hmm," was all I could manage to say.

"Well come, then. We need to be up. Light is already breaking in the camp," she said.

Indeed, outside of our tent, I could see light and hear others already up and about.

Suddenly, something hit me in the ribs. I looked and saw a little foot pushing against my side. Jacobi Arturius lay between us, stretching to give rise to the new day.

I sat up then bent down and kissed the boy's cheeks then looked at Irena. "How do you feel today?" I asked.

"Well," she replied. "The salve is quite good."

"Take a deep breath," I said.

"What?"

"Please. Take a deep breath."

She sighed, a bit annoyed, but did as I asked. The rattling wasn't quite as prominent, but it was still there. Or, *perhaps she has found a way to mask it,* I thought, smiling to myself. *That would be typical of her.*

"Thank you. All right, then," I said letting go of the matter. I got off of the sleeping pallet and froze. Something...something...a wave of foreboding washed over my entire being.

Irena was watching me. "Longinus?"

I said nothing; could not even move. There was no vision, nothing other than a...feeling; as if a squashing weight had just been placed on me.

Do not worry, Longinus, said the voice in my head, His voice. *All will be as it should.*

"My love, you're frightening me," said Irena, now standing before me, touching my arm.

Slowly, the feeling left me. I looked at her and smiled. "It's fine. I'm fine. Just an odd feeling, but it's gone," I said.

"What kind of odd feeling?" she pressed.

"Worry not. All will be as it should," I said, echoing the voice within.

She gave me that look of annoyance once again, but let the matter rest.

"Shall we join the others?" I asked.

"Hah, nah, gah," giggled Jacobi Arturius as he played with his toes.

"You go ahead," Irena said. "I'll get the little prince presentable."

Something in her phrasing caught me off guard, creating in my mind an image of a future King in a future land that I, Longinus, was related to. "What did you say?" I asked.

"What?" she replied, not having heard my question over the lad's laughter.

The image in my mind was quick and fleeting. "Never mind," I said. "I'll go help the others get ready." I left the tent wondering about the meanings of the images and visions I'd had that morning.

The day proved to be as beautiful as the preceding one. Nicxa was not far, not as far as Paulonius had thought. It was perhaps only a week away at most, at least according to the two old women we met on the trail. They took to bickering between themselves when they could not agree on the exact distance. They were sisters as it turned out and the elder of the two said that it was six days hence; the younger, seven.

We thanked them for the information, though I'm sure they did not hear, for as we moved off, they were behind us in the middle of the trail, facing each other, hands on hips, each yelling to convince the other that she was right.

All we could do was bless them, laugh and go on.

Later in the day, I was riding alongside of Paulonius and Fracix. Fracix was commenting on where we should stop for the night.

But his voice began to fade in my mind. It quickly became as a distant ring in my ear. Something else was attracting my attention; something from a source outside the realm of the physical.

The feeling of foreboding crept into my being again, but this time, there was a specific reason for it; we were being watched. There was no one in the bushes, no one in or behind the trees, of that I was sure. It was not that kind of reconnoitering work.

This was the work of one who understood the laws governing remote viewing: a *magician*, a *sorcerer*, as the layman would say. In other words, someone was looking into dark waters or a flame to view us from a distance.

An interesting side effect of that type of magic, or so I had been told by Detrom at one point, was that more often than not, it took a part of the viewer with it; part of his or her energy. You often could *feel* the personality of the one performing the remote viewing.

In this case, I knew exactly who was watching us. "Draco," I whispered as I stopped Macha.

The others stopped with me.

"What did you say?" asked Fracix.

"Where is he?" asked Paulonius nervously, drawing his sword as he spun his mount in survey of the area.

"He is not here, Paulonius. Not in the flesh, anyway." I explained. "Yet he watches us all the same," I said, again trying to feel Draco's presence.

Neither of the men questioned my assertion. They simply took it as truth.

"Don't worry, even if he watches us from afar, he does not know our plans," I continued after a moment, as much to convince myself as to assure Fracix and Paulonius. I let the matter drop for now, focusing my attention back to our immediate needs. "Speak naught of this to the others. We'll be on the boat soon enough and out of here altogether. Agreed?"

"Yes," said Paulonius.

Fracix, however, remained silent. For the first time, I sensed that there was something simmering in this one, a rage that was just below the surface, but mostly kept in check, except when I mentioned the name *Draco.*

"Fracix?" I said. "What say you?"

"Of course, I won't say anything," he replied.

"Is there anything you want to say to me?" I asked.

He hesitated, then said, "I will kill Draco if I can," he confessed.

This actually explained a lot. I had started to wonder why this man had *really wanted* to come with me. It's true that he had said he did not have anything or anyone to go back to, and I had taken him at his word. But now I could see that wasn't the only reason.

"You stayed with me believing that Draco would probably continue to chase me. That way, you'd eventually have a chance at him, is that it?" I asked, accusation dripping from my words.

"No, sir! I mean...that was not my intention in staying with you. Please, you must believe me," Fracix pleaded.

I said nothing for a moment, letting him ponder my silence. But then I softened. I liked Fracix, truly I did. "Perhaps you don't really know your mind. But then, who among us does?" I asked rhetorically.

"Yes, sir," he said, bowing his head in shame.

"It doesn't matter. I'm glad to have you here, regardless of the reason," I said, smiling. "And I've told you before, don't call me sir." With that, I nudged Macha back into motion and we headed down the trail once again.

That night, I slept peacefully and the following night, as well. In fact, the next few days were uneventful as we traveled down the trail. We ran into several people, locals of the surrounding area, as well as others traveling on the trail, but never got wind of any Roman patrols, even though either Fracix or one of the other men was constantly scouting the way ahead.

Even so, I could not shake the feeling of being watched. Draco's presence I felt, but another's too—a Mage of some kind, one of Rome's pretentious Priests of Apollo or the like. They were working together to find me, the spear, and the Rood.

No matter. I did not sense they were anywhere near us. Surely, we would make the port and be away before they could catch us.

We started on our way on yet another bright, crisp, clear day. Fracix and one of his men went on ahead to scout, as was the usual routine. They had not been gone long when we smelled something in the air: the ocean. Excited murmurs ran through the group as it was now apparent that this phase of our journey would end soon. As if to confirm this, two gulls circled above us, chirruping to one another.

"I should ride on ahead, make sure the ship's there. We're earlier than I thought we'd be, you know," said Paulonius as he came up alongside me, his mount dancing beneath him. Macha snorted in annoyance at the other horse's exuberance.

"Well, if you think it's necessary," I said.

"I think it's a good idea. Hopefully, it's already there. If so, I can encourage the captain to ready sail. The sooner we leave this land, the better," he added.

"All right, then. Be off," I said, as he kneed his mount to a near gallop.

"Wait!" I called.

He stopped and spun around.

"How will we find you? Where shall we meet?"

"Of course, sorry! Ask for me at the Porpoise Inn. It's a few streets in from the docks. You'll come to it first before you see the boats," explained the lad.

"See you there, then," I said.

With that, Paulonius was gone.

A short while later, Fracix and his man came back. They had gone as far as the top of a grassy green hill on the outskirts of Nicxa, which overlooked the port city and the bay. Fracix was confident that we would make our destination by late afternoon. We did not stop for the midday meal, but ate on the trail.

As Fracix had predicted, when the sun was nearly touching the earth towards day's end, we crested and descended the grassy green hill and headed into the city by the water.

It was easy enough to find the Porpoise Inn: a large building made of brick and wood. It had the look of a well-made, Roman-engineered structure. The sign hanging in front had a huge dolphin or porpoise painted on it. We passed several Roman patrols scurrying here and there on the way to the inn.

I had dismounted upon entering the city and walked in with the rest of our party on foot. I pulled my cloak up around my head, but that was probably unnecessary, for not one person, legionnaire or otherwise, paid us any mind. Everyone we passed seemed oblivious to all else except for their own mission of the moment.

The city was crowded, smelling of humanity and the sea, but it was exhilarating. The closer we got to the inn, the more anxious I was to be away on the boat. The next step to that was asking after Paulonius at the inn. I told the others to wait outside the Porpoise Inn while Fracix and I went inside. I thought about bringing the spear in with me, but decided that fewer arms were better. So it remained secured in its place on Macha's side.

The inside of the Porpoise Inn was a contrast from its outward appearance. Outside, the structure looked strong, even dignified, promising an ample bill of fare and comfort within. But it seemed a questionable promise. The main room was dimly lit and smoky from cooking fires. Various sorted types—dirty, nearly rag-clothed sailors, filled the nooks and crannies of the place; denizens of the sea, aliens of the land. Women served those denizens with the vivaciousness akin to the *professionals* which they probably were. Surprisingly, there were also a couple of tables filled with legionnaires, drinking loudly and playing equally as hard with the serving wenches as the denizens were.

The Centurion in me wanted to walk over to their tables and box their ears, demanding to know who their superior officers were. Of course, I was not about to do that. Instead, Fracix and I stealthily made our way to the right of the room, to what appeared to be a counter for guests to inquire for accommodations.

The robust woman behind the counter grinned toothlessly as we approached. "How may I help you?" she asked in Latin, with surprising articulation. It caught me off guard. For the most part, I had been speaking in the Celtic tongue for a few years now. I simply assumed someone in her station would not know Latin very well, if at all.

"We seek a friend," I said.

"Don't we all," she replied coyly, batting her eyes at Fracix.

"Uh, yes, well this friend's name is Paulonius," I said.

"Here now, woman. The legionnaires at table four need another round. Go," said a tall man, wearing a mead and beer splattered apron. He swatted the woman's ample rump. She sighed, obviously disappointed, but left.

The man seemed of sixty-some-odd summers, but still had a commanding presence. "Whom do you seek?" he asked in northland Celt, Dosameenor's dialect.

"Who are you?" Fracix asked, a little too gruffly and unnecessarily. If the man answered, courtesy dictated that we identify ourselves, as well. If it came to that, obviously, I would have to lie.

"The owner and proprietor here, Jamsonis," the man said with a smile. "Don't be fooled by the raucousness here right now. Three ships just came in, you understand. I keep a good place with very clean and nicely appointed rooms, providing of course, you have the means."

We had little to trade and even less money. I would have to sell Macha. Indeed, all our horses would have to be sold before the voyage.

"We have the means. But before we discuss that, let's see if there is even a need," I said. "We're looking for a lad named Paulonius."

Jamsonis' eyes lit up. "Ahh," he said. "Yes. He gave me instructions to have you wait here in a couple of our rooms. Your ship is readying herself for passage. You are to leave on the high tide at midmorning on the morrow," he said. "Your man Paulonius will meet you here later this evening."

"I see," I said, pleased, but rather surprised he knew so much.

"I know Paulonius. He grew up very near my home, you understand," Jamsonis offered.

"I did not know that," I said. "Listen, my friend, we cannot pay you for the rooms until tomorrow. We have fine animals but need to sell them before we leave."

"I can help with that. Are they horses, oxen?"

"Horses."

"Good animals?"

"Yes, especially one that I'm loath to part with," I said.

"I understand. I can get you the most *denarii*. I deal exclusively with the Roman Garrison here, you understand. I'll even be your middle man—show the beasts to the garrison commander myself," he said.

Something in his tone gave me indication that he knew I wanted anonymity. I was not sure how much Paulonius had told his childhood acquaintance, but something told me that he could be trusted. "That would be good," I said. "Perhaps first thing in the morning?"

"I don't know that the commander is available then. Perhaps tonight? Later, of course, after you've spoken to Paulonius," Jamsonis offered.

"Tonight? He would do business at night?" I asked.

"He prefers it, actually."

"Very well," I said.

"I'll show you the rooms myself," said Jamsonis.

I sent Fracix to fetch the others while I followed the proprietor.

We all fit into two fairly large rooms that connected through a large door. The rooms were *scrumptious*, according to Leona, complete with easy access to the baths in the building next. After visiting the baths myself, I snuggled in for a nap with Irena and Jacobi Arturius. Leona and Jenus shared our room; everyone else was in the other. Two of the men were outside the doors at all times, keeping watch in shifts.

I was awakened around midnight by the sound of coughing; Irena was having a rough night.

"I'm sorry, my love," she said. "I fear I keep everyone awake."

"Don't worry," I soothed. "The salve no longer works?"

"Sometimes better than others," she answered.

I kissed her then, a simple, loving peck on the lips. Something wiggled against my side; Jacobi Arturius rolled over in his peaceful sleep, oblivious to the cares of the rest of the world.

"He's beautiful, is he not?" Irena asked in a rattling whisper.

"As beautiful as his mother," I replied.

"I was thinking more like his father," she said. She coughed again, though gently, quietly.

"That chill should have left you by now," I said.

She started to protest, but stopped when I threw up my hand.

"Before we leave tomorrow, we are going to seek out a doctor. I'm sure there's one around here," I asserted. I would not be silenced this time about the matter.

She opened her mouth to speak, but was halted by a knock at the door.

Leona answered it. "'Tis master Paulonius," she said.

"Come in," I said, getting up off the bed.

Paulonius entered with Jamsonis right behind. "Are you comfortable?" asked Paulonius.

"Quite," I replied. "Good to see you."

"And you," replied Paulonius. "All is ready. We leave top of the eleventh hour in the morning." He turned to the proprietor.

"And here is the money for your horses," Jamsonis said, stepping forward and holding out two bags of coin.

It appeared to be much more than I expected. "Thank you. This is...generous."

"My pleasure. The garrison commander fell in love with yours, you understand—your Macha. I saw it in his eyes. So, I held out for a good price, a very good price," he said with a chuckle.

I would miss Macha. I had said my goodbyes earlier when first I showed her and the others to Jamsonis. I only prayed that she went to a good home.

"Ah, I know that look, my friend," Jamsonis said, staring straight at me. "Fear not, the commander is a good man. Macha will be loved and pampered."

I believed him. "Thank you for that also." *I shall have to tip this man well when we leave,* I thought. Indeed, Fracix's men too. I now had enough coins for it.

"There is something else," I said, after a moment. "A doctor. For my wife's cough."

"Well, Chefren the physician travels with us tomorrow. He's on his way home," Paulonius put in. "He's renown in Greece and Egypt and much of Rome. Do you wish to see him now, my lady?" he asked of Irena.

"No, no. Do not disturb him at this hour. I will see him tomorrow," she answered, looking at me, playfully challenging me to protest.

"The morrow is fine," I said to Paulonius, but looking at Irena. "Tomorrow is fine."

Tomorrow came quickly. Now that the day was here, I was more anxious than ever to be away. Our things, such as they were, had been stowed aboard the vessel early, before dawn. I only carried a shoulder skin of water, a sleeping Jacobi Arturius and the spear, wrapped in a sheathing of cloth. Irena walked at my side, hand on my arm, the other women and men just behind us. We were all following an excited Paulonius down to the docks.

"You'll see. The ship is as strong as...well, you'll see. And the rooms you have aboard are very comfortable," said Paulonius.

I was not paying attention to the lad. The feeling of foreboding was back; of being watched. This time, however, it did not feel as though the viewers were all that far away.

I looked around. Roman soldiers were here and there in clumps. Some would look at us as we passed; others would simply glance, then look away, at other citizens making their way about. None of them seemed to be paying undue heed to our group.

"Did you hear me?" Paulonius inquired.

"Uh-huh," I said absently, still scanning the crowds for...what I was not sure.

Then I saw it; a darkly-cloaked figure some twenty or so yards away, darting in and out of the people, all the while keeping pace with us. He—I assumed it to be a man for the figure's size—disappeared behind a large vending cart. When he did not reappear on the other side of it, I handed Jacobi Arturius to Irena. "I'll catch up to you in a moment," I said.

"Where are you going?" she asked.

"I just need to check on something." With that, I hurried off.

I quickly walked over to the cart and stepped behind it. The cloaked figure was nowhere to be seen. It was as if he had vanished into thin air. My first thought was of Draco. Perhaps he was not as far away as I had *felt* him to be during the remote viewings I sensed that he was conducting. Or, perhaps the cloaked figure I'd just seen was his apparition; his projected self. I thought this latter point hardly probable. I spent another minute or two looking over the immediate area. He was not there. It was time to leave.

I quickly caught up to the others.

"What was that for?" Irena asked, concern etched on her brow.

"I thought I saw something, someone," I replied honestly.

"Shall I take a couple of the men and go back and look again?" Fracix offered, having run up to meet me at my return.

"No, no. 'Tis not necessary," I replied. "I don't believe there to be any danger." I smiled, changing the subject. "Besides," I continued. "I have released you and your men. You are free to go home!"

It was true. I had given them all coin. It was a small gesture of my appreciation for their service.

"You are not yet away on the boat," Fracix explained. "They are your men until that time."

"All right then, but all's well," I asserted, while at the same time looking back to where we had just come from, attempting to catch again a glimpse of the cloaked figure. Still, he was not there.

We arrived at the docks. I said thank you and farewell to Fracix's men. Fracix, himself, was still determined to accompany us to Antioch and I made it clear that he was welcome.

Several large vessels appeared ready for the sea; ready to depart at or near the same time as us. Roman patrols were walking the docks, but not harassing anyone; simply observing. Many smaller boats, fishing boats and the like, appeared to be readying themselves for a day on the water, as well.

"Come," said Paulonius, "do you not recognize her yet?"

I was not sure of what the lad was talking about. But then I saw it: the Boar banner flying on the mast of the ship we were about to board. Standing at the plank, a one-man welcoming party, her Captain; Ventrix.

"'Ello, my friends!" exclaimed Ventrix, when he caught sight of us.

"Hello," I said as we boarded. I embraced him as a brother. "Captain Ventrix! What a surprise. I am so pleased to see you!" And I truly was. He had been marvelous to me and Jacobi and Dosameenor, and to Irena as well, as it turned out. He had been nothing but a very caring, good friend to her back in Najaffi.

"My lady Irena," he said with a respectful bow when he saw her.

"Stop it, Ventrix. We've known each other too long for such formalities. How are you, my friend?" she said, kissing the old salty dog on each cheek.

"I am well. I am well," he said. "But come. It is time. We must be underway. Me first mate will show you to your rooms below, or actually, why don't ye do it, Paulonius, my boy?"

"I'd love to," Paulonius said. "Follow me."

"We will meet for midday meal in two hours, yes? Much to talk about!" said Ventrix.

"Indeed. I look forward to it," I said, and followed Paulonius below deck.

The rooms were spacious, considering we were aboard ship. Irena and I and Jacobi Arturius shared one room. Leona, Jenus and Fracix shared another. Although, throughout the voyage, Fracix actually ended up sleeping most often on the deck with the ship's crew. Once we had settled in, there was a knock at the door. I opened it and there stood a dark-skinned short man clothed in a white silk tunic. His head was shaved as was his face, lending him to look more like an Egyptian priest than anything else. The bag he carried, however, was not that of a priest.

"I am Chefren, the Physician," he said with kind eyes. "I understand your wife is not well?"

"Uh, yes. Please come in," I said, standing aside for him to enter. "Irena, this is Chefren," I told her.

"Thank you so much for coming. I hope it is not too much trouble?" Irena inquired.

"No, no not at all," said the physician. "Shall we begin?"

To start with, he listened to her breathing, using a conical device. The small end went in his ear; the larger end against Irena's upper chest, all the while having her take deep, rattling breaths. He then listened from her back.

After a couple of other procedures, he asked her to hack and cough purposely, to draw up mucus from deep within the lungs, instructing her to then spit the slimy substance into a small glass bowl. He visually examined the stuff, smelled it, too, and even dipped his fingers into it to feel its properties.

Next, he requested a urine sample. Irena squatted while we turned our backs, and piddled into a glass cup. She stood and offered the physician the sample. Chefren eyed the liquid carefully, smelled it, and even tasted it.

"Well, my lady, you do not have the lung disease; yet," Chefren concluded.

"What does that mean?" I asked, bristling at the vagueness of his statement.

"She has a high-grade chest chill, it's true, but the liquid within her lungs is pooling, not flushing itself out. I have seen cases where this has led or been the precursor of the lung disease," he answered.

"Will it happen to me?" Irena asked, alarmed.

"Not likely. I said it the way I did to frighten you."

I was confused and a little angry. What game was this doctor playing?

"Please, forgive my bluntness," he said, "but you have not been taking care of yourself, have you?" It was more a statement of fact from the man, than a question.

Irena looked at me sheepishly. I simply smiled. I liked this doctor's way, after all. Maybe she would listen to *him*.

"Well..." she began.

"No, she hasn't," I volunteered. "We've been traveling, 'tis true, but—"

"Longinus—" she began to protest.

"It's fine," said Chefren. "The past is done. It does not matter now. Here," he said, holding out a small pouch to Irena. "It's an herb to mix with tea. Use a pinch in the morning, one in the afternoon and one before bed. It will help you rest and rid you of the chill before it *does* become something more. Besides, you will need your rest now more than ever. In fact," he said looking off, now clearly speaking to himself, "that obviously, at least in part, explains why the chill's held onto you so long."

"I don't understand," I said.

"Why, my dear friends," the doctor said, sounding surprised. "You are going to have another child. Truly, you didn't know?"

I looked to Irena.

"My cycle is late, to be sure, but I thought it due to the illness," she explained, wonder and excitement tingeing her voice.

"No. You are with child," Chefren said again.

Silence filled the room for a moment. "Well!" I finally said, laughing.

I crossed the floor and hugged Irena, picking her up off the ground.

"Careful," the doctor chided playfully. "I will take my leave of you, now. We depart in moments and I always like to be on deck when we set off."

I turned to the man. "Thank you, doctor. Thank you so much."

"Yes, thank you," Irena said. "Longinus, why don't you go with him?"

"Uh, I suppose I could. Are you trying to get rid of me?" I teased.

"Yes. Let me make the room presentable," she replied.

"All right, then. After you, doctor," I said, motioning to the door.

Up on deck, Paulonius was helping Ventrix with his duties.

I stopped them both briefly and told them that I was going to be a father twice over. They both laughed aloud in happiness.

"Excellent, my friend!" exclaimed Ventrix.

I let them go about their business as Chefren and I stood at the stern, watching the people on the docks as we pulled away.

A crowd milled about near the slip from which we had just launched. A shadowy figure weaved in and out of the people, coming to a halt near the water. It was the cloaked figure I had seen earlier.

He appeared to be staring right at me, but I could not tell for sure; the cloak's hood was covering his head. Slowly, he removed the hood and I stared straight into his eyes; the eyes of the Dark Druid Draco.

Sailing was smooth. We had several stops to make for cargo and passengers along the way. The first was a quick stop not too far from our initial point of departure on the island of Corsica. Ventrix had a shipment of spices and herbs to pick up. We made the pick-up and were away again before long. The stop had been completely uneventful.

I told Ventrix and Paulonius about my sighting of Draco. There was no accounting for his being there other than simply following us on the land and by way of remote viewing. He had appeared to be alone on the dock, but that was far from certain. It would also be easy enough to find out where the ship flying the Boar was destined and follow her. "Be not concerned, my friend. You are safe here, and we are not followed. I've had my men in the nest since we left," offered Ventrix as we sat at his table the next evening eating.

Even so, my mind was not eased.

"You have powerful magic now, yes? Or so I heard," he said, changing the subject.

I looked at Paulonius.

"You've been gone awhile. As you know, more than few have begun to mythologize you," Paulonius explained.

"Some say you speak to Jesu—you do God's work in *his* name and you preach *his* teachings," added Ventrix. "Is it true?"

I thought for a moment about how I should answer this. "I speak to Him, in a way. I believe He exists in all of us. As for doing God's work, I suppose you could say that too, in a way. I use the natural laws of the universe to achieve results that could not be achieved otherwise. If you believe this is God's work, then so be it," I said. "I do not preach Jesu's teachings. I don't even know most of His teachings. In fact, I don't teach or preach anything."

Ventrix looked confused, and disappointed, as well.

"Sorry. I don't wish to perpetuate a false belief," I said.

"It may not matter," Paulonius put in. "Folks are going to believe what they will, no matter what you say. And I'm sure Draco and his cronies are aiding in the spreading of rumors about you, too. Rome will think you could be a threat down the road. It'll make them want to catch you, all the more."

"Hah! That won't happen," Ventrix chimed in.

We fell silent for a while.

"How is lady Irena?" Ventrix asked.

"Fine, fine. Resting," I replied.

"Good. Good," said Ventrix. "We were good friends for a long time, you know. I mean, *just* friends, mind you, not—"

"I know, Ventrix," I said, laughing. "She's told me all."

We finished our meal talking of things of the world. By the time I retired, Irena and Jacobi Arturius were fast asleep.

XXVIII

Our final stop before continuing the last leg of the sea trip, which was also the longest, was at Sicilia. A Roman officer, a Prefect no less, came aboard with several legionnaires, commandeering passage to Antioch. It was unusual, but certainly not unheard of. Apparently, the only Roman military vessel in the area was dry-docked. Since the Boar was heading to Antioch anyway, the commandeering was inevitable. Unfortunately for Ventrix, it meant relinquishing his cabin to the Prefect. None of us aboard the ship were comfortable with the Roman military with us, but there was nothing to be done about it.

The legionnaires and their Commander kept to themselves; too much so, I thought. They seemed to be going out of their way to avoid contact with us, or perhaps were under specific instructions not to interact with us at all. That in and of itself would have been fine, except for the fact that on several occasions over the next few days of the journey, I saw more than one of them in a huddled whispered meeting. During this time, they would sneak peeks at me or Irena when she was out of our room, averting their gaze quickly if they thought I or someone else would catch them watching. It was very strange.

At first, I thought I might simply be imagining things, making something out of nothing. But the spear was beginning to say otherwise. It was constantly aglow. On the one occasion I took it up on deck, it began to shake violently. I immediately took it back to our room and wrapped it up tight.

Then one night, Paulonius approached me when I was at the bow. It was late. I normally would have been with Irena, but something compelled me to the deck. He was scared, I could see it in his eyes, feeling the distress seeping from his pores.

"What news?" I asked, keeping my voice even.

He looked around to make sure we were not being watched or listened to. "The Prefect summoned Master Ventrix to dine with him," he said in a whisper.

"Not unusual. Ventrix is the owner and captain of the vessel," I pointed out.

Paulonius ignored the point. "The conversation revolved around you. Or at least, the Prefect tried to make it so."

"Explain."

"He wanted to know who you are, who is traveling with you," said the lad.

"Again, that is within protocol, as well…" I began.

"He joked that perhaps you were the 'traitor Longinus,'" Paulonius blurted out, almost too loudly.

"Calm yourself," I said.

"I tell you, they came on board for you, these soldiers did," said Paulonius.

"You don't know that—"

"Then why, by the gods, would the Prefect make such a joke? Draco is looking for you. Rome is looking for you. They are all working together!" Paulonius said, exasperated.

"Stop it! You sound like a hysterical little girl," I reprimanded him.

He was right, though, and I knew it. I had sensed for some time that the net was closing around me. Two things warred within me: the soldier and the Druid—the man wanting to fight and the sage who knew that there was a much bigger vision unfolding here. *All will be as it should,* the voice had said. But what of Irena and my son and my unborn child? And what of the spear? I could not let Rome or Draco, especially, ever get to Irena and the spear.

"What did Ventrix tell him?" I asked.

"He said he didn't know you—that your passage was arranged by a contact in Gaul. That you are a merchant with family in Antioch," replied Paulonius.

"What name did he give for me?"

"He didn't. He pretended not to remember, claimed he never kept records of passengers because he hardly ever had them."

"What about Irena? What relationship did he give us?" I asked, anxiety lacing my voice.

"None. Said you were sharing the room for belongings but that the lady and her child slept there alone, you with the crew mates," said the lad.

"What if the Prefect asks the men?" I asked.

Paulonius smiled. "They know who you are—have heard about you and the spear, too. Every one of them was serving aboard when you were here before and remember you. They love you the way they loved the old man Jacobi and would do or say anything for you, or nothing at all if it meant protecting you."

I was shocked. "I had no idea."

"And that's the way it is supposed to be. It's what Ventrix instructed them to do; pretend like you're not here, draw no attention to you and yours whatsoever," he explained.

"And they can be trusted?" I asked.

"To the death. Remember, I know them, too."

The sound of the waves lapping against the prow filled my ears, the noise of the flapping sails their counterpoint.

I knew I must speak with Irena immediately. I had to tell her what was happening, or seemed to be happening. It would be necessary to separate for now for the safety of all, at least until we made landfall; at least until the Prefect and his men were gone. "Thank you, Paulonius. You would do best not to be seen with me anymore for a while. I must tell Irena."

"Please, Longinus, let *me*. Stay here. I'll come back in a few moments. I'll explain everything to her. Give them no reason to question lady Irena by perhaps seeing you go to her."

I thought about it for a moment. She was the love of my life. I could not, would not, send another to do this. "Thank you lad, but no. I will be quick, but I must do this. Wouldn't you in my place?"

I could see him thinking of Genevieves and the twins. "Yes, of course. But be swift."

I snuck below deck, casually but with stealth. I saw no one as I slipped into our room and sat on the bed. "Irena, my love," I said gently.

She awakened slowly. Irena was getting more and more beautiful every time I looked at her. "Come to bed, my love," she whispered sweetly.

It pained me. In that moment, I wanted nothing more than for us to be away, to have a spread of land, a home, a hearth. A place where I could watch my children grow, and I could grow old with my love. With sad discipline, I pushed the wonder-filled thought aside. "I cannot, my dearest. Are you awake enough to listen?" I asked with some urgency.

"What is it?" she questioned, alarm in her voice.

I explained to her all that Paulonius had told me. She did not like my idea of separating for the protection of her and Jacobi Arturius, but managed to come around to it after some convincing. "There's one more thing," I said. "You must keep the spear. It is wrapped and stowed behind a loose panel near the door," I said, nodding to our room's entrance. "Take it and keep it with you until we are safely off and away from the ship."

"You don't want it with you?" she asked.

"They will recognize it for what it is: a Roman issued Centurion's lance," I explained. "And by that, the Prefect will know who *I* am. Keep it with you."

"Of course. Oh Longinus," she said, fighting back tears.

"Stay strong, my love. This will all be over soon," I added, as much to convince myself as to reassure her.

We embraced. I stayed in her arms for awhile, savoring every second of her presence; every nuance of her smell. After a few moments, I kissed her passionately on the mouth, kissed my sleeping son on the head, and slipped out of the room.

Flying, I was, once again above the small misty isle in the lake of the larger island of Britain.

Jesu was with me on this flight, whispering into my soul. "All is as it should be, Longinus. There is no beginning, there is no end. Only changes in form, only changes in levels of being, of awareness, of growth."

Next, I saw that I was performing a ritual in the form of some future smaller self: a priest of the Druidic sect on that same misty isle. Jesu was there, too, standing next to me assisting in the ritual. He was not a physical form, though, but a vaporous presence. He was there briefly, then faded from sight.

"Land ahead! Land ahead!" came the voice from afar. "Land ahead!"

The priest that was myself in this future life, this future realm looked up as if he heard the call.

"Land ahead!!" came the voice again. My future self and life faded from view.

I awoke. Neck aching. I had slept yet again on the hard wood of the deck, starboard side, near several of the shipmates. They were all awake and looking at the posted lookout perched on the mast. "Land ahead!" yelled the lookout again.

"We make land, Merlin," whispered the man next to me.

"Please don't call me that," I said.

"Sorry, sir. Me apologeeze, Master," said the grizzled old fool. "I remember you."

I concluded that the old man was a few candles short in the head. I had spent the previous night next to him, as well, yet he acted as if he had just seen me for the first time, or at least for the first time in a long time.

"Shut up!" said one of the other mates, clocking the first one in the head. This one was muscled and young. "Shut up. You know what you were told."

"Sorry," the old man said again.

I looked across the deck. Some thirty feet way, on the port side, two of the legionnaires were sitting on the deck staring straight at me. Had they heard the exchange? At least the old man had not called me Longinus.

"Means we land in a couple of hours, don't you know," said the old man, referring to the sailor calling out the land sighting.

"Hmm," I said looking out to the horizon.

I kept to myself for the next hour, to keep low and make sure that I was the last one off the ship. My plan was interrupted, though, when a legionnaire approached me as I was making my way to the cargo hold. "The Commander wishes a word," said the soldier.

I knew that tone well. It was an order, not a request for my presence. Thus, it was pointless to resist.

"Lead the way," I said, meeting his eyes.

I was taken to Ventrix's room, the captain's cabin, and ushered in. The Prefect was seated at an oak wood table perusing papers and maps. "Leave us," he commanded to the legionnaire. The soldier exited, leaving the Prefect and me alone in the room.

I stood there silently for five minutes. Ten minutes. The Prefect never even glanced at me or acknowledged my presence in any way. The arrogance of the man was revolting.

Finally, I lost my patience. "Your man said you wished a word. Would you share that word before we make landfall?" I asked sardonically.

After yet another three minutes, he finally looked up and studied me for another minute or so. "No," he said flatly. He then smiled, malice dripping from his lips. He made a brushing motion with his hand, as if brushing dirt off the table—as if brushing me away. "You may go now," he said at the same time.

I felt myself growing angry. It was all I could do to keep myself contained. I backed out of the room slowly and returned to the deck, to the spot where I had been that morning.

"What did he want?" Paulonius asked from behind.

"To look me over. To see if it was Longinus who stood before him," I answered.

Paulonius stood with me for the remainder of the trip. We docked in Antioch at midmorning. The lad, who insisted on staying with me all the way to our *final destination*, as he put it, and I, remained until all the others had disembarked.

We stood near the main sail mast and watched as one by one, the passengers left. Irena sneaked a look at me, at which point Jacobi Arturius saw me too. The boy yelled something unintelligible, but something that I knew to be, "Da!" Irena turned the boy's face away and quickly left the boat.

Lastly, after all but the ship's crew left, the soldiers went. The Prefect looked back at me, once again smiling malevolently, as he walked off.

I waited for about thirty minutes. The soldiers disappeared into the crowds on dock. Ventrix was still aboard seeing to the unloading of cargo. Our eyes met. I mouthed the words *thank you*, and Paulonius gave a nod to the captain, his former master. It angered me further that I could not give the man a proper thank you and goodbye. But things being what they were, it was clearly best to feign unfamiliarity.

Together, the lad and I left the ship. We made our way through the crowd, working ourselves to the center of town. This port city was not unlike any other; similar smells and many people. The difference here, however, was that there seemed to be a large contingent of Roman soldiers; many more so than any other place we'd been recently. Certainly more than I was expecting.

Still, we proceeded unhindered. After a few minutes of walking through the people, I spotted Irena, holding Jacobi Arturius, up ahead in the distance, perhaps fifty yards away, Leona and Jenus right next to her; Fracix and two dock workers carting our belongings behind them.

They seemed to be heading toward a couple: an older man and…Mary! I assumed that the man was Joseph, the Joseph of Arimethea of which Paulonius had spoken.

I was about to call out to them when I was grabbed from behind. Strong hands seized my upper arms and spun me to face a platoon of Roman legionnaires led by the Prefect from aboard ship. Standing behind the platoon was the darkly cloaked figure, hood off, of Draco. *How did he get here? Dark, negative use of the Laws, no doubt,* were my first thoughts. Stupid, that. Of all the things to be concerned about in that moment…

"Centurion Longinus, traitor to Rome, preacher of the alleged Christ's doctrine against Rome, murderer of Roman Officers, Dark Sorcerer who seeks to destroy Rome…shall I go on?" yelled the Prefect as he stepped up to me eye-to-eye, spewing his words into my face and his spittle along with it. His mouth curved into that now familiar malicious grin.

This time I lost control. I hit him square in the face with my fist. I had always been told that I was unaware of my own strength. It must have been true, or else I had Otherworldly power coursing through my being in that moment, for the

Prefect's nose was more than splattered; it was no more at all. In fact, the whole front of his face had caved in from my blow, as if I had hit him with a fist of iron, or an anvil. The Prefect went down in muffled screams of agony, dieing within seconds.

Immediately, the soldiers drew their weapons and advanced.

"Hold!" came the command from their rear, freezing the legionnaires in their tracks.

It had not come from Draco, but from the one who stood next to him. I had not seen him before. He was dressed as an officer; not just any officer, but a General, judging by the scarlet cloak he wore.

And then there were the others. There were two behind the General, who were dressed in the traveling togs of Roman officers. But their cloaks were the purple of the Praetorian Guard.

"Centurion Longinus," began the General in a deep, authoritative voice honed by decades of commanding others. "You've heard the charges put to you. And you may now add murder of a Prefect to it..." he said, glancing down at the officer I had just killed, "...as well as murder of a Tribune. Am I right, Master Draco?" he asked offhandedly, as he looked at Draco and back to me. "Will you not come peacefully, or do we have to kill you here and now?"

"I did not kill the other officer, the Tribune. Your man Draco, here, did. But, what difference if I come peacefully or not? You will kill me anyway," I replied.

"Now, now. No need for such pessimism. You don't know that," he said, softening his tone. He looked at Draco. "Is that true? Did you kill the Tribune in the forest, then blame this poor fellow?" he asked, with utter sarcasm. He turned his attention back to me. "Ah, well, Longinus. Never mind that. You and I simply need to...talk."

I had not drawn my short sword, but was in a fighting stance. I looked to my left and saw for the first time that Paulonius was being held by three legionnaires, one of whom had him in a choke-hold. I relaxed and looked to the General, nodding my head.

"Splendid. Move out," he said and the soldiers escorted Paulonius and me away. I peered over my shoulder trying desperately to catch sight of Irena. I could not see her, but I felt her watching me. I felt them all watching me.

XXIX

I came awake in a dank cell somewhere below the city, alone. Paulonius was not with me. My head throbbed. A lone barred hole at the top of the wall near the ceiling, about a foot in diameter, was my only source of air from the world. The hole was at ground level outside and let in only enough light, or darkness as the case might be, to tell me that it was deep night.

How many days I had been there, I did not remember. I had not eaten in days—that much I did remember. Water had been scarce, I believe. A little rain had seeped in through the hole, I think. That had helped. I had been whipped and beaten severely and often; that much I knew. *Why?* I wondered. Oh yes, the spear.

I had a wife, too. I called her my wife. She was the only woman I had ever loved; the only one I ever would love. We had started a life together. Irena.

I had a son too, Jacobi Arturius, and another babe on the way. Life was good. Except for this place. I was stuck in this place. I could end this myself easily enough.

Gradually, I came to my senses, letting go of the delirious thoughts. The General wanted the spear. The Prefect I had killed had been under orders to make sure that I was indeed Longinus, and to covertly escort me to Antioch, where Rome would exact her revenge on me and take the spear. Draco had bartered some kind of deal with them, no doubt to get the spear for himself eventually. I remembered during one of the interrogations that Draco had claimed to be the only one other than I who knew how to wield its powers. He lied.

I had told my interrogators over and over that I had tossed the spear. It was no longer with me; that it was in Gaul.

"You lie!" had been the response from one of the interrogators. "You lived in a mist enshrouded village that you created through the lance's magic!"

"And the 'magic' stopped, which is why the mists left us and I left the spear," I had said.

Fools. I almost had them convinced.

I looked down at my wrapped hand, blood seeping through the bandages. Two of my fingers were now missing. A memento from the torturer, was that.

"Can you not grow another? You are the great Longinus. Perform a miracle for us, I command you!" my tormentors had teased.

In the end, they had received nothing from me; no information, no spear, no miracle. I suspected that even they were getting bored.

But had my powers, my abilities, abandoned me? Every time I had been thrown back into this cell, I had tried to conjure up a mist in which to escape in when next they came for me. I had also tried to control certain of the Otherworld elements to do my bidding; to aid me in masking an escape from this place. Nothing had worked. I could no longer even focus to go to that place within which Jacobi and Detrom and Jesu had taught me to access; that Higher place within that was my Truest Self. I had never felt so alone.

I was angry and numb. I cared for naught any longer.

Yet, that was not true. I cared about Irena, my son, my unborn child and all that I'd learned. And I cared that I would not be able to pass on the knowledge I had learned.

I wept. I slept. I dreamt.

Floating, I was, above myself in the dank cell. I looked down and saw my own huddled figure there on the floor, and realized I was not in my body. I was not dead, though. I could see the white cord attached to the body lying there and ascending up to the vaporous form that was me. It reminded me of the night of my initiation at Detrom's Temple mound.

"Strange, isn't it?" He said.

I turned my astral form and saw Jesu.

"We place so much attachment to the physical form, yet at its earthly end, it is nothing," Jesu said.

"I am not dead yet," I said.

"You might as well be. You are too attached to the form of things. You have forgotten much. But that happens when we're in the physical," He said.

"We love things, people. They become a part of us," I countered.

"Yes, but that attachment is only in the context of the physical realm. You've lost sight that existence is forever in one form or another. If you choose it, your loved ones will always be with you and you with them, not just here on the earth plane," He said.

I said nothing; just looked with sadness at my physical form down below.

"Be at peace, my friend," said Jesu.

"I just didn't want them to get the spear," I said.

"I know. It is a powerful conduit. But they won't retrieve it. It is already gone from this place," He said.

I didn't question him as to what he meant.

"Let go now. Release all attachments—to this life, to that body, all of it, and simply Trust. Non-attachment is the essence of peace and happiness. Achieve this, and cross over with ease," He said as he faded.

I awoke huddled on the floor of the cell. Had I only dreamt the floating with Jesu? No. Its reality was palpable. I could feel it still.

Sunlight was streaming in through the little hole. Seabirds were calling to one another outside. A beautiful day, it seemed. It did not matter what happened to me. I was at peace.

They were coming; I could hear the footfalls. Guards marched in unison down the hall that led to my cell. There were four of them. They stopped in front of my barred door.

"Good morning, gentlemen," I said cheerfully, even energetically, though I struggled through the pain to get up. They looked at each other, not sure if I were mad or if I was displaying a miraculous recovery.

"Afternoon, more like," said one of them, a Centurion. "But not good for you, I'm afraid."

"More interrogations?" I asked.

"No. Done with that, we are," he said.

"Master Draco won't like to hear that," I said.

"Humph," said one of the others in contempt. "That one's gone, left this morning. Disagreed with the General, he did."

"Over what?" I asked, already knowing the answer.

"Enough outta you!" the Centurion said, slapping me in the face.

"Chain 'is legs, then bring 'im up and tie the wood to his arms and shoulders. You know the drill," the soldier said to his companions.

The sun was indeed bright. The day was hot. It was also beautiful. The colors on the trees and flowers were vibrant as I had never before seen or noticed. The smells were more luxurious than I remembered smells ever being. The twilling of the birds were all meant for me; for me to truly understand the beauty and diversity of the Creator and the Created.

The wood they tied across my shoulders—the cross piece to my crucifix—was heavy, blood-stained and splintered. I felt it dig into my skin as the ropes were tied to my wrists; felt my own blood begin to trickle down my back, my arms, and add to the wood's collection of stains.

"Move!" the Centurion called. We began a slow march to a hill some four hundred yards away. I knew it was our destination, for several other crucifixes dotted the landscape at the top of the hill. As we moved along, we passed a table in the shade of a tree at which several officers were seated, taking afternoon drinks. One of them was the General.

Though I was hunched over from my burden, I could still make eye contact with him. It was unavoidable.

"Halt!" he ordered.

We complied, the Centurion poking me in the ribs to hold me upright. I all but fell over backwards, straining painfully and terribly to keep from doing so.

"Centurion Longinus," said the General, as he and the other officers got up and walked the short distance to us.

"Yes, sir," I replied.

"You seem chipper for a man about to be crucified," he stated.

"It matters not what you do to me," I said.

"You are not afraid to die?" he asked.

"No reason to fear. 'Twill not be the end," I said.

"Maybe his spear will magically appear and save him," said one of the other officers, inciting a round of laughter from the others.

Even the General laughed. "The spear matters not. Our idiotic priests claimed it to be powerful, as did that stupid sorcerer. What was his name?"

"Draco," said the other officer.

"Yes. Him. Ridiculous. A hunk of wood and metal. Absurd what fools will believe. I'm simply tired of you, Longinus. Time to make an example of you. Yet, you are not afraid, I truly see that."

"No. In fact, you honor me," I said.

"How's that?" asked the General. His demeanor had shifted to that of one who was now being insulted.

"You crucify me."

"Are you daft? How is that honoring you? I could see if we were to allow you to fall on a blade, but—"

"Because you crucify me the way we crucified *him*, Jesu," I said.

They all fell silent.

"You think this is a joke?" the General was enraged. "We shall solve that. You, Centurion," he said turning to the officer that had been leading me, "you will crucify this one upside down, do you hear me?! Hang him upside down on the cross!!"

"Yes, sir!" replied the Centurion.

With that the General turned on his heels and went back to his table in the shade, the other officers following in his wake.

The weight was crushing my lungs. I could no longer feel my feet or lower legs. Nor could I feel my hands. Where the nails were driven through my wrists, a stinging sensation was all there was. My head pounded fiercely. Blood was in my eyes. I don't know how long I had been there. It was night, I could tell. The immediate area was lit by torches. I craned my neck to view the crucifix next to mine. From my inverted position, all I could see were feet: Paulonius' feet.

He was hanged with me, next to me. He had been bloodied and missing all his front teeth when I had first arrived at the hill. He had already been attached to his cross and was lying on the ground before being hoisted to the upright position. His guards had abandoned him for the moment, drinking water and taking a break from their duties.

"I said not a word to them. Not a word," he whispered to me as I fell to my knees next to him.

"Thank you, my friend. For everything," I had replied.

He was dead now. I heard his last rasping breaths during my previous waking moments.

Something was moving in the torch light. A guard? Yes, a few yards away. A lone guard of the dead and dying.

But there was someone else. My eyesight was nearly gone because of the blood and pressure on my head. Someone was trying to get my attention. A figure crouched on the edge of the hill behind the guard. I did my best to focus my eyes.

The figure held a torch near her face. Irena. My love, my life. Was I dreaming? No, it was *her*.

I tried to call out, but I had no voice.

She made no noise, but tears streamed down her face. I craned my head again to try to see her right-side-up, but I could not move.

She was saying something, or mouthing something. I was in a daze; could not hold on much longer. What was she trying to say?

Then, I could see it, in my mind's eye, I knew what she was saying; could hear her in my heart: "I love you, Longinus."

"You are my heart, my soul, my love," I replied to her in my mind.

I left my body then for the last time. I would be Longinus no more.

EPILOGUE

It was 322 in "The year of our Lord," as the Christian monks would say. Their monastery was across the lake and up the hill. The lad did not have much contact with them.

He was growing up on the Island of Britain, in the realm of Avalon amongst the Druid priests and priestesses.

Ten summers he was, with long auburn hair and a thin frame. One beautiful day, he rummaged through the partial ruins of an abandoned underground sanctuary temple.

Going into this old place in and of itself was not unusual. The young lad loved coming to it. It was his sanctuary. He'd spend hours there digging, looking for precious relics from the past or just sitting in silent meditation, imagining that he was participating in some ancient rite.

On this day, however, he decided to venture deep into the very back portion of the temple, to its most inner sanctuary; a place he did not usually visit, and, in fact, had not visited in many a summer because it was so deep within that it was always shrouded in darkness. But something compelled him to go there. So, the lad took a torch on this day.

Shadows jumped to and fro as he entered the inner sanctuary. The smell of must and age filled his nostrils. When his green eyes adjusted to the darkness and torchlight, he noticed something under one of the toppled stones in the very back of the place. It looked to be wrapping of some kind. The boy placed the butt of the torch in the sconce hole of a nearby wall and attempted to move the stone trapping whatever it was that was beneath. He used all of his might. It was useless. Then he realized that what he took to be a stone was actually a large sarcophagus tipped on its side. *Have I found a body?* he wondered.

He decided that the portion of the stone on the wrapping was the lid of this sarcophagus. Breaking it might be possible. The young lad picked up a nearby fragment of hewn rock and threw it hard at the lid. A loud cracking sound filled the room, as well as a cloud of powdered granite and dirt. There was nothing in the sarcophagus, but the item that had lain beneath the crumbled remains of the lid was now easily retrievable.

The boy pulled on the wrapping and dragged the thing free. It was long and thin, certainly not a body. Suddenly, he felt a tension grow within him as he touched the wrapping, trying to feel what was inside.

A treasure perhaps! he thought with excitement. He remembered a story, a legend really, of a man who visited this place three centuries earlier. He was from the Christian's Holy Land and had come with a woman and two children—boys, if the lad remembered correctly—and three treasures that purportedly had belonged to the very first Christian.

Could this be one of those treasures? Slowly, carefully, the lad unwrapped the thing.

A spear it was. An old Roman lance. He held it. It felt strangely...familiar.

He stood at mock attention, spear at his side pretending to be a Roman legionnaire. After a moment the boy looked closely at the thing. The shaft was still strong, but it was splintered in spots. The blade at the tip was bent slightly and the whole of the metal was stained with rust, and something else. The boy drew the blade close to his face and squinted his eyes to try and make out what, besides rust, was on the blade. *It looks like blood!* he thought.

Then a strange thing happened: the spear vibrated in his hands, and its tip began to glow softly. It was as if the thing was alive and simply waking up from a long nap.

He dropped it with a start. After a moment, the spear stopped the vibration, ceased its glowing.

The lad picked it up again. *A fine weapon this is*, he thought to himself. *But I'm not a soldier.*

The boy thought for a moment, then realized it would be wonderful for another purpose.

He looked at the spear and said in a loud voice, "I declare you the wizard's staff!" His words echoed off the cavernous walls. He held the spear high for a moment, vertically, blade pointing up, then brought it down, tapping the shaft's butt end on the ground three times to make his declaration so.

"Hello!" called the female voice from outside. "Master Merlin, is that you? Are you in there?"

"Yes, priestess!" answered the boy.

"Come. Time for studies," the priestess called back.

The boy wrapped the spear back up and tucked it under his arm. He took his torch and treasure and headed out of the ancient temple.

Other Inspirational Books from Purple Haze Press Publisher

You Are What You Love
By Vaishali

You Are What You Love is the definitive twenty-first century guide for spiritual seekers of timeless wisdom who have hit a pothole on the way to enlightenment and are searching for the answers to the big questions in life: "Who am I?" and "Why am I here?" Author Vaishali explores mystic Emanuel Swedenborg's philosophy of gratitude and love. She expands this wisdom by associating it to traditional sources including Christianity and Buddhism. Through storytelling and humor, the focal point of the book "you don't have love, you are love" is revealed. A compelling read to deepen your understanding of Oneness.

Paperback, 400 pages, ISBN 978-0-9773200-0-4, $24.95

You Are What You Love Playbook
By Vaishali

You Are What You Love Playbook is a playtime manual offering practical play practices to invoke play into action. Included is step-by-step guidance on dream work, a 13-month course in how to practice playful miracles, and a copy of the author's lucid dreaming diary. The perfect companion to *You Are What You Love.*

Paperback, 124 pages, ISBN 978-0-9773200-1-1, $14.95

You Are What You Love, Book on CD
By Vaishali

The book on CD is an 80-minute condensed and abridged version of its 400-page book counterpart. The book on CD is read by the author and is as entertaining and fun to listen to as the text is to read. The CD format is perfect for deeper integration of the highly penetrating Spiritual wisdom offered.

CD, ISBN 978-0-9773200-2-8, $14.95

Available at your favorite bookstore, online,
or at www.youarewhatyoulove.com.